COUNT THE HELMETS

COUNT THE HELMETS

The Story of the 1985 Falcon Football Team

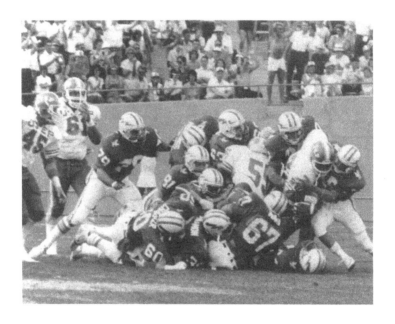

*Leaders of Character
in a
Culture of Commitment
and a
Climate of Respect*

Neal Starkey

Copyright © 2018 by Neal Starkey.

HARDBACK: 978-1-949169-26-3
PAPERBACK: 978-1-949169-25-6
EBOOK: 978-1-949169-27-0

All rights reserved. No part of this publication may be reproduced, distributed, or transmitted in any form or by any electronic or mechanical means, without the prior written permission of the publisher, except in the case of brief quotations embodied in critical reviews and certain other noncommercial uses permitted by copyright law.

Ordering Information:

For orders and inquiries, please contact:
1-888-375-9818
www.toplinkpublishing.com
bookorder@toplinkpublishing.com

Printed in the United States of America

Contents

Prologue xix

Part One: The History 1
Part Two: The Games 61

Chapter One: The Miners 63
Chapter Two: The Cowboys 81
Chapter Three: The Owls 89
Chapter Four: The Lobos 102
Chapter Five: The Fighting Irish 120
Chapter Six: The Goats 152
Chapter Seven: The Rams 168
Chapter Eight: The Utes 189
Chapter Nine: The Aztecs 211
Chapter Ten: The Black Knights 236
Chapter Eleven: The Cougars 271
Chapter Twelve: The Rainbows 294
Chapter Thirteen: The Longhorns 320

Part Three: Leaders of Character 331

Benji 53 333
Crew/Description 335
Actual Transmissions 336
Epilogue 351
About the 1985 Falcons 351
1985 Falcon Football players 370
A Toast to the Host 401
Leaders of character 404

To **Sharon**: you're <u>still</u> the one!

To **Tracie** and **Mitch**: Keep making a difference!

High Flight
by John Gillespie Magee, Jr.

Oh, I have slipped the surly bonds of earth,
And danced the skies on laughter-silvered wings;
Sunwards I've climbed and joined the tumbling mirth
Of sun-split clouds – and done a thousand things
You have not drefamed of - wheeled and soared and swung
High in the sunlit silence, hovering there,
I've chased the shouting wind along and flung
My eager craft through footless halls of air,
Up, up the long delirious burning blue
I've topped the wind-swept heights with easy grace,
Where never lark, or even eagle, flew;
And, while with silent, lifting mind I've trod
The high unsurpassed sanctity of space,
Put out my hand, and touched the face of God.

"Football at the Air Force Academy has been one of the primary forces that shaped my life. I can't say it taught me many new values, because I played in a very good high school program that shared the values of AF, but I can say that it honed, reinforced, and sharpened those values in a way that will hopefully ensure I will never lose sight of them. Playing there taught teamwork, discipline, the importance of execution, and spirit. Most important to me, it taught persistence. I am most proud of the fact that no Air Force team I was on ever gave up. Whether we were winning the game by 20 or losing by 20 with two minutes to go, we were still trying our best, still not giving up. If it was the last play of the game, we were still going to take your head off, because that's just what we did. These values, particularly persistence, have paid off in training, in flying fighters, in war, in coaching, in marriage, and in every facet of my life."

Steve Hendrickson, former AFA cadet and football player, a retired USAFR Lt. Col., Air Force career included flying combat missions in the F-111, F-15, and F-16, now an international pilot for FedEX. Steve and wife, Sharon have three daughters and live in Poquoson, VA.

"Count The Helmets" – *How it all started, as told by Mike Bohn and Neal Starkey.*

On Saturday, August 31, 1985, the Air Force Academy Falcons defeated the University of Texas at El Paso (UTEP) Miners football team by a score of 48-6 at Falcon Stadium in Colorado Springs, CO.

The next morning, Sunday, September 1st, the author of this book (Neal Starkey), opened his copy of the Colorado Springs Gazette newspaper to the Sports section to read all about the wonderful game he had watched the Falcons play the previous day.

To his amazement, he saw the picture shown above, and thought, "That's the best football picture ever taken!"

Neal is a 1968 graduate of the academy, and he had grown up playing football in Texas, before coming to Colorado Springs, where he was the captain of the '67 Falcons, received

All-America honors in both 1966 and 1967, becoming the first two-time All-America football player at the AFA.

In addition, he coached football at the academy for four years, including one year as the head coach of the USAF Academy Prep School.

The point being, he's seen a lot of football over the years, thus his assessment of "The best football picture ever taken!"

On Monday morning, Neal went down to the old Gazette Telegraph location on East Pikes Peak Avenue in Colorado Springs, and asked to speak to anyone from the Sports Department who could tell him who the photographer was for this wonderful picture, and what steps must be taken to get a negative of that photo.

A gentleman came out to the desk and heard his request, then went back behind the doors for about 10 minutes before returning, saying there were several groups of photographers at the game . . . some from the Gazette, some from the Air Force, and even some freelance photographers that help for the bigger games, like the first game of the season . . . but nobody raised their hand or offered a name of who it might have been. Then he said, "However, here are two negatives of that photo if you'd like them." And he handed them to Neal and walked back behind the doors.

The original negatives for "The Picture" . . .
later to become "Count The Helmets".

Neal took the negatives to the closest copy shop he could find and had an 8x10 black and white photo made, which he promptly took out to the academy, and gave to Fisher DeBerry . . . saying, "Coach, I think this is the best football picture ever taken, and it's your team!"

Coach DeBerry admired the picture for a minute, taking time to count all 11 Falcon football helmets w/lightning bolts, and then said he had to agree, he'd never seen a better football picture.

One picture, an action shot, captures all 11 defensive players for the academy on, or moving rapidly to, the poor UTEP ball carrier. All 11 in one frame. Not posed. It's an action shot. It's the best football picture ever taken!

Fisher thanked Neal for the picture, and later that day, took it out onto the practice field, where he called his team and coaches together and shared it with them, noting that this was certainly an excellent example of Teamwork, and if they continued to perform with that level of focus, execution, and commitment this might be the start of a very special season.

After practice, Coach DeBerry took the picture off his clipboard and set it on the top of his desk, really not thinking a lot about it for quite some time.

Two days later, Associate Athletic Director Mike Bohn stopped by to get Coach DeBerry to drive him up to Denver for his weekly Wednesday luncheon with the Denver Quarterback Club. Mike noticed the picture on Fisher's desk, and asked if he could borrow it for a few days . . . he had something in mind.

As the key guy in the AD's office responsible for promotions designed to increase attendance at all AFA athletic functions, Mike immediately recognized a unique opportunity for the AFA football program.

He quickly reached out to several associates within and outside the academy, sharing the picture and asking for suggestions. As the season moved forward and the Falcons continued to win, impressively, the ideas for utilizing "The Picture" began to get better, and better.

One gentleman, Frank Aires, volunteered in the Falcon Stadium Press Box during the season, but his day job found him working at the Olympic Training Center near downtown Colorado Springs. Frank mentioned that "The Picture" would be great inspiration for a color portrait, and he had just the candidate in mind.

A Czech-national, named Oliver J. Stankovsky, had painted an extraordinary, full-color lithograph/portrait for the U.S. Olympic Hockey organization to help them celebrate "The Miracle on Ice", and he felt he would be a good choice for the AFA Football project.

Mike asked Frank to track down and contact Mr. Stankovsky, explain a little about what the group had in mind and see what feedback he might share.

Well, Frank did a great job, because not only did Mr. Stankovsky like the idea, he said he would do it for free, largely due to the warm feelings he had for the United States from his experiences in WWII and later in the Cold War, and also the very good experience he had with the U.S. Olympic Hockey team.

At this point (some of the details are starting to get a little fuzzy after thirty years!) the group was ready to put some ideas on paper, and they needed the help of professionals. They felt that a multi-colored portrait, signed by the artist, mounted, framed and numbered would be an appropriate "acknowledgement of contribution" for all the folks who were part of the '85 Falcon Family. Now, they needed someone who could handle concepts for layout, printing, colors, etc. A local company had done some great work previously for the academy, so Jim Heisley, the founder and owner of Heisley Advertising in Colorado Springs, was contacted, briefed on the concept, and quickly joined the team.

The final, critical piece of the project... the funding, was next on the list of things that had to happen to make this project work. Fortunately, several members of the AFA planning team had very good relationships with Rouse Properties, Inc. (RPI), the owner of the Citadel mall in Colorado Springs and a Falcon sports sponsor since opening their doors in 1972. With a few phone calls and the promise of some special perks, the deal was done, largely due to the support received from RPI's GM for the Citadel Mall, Mr. Joe Naketa.

The project was formally launched . . . a real team effort.

RPI's Director of Marketing, Mr. Gary Butcher, coordinated the design with the schedule, and Oliver Stankovsky completed his master lithograph/portrait on time, and then he and Mrs. Stankovsky flew to Colorado Springs where he personally signed and numbered all 500 pieces before they were mounted and framed.

In the meantime, the Falcons finished their season 12-1, beat Texas in the Bluebonnet Bowl, and finished 1985 as the 5th best Division-1 football team in the nation.

Portrait #1 was given to head coach Fisher DeBerry, who promptly gave it to Athletic Director/Colonel John Clune, without whose never-flinching support, none of this would have happened.

After leaving the academy, Mike Bohn's career led him through increasingly more responsible jobs at the College

Football Association (CFA), Colorado State University, the University of Idaho, San Diego State University, the University of Colorado, and he is now the Athletic Director at the University of Cincinnati (whose Bearcat football team played Virginia Tech in the 2015 Military Bowl) and has always had portrait #73 hanging in each of his offices throughout his career.

Neal Starkey left the Air Force after medical issues with a spinal cord injury/blood clot he received from playing football at the academy (ironically!) disqualified him from Pilot Training (his #1 reason for attending the AFA) and he began a 35+ year career in the Computer, Defense and Aerospace industries. When the technology allowed, he had the negative of "The Picture" converted digitally, which allowed him to share the picture electronically. He also put the picture (which he calls: "Count The Helmets") on the back of every business card he has ever used throughout his career(s), using it to help him "measure" potential business partners through their reaction to the picture . . . it's all about Teamwork!

During a recent phone call, Mike Bohn told Neal that he had one extra portrait . . . #500, that had been sitting in a trunk in his basement all these nearly 30 years, and he was sending it to Neal in Colorado Springs, to hang on his wall . . . 30 years later.

"The best football picture ever taken!" is now called "Count The Helmets". It has gone full circle, and remains an anonymous, tangible tribute to the dedication, commitment and success of the '85 Falcon football team.

May the lessons learned from these very true stories of character, leadership and commitment help current and future generations at the United States Air Force Academy succeed as they serve America.

Portrait #63/500, courtesy of USAF BGen (Ret.) Orwyn "O" Sampson

Prologue

"Upon the fields of friendly strife are sown the seeds that upon other fields, on other days, will bear the fruits of victory."

General of the Army, Douglas MacArthur

USAF Captain Roger Clinton Locher is a former F-4D Phantom weapons officer and pilot who, on May 10, 1972, during the Vietnam War and "Operation Linebacker", was shot down only 64 km (40 miles) from Hanoi, North Vietnam, and only about 8.0 km (5 miles) from Yên Bái Airfield. Locher was on his *third combat tour* and had *over 407 combat missions*. He was *one of the leading MIG killers in Vietnam with three kills.*

Locher successfully ejected at about 2,400 m (8,000 feet) but because the remaining planes were busy with the other MiGs, and due to smoke, no one saw his parachute canopy. Two Mig 19s (quite likely the ones that had just shot him down) buzzed Locher as he descended, so he knew the enemy was aware he had survived.

Locher was afraid to use his URC-64 rescue radio as he parachuted because it was difficult to remove from the zippered pocket of his survival vest and he was not sure he could get it back in. He figured out his rough location and managed to steer his chute about 1,800 m (2,000 yards) away from the plane burning below him and towards a nearby mountain side. After he landed, he couldn't hide his parachute because it was stuck in the trees overhead.

He removed a couple of essential items from his survival pack and left the remainder behind. His survival vest contained a pistol, two pints of water, a first aid kit, insect repellent, mosquito netting, and a knife. He knew from prior briefings that he could not expect Search-And-Rescue this deep in North Vietnam, north of the Red River. Once on the ground and under the trees, he could not hear any jets overhead. He also knew his radio could not penetrate the dense jungle canopy overhead.

Locher listened to hear if a search party was looking for him. He camouflaged his trail for about 91 m (100 yards) and then climbed the eastern side of the mountain to its peak. He got his bearings and then hid in bushes on the west slope. For three days, Locher listened as a search party of local farmers beat the bushes up and down the east side of the mountain, searching for him. He hid in a brush pile and at one point over the next three days, a boy came within 9.1 m (30 feet) of his hiding place. In the evening he returned to the peak. On the second day he picked up radio traffic from American aircraft almost 160 km (100 miles) to his south, but they did not hear his radio beeper or voice.

He decided his best chance for rescue was to cross the forested, hilly terrain and get to the heavily cultivated Red River Valley swim the river, and work his way to the sparsely inhabited mountains to the south. He figured it would take him 45 days. He traveled only at first light and at dusk, avoiding the local farmers, and living off the land.

He was able to find plenty of water but only occasionally fruit and berries to eat. He evaded capture and covered over 19 km (12 mi), gradually losing 30 pounds (14 kg) and his strength. On the 10th day he came within 1.5 m (5 feet) of being discovered. Following a well-used trail early one morning, he suddenly had to evade local farmers. He hid in a nearby field where there was little concealment, but pulled leaves and debris over himself. He lay there all day as children from a village he discovered a short distance away played in his vicinity. At one point a water buffalo nearly stepped on him, and a boy came to fetch the animal, only a few feet from Locher. That evening he spotted a hill near the village alongside the Red River, the last hill before the wide open fields of the Red River basin.

He hid on the hill for the next 13 days and watched for American aircraft. On June 1, 1972, he was finally able to contact a flight of American jets overhead, calling, *"Any U.S. aircraft, if you read Oyster 1 Bravo, come up on Guard"*. USAF Captain Steve Ritchie, in one of the F-4 aircraft overhead and who had witnessed Locher's jet fall out of the sky, remembered Locher's call sign and answered his call. Locher calmly responded, *"Guys I've been down here a long time, any chance of picking me up?"* Ritchie replied, *"You bet!"* Locher's transmissions left some Americans who did not hear his call in doubt about the authenticity of his message, and they believed that the NVA may have manipulated a POW into impersonating him, setting a trap for the would-be rescuers.

A Search-And-Rescue mission of several A-1E and two HH-53 with F-4 and F-105 fighters providing air protection was launched that same day but was driven off by heavy anti-aircraft fire and MiGs. The A-1 Skyraider and HH-53C pilots came under attack from a MiG but eluded the enemy fighter in a narrow canyon. The rescue force then dodged missiles, another MiG and gunfire, but failed to get through to Locher that day.

On June 2, 1972, **General John Vogt**, commander of the 7th Air Force, consulted with Army MACV commander General Frederick C. Weyand. ***Vogt canceled the entire strike mission set for Hanoi that day!*** He dedicated all the available resources, over 150 aircraft, to rescuing Locher. The direct task force of 119 aircraft included two HH-53 rescue helicopters, bombers, and an array of F-4 escorts, EB-66s, A-1Es, F105G Weasels, and KC135 tankers.

Vogt said, "I had to decide whether we should risk the loss of maybe a dozen airplanes and crews just to get one man out. Finally I said to myself, Goddamn it, the one thing that keeps our boys motivated is the certain belief that if they go down, we will do absolutely everything we can to get them out. If that is ever in doubt, morale would tumble. That was my major consideration. So I took it on myself. I didn't ask anybody for permission. I just said, **"Go do it!"**" General John Vogt was a ***leader of character***.

The Yên Bái MiG airfield, about 97 km (60 miles) northwest of Hanoi, was one of the most important and well-defended Vietnamese People's Air Force airbases in North Vietnam. The aircraft bombed and strafed around Yên Bái airfield for two hours, reducing enemy opposition so that the helicopters could get in. Capt. Ronald E. Smith in an A-1E guided Capt. Dale Stovall, piloting a HH-53 "Super Jolly Green Giant" from the 40th Aerospace Rescue and Recovery Squadron, to

Locher's position. Only when Locher rose out of the jungle canopy were all of the Americans sure it was him. Despite their proximity to Yen Bai airfield, no aircraft were lost during Locher's rescue. "We shut down the war to go get Roger Locher," Stovall later said.

Locher was flown back to Udorn. The first person to greet him was General Vogt, who had flown up from Saigon in a T-39. Capt. Locher had successfully evaded capture for 23 days, a record for the Vietnam War. The evening of his return, he was greeted at the Officers Club by hundreds of individuals with an ovation lasting 20 minutes.

USAF Captain Dale E. Stovall, an All-American Track and Field athlete at the United States Air Force Academy, Class of 1967, figured prominently in several search and rescue operations during the Vietnam War. A member of the 40th Aerospace Rescue and Recovery Squadron based in Thailand, on June 2, 1972, he recovered Captain Roger Locher from deep inside North Vietnam, *the furthest any airman was ever rescued from inside enemy lines*. For his efforts in rescuing Locher, Stovall was awarded the *Air Force Cross*, which described how "he willingly returned to this high threat area, braving intense ground fire, to recover the downed airman from deep in North Vietnam." Stovall was also recognized with the *1973 Jabara Award* for Airmanship, *two Silver Star awards* and *two Distinguished Flying Cross awards* for other combat rescues among the 12 successful rescue missions he accomplished during his tour in Southeast Asia. Dale Stovall was a *leader of character* who later retired from the Air Force as a Brigadier General on June 1, 1993.

USAF Captain Richard Stephen (Steve) Ritchie was born in Reidsville, North Carolina, the son of an American Tobacco

Company executive. He was a star quarterback for Reidsville High School, despite breaking his leg twice. In 1964, he graduated from the United States Air Force Academy, where, as a "walk-on", he became the starting halfback for the Falcons varsity football team in 1962 and 1963. Interestingly enough, as a 1st Class (Senior) cadet at the Academy, Ritchie was directly involved in the training and motivation of several members of the USAFA Class of 1967, including a young "Doolie" from Toppenish, WA named Dale Stovall.

Ritchie entered pilot training at Laredo Air Force Base, Texas, and finished first in his class. His first operational assignment was with Flight Test Operations at Eglin Air Force Base, Florida, where he flew the F-104 Starfighter. Two years later he transitioned into the F-4 Phantom II at Homestead Air Force Base, Florida, in preparation for his first tour in Southeast Asia.

For his ***first combat tour***, Ritchie was assigned to the 480th Tactical Fighter Squadron, 366th Tactical Fighter Wing at Da Nang Air Base, South Vietnam in 1968. Ritchie flew the first "Fast FAC" mission in the F-4 forward air controller program and was instrumental in the spread and success of the program. He completed ***195 combat missions***.

In 1969, he was selected to attend the Fighter Weapons Course at Nellis Air Force Base, Nevada, becoming, up to that point, the Air Force Fighter Weapons School's youngest-ever instructor at age 26. He taught air-to-air tactics from 1970 to 1972 to the best USAF pilots, including Major Robert Lodge, a 1964 classmate of Ritchie's at the USAF Academy, who later became his flight leader in Thailand and shot down three MiGs himself before being KIA over North Vietnam on May 10, 1972.

Ritchie volunteered for a ***second combat tour in 1972*** and was assigned to the 432nd Tactical Reconnaissance Wing at Udorn Royal Thai Air Force Base, Thailand. Flying F-4 Phantom IIs with the famed 555th ("Triple Nickel") Tactical Fighter Squadron he shot down his *first* Mikoyan-Gurevich MiG-21 on 10 May 1972, scored a *second* victory on May 31, a *third* and *fourth* on July 8, and a *fifth* on August 28 . . . ***110 days . . . 5 kills***. All of the aircraft he shot down were MiG-21s, and all were shot down by the much-maligned AIM-7 Sparrow radar-guided air-to-air missile.

Ritchie commented:

> "My fifth MiG kill was an exact duplicate of a syllabus mission (at Fighter Weapons School), so I had not only flown that as a student, but had taught it probably a dozen times prior to actually doing it in combat."

USAF Captain Steve Ritchie became the United States Air Force's ***first and only pilot ace of the Vietnam War.***

After completing ***339 combat missions totaling over 800 flying hours***, Ritchie returned from his second combat tour as of ***the most highly decorated pilot in the Vietnam War.*** His combat achievements earned him the ***1972 Mackay Trophy*** for the most significant Air Force mission of the Year, the Air Force Academy's ***1972 Jabara Award*** for airmanship, and the ***1972 Armed Forces Award***, presented by the Veterans of Foreign Wars for outstanding contributions to the national security of the United States. Steve Ritchie retired from the Air Force in 1999 as a Brigadier General... and a true ***leader of character.***

Steve Ritchie's Decorations include:

Command pilot (3,000 + hours)
Air Force Cross (second highest United States Air Force award)
Silver Star (plus three oak leaf clusters)
Distinguished Flying Cross (with nine oak leaf clusters)
Air Medal (with 25 oak leaf clusters)
Air Force Outstanding Unit Award (with Combat "V" for Valor)
National Defense Service Medal (two awards)
Vietnam Service Medal (with three campaign stars)
Air Force Longevity Service Award (with eight oak leaf clusters)
Vietnam Air Gallantry Medal (with Gold Wings)
Vietnam Campaign Medal

To watch an 8 minute video of BG Steve Ritchie telling this story in his own words, click on:

http://www.youtube.com/embed/QvRcP4go-eg?feature=player_embedded.

Roger Locher lives in Sabetha, KS.
Steve Ritchie lives in Bellevue, WA.
Dale Stovall lives in Missoula, MT. (Wikepedia)

Leaders of Character,

in a Culture of Commitment

and a Climate of Respect . . .

it's a matter of choice!

PART ONE

THE HISTORY

Our nation has five outstanding, undergraduate Service Academies:

The United States Military Academy   (USMA) (established 1802)

The United States Naval Academy   (USNA) (established 1845)

The United States Coast Guard Academy   (USCGA) (established 1876)

The United States Merchant Marine Academy   (USMMA) (est. 1943)

The United States Air Force Academy   (USAFA) (established 1954)

These are ***Institutions of higher learning, with a higher calling: to serve our nation*** . . . not the way many of our nation's politicians "serve" this country, but by actually committing themselves to the values that will best prepare them to step into "harm's way" on behalf of the United States of America.

These clean-cut, highly-educated, multi-talented, goal-oriented men and women have chosen to leave their homes, their friends and their unique cultures, and dedicate themselves to strict codes of conduct - integrity, education, leadership, teamwork and competition . . . the ***first steps*** to building ***leaders of character*** . . . to position themselves as potential officers in America's military organizations.

All Cadets and Midshipmen live in an environment, a culture if you will, of strict rules and intense competition, having every facet of their lives observed, measured, and evaluated against everybody else. They expect, and are expected, to excel at:

- How well they do in the classroom.
- How precisely they march to meals and in parades.
- How clean and orderly their rooms and uniforms are each day.
- How well they memorize endless volumes of required "knowledge"*.
- How well they lead/follow/interact with their fellow students.
- How well they "live the values" of Honor and Ethics.
- How well they perform in intermural/interscholastic athletics.
- How well they handle all this . . . plus just a little adversity!

* ***Contrails*** *is a small handbook issued to new cadets entering the United States Air Force Academy. It contains information on United States Air Force and United States military history; Academy history; notable Academy graduates; aircraft, satellites, and munitions in the current U.S. Air Force inventory; transcripts of important national documents such as the Preamble to the Constitution and the full national anthem; and famous quotes, which are usually patriotic or leadership-related. Cadets in their fourth class (freshman) year are* **expected to learn <u>all</u> of the information from Contrails, and be able to recite it verbatim . . . *often under severe verbal and physical duress*.** *Contrails has traditionally been published in the class color—Blue, Silver, Red, or Gold—of the freshman class.* (Wikepedia + ***"tweaks by the author"***)

Recruited athletes, about 23% of any in-coming class, are just ordinary cadets and midshipmen for about 20 hours each day . . . the other four plus hours they dedicate themselves to their chosen craft . . . with vigor!

These are generally not High School All-Americans. They don't have questionable academic qualifications and they have absolutely no desire to leave school early without their college degree and commission! At an academy, these young men and women actually count days until graduation and being sworn into their chosen service as a new officer... not the days until their specialty-sport drafts new players into their system . . . the higher the draft, the bigger the paychecks!

Academy cadet-athletes are all amateurs. They have not been offered any of a wide variety of "special deals" to say "YES" to an academy and "NO" to other traditional colleges or universities also seeking their talents.

And they are <u>all</u> very talented, most with tremendous "upside" potential, some having turned down opportunities to go to one of the premier schools . . . but having one or two of that "quality" athlete on any specific Academy Intercollegiate team in any specific year is a luxury, indeed.

Academy Intercollegiate cadet-athletes want to be contributing members of a Team.

Academy Intercollegiate cadet-athletes want to make their school proud.

Academy Intercollegiate cadet-athletes want to make their nation proud.

Academy Intercollegiate cadet-athletes want to make their Mom (and Dad) proud!

Academy Intercollegiate cadet-athletes depend on Teamwork.

Academy Intercollegiate cadet-athletes expect and train to WIN.

Academy Intercollegiate cadet-athletes never quit.

This is a ***culture of commitment***, and not everybody can live here!

In fact, if you don't think you can adapt to this culture . . . do ***not*** come here!

If you think you can, be prepared to swear to the following:

> *I do solemnly swear that I will support and defend the Constitution of the United States against all enemies, foreign and domestic; that I will bear true faith and allegiance to the same; that I take this obligation freely without any mental reservation or purpose of evasion; and that I will well and faithfully discharge the duties of the office on which I am about to enter: So Help Me God.*
>
> —Commissioning Oath of Office

The officer's commission and oath of office has a meaning attached to it like no other known document or commitment. The commission or oath of office is more than a "handsome framed parchment that once hung proudly on the young officer's office wall but which may now be moldering somewhere in an old packing box."11

As Colonel (now BGen retired) Orwyn Sampson* pointed out in his analysis of the military oath of office, the oath is to be taken seriously:

> "It embodies the principles of liberty for all men and women. It represents an ideal that has been tried by fire and found to be genuine, lasting, and valuable. The individual's complete loyalty is tied up in the commitment. It is clearly and without question a commitment to excellence and an allegiance to God."
>
> (11 Matthews, Lloyd. The Need for An Officer's Code of Professional Ethics. Army 44:20-29 March 1994. pp.22.)

* BGen. (Ret.) Orwyn Sampson. 33 year military career. Professor Emeritus of Biology at USAFA. Masters degree from UCLA. Ph.D from University of Oregon. Guest lecturer at NASA. Head Gymnastics coach at AFA. Football and FCA Officer Representative. Retired inventor, involved in a multitude of projects: writing, speaking, FCA, Campus Crusade, church and civic groups. Retired with wife, Diane, in Colorado Springs, CO.

In addition, the quote shown below, from **_Contrails,_** clearly sets measurable expectations for any prospective cadet/midshipman candidate to help them better understand this warrior culture they are considering joining, and help them decide if a service academy culture is the right choice for them:

The American Fighting Man's Code of Conduct

I

I am an American Fighting man. I serve in the forces which guard my country and our way of life. I am prepared to give my life in their defense.

II

I will never surrender of my own free will. If in command, I will never surrender my men while they still have the means to resist.

III

If I am captured, I will continue to resist by all means available. I will make every effort to escape and aid others to escape. I will accept neither parole nor special favors from the enemy.

IV

If I become a prisoner of war, I will keep faith with my fellow prisoners. I will give no information nor take part in any action which might be harmful to my comrades. If I am senior, I will take command. If not I will obey the lawful orders of those appointed over me and will back them up in every way.

V

When questioned, should I become a prisoner of war, I am required to give name, rank, service number, and date of birth. I will evade answering further questions to the best of my ability, I will make no oral or written statements disloyal to my country and its allies or harmful to their cause.

VI

I will never forget that I am an American Fighting man, responsible for my actions, and dedicated to the principles which made my country free. I will trust in my God and in the United States of America.

These words are not found in the small print on the bottom of the last page of some organization's mission statement.

These words define the real reason young men and women ultimately decide to attend, persevere and graduate from a service academy.

These words define a ***culture of commitment*** that requires outstanding ***character***.

It takes a lot of ***character*** to handle all this.

> *"When a team takes to the field, individual specialists come together to achieve a team win. All players try to do their very best because every other player, the team, and the home town are counting on them to win. So it is when the Armed Forces of the United States go to war. We must win every time. Every soldier must take the battlefield believing his or her unit is the best in the world. Every pilot must take off believing there is no one better in the sky. Every sailor standing watch must believe there is no better ship at sea. Every Marine must hit the beach believing that there are not better infantrymen in the world. But they all must also believe that they are part of a team, a joint team, that fights together to win. This is our history, this is our tradition, this is our future."*
>
> —*General Colin L. Powell*

So, what is character?

Character is a life-long series of choices that become a pattern of behavior, thoughts and feelings based on universal principles, moral strength, and integrity – plus the guts to live by those principles every day.

Character is evidenced by your life's virtues and *"the line you never cross."*

Character is the most valuable thing you have, and nobody can ever take it away. *You have to give it away*!

How do we measure the *character* of an individual, a Cadet, a Midshipman, an officer?

The New Webster's Dictionary simply defines *character* as:

"The total quality of a person's <u>behavior</u>."

Not your thoughts, or your hopes or your aspirations…*<u>your behavior.</u>*

When notable, historical personalities were asked for their definitions of *"character"*, they said:

> *"Nearly all men can stand adversity, but if you want to test a man's character, give him power."*
>
> - Abraham Lincoln, President

"Character is, in the long run, the decisive factor in the life of individuals and of nations alike."

- Theodore Roosevelt, President

"If it is a cliché to say athletics build character as well as muscle, then I subscribe to the cliché."

- Gerald Ford, President

"Be more concerned with your character than your reputation, because your character is what you really are, while your reputation is merely what others think you are."

- John Wooden, UCLA basketball coach

"Hold yourself responsible for a higher standard than anybody else expects of you. Never excuse yourself."

- Henry Ward Beecher, Congregationalist clergyman, social reformer

"The true test of civilization is not the census, nor the size of cities, nor the crops, no, but the kind of man the country turns out.

- Ralph Waldo Emerson, American essayist, philosopher and poet

"Faced with crisis, the man of character falls back upon himself."

- Charles DeGaulle, French President

"At some point, how you act is just who you are."

- NHL Penguins Captain, Sidney Crosby

"Love never fails, character never quits, and dreams do come true."

- Pete Maravich,
professional basketball player

"Most people say that it is the intellect which makes a great scientist. They are wrong: it is character."

- Albert Einstein,
mathematician, physicist, philosopher

"The measure of a man's character is what he would do if he knew he never would be found out."

- Baron Thomas Babington Macauley,
English historian and statesman

"You can easily judge the character of a person by how they treat those who can do nothing for him/her."

- Anonymous

"I had said that if we lose some games it's a disappointment, but if we lose our character, it's a disaster."

- LtGen Michelle Johnson,
USAFA Superintendent

"Watch your thoughts; they become words. Watch your words; they become actions. Watch your actions; they become habits. Watch your habits; they become character. Watch your character; it becomes your destiny."

- Hon Sheila E. Widnall,
Secretary of the Air Force

"Never, never, never give up!"

- Winston Churchill, Prime Minister

When we look for what "the best" minds of the 21st century have to say about *"character"*, the work done by both the *"Josephson Institute"* in Los Angeles, CA, and the *"Love and Logic Institute, Inc."* in Golden, CO quickly rise to the top.

Each has researched and developed ***character-based*** papers, tutorials, consultations and clinics for nearly every segment of the population over the past 30+ years.

Interestingly, both programs are built on the premise that if an adolescent/pre-adult hasn't chosen to live by specific, very basic character traits, and the value system listed below, by the time they reach their teens, they will have an extremely difficult time conforming completely to a different culture, a "new normal", no matter how stringent or long the behavior modification.

"The Six Pillars of Character"©2012 Josephson Institute (Reprinted with permission, www.JosephsonInstitute.org), targeted at the most basic (juvenile) level of understanding, presents *"character"* in a manner that is most easily

understood by children from all cultures, and is therefore, *most easily transferrable to all other levels of maturity*, from which all professions may choose:

Trustworthiness: ("Duty, Honor, Country" USMA and "Integrity first!" USAFA)

Be honest • Don't deceive, cheat, or steal • Be reliable — do what you say you'll do • Have the courage to do the right thing • Build a good reputation • Be loyal — stand by your family, friends, and country

(The Honor Code at the United States Air Force Academy reads: "We will not lie, steal or cheat, nor tolerate among us anyone who does.")

Respect:

Treat others with respect; follow the Golden Rule • Be tolerant and accepting of differences • Use good manners, not bad language • Be considerate of the feelings of others • Don't threaten, hit or hurt anyone • Deal peacefully with anger, insults, and disagreements

Responsibility:

Do what you are supposed to do • Plan ahead • Persevere: keep on trying! • Always do your best • Use self-control • Be self-disciplined • Think before you act — consider the consequences • Be accountable for your words, actions, and attitudes • Set a good example for others

Fairness:

Play by the rules • Take turns and share • Be open-minded; listen to others • Don't take advantage of others • Don't blame others carelessly • Treat all people fairly

Caring:

Be kind • Be compassionate and show you care • Express gratitude • Forgive others • Help people in need.

Citizenship:

Do your share to make your school, community, country better • Cooperate • Get involved in community affairs • Stay informed; vote • Be a good neighbor • Obey laws and rules • Respect authority • Protect the environment • Volunteer

Jim Fay, co-founder of "Love and Logic Institute, Inc." has developed twelve *"Pearls of Wisdom"* that are helping people/organizations move successfully through character-building/behavior-modification programs . . . from one culture to another.

Pearl-1 actually helps people better understand just how long this process takes, stating: *"It takes one month to change a behavior for every year it existed in its old form."*

Bottom line, it is very, very hard to change the basic value system from one culture to another, and it takes a very, very long time. In the case of cadets/midshipmen at the nation's service academies (given entrance age requirements/limits between 18-23 years) you're talking about nearly two years to completely change from one culture to another . . . if you're lucky!

It's for this very reason that most organizations/institutions that choose "honor/integrity" as one of, if not the most important building block of their core values, set themselves up for many disappointments along the way . . . scandals, from petty to extreme, all the same under honor codes that all have sworn to, not fully understanding the degrees of difficulty that should/could/would one day determine the fate of an individual, an institution, a nation.

Choosing to set the bar at, "*Integrity first!*" sends a message to all that, because we do know that many will certainly fail along the way (traditionally about 30-35% of each class that enters does not graduate, for a variety of reasons), being part of those that stay the course and graduate with integrity will make all of us stronger . . . individually, and as a Team, serving our country.

Leadership is often evident from childhood.

Character, by definition, is built into an individual over the months, years, and decades, a telling summation of his/her choices in life.

Neither is possible without integrity.

Leaders of character are rare, but essential to the continued success of most organizations, especially when times are tough.

The United States of America has been blessed with an ever-growing number of *leaders of character*, stepping up to virtually every challenge, no matter how daunting . . . including the Great Depression and the Dust Bowl, both leading up to the start of World War II.

You may recall the economic status of most countries around the world in the mid-to-late 1930's was weak at best. "Black Tuesday", the day the U.S. stock market crashed, occurred on October 29, 1929, the start of the Great Depression in the U.S.

In most countries of the world, recovery from the Great Depression began four years later, in 1933. In the U.S., recovery began in early 1933, but the U.S. did not return to 1929 GNP levels for over a decade and still had an unemployment rate of about 15% in 1940, albeit down from the high of 25% in 1933.

When the European war began in earnest on September 1, 1939, with the German invasion of Poland, the United States' President, Franklin Delano Roosevelt, was struggling to deal with the worst economy in the history of the Republic. The last thing he wanted was to be drawn into another World War.

America was not ready, economically, militarily, or mentally!

And then, on Sunday morning, December 7, 1941, the Japanese Empire declared war against the U.S. and with a sneak attack, devastated most of our Pacific Fleet while docked at Pearl Harbor, Oahu, Hawaii. (Fortunately, all the carriers were at sea or in dry dock elsewhere for repairs.)

Indeed, **World War II** for the United States of America started on "a day that will live in infamy" and soon would become the ultimate challenge to American ***character*** and its ***leadership***.

We desperately needed "***leaders of character***".

When the U.S. declared war against the Axis Alliance (Germany, Italy, Japan) the U.S. Army ranked ***seventeenth*** among armies of the world in size and combat power . . . just behind Romania!

It numbered 190,000 soldiers.

When mobilization had begun in late 1940, the Army had only 14,000 professional officers. The average age of majors—a middling rank, between captain and lieutenant colonel—was nearly 48; in the National Guard, nearly one-quarter of first lieutenants were over 40 years old, and the senior ranks were dominated by political hacks of certifiable military incompetence. Not a single officer on duty in 1941 had commanded a unit as large as a division in World War I. At the time of Pearl Harbor, in December 1941, only one American division was on a full war footing.

Fortunately, the U.S. Army also included the newly created Army Air Corps, which in turn embodied what would soon become the single greatest military disparity between us and our enemies: our ability to flatten fifty German cities, to firebomb Tokyo, to reduce Hiroshima and Nagasaki to ashes . . . bringing an end to World War II.

Those fleets of airplanes—a thousand bombers at a time attacking enemy targets—are perhaps the most vivid emblem of the "arsenal of democracy" that outfitted our military and, to some extent, our military allies.

The United States built 3.5 million private cars in 1941; for the rest of the war, we built 139. Instead, in 1943 alone, we built 86,000 planes (about 30% of the nearly 276,000 military aircraft built throughout the war)*, 45,000 tanks, and 648,000 trucks. We made in that one year 61 million pairs of wool socks; every day, another 71 million rounds of small-arms ammunition spilled from Army munitions plants.

Henry Ford was determined that he could mass produce bombers just as he had done with cars, so he built the Willow Run assembly plant in Michigan and proved it. It was the world's largest building under one roof at the time.

The "youtube.com" selection below will absolutely blow you away - **one B-24, costing $215,516 in 1943 dollars, rolling off the assembly line every 55 minutes**, *and Ford had their own pilots to test them!!*

ADOLF HITLER HAD NO IDEA THE U.S. WAS CAPABLE OF THIS KIND OF THING.

http://www.youtube.com/embed/iKlt6rNciTo?rel=0

The **character** of America allowed us to build a war machine that was "a prodigy of organization," in Churchill's phrase, derived from a complex industrial society. To service those planes and tanks and trucks required a vast army of support troops within the larger Army, an army that benefited from "the acquaintance of Americans with the gadgetry of American life," from what the historian Russell Weigley called a "confidence born of familiarity with the machine age." All of this gave the U.S. Army mobility unmatched by any of our adversaries, a mobility that permitted the rapid movement and concentration of firepower. The German army by contrast relied on hundreds of thousands of horses to pull their artillery and to haul supplies.

Meanwhile the U.S. Navy was exploding with comparable growth, adding eight (8) Battleships, twenty-three (23) Fleet Carriers, seventy-one (71) Escort Carriers, forty (40) Cruisers, two hundred sixty-five (265) Destroyers, and one hundred seventy-eight (178) Submarines between Pearl Harbor (12/7/1941) and V-J Day (8/14/1945).

Much of the battlefield success throughout World War II came directly from the men who had been selected and trained to be ready to take on the incredibly important ***leadership*** roles of our military establishment, former Cadets from the United States Military Academy (West Point), established on 16 March 1802, and former Midshipmen from the United States Naval Academy (Annapolis), founded as the Naval School in 1845. These men became the "face" of American military power, displaying the ***character***, intelligence, and trustworthiness required by American citizens. And they have never let us down!

West Point's motto is: "Duty, Honor, Country"

Nearly 500 West Point graduates died in WWII.

There have been 224 four-star generals in the history of the U.S. Army.

196 (87.5%) of them graduated from West Point.

Only five men in American history, four of whom were West Point alumni, have been promoted to the five-star rank of General of the Army.

These men were *leaders of character*:

>General of the Army George C. Marshall/VMI - 1901
>General of the Army Douglas MacArthur/USMA - 1903
>General of the Army Henry H. Arnold/USMA - 1907
>(Re-designated General of the Air Force on May 7, 1949)
>General of the Army Dwight D. Eisenhower/USMA - 1915
>General of the Army Omar N. Bradley/USMA – 1915

Annapolis' motto is: "Through Knowledge, Sea Power"

686 Naval Academy alumni died in WWII.

There have been 258 four-star admirals in the history of the U.S. Navy.

227 (87.9 %) of them graduated from Annapolis.

Only four men in American history, all Naval Academy alumni, have been promoted to the five-star rank of Admiral of the Fleet (the navy equivalent of General of the Army or the British Field Marshal rank).

These men were *leaders of character*:

>William Leahy/USNA-1897
>Ernest King/USNA-1901
>Chester Nimitz/USNA-1905
>William Halsey/USNA-1904

These four radically different men were the best and the brightest the navy produced, and together they led the U.S. Navy to victory in World War II, establishing the United States as the world's greatest sea power.

The following two quotes help us better understand how important the concepts of *"commitment"*, *"character"*, *"leadership"*, and *"teamwork"* are to graduates of military academies, for over 212 years . . . most easily observed here at home with athletic competition while they were still matriculating at their respective academies:

General of the Army George C. Marshall, Chief of Staff during World War II was known to have said, *"I want an officer for a secret and dangerous mission. I want a West Point football player."* Each Army football player passes this sign as they go out onto the playing field.

General of the Army Douglas MacArthur wrote, *"Upon the fields of friendly strife are sown the seeds that upon other fields, on other days, will bear the fruits of victory."*

With this amazing tradition and heritage of service to our country, it's no wonder that every facet of "Academy" life at both West Point and Annapolis was not only competitive, but also hugely successful . . . especially their respective football programs.

An abundance of young men with a wealth of talent, *character*, and *leadership* skills launched "Academy" athletic teams into the public's awareness, and eventually to a new generation known as the "Baby Boomers"!

Army vs. Navy

Army football began in 1890, when Navy challenged the cadets from Army to a game of the relatively new sport. Navy defeated Army at West Point that year, but Army avenged the loss in Annapolis the following year. The rival academies still clash every December in what is traditionally the last regular-season Division I college-football game.

Army's football team reached its pinnacle of success under Coach Earl Blaik when Army owned *"the fields of friendly strife"*, winning three consecutive national championships in 1944, 1945 and 1946, and produced three Heisman trophy winners: Doc Blanchard (1945), Glenn Davis (1946) and Pete Dawkins (1958). The West Point football team still plays its home games at Michie Stadium, where the playing field is named after Earl Blaik.

Likewise, Navy's 1926 national championship team was loaded with talent, **character**, and competitive spirit . . . but they were not alone.

Three undefeated teams with nearly identical records would cause a stir among fans and pollsters today, but this was not the case when Navy earned its lone national championship in 1926, as the Midshipmen shared the honor with Stanford and Alabama. A 7-7 tie between Alabama and Stanford in the 1926 Rose Bowl gave Stanford a 10-0-1 mark, while the Crimson Tide and the Midshipmen each had identical 9-0-1 records.

The 1963 Navy Midshipmen football team was led by head coach Wayne Hardin in his fifth year, finished the year with an overall record of nine wins and two losses and with a loss against Texas in the Cotton Bowl Classic.

It was in the 1963 Army–Navy game that "instant replay" made its television debut.

Quarterback Roger Staubach won the Heisman Trophy and the Maxwell Award while leading the Midshipmen to a 9–1 regular season record and a final ranking of #2 in the nation. He led Navy to victory over their annual rivalry with Notre Dame, which would be the Midshipmen's last win over Notre Dame until 2007. In the Crab Bowl Classic, Navy defeated Maryland by a score of 42–7. Second-ranked Navy accepted an invitation to play in the 1964 Cotton Bowl Classic versus #1 Texas, only the second #1 versus #2 bowl game in college football history. Unfortunately for Navy, the Longhorns won the game 28–6.

Meanwhile, back in the Pentagon, it was clear that air power was and is an essential component of any nation's fighting machine, and the U.S. was already underway with plans to turn the Army Air Corps into a full-blown, very robust United States Air Force (July 26, 1947).

The United States Air Force Academy couldn't be far behind!

The site selection committee chosen to pick the home for the AFA and all future graduates, included General Hubert Harmon, General Carl Spaatz, General Curtis LeMay, Reserve Brigadier General Charles Lindbergh, Mr. Virgil Hancher, and Mr. Merrill Meigs.

On June 24, 1954, Colorado Springs, Co was chosen as the new home for the United States Air Force Academy, after a grueling down-select process that started with over 400 "potential" sites across twenty-two states . . . just beating out Alton, Illinois (near St. Louis) and Lake Geneva, Wisconsin, about 100 miles from Chicago.

Soon after President Dwight Eisenhower signed the Academy Act (with some encouragement from his wife, Mamie, who just happened to be a Denver, CO native), General Hubert Harmon, the Academy's first Superintendent, signed General Order #1, activating the Air Force Academy, on August 14, 1954.

For its first three years, the Air Force Academy was located at a temporary site on the east side of Lowry AFB in Denver, CO, under the command of General Hubert Harmon, who had been recalled from retirement to be the first "Super" (Superintendent).

Construction on the permanent location (18,000 acres) north of Colorado Springs began in 1955 and was sufficiently complete for the Cadet Wing to move in August of 1958.

Army and Navy, aka West Point and Annapolis, were not impressed with the newest Academy. "Tradition" became a central point of discussion between the three Academies, including many of the professors at the Air Force Academy, most of whom were from, you guessed it, West Point or Annapolis.

Since day #1, Air Force Cadets have taunted their "older" brothers, saying that, "both West Point and Annapolis possess more than a century and a half of tradition, *unhampered by progress!*" To which the Cadets and Midshipmen respond, "West Point and Annapolis don't have to prove themselves to the world, they are stabilized. The Air Force Academy can't make that statement for another 100 years!"

The '59ers - It helps to get off to a great start!

Three hundred and six members of the AFA Class of 1959 were sworn in as Cadets at the newly-opened United States Air Force Academy at their temporary site at Lowry Air Force Base in Denver, Colorado on July 11, 1955. On June 3, 1959, 207 members of that class graduated and were sworn in as 2nd Lieutenants (Twenty went on to become General officers . . . nearly 10% of their Class). The <u>first</u> graduates of the United States Air Force Academy set the "bar" very, very high.

Among their many, many, many accomplishments, we find one special group of about 40 cadets, members of the Air Force Academy classes of 1959, 1960, and 1961, who over-achieved, by any measurement.

The 1958 AFA Falcon Football Team.

Not many people get to be the first to do anything. And of those that do, very few actually set the mark so high . . . with outstanding **commitment**, **character**, **teamwork**, and **leadership** . . . that for generations, people would agree that what they accomplished would never be matched. The bar had been set. A tradition had begun!

Such was the *character* of the 1958 Falcon Football team.

The 1958 Air Force Academy Falcon Football Team

Bob Collins
Rocky Mountain News
Oct. 5, 1958

"October 4, 1958, that's the date the Air Force Academy came of age. It's the day the Falcons met the challenge of athletic greatness and passed with flying colors. The yardstick was applied by the touted Iowa Hawkeyes, proud standard bearers of the greatest football conference of them all, the Big Ten. The score was 13-13 and the result transcends sports in its effect on the Academy.

All sports tradition at the Academy now starts with this game. No matter what happens to the rest of the season or in seasons to come, they'll still go back to this game in Iowa City when the Air Force Academy made its mark in the face of great odds."

Under the direction of Head Coach Ben Martin, a charismatic, multi-sport scholar-athlete and 1946 graduate of the United States Naval Academy, the 1958 AFA-Iowa football game was ***the first of many firsts*** for the very young Air Force Academy football program.

The 1958 Falcons beat Detroit-Mercy (37-6), tied the Iowa Hawkeyes (13-13), destroyed Colorado State (36-6), beat Stanford (16-0), edged out Utah (16-14), barely beat Oklahoma State (33-29), squeaked by Denver (10-7), beat Wyoming (21-6), crushed New Mexico (45-7), outlasted Colorado (20-14), and played TCU to a 0-0 Tie in the 1959 Cotton Bowl.

That's a 9-0-2 record, a .909 winning percentage, with eight games on the road . . . leading to a year-end 6th place national ranking (AP Poll).

In the Cotton Bowl, as during the '58 season, the Falcons relied on the leadership/running/passing of talented QB's Rich Mayo and John Kuenzel, the hard running of a stable of memorable names: Steve Galios, Mike Quinlan, Monte Moorberg, Phil Lane, Larry Thompson, Eddie Rosane and George Pupich, and the timely pass receiving of ends Bob Brickey and Tom Jozwiak.

Meanwhile, #33, Charlie May, a talented Fullback/Linebacker, went on to become the only senior (class of 1959) member of the team to attain the rank of General Officer, a Lieutenant General (three stars) at that! Charlie and wife, Barbara live in Shepherdstown, WV.

In addition, guard Ruben A. (Randy) Cubero (Class of 1961), weighing in at 5-foot-10 and 173 pounds, wearing #67, and described in the national media as "the smallest Guard in major college football today," went on to be a combat pilot, veteran of the Vietnam War and the first Hispanic Dean of Faculty at the United States Air Force Academy, retiring with the rank of Brigadier General in Colorado Springs with his wife, Janet.

Upfront, Air Force's first consensus All-American and College Football Hall of Fame member, Brock Strom, and Cotton Bowl Outstanding-Lineman-of-the-Game, Dave Phillips, paved the way, keeping All-Everything (and future Dallas Cowboy All-Pro and NFL Hall of Fame member) defensive lineman Bob Lilly at bay for sixty very long minutes.

Army vs. Navy vs. Air Force

The Air Force Academy football program was on the map, and subsequent teams leveraged what the '58 Falcons did, and built their pieces of the legacy, starting with key games against both Army and Navy. The current-to-date records show Air Force leading both series . . . 34-14-1 against West Point, and 28-19 against Annapolis. The 1966 Falcons were the first Air Force football team to beat both Army (14-3 on November 6, 1965 at Soldiers Field in Chicago) and Navy (15-7 on October 1, 1966 at Falcon Stadium in Colorado Springs).

The Commander-in-Chief's Trophy symbolizes football supremacy among the nation's three major military academies. The 170-pound, three-sided trophy stands 2.5 feet tall and is engraved with the seal of each Academy. It also displays a sculptured model of the mascot of each school.

The Commander-In-Chief's Trophy

The trophy is presented annually to the service academy with the best won-lost record in inter-service football competition. The year in which the trophy is won is engraved on a plate on the appropriate Academy's side of the trophy.

Named in honor of the President as Commander-in-Chief of the U.S. Armed Forces, this rotating trophy is sponsored by the alumni associations of the three academies.

The idea for the establishment of an inter-service football trophy originated with the late General George B. Simler, commander of the Air Training Command and a former Air Force Academy athletic director. General Simler proposed the idea to the AFA Association of Graduates in early 1972. The Association in turn proposed the project to the alumni associations at West Point and Annapolis.

Although both Army and Navy were initially reluctant to consider any proposal that might diminish the importance of the Army-Navy football game, Lt. General Albert P. Clark (AFA's 6th Superintendent) kept hammering away at his counterparts at West Point and Annapolis, and eventually the idea caught on. The 1972 season was chosen as the appropriate time to establish the tradition in-as-much as it marked the first year of round-robin competition in football between the three academies.

Army captured the trophy that first year. Navy took possession of it in 1973 and held it through the 1976 season. Army regained the trophy in 1977. Navy won it back in 1978 and held it until 1982.

The Falcons defeated Army and Navy in 1982 and 1983 to claim possession of the trophy for the first time since it was established. The 1984 season saw the trophy return to the Black Knights, and the Falcons didn't like it at all.

Head Coach Fisher DeBerry challenged his Team at the beginning of the 1985 season to win back the coveted Commander-in-Chief's Trophy. Things looked promising for the Falcons as they defeated the highly touted Midshipmen in Annapolis on October 12th by a 24-7 margin.

The trophy wasn't theirs yet, however, because the Black Knights of Army were coming off an excellent 8-3-1 season and an appearance in the Cherry Bowl. Army invaded Falcon Stadium on November 9th. A sell-out crowd watched as the Falcons routed Army 45-7.

"Our number one goal *always* is to beat Army and Navy," said DeBerry.

In 1985, the Falcons regained possession of the Commander-in-Chief's Trophy and won a portion of the WAC title. (Courtesy, Ronald Sapp)

To date (2014), the record shows:
Air Force Falcons   18
Navy Midshipmen/Goats   14
Army Cadets/Black Knights/Mules   6
Shared Award   4

Much of the success the Air Force Academy has had against both Army and Navy over the past three decades can be directly attributed to the Falcon's adoption of the Wishbone offense (and several variants). According to Wikipedia, "The wishbone formation, also known simply as "the 'bone", is an offensive formation in American football." The wishbone offense first debuted in college football on September 21, 1968 when the University of Texas, coached by Darrell Royal, played the University of Houston. The style of attack to which it gives rise is known as the wishbone offense. Like the spread offense in the 2000s, the wishbone was considered to be the most productive and innovative offensive scheme in college football during the 1970s and 1980s."

Actually, the Texas Wishbone offensive concept was introduced by new Texas offensive coordinator, Emory Bellard, in the summer of 1968, at the Texas High School

Coaches Association (THSCA) Convention held in Dallas, Texas. The THSCA is the largest football conference in the country, with more than 35,000 attendees, and Coach Bellard was on the agenda in one of the smaller (<250) meeting rooms to introduce "the new Texas offense, the Wishbone"... which he considered to be ". . . the soundest offense that's ever been put together" About 150 current and former Texas HS and College football coaches were on hand to see Coach Bellard draw a series of X's and O's on the large, green chalkboard. It looked like an inverted "Y", and he proceeded to show where all the O's were moving and he said, " . . . and if we're going to run the ball to the left, we're not going to block anybody on the left side of the line."

Eyes opened wide. Heads turned. Mouths silently spoke, "what?"

About 20 well-educated football coaches excused themselves from the room.

Then Emory said, " . . . and if we're going to run the ball to the right, we're not going to block anybody on the right side of the line."

Another 50 been-there-and-done-that football coaches left the room, hoping to get a good seat in the big auditorium where Tennessee Head Coach Johnny Majors would soon use his own set of X's and O's to explain the new Vol's passing game for the upcoming '68 football season.

In the Fall of 1968 Head Coach Darrell Royal became the first coach to install the Wishbone formation in a backfield led by a group of players that became known as the "Worster Bunch" consisting of All-American's Steve Worster, James

Street, Billy Dale, Chris Gilbert, and Cotton Speyrer. With this powerful new offense in effect, the 1968 Texas team went 9–1–1 with a demolishing 36–13 victory over Tennessee in the Cotton Bowl Classic, one of the most complete and lopsided wins in all statistics since the 1941 Texas win over Oregon, 71–7.

One year later, the Texas High School Football Coaches Association (THSFCA) conference was held in Ft. Worth, Texas. When Texas offensive coordinator Emory Bellard arrived 15 minutes early at the largest (>5,000) auditorium in the complex to present, "The new Texas offense . . . the Wishbone"... the folks standing at the back and in the aisles pushed the attendance to over 8,000. Nobody left early.

Texas began the 1969 season by defeating all opponents by an average score of 44 points. The final game of the regular season had No. 1 Texas against No. 2 Arkansas in the true "Game of the Century" for the 100th year of college football. The game saw Arkansas leading throughout the game when the Longhorns came from behind in the 4th quarter to win 15–14, capturing their second officially recognized National Championship in which President Richard Nixon declared Texas the champion after the game. Texas would then go on to face and defeat Notre Dame in the 1970 Cotton Bowl Classic which solidified Texas' place as the No. 1 team in all of college football . . . again . . . running the Wishbone.

The Wishbone offense, and variations thereof, dominated junior high, high school, and college football for nearly two more decades . . . most notably by the Oklahoma Sooners and the Air Force Falcons. In fact, Oklahoma Head Football Coach, Barry Switzer, visited two spring training sessions at Air Force hoping to better understand the timing and coordination the Falcons displayed as they ran the country's newest, most powerful option offense . . . the Wishbone, and later the "Flexbone".

Other schools and other coaches, offensive and defensive alike, paid attention to what made the Wishbone work so well, and ways to stop it! They all quickly realized that the complexity involved in successfully running the Wishbone offense required not only good athletes, but also very *smart* players . . . a combination of traits that were not found at most Colleges and Universities around the nation . . . but abundantly available at the nation's service academies . . . especially Air Force!

Air Force Head Coach Ken Hatfield, like many before him, was trying to come up with offensive and defensive schemes that would allow his always-undersized Falcons to be more competitive . . . and in 1980, the Wishbone looked like a candidate to help the Falcons put more points up on the board.

After an extensive search within the Wishbone-savvy coaches around the country, Hatfield interviewed and hired Fisher DeBerry in 1980 as the Air Force Academy quarterbacks coach. DeBerry had earned his coaching stripes, including six years of coaching and teaching in the South Carolina high school ranks, then, returning to his alma mater, Wofford College, where he coached for two years as an assistant when the Wofford Terriers won 21 consecutive games and were ranked first in the NAIA.

For the next nine years, 1971 to 1979, DeBerry was an assistant coach at Appalachian State University, where he learned about and implemented their version of the Wishbone. While DeBerry was there, Appalachian State was ranked in the top 10 nationally in rushing, total offense or scoring offense three times. In 1974, the team ranked sixth nationally in pass defense when he was defensive coordinator.

The next year at Air Force, DeBerry was promoted to offensive coordinator. By 1982**, Air Force had fully implemented the Fisher DeBerry-version of the Wishbone (The Flexbone) and quickly posted an 8-5 record and beat Vanderbilt in the Hall of Fame Bowl while averaging 30.4 points per game. After the Falcons' 10-2 season in 1983, Hatfield won both the Bobby Dodd Coach of the Year and the 1983 American Football Coaches Association (AFCA) Coach of the Year awards, and, after much soul-searching, left Air Force for Arkansas, his Alma Mater, fulfilling a life-long dream. Fisher DeBerry was promoted to head coach, and during his tenure as head coach, Air Force won at least eight games in 11 different seasons. DeBerry's first team, in 1984, was 8–4 and beat Virginia Tech in the 1984 Independence Bowl. The next year, the Falcons won 12 games, and were ranked as high as #4 nationally until a 28–21 loss at BYU. In the final Associated Press poll, the Falcons ranked #6.

Air Force Bowl Results (10-12-1) and Winning percentage by Head Coach:

Head Coach: Ben Martin (96-103-9) = 46%

Season	Bowl	Opponent	Score	W/L
1958 (9-0-2)	Cotton	TCU	0-0	T
1963 (7-4)	Gator	North Carolina	0-35	L
1970 (9-3)	Sugar	Tennessee	13-34	L

Head Coach: Bill Parcells (3-8) = 27%

Season   Bowl   Opponent   Score   W/L

No Bowl Games

Is it easier to win in the NFL, coaching the New York Giants, the New York Jets, the New England Patriots, and the Dallas Cowboys . . . or at the Division I-A collegiate level, coaching the Air Force Falcons?

Head Coach: Ken Hatfield (26-32-1) = 44%

Season	Bowl	Opponent	Score	W/L
1982 (8-5)**	Hall of Fame	Vanderbilt	36-28	W
1983 (10-2)	Independence	Mississippi	9-3	W

Head Coach: Fisher DeBerry (169-107-1) = 61%

Season	Bowl	Opponent	Score	W/L
1984 (8-4)	Independence	Virginia Tech	23-7	W
1985 (12-1)	Bluebonnet	Texas	24-16	W
1987 (9-4)	Freedom	Arizona State	28-33	L
1989 (8-4-1)	Liberty	Mississippi	29-42	L
1990 (7-5)	Liberty	Ohio State	23-11	W
1991 (10-3)	Liberty	Mississippi State	38-15	W
1992 (7-5)	Liberty	Mississippi	0-13	L
1995 (8-5)	Copper	Texas Tech	41-55	L
1997 (10-3)	Las Vegas	Oregon	13-41	L
1998 (12-1)	Oahu	Washington	45-25	W
2000 (9-3)	Silicon Valley	Fresno State	37-34	W
2002 (8-5)	Emerald	Virginia Tech	13-20	L

Head Coach: Troy Calhoun (59-44 = 57%)

Season	Bowl	Opponent	Score	W/L
2007 (9-4)	Armed Forces	California	36-42	L
2008 (8-5)	Armed Forces	Houston	28-34	L
2009 (8-5)	Armed Forces	Houston	47-20	W
2010 (9-4)	Independence	Georgia Tech	14-7	W
2011 (7-6)	Military Bowl	Toledo	41-42	L
2012 (6-7)	Armed Forces	Rice	14-33	L
2013 (2-10)	None			
2014 (10-3)	Idaho Potato	Western Mich.	38-24	W

So what makes the Air Force Academy special?

First, you need to know and understand that, *"The mission of the United States Air Force is to fly, fight and win . . . in air, space and cyberspace."*

Second, *"The mission of the United States Air Force Academy is to educate, train, and inspire men and women to become **officers of character** who are motivated to lead the United States Air Force in service to our nation."*

Third, *"The mission of the United States Air Force Academy Athletic Department is to **teach leadership** in a competitive environment and **to build character** by providing all cadets a realistic leadership experience in a mentally and physically challenging environment . . . molding future officers through athletics."*

And finally, *"The mission of the United States Air Force Academy Football Team is made up of three complimentary parts:*

> <u>*Part Number 1*</u>: *to develop on-field competitive spirit,*
> <u>*Part Number 2*</u>: *to instill within our cadets lifelong resolute **character** traits, and*
> <u>*Part Number 3*</u>: *to prepare each team member for service and **leadership** to help our country."*

<u>**The Bottom Line**</u>: *"The Air Force Academy shall produce **leaders of character** who are exceptionally well-prepared to lead in a complex, challenging, technically sophisticated and ever-changing geopolitical environment."*

The 1985 Air Force Falcons are right up there with the 1958 Air Force Falcons when it comes to **character** and *leadership* . . . hard-working, smart, talented overachievers whose uniqueness can be traced right back to their Head Coach.

Head Coach Fisher DeBerry, along with the young but highly-motivated assistant coaches and trainers around him, was the perfect solution for the youngest Academy that was still struggling with how to recruit, train, and prepare outstanding young athletes to become "***winners***" while ***maintaining all the core values*** that are so important for the USAF Academy, the U.S. Air Force, and the nation.

Fisher DeBerry, the winningest coach in Air Force football history, was a steady influence on his players, on and off the field. He realized that his football teams were a "culture-within-a-culture-within-a-culture", and teaching the essential "rules of engagement" would be the glue that held everything together and kept everybody connected and focused on their objective(s).

After every game for twenty years, when only team and coaches are allowed in the locker room, his players know that he will emphasize the things that matter most, certainly not their standing in the Mountain West Conference or what the press is saying this week.

DeBerry takes the words from his book, For God And Country, very seriously and knows how to impart values that his players can live by. Whether they win or lose, the first item on the agenda is to thank God for the opportunity of playing the game and for the lessons and values that will make them better officers and better people.

On his wall hangs a plaque that reads, *"A coach's success is not measured by wins or losses, but by the men his players become."*

"The fact of the matter is we all have baggage that we have to deal with and that's the key: Deal with it, whether it means discussing it in counseling with a therapist or with the minister from your church. You can overcome your past. By the same token, you can build on the things that were good in your life and the good things that you picked up from those who raised you." ("For God and Country" by Coach Fisher DeBerry.)

The men his players have become include hundreds of guys who went on to serve their nation and honor their coach. Today, after each game, he'll be telling them just what I'd want him to tell my own son, "Go to church tomorrow, call your mom and daddy and tell them you love them, and remember who you are." (Artsy-Asylum)

**The Team behind the Team
1985 AFA Falcon Football Staff**

<u>Back row, going from left to right:</u>

Cal McCombs, Ken Rucker, Jim Bowman, Charlie Weatherbie, Carl Russ, Tom Miller, Darrell Mastin, Jim Conboy, Jim Grobe, Rick Brown

<u>Front row, going from left to right:</u>

Jack Culliton, Sammy Steinmark, Bruce Johnson, Fisher DeBerry, Bob Noblitt, Dick Ellis, Jack Braley, Dick Enga

For Fisher DeBerry, this was an easy challenge to step up to. Fisher didn't have to change anything about who he was and what made him tick. And he quickly assembled a talented staff with the same values and motivation (from <u>For God and Country</u>):

> **Keeping The Faith** – "The greatest test of a person's faith is when they find themselves on a fence. Does a person jump to the other side of the fence when there's a chance for social and popular approval? Or does he/she stand by his/her beliefs knowing that as a religious person, a person of faith, he/she might have to endure criticism and grief? It's hard when there's pressure, but that's a test of your faith, and you'll find out how true and deep your faith runs on those occasions."
>
> **Character** – "Character is a summation of who you are as a person. Character is how you act and who you are when no one else is looking. The accountability and standards you are raised around, and what comes from within, determine your character. You can't tell someone in words about your character. However, your words and actions

tell all anyone needs to know about you and your character."

Teamwork – "Teamwork is commitment. It means everyone is committed to the same thing. You can't be successful without it. The epitome of teamwork is when you have a group of people who don't care about getting the credit."

Dedication and Discipline – "Dedication, discipline and commitment go hand-in-hand. Dedication means being disciplined enough, and willing enough to do whatever it takes to see the job completed."

Optimism – "If you aren't optimistic, the sky is not as bright. The days seem longer. The simple pleasures are overlooked. Folks focus on what they don't have instead of what they do have. Optimism is a key to achievement, and it says a lot about your character as well."

Realizing Potential – "Potential isn't worth a hill of beans if it is not actualized. We talk about the potential to be a good team, but potential is one thing. Actualization is something completely different. A lot of hard work and sacrifice . . . those are the necessities to realize potential. The teams that are good at the little things and intangibles are going to be successful – not the most talented. That's why character is so important. Character is the essence of life and of being successful, and once you achieve a goal, you feel a sense of pride. There's nothing more exciting than seeing your highest goal within your grasp. It's not just a testament to how far you've come. It says a lot about who you are, the sacrifices you've made, and the hard work you've displayed."

Leadership – ". . . the Academy exists to produce leaders for the Air Force, who in turn protect our country and our freedoms. That's why what we're doing is so meaningful every single day. A leader can help someone do something that they didn't think they could do. A good leader can instill and develop confidence in those around him or her. Leaders are willing to step out front and not worry about criticism or people questioning and abusing them. Hopefully, the way you do things – the way you live your life and interact with people – will make others want to follow you. When they want to follow you, then you've found the definition of leadership."

Commitment – "Commitment is part of who you are. If you give someone your word, you have to realize what that means. Your word is the most prized possession you have. Commitment is finishing what you begin."

Loyalty – "To me, telling someone that they are loyal is the greatest compliment you can give."

Balance – "You have to have balance in your life, a sense of being well-rounded. If you focus in just one area, you can get so overwhelmed and so engrossed that you don't see or appreciate other things. However, if you have balance and can enjoy other things, you will be happier and can achieve meaningful things in many areas of your life."

Perspective and Prayer – There are always hiccups during the course of a long football season, some of which require the services of an experienced chaplain, which has been part of AFA football program since 1984. "The chaplain also leads our team for Share Time on Friday nights before a game and gives thanks for our gifts and opportunities. It's a time for us to keep the game in its proper perspective. We have a lot of athletes, often members of the Fellowship of Christian Athletes (FCA), or coaches who come in and share their thoughts with us."

Steps To The Top – "If you are going to be successful, you can never forget about the fundamentals, the little things. You have to be committed to the fundamentals. If you excel at the fundamentals and 'little' things, you will win most of your games on the field and in life.

We want our players and staff to 'expect to win.' I believe you win with good people and positive attitudes. We want the tradition and the expectations in the program to be high.

You have to dream big. You have to have big visions and not limit yourself. If you dream it and can envision it – and if you are willing to put forth the effort – we can do anything."

Making A Difference – "We don't have egos on our team or among our coaching staff. We all have a job to do. No one job is more important than the other. Every single day our players and staff pass by a sign that reads, *'You make the difference.'* That means no matter what your job is, it is your attitude toward your responsibility and your commitment to excellence that is going to contribute to this team. Everyone has a job to do on every play and we expect everyone to take exceptional pride doing the jobs with quality and pride."

They say that *"A picture is worth a thousand words."*

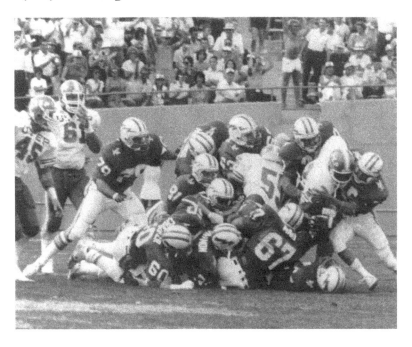

The picture above, and on the front cover of this book, "Count The Helmets", shows an actual play from the 1985 Falcon football game against the University of Texas @ El Paso (UTEP) on August 31^t, 1985, played in Falcon Stadium in Colorado Springs, CO.

Often referred to as, "The best football picture ever taken!", this one photograph captures eleven young men who, like the rest of their Team, as integral parts of the USAFA Cadet Wing, have chosen to dedicate themselves to a ***culture of***

commitment and ***a climate of respect and unselfishness*** that leads directly to a level of ***TEAMWORK*** that produces extraordinary results.

How else can you get that picture? On that one play, all eleven AFA players had to know exactly what their respective jobs were and then execute it perfectly, together with all their teammates, at just the right time!

No other picture with this level of execution exists, anywhere, but at the AFA.

The 1985 Air Force Falcons set the standard for demonstrating ***character, leadership, un-selfishness, commitment, excellence*** and ***teamwork*** like no other team in AFA history, not even the beloved and undefeated Class of 1959!

The 1985 Air Force Falcons were indeed a "Band of Brothers", much like Shakespeare's Henry V. saying, "We few, we happy few, we band of brothers!"

Under the direction of Fisher DeBerry, and after choosing to live-work-play under his rules, the '85 Falcons were a happy group, a living "brotherhood" in every sense of the word, and long, long before Stephen E. Ambrose's 1992 book of the same name or HBO's ten-part, 11-hour miniseries that debuted on September 9, 2001 . . . virtually re-setting the bar for ***character, leadership***, and ***teamwork*** for <u>***all cadets***</u> at the AFA.

Denver Post sports writer, Jim Armstrong, covered the Falcons from the early 80's, reported on the '85 Falcons each week, and in retrospect, wrote and published an article in the Post that best explains this special group of Academy athletes:

Band of Brothers: 1985 Falcons

Team shares a special bond and a legacy that still soars to this day.

By Jim Armstrong
The Denver Post
November 1, 2009

Terry Maki remembers it as if it were yesterday. The chaos in the cockpit, the sense of imminent disaster, the flashes of enemy fire cutting through the darkness toward the helicopter.

"We were 50 feet off the ground," Maki said. "The helicopter drowns out most of the sound and light, but there were a lot of anxious folks in that helicopter. I really thought, at one point, we were going to be shot down."

Maki doesn't particularly like talking about that day in Iraq, or any of his military experiences for that matter. It's all part of the code of a Special Forces officer. He will, however, acknowledge a certain box in his name in Montana, one filled with medals to honor a man filled with meddle.

"I have a few, yeah," he said.

The Distinguished Flying Cross, the Bronze Star and the Meritorious Service Medal, just to name a few.

Before he became a real-life Rambo, a man who infiltrated enemy lines with the Navy SEALS and Army Rangers, Maki was a heck of a linebacker at the Air Force Academy. What Dick Butkus was to the Chicago Bears of the mid-1960s, Maki was to the Air Force Falcons of the mid-1980's.

"One tough son of a gun," said his coach, Fisher DeBerry.

Maki had a lot of company on the 1985 Air Force team that finished 12-1 and ranked No. 5 in the nation. With each passing year, the pile of evidence grows higher, one that points to that season as the greatest in school history.

Funny thing, though. Time also has revealed the special nature of that team, and the player's lasting legacy has little to do with setting academy records for victories, or points scored, or interceptions, all of which they accomplished, but what they did after leaving the academy.

Maki was asked about his most prized piece of memorabilia from his days in the armed forces. He didn't mention any of his medals, but rather a helmet signed by DeBerry and members of the 2006 Air Force football team, DeBerry's last at the academy.

"They sent it to me for my retirement," Maki said. "That was really cool."

A special blue-collar group

They had nicknames for each other. Smaki. Sid Vicious. Fat Joe. Spike. Scooter. Horsehead. Bandstand. They spent countless hours together, squeezing in impromptu film sessions between late-night study-thons involving such core courses as astronautical engineering and aeronautical engineering and statistics. And they had an unconditional commitment to each other, a bond they still feel to this day, with their hair thinning and graying.

"We had blue-collar players who bought into our foundation, which was family and brotherhood," said DeBerry, who won the 1985 Bear Bryant Award as the national coach of the year.

"They didn't want to let each other down. That's what made that group."

*Added wide receiver **Tyrone Jeffcoat**, one of the few black players on the team: "I don't know if people understand how tight we were as a group. We transcended race and background. We broke down a lot of the sub-cliques that may have existed in previous classes."*

But there was no discounting the role played by the rigors of everyday academy life.

"The adversity of the situation brought us all together," Jeffcoat said. "You depend on teammates. They're your brothers. You lean on them, tell them about the bad days and the good days. We had real strong bonds because those guys see you at your most vulnerable. There's a certain degree of intimacy that comes with that."

*All-American safety **Scott Thomas** stays in touch with former teammates via the internet and when he gets the chance he travels to Colorado Springs for reunions from Sheppard Air Force Base in Wichita Falls, Texas, where he serves as a Squadron Commander.*

We pick up right where we left off, even if we haven't spoken to each other for a year," Thomas said. "There are so many guys I'm proud of on that team. I mean, look what they've done with their careers."

*Only one player on the 1985 team, sophomore defensive tackle **Chad Hennings**, played in the NFL. But then, that was by design. Air Force graduates are supposed to aspire to stars on* *their shoulders, not on their helmets, as Hennings wore with the Dallas Cowboys.*

If Hennings was the exception among those players, doing great things in the service of their country was the rule.

Some of those players became majors, several rose to colonel, most if not all ahead of the age curve – under the zone. Panama, Bosnia, Afghanistan, Somalia, Iraq, to name a few. One, **Richard Clark***, is a brigadier general in his mid-40s. Another,* **Mike Chandler***, went on to command the Thunderbirds. Another,* **Brady Glick***, has spent more hours in an A-10 fighter plane than any other flier in Air Force history.*

They didn't just fly A-10s. They piloted C-141s and F-16s, even Air Force 2. They led troops that ultimately vanquished Manuel Noriega from Panama and Saddam Hussein from Baghdad. They tracked down terrorists, carried supplies for starving refugees, escorted the vice president and secretary of state around the world, and took part in more operations than Hawkeye and Trapper John – Operation Desert Storm, Operation Anaconda, Operation Desert Fox, Operation Desert Shield and Operation Just Cause among them.

John Ziegler*, a defensive tackle on that team, is now Col. John Ziegler. He landed in Iraq in 2006, where he worked counterintelligence and special investigations to identify and locate terrorists.*

"There's not a lot I can tell you," Ziegler said. "There were a few we had our eyes on and we were able to . . . keep tabs on them. I was watching a video feed from a Predator, and to be able to see our guys flying around a house I had been watching a month earlier, it was kind of rewarding."

Maki saw his share of combat

Maki was deployed nine times from the late 1980s into the early years of this decade before retiring from the military to coach high school football in Montana. Name just about any Middle East conflict and he saw it, sometimes behind enemy lines with his Special Forces brethren. And yes, he witnessed more than his share of casualties. That's why he's not comfortable talking about his military experiences.

"It's personal when you lose forces, men who put their tails on the line every day. You're talking about the bravest Americans you can imagine. The best of the best, each one of them."

Scott Thomas *has a similar story, having been rescued behind enemy lines in Iraq after being forced to bail out of his F-16 when the engine caught fire. U.S. Special Forces arrived 2 ½ hours later, but the mission wouldn't have been successful if some of those missiles whizzing past the helicopter had found their mark.*

"I never thought I was going to die," said Thomas, now a lieutenant colonel. "There were a couple of long hours of wondering, but I always had confidence in everybody around me. That comes from what's instilled in you after being part of a team with that academy group."

Thomas isn't alone. To a man, members of the 1985 team interviewed by The Post credited the experience of playing football at the academy with helping to mold them into the officers they became.

"We had a lot of leadership courses, but I firmly believe that nothing taught you more about leadership than playing football at the academy," said **Bart Weiss**, *the quarterback on the 1985 team. "It taught you to identify people's strengths and*

weaknesses. You learn that you're going to take a physical and mental pounding, but you can't get down. Because you're not always going to play on 72-degree sunny days."

Maybe it was meant to be that Maki, a retired lieutenant colonel, would teach those lessons himself to high school football players. He's coaching in Florence, Montana, population 1,000, where he and his players were preparing this past week for a Class B state playoff game Saturday night. The name of his team? What else?

The Falcons.

Terry Maki . . . developing the next generation of leaders in Montana.

"Leaders of Character."

It starts at the top.

Lieutenant General Michelle Johnson is a 1981 graduate of the Air Force Academy, a Rhodes Scholar, an All-American athlete, a Command pilot, a wife, a mother and the first female Superintendent of the USAF Academy.

She acknowledges many of the problems that the Academy is facing today (Honor, Sexual abuse, Character, Leadership, Sequester, Religion, etc.) and goes on to say, "The Academy will embrace the necessity of making decisions that may reshape the institution but will remain committed and capable of producing top-quality Lieutenants for our Air Force and the nation."

Reflecting back on her four years at the Academy and thirty-three-plus years serving in the USAF, she talks about the "essence" of the Academy and what makes it, and its graduates, unique.

At the top of the list of key components, identified by the person who will be leading the USAF Academy for the next 3-4 years are:

- Developing *Character* and *Leadership*
- Focusing on the AF Mission in Air, Space and Cyberspace
- Immersing Cadets in a Total Experience
- Competing at all levels
- Exposing Cadets to AF Professional Culture
    - Internalizing the Air Force Ethos*
    - *Leadership Character*
    - Professionalism
    - *Teamwork*

*A Greek word meaning "**character**" that is used to describe the guiding beliefs or ideals that characterize a community, nation, or ideology.

LtGen Johnson's successful experience as a cadet, an officer, a pilot, and now the leader of the USAF Academy, provides her with first-hand experience with how important "**character**" and "**leadership**" are to every organization at the Air Force

Academy, and she is looking to the very-visible and morale-setting AFA Falcon football teams to be ***leaders of character***, showing the rest of the Academy what it means to: *"... inspire men and women to become **officers of character** who are motivated to lead the United States Air Force in service to our nation."*

General Johnson reminds us:

> *The Core Values of the United States Air Force Academy:*
>
> – *Integrity first.*
> – *Service before self.*
> – *Excellence in all we do.*

#USAFAValues: *The blueprint for reshaping the "essence" of the USAF Academy may very well be found by examining the pieces of the puzzle that was the 1985 Falcon football team, culminating in a 12-1 season that came within four seconds and four yards of moving on to the national championship game, and launching a "band of brothers" into proud, distinguished service to their nation.*

PART TWO

THE GAMES

Chapter One

The Miners

"The greater danger for most of us lies not in setting our aim too high and falling short but in setting our aim too low and achieving our mark." --- Michelangelo

Aug 31, 1985   **AFA vs. Texas-El Paso**   **W 48-6**

UTEP hoped to field a team that would be competitive. Coach Bill Yung had worked hard on a struggling program. The Air Force game was their first test. They failed.

On the Falcon's first possession, they went 47 yards in only 1:38. Quarterback Bart Weiss had 37 of the yards and scored the touchdown. Three minutes later the Academy scored again and never looked back.

Mike Burrows/GazetteTelegraph:

If you're a believer, spread the word. If you're a non-believer, prepare to spread the word.

This Air Force Academy football season is going to be interesting.

Teams normally hang their heads when they commit four turnovers.

Teams normally don't do well when they trail in possession time by almost eight minutes.

Air Force did both Saturday.

But Texas-El Paso couldn't have picked a worse day to show up.

The crowd of 38,500 saw a 48-6 rout that favored the Falcons from the very start.

Either Air Force is going to make noise in the Western Athletic Conference comparable to those F-15s that zoomed overhead prior to the kickoff, or UTEP is horrible.

There was a little of both on a 90-degree afternoon that Air Force now hopes will serve as a launching pad to its first WAC title.

The Miners trailed after one quarter, 17-0, and never threatened while dropping their fifth consecutive game to the Falcons.

Consider these AFA heroics:

- The Falcon's wishbone finished with 225 rushing yards and 150 by passing.
- Mark Simon, an emerging star, averaged 53.6 yards on three punts.
- Tom Ruby, virtually an unknown quality, kicked field goals of 31 and 27 yards when drives stalled and easily handled five extra-point tries.

- Bart Weiss, the first-team quarterback, completed five of six passes for 132 yards, including a 60-yard scoring strike to halfback Kelly Pittman. Incredibly, the long TD put UTEP into a 14-0 hole less than seven minutes into the game.
- Safety Scott Thomas and linebacker Terry Maki combined for 23 tackles. Cornerback Dwan Wilson set an AFA record with his 10th career interception.
- At its best, the AFA defense suffocated UTEP. At its defensive worst, the Falcons looked formidable.

Mike Burrows/GazetteTelegraph:

Touchdowns tend to make you smile a lot. They can lift you to cloud nine. And when you get there, you never want to come down.

Randy Jones, an Air Force Academy halfback, scored a touchdown Saturday at Falcon Stadium.

It was somewhat lost in an avalanche of points when Texas-El Paso absorbed a 48-6 setback.

But there Jones was, in the locker room afterward. Wide smile. Cloud nine resident.

All for a one yard score late in the second quarter that gave the Falcons an impressive 27-0 halftime lead.

To be sure, Air Force had more glamorous stars Saturday, but nobody's joy matched that belonging to Jones.

You'd wear the look of a hero, too, if you'd just scored the first touchdown of your four year career, especially after a painful back injury forced you to the sideline for all of last season.

That description fits Jones, a 5-foot-11, 193-pound senior from Corpus Christi, Texas.

"My first touchdown. I'll never forget it," he said, beaming. "It really was a long time coming. I was beginning to think I'd never get one here."

"Your first goal is to make sure the team does well. But I like to do well, too. When you score, it does nothing but build your confidence."

Few of the Falcons are respected more than Jones. He was a starter two years ago as a sophomore before a disc problem crashed his junior season.

It's been a long road back. His role, at least for now, is coming off the AFA bench and providing a spark when needed.

"We can only start two halfbacks at a time," said Ken Rucker, the AFA running backs coach. "But we look at Randy like he's a starter. It was great to see him get the touchdown, considering what he's been through."

"We know what he can do. Just like we know what (senior starters) Greg Pshsniak and Kelly Pittman can do. All three are quality players and all three are considered starters."

All three had a hand in Saturday's wishbone explosion.

Interestingly, Air Force's top three halfbacks combined for only 40 yards on eight carries. Their ball-carrying action was that limited.

Still, they helped launch the AFA attack with crunching blocks on the corners, and no halfback at the academy blocks better than Jones.

Need proof?

When Pittman danced 10 yards with a pitch from quarterback Bart Weiss for a third-quarter touchdown, padding the Falcon's lead to 34-0, Jones flattened a UTEP defender to open the door.

Halfbacks who can block make for a dangerous wishbone.

UTEP simply got in the way and suffered the consequences.

"We've worked awfully hard to get better," said Pittman, a 5-9, 190-pounder from Houston. "We take a lot of pride in our ability to block."

Ralph Routon/The Colorado Springs Gazette:

An impact player, this Arkie. A winner from Wynne.

A gifted schoolboy quarterback suddenly became a gift to the Falcons' secondary.

No fooling.

A year ago, he led Air Force with five interceptions, a total that tied for the Western Athletic Conference lead. On a defense that ranked as the WAC's best, he made 49 tackles, giving him a three-year total of 140.

"I know I was a different person after that BYU game back in '82," Wilson said. "We were burned a few times, but I learned so much that day. I learned I could play. It's amazing how one day can change you. When we came back and won that game, I suddenly felt like I had all the confidence in the world."

Sam Garza, the Texas-El Paso quarterback, should have known better. There was 7:44 left in the second quarter of the AFA-UTEP opener eight days ago, and Wilson was lurking in the territory.

Garza fired. Wilson intercepted, and the Falcons went on to pound the Miners, 48-6.

The school record was his.

"I'd like to get one every game," said Wilson, now a 6-foor-1, 185-pound senior. "If I get 10 or 11 more, that's not really a whole lot considering how many passes you see in the WAC. I want to push this record up high, to establish it with some credibility. That's one of my goals now."

Don't sell him short.

Air Force doesn't, with good reason. The Falcons got one of their best defensive backs in history practically by default.

Wilson's hometown, Wynne, is in the rural rice and cotton country of northeast Arkansas, near the Tennessee and Mississippi borders. He was weaned on the Razorbacks, and grew up wanting to play for the University of Arkansas in Fayetteville.

One problem. The Hogs didn't think he warranted a scholarship.

So Wilson looked elsewhere. Oklahoma State offered a scholarship, and Wilson took his recruiting trip to Stillwater with a lineman from Little Rock named Leslie O'Neal.

O'Neal, a consensus all-America defensive tackle at OSU last season, is now chasing the Outland Trophy and Lombardi Award.

Wilson is chasing a dream, though he's been living it every day for the past three years.

"Just like everybody else growing up in Arkansas," he said, "I wanted someday to play for the Hogs. But even more than that, I just wanted to play major-college football. That was my No. 1 dream, and there are times even now when I have a hard time believing I'm really at this level. Besides OSU and Air Force, nobody very big wanted me. I thought I'd go to OSU, then I visited the academy.

"It was like nothing else mattered. It was love at first sight. It's funny, but six or seven years ago I'd have said somebody was crazy to think I'd end up here, training to be a pilot and playing football at a place like this. It's crazy, but I love it. One visit here and OSU was out the window.

"I don't come from a military family. My sophomore year in high school, I knew nothing about the academy. Now it's my life, or at least a very big part of my life. Crazy, isn't it?"

Yeah, and the Falcons are loving every minute of it.

"All Dwan wants is to play hard and win," said Cal McCombs, the AFA secondary coach.

"The thing I always stress is, 'Do your job, and use the proper technique when you do it.' Dwan's a great example of that. He's always prepared. What's special about Dwan is that even though he broke into the starting lineup as a freshman, he's never stopped trying to be a better football player. He could sit back and relax a bit. But, you'll never see him do that."

In the veteran AFA secondary, no one sits back. Wilson is only one of four seniors. The others are safety Scott Thomas, cornerback Tom Rotello and Falcon back A.J. Scott. Few secondaries in the country can match their experience.

And there may be none capable of matching their togetherness.

"Scott Thomas is our star," Wilson said. "He's the all-America candidate, and deservedly so. But I think we're all pretty capable of doing well. At the same time, none of us is jealous of the other. We're about as close a group as you'll find."

It's easy to make note of Wilson's contribution, McCombs said.

"He keeps the attitude going. He's happy when the others are happy. If Dwan had his way, he'd rather have the other three guys get all the ink, all the recognition."

Bruce Johnson, AFA Defensive Coordinator:

"We didn't play great the entire game, but when the chips were down, we responded well. It feels good for us to do so well in a blood-and-guts kind of game, when they are trying to line up and whip us."

Fisher Deberry, AFA Head Coach:

"I worried a lot about this game," said Fisher DeBerry, the AFA Head Coach. "I just didn't know what to expect. I really thought it'd be a nail-biter right down to the very end.

"But I thought we had a big edge in quickness, and I thought we were downright dominating in the kicking game. Simon is a great punter. Ruby is emerging, too.

"We capitalized on mistakes. UTEP gave us a lot of help. Our defense was outstanding. As far as I'm concerned, give the defense credit for this win. They were exceptional most of the time."

Ralph Routon/The Colorado Springs Gazette:

Their lockers sit together in a busy corner of Air Force's football dressing room under Falcon Stadium.

So close, just as the lives of Bart Weiss and Brian Knorr have been so entwined the last three years.

Weiss and Knorr, the Falcon's senior quarterbacks, have taken their turns at maturing into Air Force's wishbone offense during their concurrent cadet-athlete careers. Both have been heroes, and both have suffered tough defeats. At different times, each has operated the triple option with flawless poise.

Now it is their final season, and at this stage Weiss and Knorr have to qualify among the very best 1-2 college quarterback combination in the nation. Either could start for any run-oriented offense in America. Unfortunately for them, they must share the playing time this fall as the Falcons aim for more big-winning rewards.

But there is no animosity. Both know anything could happen. They also realize Air Force probably will need two quarterbacks, somewhere in the 11 games ahead, if this is to be a memorable football autumn at the academy.

Saturday, as the Falcons embarked on their new schedule with a surprisingly easy 48-6 romp past Texas-El Paso, Weiss and Knorr again divided the time and the production. Weiss, the starter since Knorr's shoulder injury in the fourth game of 1984, led the way to a 34-0 lead and scored a touchdown. Knorr guided the No. 2 offense to the final 14 points, and his touchdown came on a slick 25-yard run.

AFA Notepad:

Krazy George, the well-known professional cheerleader, made his presence known throughout the day at Falcon Stadium. Midway through the first quarter, he initiated the first true "wave" ever done in Colorado Springs, and it lasted for more than five minutes. Trouble was, Air Force was on offense at the time, and "waves" are supposed to be done when the home team is on defense.

Krazy George also had huge groups of the crowd chanting and clapping in unison, with several effective back-and-forth cheers led by "tastes great . . . less filling."

****

Air Force officials announced the crowd as 38,500 and called it the third-largest attendance for a home opener in AFA history. But press box veterans figured the crowd closer to the 31,000-32,000 range, though Air Force has not been known for padding its figures in recent seasons.

But, with 38,500 as the announced count, Air Force definitely is in position to average more than 40,000 for its six home games this fall, something that hasn't happened since 1972.

****

Air Force's defense, which was the dominant force all afternoon, succeeded on many counts Saturday. But perhaps the most impressive statistic was that the Falcons stopped UTEP's offense without a first down on eight of the Miner's first 13 possessions.

Of course, Air Force also forced UTEP into five turnovers, which gave the Falcons possession at the Miners 26, 33, 32, 46 and AFA 49. With field position like that, any team would have a good chance to win.

****

Air Force players and coaches were united in favor of the Falcons' open date this week before the long-awaited trip to Wyoming on Sept. 14. By then, the AFA injury list should be thinned out considerably.

Starting fullback Pat Evans, who sat out Saturday with a bruised knee, will return as will receiver Eric Pharris. No other Falcons were seriously hurt against UTEP, with offensive tackle Dave Sutton suffering a slightly sprained left knee (he returned in the second half).

"We've got a lot of guys, including myself, with bumps and bruises," said quarterback Bart Weiss. "We weren't so sure at first about the early open date, but now it couldn't come at a better time for the team."

Final Statistics: AFA vs University of Texas at El Paso (UTEP)

Score	1	2	3	4	Final
Air Force	17	10	14	7	48
UTEP	0	0	0	6	6

Scoring Plays:

AFA – Weiss	5 run (Ruby kick), 1/11:31
AFA-Pittman	60 pass from Weiss (Ruby kick), 1/8:29
AFA – Ruby	31 FG, 1/5:00
AFA – Ruby	27 FG, 2/4:20
AFA – Jones	1 run (Ruby kick), 2/1:50

AFA-Pittman 10 run (Ruby kick), 3/9:39
AFA – Knorr 25 run (Ruby kick), 3/5:42
UTEP – Remo 10 run, (pass failed), 4/12:18
AFA – Morris 2 run, (Camacho kick), 4/10:24

Team Statistics:

Category	AFA	UTEP
First Downs	17	15
Rush-Pass-Pen	52-225-4	64-224-12
Rushing Yards	225	224
Passing (C-A-I)	6-8-0	8-15-2
Passing Yards	150	69
Punt Avg.	53.6	35.2
Fumbles-Lost	5-4	4-3
Penalties-Yards	4-30	12-125

Individual Statistics (Leaders only):

Rushing (Att-Yds): Weiss (AFA) 13-49
Smith (AFA) 12-38
Knorr (AFA) 2-29
Harvey (UTEP) 12-55
Dixon (UTEP) 8-41
Passing (C-A-I-Yds): Weiss (AFA) 5-6-0-132
Knorr (AFA) 1-2-0-18
Garza (UTEP) 6-13-2-35

Receiving (#-Yds): Pittman (AFA) 1-60
Carpenter (AFA) 1-40
Keseday (UTEP) 2-20
Tackles: Scott Thomas – 13
Terry Maki – 10 Brady Glick – 7

The best football picture ever taken!

Dwan Wilson wraps up another Miner receiver!

Coach DeBerry shouts "encouragement" to the Falcons!

The record-setting '85 Falcon Kicking-Combo: Mark Simon (Punter & Holder), Derek Brown (Snapper), and Tom Ruby (Kicker) at Falcon Stadium.

Pre-game strategy session, Scott-to-Scott
(Yes, I know it's from the wrong game,
but the picture is too good not to use!)

Coin toss, AFA vs UTEP, August 31, 1985
(Note: Falcons' bench was on the east
side of Falcon Stadium in 1985.)

PAT vs. UTEP
Derek Brown snaps, Mark Simon holds,
Tom Ruby kicks . . . Teamwork!

WYO TODAY

SEPTEMBER 14, 1985

Wyoming's Quarterbacks

and Receivers

AIR FORCE
WAR MEMORIAL STADIUM

Chapter Two

The Cowboys

"A leader does not deserve the name unless he is willing occasionally to stand alone." ---Henry A. Kissinger

Sept 14, 1985   AFA @ Wyoming   W 49-7

Air Force had seemingly forgotten how to win in Wyoming's War Memorial Stadium. For thirty minutes it looked like history would repeat itself as the Cowboys shut down the wishbone.

Wyoming scored first and the Falcon's Head Coach Fisher DeBerry was scratching his head. He tried 11 different ball carriers in the game. Eight fumbles resulted – half were lost.

Things changed in the second half. Mike Chandler and Steve Sigler led a defense that gave the offense an opportunity to perform, and perform, and perform some more. The 49-7 score is deceptive. It was a tough game. The Cowboys always play the Falcons tough, especially in Laramie.

Ralph Routon/The Colorado Springs Gazette:

Some football games are decided long before anyone even puts on a uniform.

Exactly two hours before the opening kickoff here Saturday, Air Force's Falcons arrived at War Memorial Stadium for their game against the University of Wyoming.

They already had won. Wyoming didn't have a chance.

The clock said 11:30am, and not a single fan had come through the turnstiles. One by one, the Air Force players stepped off the bus and walked toward the dressing room. Everybody knew the way, because this was the Falcon's third straight year to visit Laramie.

They also were in a bad mood. Angry. Seething. Or maybe consumed is the right description.

I have watched Air Force play football for nine seasons. I have never seen the Falcons that intense, that ready, before.

Not against Notre Dame. Not against Army or Navy. Never. Not even close.

Usually in the past, the AFA pregame personality has been loose and relaxed. They rarely have been accused of wasting much mental energy in advance of 1:30pm. That has been their style, and it has worked wonderfully.

But this was different. This was Wyoming, which had cost Air Force many special dreams here in 1983 and 1984. Once again, the Falcons had come here without a loss and hoping to build early-season momentum.

Everybody said the Laramie Jinx didn't exist. But, they all knew, it had to end now or the jinx would become very real.

Coaches had nothing to do with the Air Force mood. Head Coach Fisher DeBerry had told the Falcons that they had a chance to enjoy an outstanding 1985 season. But, without a victory here, most of the team's ambitions would be impossible.

They wanted to make sure Wyoming didn't spoil their dreams again. So they were fired up. Lord, they were fired up!

Mike Burrows/The Colorado Springs Gazette:

Terry Maki was 6 years old in 1970 and nowhere near a football field in Libby, MT, the day Wyoming was drubbed, 41-17, by the Air Force Academy at War Memorial Stadium.

Until Saturday, that was the Falcon's last successful trip across the Wyoming border.

"A long time ago," Maki, an AFA linebacker, said. "But I guess all that's changed now."

It is.

If there ever were demons residing in Laramie, Air Force's 49-7 victory over the Cowboys forced them into hiding.

"I feel like a big weight has been lifted off my shoulders," Maki said. "This has been a long time coming. We came here with the idea of winning the game, and we did that. Nothing was going to stop us."

Not even a 7-0 deficit early in the first quarter. Not even an AFA offense suddenly stricken by a severe case of fumbilitis.

"We're coached to overcome adversity," said Maki, a 6-foot-2, 227 pound junior who finished with seven tackles – a total second among the Falcons, behind the 10 contributed by senior linebacker Mike Chandler.

"When you're down by a touchdown and the game's onbly about five minutes old, that's adversity. But we held together. This is a close group. We don't die easy."

Bruce Johnson/ AFA Defensive Coordinator:

"This bunch has a lot of maturity," said Bruce Johnson, the AFA Defensive Coordinator. "What was great to see was that we responded when our backs were against the wall.

"Any time you can face adversity like we did (Air Force fumbled five times in the first quarter, losing three) and come out of it with something positive like this, you have to feel great.

"We built a lot of *character* out there. And I believe it's going to help us down the road."

Final Statistics: AFA @ Wyoming

Score	1	2	3	4	Final
Air Force	0	14	21	14	49
Wyoming	7	0	0	0	7

Scoring Plays:

WYO – Griffin	38 pass from Runyan (Cottingham kick), 1/10:40
AFA – Weiss	1 run (ruby kick), 2/8:27
AFA – Weiss	1 run (Ruby kick), 2/4:55
AFA – Weiss	5 run (Ruby kick), 3/9:09
AFA – Smith	1 run (Ruby kick), 3/4:11
AFA – Brennan	6 pass from Weiss (Ruby kick), 3/3:16
AFA-Vallanti	26 run (Camacho kick), 3/9:39
AFA – Sigler	35-yard interception return (Camacho kick), 4/4:30
AFA – Morris	2 run, (Camacho kick), 4/10:24

Team Statistics:

Category	AFA	WYO
First Downs	29	12
Rush-Pass-Pen	68-18-3	47-21-7
Rushing Yards	340	124
Passing (C-A-I)	11-18-0	8-21-3
Passing Yards	167	95
Punt Avg.	37.5	37.7
Fumbles-Lost	8-4	3-1
Penalties-Yards	3-15	7-67

Individual Statistics **(Leaders only):**

Rushing (Att-Yds): Smith (AFA) 17-80
Lyons (WYO) 6-17
Passing (C-A-I-Yds): Weiss (AFA) 11-18-0-167
Runyan (WYO) 3-7-2-50
Receiving (#-Yds): Carpenter (AFA) 5-108
Daum (WYO) 4-42

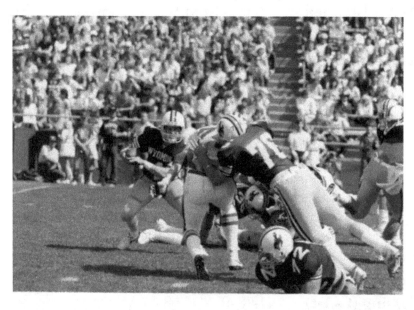

John Ziegler moves in on the Wyoming QB.

The Falcons celebrate another Sack!

Chapter Three

The Owls

"Sports do not build character. They reveal it."

and . . .

"Ability may get you to the top, but it takes character to keep you there."

John Wooden

Sept 21, 1985   **AFA vs. Rice**   **W 59-17**

The wishbone worked well and often against the Rice Owls. Quarterback Bart Weiss led the offense with 172 yards of the total 406 rushing yards gained.

Fullback Johnny Smith carried the ball through huge holes for 133 yards in the first half, and the Falcons ended the game with 505 total yards.

Punt returner Scott Thomas provided some excitement as the first half ended, running back a punt for a 72 yard touchdown.

Terry Maki led the Falcons in tackles keeping the Owls back on their heels all afternoon.

Mike Burrows/The Colorado Springs Gazette:

If the Air Force Academy has seen more productive days on the football field, then let those days speak now or forever hold their peace.

But don't tell the Rice Owls.

The victims of a 59-17 waxing, they were thankful Saturday just to get out of Falcon Stadium with their hides intact.

They wouldn't believe it anyway, this note that Air Force has had bigger explosions on the scoreboard, and recently, too.

Think back to 1972, and you recall the Falcons' 68-6 thrashing of Davidson. Just a year ago, Air Force steam-rolled Northern Colorado, a Division II school looking for a nice payday, by a score of 75-7.

Both routs took place at the same cemetery plot that, naturally, had ample room for Rice.

The Owls merely reared back, let fly, and crashed.

Loudly.

They probably didn't even know they'd just become Air Force's third consecutive 42-point victim in a 3-0 season for the Falcons.

Rest assured, knowledge of algebra and ownership of a calculator weren't needed to realize Air Force's triple-option running game emerged superior to Rice's vaunted passing attack.

AFA quarterback Bart Weiss scored three touchdowns for the second straight week and rushed for a career-high 172 yards on 14 carries while directing a turnover-free wishbone attack. This performance earned the 6-foot, 172-pound senior from Naples, FL the Western Athletic Conference's offensive player of the week.

Johnny Smith, the Falcons' junior fullback, also had a career-best day – in the first half alone. By the time Air Force had shot to a 31-10 lead at halftime, boosted with 24 points in the second quarter, Smith had 133 yards on 11 carries. That's the way he finished.

Scott Thomas, Air Force's do-it-all safety, broke loose for his first special-teams touchdown when he returned a Steve Kidd punt 72 yards on the final play of the first half.

Thomas' great wall of blockers resembled another Great Wall and enabled the All-America candidate from San Antonio, Texas to dash past a jubilant AFA bench en route to the end zone. With him went Rice's dream of an upset victory.

The crowd of 33,868 respectfully asked to be excused when Air Force lifted its lead to 52-10 with 2:50 still left in the third quarter on a two-yard run by reserve fullback Grant Morris.

It's worth noting that Morris' touchdown was preceded by linebacker Kevin Martin's block of a Kidd punt. It was that kind of day for the Owls, who surrendered 503 total yards to the Falcons. Included were 406 rushing yards compiled by 13 backs.

Air Force's defense gave up 390 total yards to the Owls' blitzkrieg offense. But that figure was ballooned considerably with 1:20 left in the game when Elliston Stinson, a wide receiver with world-class sprint speed, scored against the AFA reserves on a school-record, 86-yard strike from second-team quarterback Kerry Overton.

Scott Smith/The Colorado Springs Gazette:

"Wishbone Wizards" – Air Force fullback Johnny Smith jogged down the runway toward the locker room, oblivious to his pursuer. As Smith neared the doorway, he was slowed by a merry-mass of blue shirted teammates, all trying to funnel their way through an opening not designed for madding crowds. Smith slowed to a walk, his smile expanding in the wake of the Falcons' 59-17 thumping of Rice.

His mind was elsewhere. Perhaps he was thinking about his 133 rushing yards. Perhaps he was contemplating the considerable glory created by a third consecutive 42-point blowout victory. Perhaps he was reliving his three long runs (40, 38, and 27 yards), all of which ended with him being dragged down from behind, short of the goal line, after bursting untouched into the Owl's secondary.

Whatever, Smith never saw it coming.

Boom. He was blind-sided – grabbed from behind, his arms pinned to his sides by a strong embrace. His surprise turned to joy as he turned and recognized his post-game tormentor: His Dad. They exchanged an emotion-charged hug and Smith proceeded into the locker area. Both men smiled.

Mike Burrows/The Colorado Springs Gazette:

Now the $64,000 question: Do the high-flying Falcons deserve to be in the Associated Press Top Twenty?

"I don't worry about things like that, seriously," Fisher DeBerry, who now has an 11-4 coaching record and six-game win streak in his second year at the academy, said Sunday. "We'll let the people that do the picking decide where we stand.

"Besides, the poll doesn't mean a whole lot right now. Yes, I think we're deserving. But I also think the poll that means the most is the one you see at the end of the year."

Free safety Scott Thomas, defensive tackle John Ziegler, and cornerback Tom Rotello agreed.

"Where would I vote us? That's a good question," said Thomas, who returned a Rice punt 72-yards for a first-half touchdown in Saturday's landslide whipping of the Owls. "I think we probably should be in there somewhere, but exactly where is tough to say.

"I don't know how good everybody else is. We're good, I know that. But I don't think the poll means very much right now. If we get in, that's great. But we know we've still got a lot of games to play.

"We have to be patient."

Air Force had five sacks of Rice quarterbacks Saturday, and Ziegler got one. Rice sophomore quarterback Mark Comalander threw two interceptions, and Rotello got one. Rotello now has two, tying the junior from Denver with junior free safety Steve Sigler and senior cornerback Dwan Wilson for the team lead in interceptions.

"I don't know about the Top Twenty yet," Ziegler said. "There's a lot of season left and a lot of things can happen. Maybe we are that good. At least I hope so. But I wouldn't be that disappointed if the rankings leave us out this week. It's the end of the season that matters most to us."

"Sure we deserve it," Rotello said. "We're hot right now. But we don't get depressed if we're not in it this week. We've got to keep doing this every week. I don't expect us to win by 42 points every week. But we do have the capability to win every week. I think the ranking will take care of itself."

Critics will say the Falcons have yet to face a test.

True.

Critics will say Rice's defensive line, which surrendered a combined 305 rushing yards to quarterback Bart Weiss and fullback Johnny Smith, couldn't have stopped a little girl pulling a little red wagon.

OK, that's stretching it.

Three routs of three sub-par teams. But the Falcons aren't just walking to wins. They're burying teams alive.

They're hot, like Rotello said.

Air Force still ranks No. 2 nationally in per game scoring with an average of 52 points. And the Falcons now rank No. 15 in total offense with a per-game average of 449.7 yards.

Ralph Routon/The Colorado Springs Gazette:

Go ahead, Air Force, take a bow. Enjoy the moment. Soak in the applause. Feel proud.

You deserve it.

Monday brought a double dose of special national recognition for Air Force Academy football. Part Three came this morning (Tuesday, September 24, 1985), but it wasn't even absolutely essential. Just icing on the cake.

Air Force officially returned to the nation's college elite, that superior group of acknowledged powers who make up the wire-service rankings and earn the national TV appearances.

After their impressive 3-0 start including that many 42-point victories, the Falcons have been ranked No. 18 in America by United Press International's weekly poll. Several hours before that announcement Monday, ABC-TV decided to schedule Air Force vs. Notre Dame as the network's sole nationally televised game on October 5th.

Today, the Associated Press rankings (including two probation teams, Florida and SMU, that are ineligible for the UPI list) placed Air Force in the No. 19 spot, just behind Southern Cal.

Those things may not seem like much to the disinterested observer. After all, Air Force has been a consistent winner since 1982, including those three straight bowl victories and conquests of Notre Dame.

But in reality, Monday's news will have a huge impact inside the AFA program. Humility reigns supreme from head coach

Fisher DeBerry down to the greenest freshman. But everyone still has thirsted for more national credibility.

Confidence is no problem. Ever since those first milestone wins over Notre Dame and Brigham Young in 1982, the Falcons have considered themselves capable of beating (or losing to) anybody.

Final Statistics: AFA vs. Rice

Score	1	2	3	4	Final
Air Force	7	24	21	7	**59**
Rice	3	7	0	7	**17**

Scoring Plays:

AFA – Weiss	10 run (Ruby kick), 1/13:15
Rice – Hamrick	54-yard Field Goal, 1/8:17
AFA – Pittman	7 run (Ruby kick), 1/3:38
AFA – Ruby	37 FG, 2/6:33
Rice – Brinkley	61-yard pass from Comalander (Hamrick kick), 2/5:55
AFA – Weiss	6 run (Ruby kick), 2/2:24
AFA – Thomas	72-yard punt return (Ruby kick), 2/:00
AFA-Pittman	3 run (Ruby kick), 3/12:29
AFA – Weiss	14 run (Ruby kick), 3/8:22
AFA – Morris	1 run, (Camacho kick), 3/2:50
AFA – Evans	2 run (Camacho kick), 4/13:09

Rice – Stinson 86-yard pass from Overton (Hamrick kick), 4/3:24

Team Statistics:

Category	AFA	Rice
First Downs	19	21
Rush-Pass-Pen	58-7-4	25-48-3
Rushing Yards	406	36
Passing (C-A-I)	5-7-0	23-48-2
Passing Yards	97	354
Punt Avg.	51.2	32.1
Fumbles-Lost	1-0	0-0
Penalties-Yards	3-27	4-38

Individual Statistics (Leaders only):

Rushing (Att-Yds): Weiss (AFA) 14-172
Smith (AFA) 11-133
Brinkley (Rice) 7-29

Passing (C-A-I-Yds): Weiss (AFA) 5-7-0-97
Comalander (Rice) 19-37-2-237

Receiving (#-Yds): Carpenter (AFA) 2-32
Stinson (Rice) 3-117

Tackles: Terry Maki (AFA) – 7
Scott Thomas (AFA) – 6
Evans (Rice) – 8

Safety Scott Thomas takes aim at another Rice Owl!

DeBerry counsels future AFA Head football coach.

Kevin Martin blocks another punt!

Fullback Johnnie Smith breaks away for another long gainer.

QB Bart Weiss executes Option #2 for 6 more points!

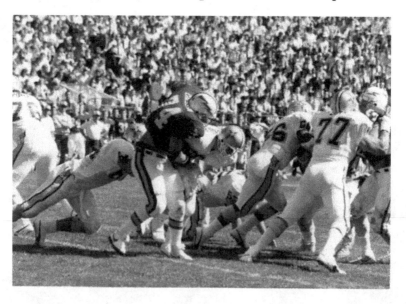

DT John Ziegler hanging out in the Owls' backfield.

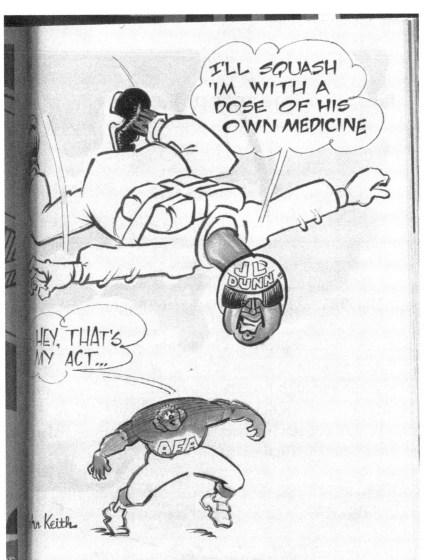

New Mexico vs Air Force

Chapter Four

The Lobos

"Football is like life --- it requires perseverance, self-denial, hard work, sacrifice, dedication and respect for authority." --- Vince Lombardi

Sept 28, 1985   AFA @ New Mexico (Night)   W 49-12

It was starting to look easy. The wishbone was well oiled and running smoothly. Quarterback Bart Weiss and receivers Ken Carpenter and Hugh Brennan showed the Lobos and anyone else who cared to watch that the Falcons had more than a running game. Even halfback Randy Jones completed a pass for a touchdown. Total passing yardage: 240.

With 580 total yards, the best of the early season, the Falcons put the Lobos away early. It was no contest.

Mike Burrows/The Colorado Springs Gazette:

The much-awaited test still has not found its way into the Air Force Academy classroom.

And we're now four games into the season, folks.

Air Force unleashed a monstrous offensive attack again Saturday night. The only difference was in the name of the victim.

In weeks past, it's been Texas-El Paso, Wyoming and Rice that wilted under an avalanche of AFA points. This time, it was New Mexico.

The Lobos walked out of a damp University Stadium with a 49-12 noose around their necks and a crowd of 27,124 watching.

New name, same result. Yes, even the same yawn.

While New Mexico checked for casualties, the 19th-ranked Falcons managed to cast a glance ahead to this weekend's nationally televised clash with Notre Dame at Falcon Stadium.

Routs give you that luxury.

"This one is over," Air Force head coach Fisher DeBerry said afterward. "Now, it's Notre Dame. It's time to give some thought to Notre Dame.

"We're capable of winning again. We're fully aware of that. We're going to fight our guts out, I assure you. But we also know that Notre Dame will give us the fight of our lives."

All the Falcons got from New Mexico was an exhibition bout. The excitement was over at halftime, when Air Force had a 28-6 lead.

Air Force, 4-0 overall, moved its pace-setting Western Athletic Conference record to 3-0. New Mexico fell to 1-2 overall and 0-1 in the WAC.

The teams amassed nearly 1,000 yards in combined total offense, but the Falcons still won comfortably.

Air Force finished with a 580-415 edge in total yards, and the Falcons got career-best productions of 218 passing yards from senior quarterback Bart Weiss and 156 receiving yards from senior wide receiver Ken Carpenter.

New Mexico never stopped the landslide, and managed only two Joe Bibbo field goals in the first half and a 4-yard touchdown run early in the fourth quarter from reserve quarterback Ned James.

Air Force's 4-0 start is its best since 1972, when the Falcons opened with five consecutive wins.

"The key to defending Air Force is that you have to stop their running game," UNM head coach Joe Lee Dunn said after the Falcons raced for 340 rushing yards. "We didn't do a very good job of that, especially in the first half.

"They ran all over us early and made us look bad. We can't quit. We've got a long season ahead of us."

So does Air Force. The difference is that the Falcons are on a roll.

"We're not completely fine-tuned yet, I don't think," DeBerry said. "I will say I'm happy with the offense.

"And I'm very happy with the defense. I thought they were tremendous, even though we gave up some yards. We bent, but we didn't break. That's the whole key for us. That's our whole philosophy. To give up just one touchdown to an offensive team the caliber of New Mexico is just remarkable."

What New Mexico hoped to do was not fall behind early. So much for best-laid plans.

Air Force safety Scott Thomas intercepted a Billy Rucker pass on the game's third play, and Weiss immediately took the Falcons on a 12-play, 56-yard scoring drive that halfback Kelly Pittman capped at 10:07 with an 8-yard touchdown run on an option play.

Perhaps at no other time in the five-year AFA marriage with the wishbone was powerful halfback blocking more evident on a scoring drive.

The key supplier for the Falcons was reliable Randy Jones, a senior from Corpus Christi, Texas, Pittman, another senior, had three carries for 23 yards in the march and each was sprung by crunching lead blocks on the corner by Jones.

And it was a Jones block on New Mexico cornerback Troy Clewis at the 2:34 mark of the second quarter that enabled Pittman, a Houston native, to dash 62-yards past the AFA bench for a touchdown that gave Air Force its 22-point halftime lead.

Pittman had a career-high 97 yards on just six carries by halftime, and Jones had a hand – or shoulder – in much of the explosion.

New Mexico got field goals of 38 and 31 yards from Bibbo to trail only 14-6 with 12:04 left in the second quarter.

Bibbo's kick's helped cushion the blow of Weiss' 57-yard touchdown strike to Carpenter at 5:06 of the first quarter. Weiss found his favorite receiver all alone down the AFA sideline, after Carpenter streaked past UNM cornerback Pat Duncan.

Bibbo's second field goal was set up when Thomas, the nation's fifth-leading punt returner, fumbled a 40-yard Ron Keller punt at the AFA 41-yard line.

Actually, the punt first touched Air Force's Tom Rotello, then bounced off Thomas. New Mexico freshman Devin Cooper made the timely recovery, but the Lobos soon discovered they were running short of heroics on a night when Air Force continued to stamp itself as a legitimate WAC title contender.

After Keller, the national punting leader from Lakewood, hit a 38-yarder midway through the second quarter, Weiss struck quickly with a 52-yard pass to tight end Hugh Brennan that carried to the UNM 5.

Three plays later, with 5:16 left in the first half, Air Force called for its halfback pass, a traditionally productive play.

The magic worked again, and the stunned Lobos watched in disbelief.

Weiss started with an option play to his left and, under pressure, pitched to Jones, the trailing halfback. Jones pulled up and lofted a 9-yard touchdown pass to Brennan, who had no company in the end zone. Tom Ruby's third of seven AFA extra points made it 21-6.

DeBerry sent most of his starters to the bench after Weiss' score gave Air Force a 42-6 lead with 11:50 left in the game.

Mike Burrows/The Colorado Springs Gazette:

Long live the wishbone.

Or better yet, long live the passing attack that the wishbone generates, seemingly on a whim.

Sure, the Air Force Academy ground game had its moments Saturday night in the 19th-ranked Falcons' 49-12 drubbing of New Mexico at University Stadium.

Sure, AFA halfback Kelly Pittman dashed for a career-high 126 yards on only 12 carries and scored two touchdowns on runs of 62 and 8 yards.

Sure, the Falcons pounded their way to 340 rushing yards and averaged 4.8 yards per carry.

But remember, this is Air Force. Every now and then, it should make the football fly to keep its name from becoming a misnomer.

Against New Mexico, two Falcons obliged in stunning fashion.

Since the Lobos mostly were concerned with stopping the AFA backs, wide receiver Ken Carpenter and quarterback Bart Weiss lit up the cloudy Albuquerque sky.

Weiss completed eight of 12 passes without an interception for 216 yards, including a 57-yard touchdown throw to Carpenter in the first quarter.

Carpenter finished with six catches for 156 yards. AFA tight end Hugh Brennan added three receptions for 71 yards and one touchdown – all in the first half.

The yardage totals for Weiss, Carpenter and Brennan marked career-best performances.

"The pass will never be the mainstay of this offense," said Carpenter, a 6-foot-1, 180-pound senior from Fort Lewis, Wash. "But I'll tell you what. We can hurt people with the pass, like we showed tonight.

"I had a lot of fun, and I think everybody did. I don't know what it looked like from the stands, but it was a dogfight out there. New Mexico really came at us hard. They wanted to win as much as we did."

Sorry, Ken, but from the stands it looked like a laugher, one of four in the Falcon's 4-0 season.

"We looked at a lot of film of New Mexico during the week before practice, and I'd say the time was well spent. We thought we could hurt them with the pass. That's what I like about us so far. We've been able to move the football with the run and, when we've had the desire, we've moved it through the air, too.

"That makes it tough on a defense, for sure."

New Mexico never did stop Pittman, a 5-9, 180-pound senior from Houston.

He averaged 10.5 yards per carry and likely could have padded his total had he not missed much of the second half with the mismatch in full bloom.

By halftime, when Air Force had a 28-6 lead, Pittman had 97 yards on only six carries.

"Credit it to great blocking, up front and in the backfield," Pittman said. "With those blocks, I was able to get to the crease and get some yards.

"It certainly was a good night, but not just for me. We all share in something like this. I just hope we can keep it going.

"This is fun. We realize it's worth our while to keep this feeling alive."

Ralph Routon/The Colorado Springs Gazette:

"Four in a row. Four in a row. Four in a row."

That happy, incessant chant rang out from Air Force's dressing room here Saturday night at University Stadium, as the Falcons celebrated their 49-12 victory over New Mexico.

But the "four in a row" had nothing to do with Air Force's 4-0 start in the 1985 season.

It had everything to do with the Falcon's next goal at home next Saturday against Notre Dame. Three straight times Air Force has beaten the Fighting Irish, and now the Falcons will try for No. 4.

That feeling doesn't exist solely within the AFA senior class, either. Everyone feels the same way, from the most established veterans down to the newest stars.

Air Force added a name to that list Saturday night. But it didn't come as a huge surprise to anyone.

Ever since sophomore Chad Hennings moved last spring from tight end to defensive tackle, taking over the vacancy left by three-year starter Chris Funk, everybody inside the AFA program expected big things.

Against New Mexico, Hennings emerged very quickly. He had eight tackles, seven un-assisted. And the 6-foot-5, 245-pounder also had four sacks for the night.

"I've been waiting for this all year," Hennings said later while accepting congratulations from his teammates and coaches. "We worked hard all week on staying in our passing lanes, and we knew we could take a lot of pressure off the secondary if we could get to their passer."

During the first half, Hennings was everywhere. He had two sacks in a row and three in two series. As the game wore on, he received a more respectful honor when the Lobos started double-teaming him.

But that merely allowed fellow tackle John Ziegler and noseguard Steve Spewock more freedom to apply pressure of their own. As a result, New Mexico was only able to reach the end zone once despite gaining more than 400 yards.

"We guys in the defensive front worked hard in the off-season to improve our strength," said Hennings. "I think it has made a difference for us this fall."

Agreeing fully with that is Scott Thomas, the senior free safety. Thanks largely to the pass-rushing success up front, Thomas picked off three New Mexico passes (though one of them, on a two-point conversion attempt, won't count on the stat sheets).

"I was beginning to wonder if I would ever get an interception this year," said Thomas, "bus when we get pressure like that, it gives us a lot better chance. There's just no comparison between our D-line this year and in the past. These guys are just awesome.

"As for Chad, he's a mean guy and he gets after it. I don't think anybody will stop him now.

And, just four games into his first season as an Air Force starter, Hennings was happy to join in that "four in a row" chant.

"That's the big one for us now, playing Notre Dame," said Hennings, who was in high school in Iowa when Air Force began its streak against the Irish. "We'll be ready for that one."

Ralph Routon/The Colorado Springs Gazette:

Fasten your seat belts. This jet is flying.

In the language of the military, permission is hereby granted for excitement in regard to the Air Force Academy football program.

If you would prefer for the word to come from Lt. Gen Winfield Scott, the AFA superintendent, then consider it an order. With priority.

Air Force is 4-0, the Falcons probably will move up to about No. 16 in the nation this week, and Notre Dame is next.

This could become crazy soon.

Or, most likely, now.

It's time to make a few pronouncements about this Falcon team, with the hope they don't bring bad fortune. But Air Force's stunning 49-12 victory Saturday night over a capable and determined New Mexico team, it would be wrong to hold back any longer.

This could be the most wondrous autumn in AFA football history.

Air Force could go 13-0 this fall.

Yes, just as Brigham Young did last year. And we all know how the Cougars wound up.

No. 1 in the nation.

This is no place to argue whether the Falcons could beat any college team in America, nor whether Air Force could win the Big Eight or Southeastern Conference.

But if BYU could be national champion, given the system as it is now, so could Air Force.

The road won't be easy, of course. Dead ahead are two enormous challenges: Notre Dame at home, Navy at Annapolis. Nobody cares that the Fighting Irish are 1-2 and the Midshipmen 1-3. Both could end Air Force's dreams on either of the next two Saturdays.

But the Falcons have risen to a new level now, higher than at any other time since perhaps Air Force's Sugar Bowl team 15 years ago.

Look at the scores: 48-6, 49-7, 59-17, 49-12.

That adds up to 205-42, which is nothing like Air Force ever has done before.

This victory over New Mexico was legitimate, too. The Lobos had offensive talent and defensive toughness. All they needed was some breaks at the right time to build some momentum. They got some breaks, but never the momentum.

Air Force has the closest thing it has ever had to a complete team. They have developed superb depth on both offense and defense, using reserves as much as possible in each of the four games so far.

More than anything else, though, Air Force has confidence now.

Scott Thomas, the free safety who could ride this exceptional season to an all-America honor, stood in the Falcon dressing room late Saturday night and tried to define the AFA squad's feeling now.

"We don't want to lose now," said Thomas, "and we feel like we can beat anybody."

Against Notre Dame, they will have a chance to pick up new believers – millions of them. After the Irish had been smothered Saturday by Purdue, ABC-TV executives were suffering from stomach ulcers. But now they have a hot item: Air Force.

Perhaps the best thing going for the Falcons now is that they can do nothing to change their normal, grueling routine. If this were Norman, Okla., or Austin, Texas, a 4-0 start with national ranking would turn a team's life upside down. But at Air Force, the physics and engineering tests just keep on coming.

Thanks to that, the Falcons should be able to maintain a steady keel. It will be important now, but the senior class of 31 strong already has proven its ability to hold everyone else together.

They will have to get accustomed o something new this week, however.

Given the circumstances and the records, for the first time ever, Air Force will be favored next Saturday against Notre Dame. Think about that. The Fighting Irish will be underdogs to the Falcons.

So, between now and then, our city can discover and enjoy a new identity. When more than 50,000 excited people produce Air Force's largest home crowd ever next weekend, the title will become official.

Colorado Springs – football town. Home of Air Force – football power.

Final Statistics: AFA @ New Mexico

Score	1	2	3	4	Final
Air Force	14	14	7	14	**49**
New Mexico	3	3	0	6	**12**

Scoring Plays:

AFA – Pittman	8 run (Ruby kick), 1/10:07
NM – Bibbo	38-yard FG, 1/6:36
AFA – Carpenter	57-yard pass from Weiss (Ruby kick), 1/5:06
NM – Bibbo	31-yard FG, 2/2:04
AFA – Brennan	9-yard pass from Jones (Ruby kick), 2/5:16
AFA-Pittman	62 run (Ruby kick), 2/2:34
AFA – Smith	3 run (Ruby kick), 3/1:19
AFA – Weiss	1 run (Ruby kick), 4/11:50
NM – James	4 run (pass failed), 4/9:21
AFA – Knorr	1 run (Camacho kick), 4/3:50

Team Statistics:

Category	AFA	New Mexico
First Downs	27	21
Rush-Pass-Pen	70-14-3	41-41-7
Rushing Yards	340	78
Passing (C-A-I)	10-14-0	21-41-2

Passing Yards	240	337
Punt Avg.	36.5	36.2
Fumbles-Lost	5-3	4-1
Penalties-Yards	3-49	7-40

Individual Statistics (Leaders only):

Rushing (Att-Yds):	Pittman (AFA) 12-126
	Weiss (AFA) 15-53
	Smith (AFA) 13-59
	Turral (NM) 12-54
Passing (C-A-I-Yds):	Weiss (AFA) 8-12-0-218
	Rucker (NM) 8-17-2
Receiving (#-Yds):	Carpenter (AFA) 6-156
	Brennan (AFA) 3-71
Tackles:	No information

OG Steve Hendrickson leads the way for FB Johnnie Smith!

Defensive stalwart Chad Hennings goes hunting for the Lobos!

How many pushups have we done today???

RE DAME

OCTOBER 5, 1985

ON STADIUM

$2.00

Chapter Five

The Fighting Irish

"The supreme quality for leadership is unquestionably integrity. Without it, no real success is possible, no matter whether it is on a section gang, a football field, in an army, or in an office." --- President Dwight D. Eisenhower

Oct 5, 1985   AFA vs Notre Dame   W 21-15**

**Including the most important play in the history of AFA football!

Air Force was a six-point favorite, but someone forgot to tell Notre Dame. With the national television cameras running and the Irish looking for revenge, the cadets had to find a miracle to win.

Notre Dame controlled the game with a 15-13 lead. The ball was at the Air Force two-yard line with only two minutes left. Three plays later, Notre Dame attempted a 37-yard field goal. Linebacker Terry Maki broke through the line and blocked the kick. Defensive back A.J. Scott grabbed the ball in the air and raced 77 yards for the miracle finish, a 21-15 victory for the Falcons over the Irish.

Ralph Routon/The Colorado Springs Gazette:

The private audience was scheduled for 11:30am in the small corner office, and the visitor came dressed for church.

In a way, it seemed like a religious experience.

Just a few minutes late, Gerry Faust came bouncing up the hallway, his ever-husky voice preceding him.

"Sorry if I'm late," he said apologetically. "It's a big week. Come on in."

After everything else here at Notre Dame that oozes tradition and flavor, keeping alive so many memories of the past, one might expect the head football coach's office to be the same. But it really isn't. Pictures hang everywhere, and an ornate trophy cabinet dominates one wall.

But this audience was not meant to gawk at an office. It was meant to talk with Faust. Already, there had been assurances that this would not be a lengthy life-history review. Only a brief discussion about this year and this game – Notre Dame at Air Force.

Son, Faust is everything you've ever heard or read. Down-home. Comfortable. Wide-open. Charming. Honest. Instantly likable. The world may be crashing down all around him, but he still smiles and laughs through it all.

He purposely has arranged his office so that nobody can sit and talk to him at his desk. That would be pretentious, out of character. He ignored the cluttered desk, preferring the chairs and sofa instead. He propped his feet up on the coffee table, and his white socks drooped below his pant legs. Informality at its best.

Quickly, Faust took the offensive:

"From Colorado Springs, huh? We ought a talk about your team, not mine. Air Force is good. They've got the best team I've seen them have in my time here. What an offense! And that defense is much improved. They're jelling as a team early, the way we wish our team could do. We're struggling right now. Last week at Purdue, we just stunk.

"I keep telling 'em they've got to be motivated and ready to play every week. I just hope they're learned it now. It's a big game. A big game. If they can't be excited about this one, they never will be."

Whoa, Gerry. Wait a minute. This isn't a speech. Let's have a pertinent question. After three years of facing Air Force's wishbone, do you think it's better to play straight defense or try special gimmicks?

Faust just smiled, scratched his legs and said, "Now, really, do you think I'm going to answer that? I can't give away our strategy."

Just wondering, coach.

For the next 25 minutes or so, we rambled and slid through a variety of subjects – mostly soft, a few tough. He made it clear that his job security was not a concern to him, nor the latest hot rumors of his replacements. How does he pull that off? Simple. He makes his life a tight, impenetrable cocoon.

"I never read a single newspaper during the season," he said. "If I did, I'd be swayed – either way. If we were winning, I would think we were better than we are. If it was bad . . . I just don't need the grief, to see bad things magnified out of proportion."

But, he doesn't make his assistants or players live such a sterile existence.

"I feel like I'm the one who should have the common-sense approach," he said. "My wife reads the paper. Just last week she said, 'Hey, Gerry, read this one. It's honest, but it's good.' But I said, 'No, I won't read it.' I just don't need the distractions.

"But I do vote on the UPI poll, and Air Force was on my list. They deserve to be there. I didn't vote for us. We shouldn't be ranked. I think we're about 30th or 35th right now.

"You know, if Air Force had to play the kind of schedule with the physical teams each week that we have to play, I don't think they could survive physically. They'd get injured up, because of their size. But three or four times a year, they can beat anybody in the country."

Mike Burrows/The Colorado Springs Gazette:

It's practically old-home week for Air Force Academy outside linebacker Pat Malackowski even though his hometown, Valparaiso, Ind., is more than a few hundred miles away.

With Notre Dame set to invade Colorado Springs today in preparation for Saturday's AFA-Fighting Irish kickoff at Falcon Stadium, Malackowski has been thinking back to his days as a Valparaiso youth.

Days when his family would drive 60 miles East to see Fighting Irish home games at hallowed Notre Dame Stadium in South Bend.

"You bet I've seen games there," Malackowski said after the 17th ranked Falcons completed Thursday's tune-up practice amidst blustery, ice-cold winds.

"That area is predominantly Notre Dame fans. I grew up when coach (Ara) Parseghian was there, and I can remember a lot of great times in that stadium."

Malackowski, a 6-foot, 209-pound senior and one of the Falcons' defensive leaders, has gone back to Notre Dame Stadium as a player the past two years. The Falcons won both times and now own a three-game streak over the Irish.

"I never actually believed I'd ever walk in there as a player," he said. When you grow up in Valparaiso, you dream of playing for Notre Dame. But, more or less, it's usually just a fantasy. You don't expect to actually do it.

"So when you come back as a player on the other side of the field, you know it's a really wild feeling. But now we get a shot at them at our place for a change."

The sudden late-afternoon change in weather left the Falcons with cold feet and red cheeks as they wrapped up the workout. But Fisher DeBerry, the AFA head coach, looked especially poised afterward when an ABC Sports crew taped a seven-minute interview with him in his Cadet Field House office.

The interview will be shown during ABC's national telecast of Saturday's Notre Dame game.

"Shoot, it's no different talking to those guys than it is to you," DeBerry, grinning, told an office visitor.

Turning serious for a moment, he said, "I believe we're ready to play. Notre Dame can expect to see our best Saturday. If we can keep away from mistakes, we've got a chance."

Mike Burrows/The Colorado Springs Gazette:

Near death late Saturday afternoon at wildly enthusiastic Falcon Stadium, the Air Force Academy football team had no choice but to knock on heaven's door.

Lo and behold, and miraculously, two of the Falcons' own answered that knock.

It was that kind of a devilish day for too-talented, too-strong, too-big Notre Dame.

With 5:28 left in a classic thriller and emotion dripping from everyone in a stadium-record crowd of 52,153, Terry Maki and A.J. Scott convinced Air Force that it is most certainly pointed toward a dream season.

Air Force trailed, 15-13, when Maki blocked a 37-yard John Carney field-goal attempt. The ball landed in the welcoming hands of Scott, who then raced 77 yards to history down the Notre Dame sideline.

Scott's cross-country touchdown sprint lifted the 17th ranked Falcons to a 21-15 triumph, and enabled Air Force to become **only the fourth team this century** to beat Notre Dame in four consecutive years.

The disbelieving Fighting Irish dropped to 1-3. Air Force, which plays Navy this week at Annapolis, Md., rocketed to 5-0.

"I kept saying to myself over and over, 'Somebody has got to come up with the big play. Somebody has got to give us a lift,' said an emotionally wiped out Fisher DeBerry, the AFA head coach. "We got what we needed. I don't think I've ever witnessed a bigger, more crucial play than the one Terry and A.J. teamed on.

"I'm thoroughly exhausted. I'm going home to think about Navy and lay in front of the fire."

He could have used Notre Dame as firewood. The Irish's season may very well lay in ashes.

"You can't ask our players to play any better than these guys played," said Jerry Faust, Notre Dame's classy but snake bit head coach.

"We played a heck of a game against a real good team.

"Losing a game like this is real tough on the kids."

Then Faust paused, fully aware his Irish now have their backs slammed against the wall.

"I feel for them," he said softly.

Later in the evening, Air Force acquired more prestige. Its eight-game winning streak, dating back to last November, became the nation's longest in Division I-A after SMU lost to Arizona.

But the Falcon's string could have ended Saturday, too. They got all they wanted from Notre Dame. And more.

Carney field goals of 28 and 33 yards had the Irish leading, 6-0, by the 14:12 mark of the second quarter.

Another Carney field goal, this one from 40 yards, and a 2-yard touchdown plunge by All-America tailback Allen Pinkett gave the Irish a 15-10 cushion with 7:33 left in the third quarter.

But Air Force answered in both instances and hardly appeared shy in throwing the fight to the Irish.

Oh, how the Falcons fought.

In the first half, they answered with a 24-yard touchdown strike from quarterback Bart Weiss to halfback Kelly Pittman and a 20-yard field goal from Tom Ruby to lead at intermission, 10-9.

Ruby came back with a 35-yarder late in the third quarter to pull the Falcons 15-13, and the Maki-Scott heroics followed almost a full quarter later.

Weiss' play was almost spotless. The AFA senior from Naples, Fla., completed 11 of 20 passes for 142 yards and used the wishbone to run for 107 more on 17 carries.

Lost in the ruins of the Irish defeat were Pinkett's game-high 142 yards on 31 carries.

Based on the record book, Air Force had to feel confident at halftime. In the five-year Faust era, Notre Dame had been 1-11 in games it trailed after two quarters.

That ledger now reads 1-12.

"I can't say enough about our team, our spirit, our fight, our belief in one another." DeBerry said. "They never gave up, never folded. And there was a time when it didn't look good for us. Yet we never gave up hope."

With 10:16 remaining in the fourth quarter and ahead by three points, Notre Dame opened a Pinkett-led drive that carried to the AFA 2-yard line.

Notre Dame used the power of its monstrous linemen and the dancing, slashing feet of Pinkett to produce a first-and-goal situation.

The Irish moved from their 41 to the AFA 2 in just seven plays.

Four plays later, Faust sent out Carney, one of the nation's best, to add to the Notre Dame lead.

Air Force's life hung in the balance.

Maki crashed through for the block, and Scott made like Pinkett once he had Carney's ball.

Game, set, jubilation.

"It was the longest 77 yards of my entire life," said Scott, a senior strong safety.

"I was jumping up and down anyway because I made the block," said Maki, a junior linebacker. "Then I saw A.J. with the ball, and I really jumped."

Tom Rotello, an AFA cornerback, took care of the last Notre Dame player near Scott with a rollover block 25 yards from the end zone.

"I couldn't tell what happened," said Carney, a junior from Centerville, Ohio, who had made 25 of 30 career field-goal tries before the fateful kick.

"I had my head down. But I thought everything went as scheduled with the snap, hold and kick. It felt good, real good. I didn't think the kick was low. I guess we had some sort of breakdown up front."

Notably, the blocked kick was the first of Carney's career at Notre Dame.

Early on, Air Force knew all about breakdowns. And their cost.

Weiss and fullback Johnny Smith botched a handoff on the Falcon's first snap of the game. Notre Dame linebacker Robert Banks made the recovery at the AFA 16, and six plays later, Carney hit his 28-yarder.

On the Falcons' next possession, Smith opened with a 3-yard carry and Weiss followed with a marvelous 39-yard dash, off an option play, to the Notre Dame 38. Weiss came back again with an 8-yard gain, but this time lost the ball to Notre Dame linebacker Rick DiBernardo.

Late in the first quarter, Weiss misfired on a fourth-down pass to Ken Carpenter from the Notre Dame 35. The Irish methodically drove into range for Carney, who booted his 33-yarder on the third snap of the second quarter.

Air Force then set sail on a six-play, 80-yard march that Weiss capped with his floating 24-yard pass to an all-alone Pittman, who bobbled the ball before clutching it and falling to the end-zone turf.

On the Falcons' first offensive play of the second half, Weiss again fumbled into the hands of DiBernardo, this time at the AFA 42.

More than five minutes later, Pinkett's scoring blast gave the Irish their 15-10 lead.

"I take the blame for the fumbles," Weiss said. "On the first one, I got a little confused when I saw one of their linemen jump. I just didn't make a smooth handoff to Johnny. We were very sloppy at times.

"But we also knew that if we didn't panic, we'd move the football. We're confident of our ability to do that. Besides, our defense saved our butts. They won the game, not the offense."

Still, Air Force accumulated 412 yards in total offense. Carpenter, a senior wide receiver from Fort Lewis, Wash., was Weiss' favorite target, catching five passes for 62 yards.

Never was the AFA defense more magnificent than when Notre Dame had its house in order with the first-and-goal situation from the AFA 2 with 6:42 left.

On the first snap, AFA tackle John Ziegler slashed through to stop Pinkett for a 1-yard loss.

Then Dick Clark, a second-team nose guard, stopped Pinkett for a 6-yard loss.

On third down, Maki and Ziegler pounded Irish quarterback Steve Beuerlein to the stadium floor with a heavy rush, but not before Beuerlein was flagged for intentionally grounding a pass.

Watching along with DeBerry was a national television audience.

Out trotted Carney. It took Scott only 12 seconds to carry Air Force to glory.

"Our defense gave up 396 yards out there," DeBerry said. "But nobody is more proud of them than our coaches. We continually rose to the occasion.

"We were dead tired in the fourth quarter and we still kept plugging away. I can't think of anything else to say."

Being speechless was the only ideal way to describe it.

Scott Smith/ The Colorado Springs Gazette:

One man spoke of divine intervention; the other man spoke of mortal errors.

The truth undoubtedly lay obscured somewhere between an act of God and human frailty. But it was readily apparent that the analytical dissection of Air Force's remarkable 21-15 victory over Notre Dame meant little to two of Saturday's prime role players. No, for Air Force quarterback Bart Weiss and Notre Dame quarterback Steve Beuerlein, all that mattered was the end result.

Air Force won, and Weiss was all smiles. Notre Dame lost, and Beuerlein was surly.

Never mind that both offenses sputtered. Never mind that it was a day for defense, a day when quarterbacks were battered, bruised and abused. Never mind the Falcons' wishbone bobbles and the Irish's slips and stumbles.

This game, with its mirror images of defensive domination and offensive frustration, was decided by a bizarre special-teams play – a 77-yard blocked field-goal return by Air Force's A.J. Scott late in the fourth quarter. It was a play during which Weiss and Beuerlein could only watch, in jubilation and horror. And disbelief.

"It was an act of God or something on that play," said Weiss, "I was praying for something like that to happen, I really was. God's on our side or something. I really believe it."

But Bart, isn't Notre Dame supposed to be blessed by the football deity?

"Hey, I'm Catholic, too," Weiss said, smiling a gargantuan smile. "It works both ways."

For Weiss, Saturday's game was a true test of faith. The Irish defense repeatedly hammered the Falcon senior, effectively snuffing Air Force's high-powered option game. Weiss had just enough success – 107 yards rushing and an 11-of-20 day passing for 142 yards and one touchdown – to keep the Falcons afloat, but he paid dearly for it.

"They were really coming after me, more than anyone else has," he said. "It was a long game, a loooong game.

"They played a lot better defense against us than they did last year. They're so quick and strong – and they hit so hard. I feel like we should have scored more – any time you fumble a few times (the Falcons lost two fumbles) like that, you should score some more points. I'm just thankful that our defense came through so many times."

Ah, yes, the Falcon defenders. Were they the reason Notre Dame managed just one touchdown? Not necessarily, according to Beuerlein, who emerged from a lengthy post-game shower awash in disappointment and disgust.

"It seems like every time we need a big play, something happens," said Beuerlein, who was 20 of 36 for 223 yards passing. "The receivers slip. Or the fullback slips and trips me. Or the tailback and fullback run the wrong direction on a big play. Now, that stuff is going to happen from time to time. But it seems like it always happens to us.

"We had the ball down inside their 10 three or four times and we should have scored, but this stuff kept happening. Hey, I threw an interception down close to the goal line, and there's no excuse for that. It was a terrible pass; it was all my fault. The fact is, we had our chances. We just didn't do it."

Ironically, Beuerlein was on the field for one of his coveted "big plays" – he was the holder on John Carney's blocked field-goal attempt.

"But that play wasn't why we lost the game," he said. "It shouldn't have come to that point in the first place – and that's what ticks me off. We should have scored three or four touchdowns.

"Now all we can do is go back to South Bend, take a couple of days off and get back into it. I could say the same things I said last week, but you all probably have it written down in last week's notes: We've just got to pull together and win the last seven games."

AFA Notepad:

Allen Pinkett, tailback became Allen Pinkett, philosopher, in Notre Dame's somber locker room.

"Sometimes life deals you some severe blows, said Pinkett, who rushed for 142 yards and scored the Fighting Irish's lone touchdown in Saturday's shocking loss to Air Force.

"But this is no time to sit back crying and give up. We've got seven games left, seven opportunities to wear the gold helmet. We still have a lot of pride left, and I know I am speaking for the whole team.

"It's a shame . . . but I guess things happen like this. I guess it's what you'd call the breaks. Against (Air Force) it seems like it's always 50-50 on the field, but then something happens and we don't win.

"They made the point spread just right, I guess. Somebody in Las Vegas knows what they're doing."

****

When Notre Dame cornerback Mike Haywood intercepted a Bart Weiss pass on the next-to-last play of the first half, it ended Weiss's interception-less streak at 76 passes, a total that dated back to last season.

This season, Weiss has completed 40 of 63 passes for 756 yards. He has thrown four touchdown passes and one interception.

****

Scott Thomas, Air Force's excellent senior safety, had to sit out much of the first half after being "dinged" when he tackled Notre Dame quarterback Steve Beuerlein.

"I thought I was at the concession stand buying popcorn. It was weird. It took a while to get the cobwebs out, "Thomas said. "After that play, they signaled a defense in from the bench and I called the wrong defense. Then, when they had to punt, I couldn't remember what we were supposed to do. That's when I figured I'd better get out of there for a while."

****

Certainly, ABC-TV's presence had an effect on the game, which lasted longer than any other Falcon game in recent memory – 3 hours and 27 minutes. The first half lasted nearly an hour and a half, then the third quarter didn't end until 4:15p.m., which is normally when Air Force games are finished.

But nobody at Air Force complained about the exposure received by the school, including a lengthy pregame segment about academy life.

****

Scouts from a handful of bowls were present, including the Cherry, Freedom, Liberty, Holiday and Independence. From the rumor mill, the Cherry (in Pontiac, Mich.) is interested in arranging a deal for the Air Force-Brigham Young loser, and the Freedom would like Air Force vs. Southern Cal.

The Holiday doesn't have to take the Western Athletic Conference champion this year, but still is interested in the Falcons.

"They may be playing on January 1 before it's all over, though," said one of the bowl visitors.

****

Coach Dick Ellis/AFA Football Staff-Special Teams Coordinator . . . on what he remembers from "The Play" that beat Notre Dame:

"Our Notre Dame game came on the fifth week of our 1985 season. It was a beautiful Colorado day, with perfect weather conditions on October 5th. Our game had been selected for national TV coverage. Frank Broyles was the color commentator along with the famous Keith Jackson. Years later when I worked at Arkansas, Coach Broyles told me that game was on the list of his top five all-time games during his long broadcasting career. Along with the national TV audience, we had a sell-out crowd of 52,153 in Falcon

Stadium, which was the largest Air Force home attendance record at that time.

Notre Dame used their size and speed to pretty much control most of the game, but with tough Falcon play, the score was still close going into the last few minutes of the fourth quarter. With the score 15-14, the Irish mounted a sustained offensive drive that we finally were able to stall at our own 21 yard-line. With a fourth down and short, Coach Gerry Faust elected to kick a sure 27 yard field goal that would undoubtedly sealed the win for ND. This was a logical decision because their kicker was the nationally ranked John Carney, and he had already kicked FG's in the game. (Carney would later go on to a very successful 11-year career in the NFL).

All year, we had worked on blocking field goals and PAT's. Our primary focus was coming hard off the corner as the upback stepped down to seal the inside. We had blocked PAT's and FG's in past games, so our opponents knew Air Force had a good reputation for blocking kicks. Part of our strategy to blocking kicks was to also stress to our inside rushers that if the kicking team did not step down correctly, there was a chance to rush through an inside gap.

Now the stage was set. Time was running out and Notre Dame was setting up for the game clenching FG to virtually end the game in front of a national TV audience and a record sell-out crowd. We had already been close to blocking a kick with our outside rusher earlier in the game. When the ball was snapped, the Irish left up-back and the left TE seemed to be concerned about our outside rush off the corner, and did not completely seal down inside. This left just enough of an opening for Terry Maki to break through from the inside and get his hands on Carney's kick. The ball went straight up in the air. AJ Scott was rushing off the Irish left side, caught the ball out of the air, and raced down the sideline with a host of AFA blockers for a Falcon TD.

Later after reviewing the game films, there were some other interesting aspects of that play. After Terry Maki blocked the field goal, he began celebrating by dancing and jumping around, without realizing that AJ had caught the ball and was running for the score. Obviously, he had done his part with blocking the kick. Also it is of note, that AJ Scott was known for his bowlegged running style. As he was heading down the sideline for the score, he was obviously in bounds all the way, but on every step it appeared that his bowlegged right leg was out-of-bounds as he ran. His feet were on the ground in-bounds, but his knee was in the air just over the side line.

That 1985 blocked field goal has to be one of the top Air Force Academy football plays of all time. This play led to a seemly impossible comeback win over Notre Dame, on national TV and a full house Falcon Stadium. It also allowed Air Force to enter the November game at BYU, not only nationally ranked and undefeated, but with a chance to play in a national championship game."

****

<u>John Ziegler, AFA-DT, on what he remembers from "The Play" that beat Notre Dame:</u>

"AFA vs ND: National TV! Very tough game and physically demanding. During the fateful ND drive, they were wearing us down and seemingly gouging us for rushing yards all the way down inside our ten yard line. Dick Clark breaks through and makes a great tackle for a loss. Another ND play for minimal to no gain. Then on third down, Steve Beuerlein drops back to pass and rolls to his right, away from my side. Off we were in pursuit, in what had to have appeared to have been slow motion for a very tired defense. Beuerlein posted up and attempted to throw into the end zone and I hit him as hard as I could. I thought I had sacked him, but there was a flag on the field and Beuerlein was flagged for intentional grounding. With the loss of yards, ND was forced to attempt a slightly longer field goal. Terri Maki broke through and blocked the kick, which A.J. Scott skillfully caught and went off to the races for the game winning touchdown. Falcon stadium went crazy as numerous AFA players ran on the field in celebration, all I could do was walk off the field and collapse on the bench utterly exhausted. Thus the Falcons won four in a row over ND!

While Gerry Faust may have struggled as the Head Coach at ND, he should receive high marks as a person. Following our 1985 defeat of ND, Coach Faust came into our locker room, got up on a chair and addressed our team. He advised that ND was prepared and ready to play us this year and he congratulated us upon our hard fought victory. This is the one and only time that I can remember in which an opposing coach has entered our locker room and addressed our team! It was a great way for Coach Faust to show his respect for our team, the US Air Force Academy, and the US Air Force!"

****

A.J. Scott, AFA-DB, on what he remembers from "The Play" that beat Notre Dame:

"I was lined up on the right side of the defense on the press box side (West) of the field. In this standard alignment we had zone coverage for a fake FG or a muffed kick. Once the ball was snapped, I just looked into the backfield to make sure none of the backs were coming out for a pass or to block. I couldn't see anything, but I did hear the thud from Terry Maki hitting the ball. As I was tracking the ball, it looked like it went straight up into the air, but I could see that it came off to our right. I took a peek inside to see who was coming out toward me and then it came down where I was. I didn't catch it with too much of a running start; it was almost like a high punt. Back behind me were Scott Thomas and Tommy Rotello. Both were tracking the ball as I was and Scott got there about the same time as I did. As I started to head down the sideline, both Scott and Tommy turned inside to block. It was one of those perfect pictures of teamwork. Scott put his hand on my hip, and as he wheeled inside he crossed and accidentally kicked my right leg, causing me to kick the back of my left leg as I pull it through. I initially felt like I was starting to fall but hung on through the next steps. The return was 70+ yards and a lot of it was close to the sideline. I stayed as far away from the ND players as I could because the only thing worse than falling would have been getting "wacked" by one of them. Many joked that my bow-leg was out of bounds, even if I was inbounds. I don't remember much after crossing the goal-line; I just knew I didn't want to be at the bottom of the pile. The crowd in Falcon Stadium literally thundered!"

****

Terry Maki, AFA-LB, on what he remembers from "The Play" that beat Notre Dame:

"For field goals, the Defensive 'right' side of the ball looked like this (see diagram below). Kevin Martin (#85) and I worked together every game in the '85 and '86 seasons to block kicks. We would study film and try to find the guy on offense who didn't step down hard enough, or left a crease by stepping down too far. Against Notre Dame we noticed the Left End didn't step down hard enough. So Kevin Martin attacked his outside shoulder, and Chad Hennings attacked the Tackles inside shoulder to make a hole, it was REALLY close all game, we finally got the block in the 4th quarter with about 5 minutes left in the game. It was a total team effort. We were a team, and it was such a great experience to be part of a team that good. But you know what? A.J. Scott is my hero! Eleven guys could have blocked that kick, but only one could have returned it for a touchdown!"

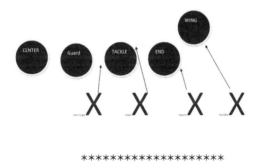

****

On May 20, 2008, Notre Dame Head Coach Gerry Faust penned a hand-written note of congratulations to A.J. Scott on the occasion of his retirement from the U.S. Air Force, after 23 years of service. The note, written on a piece of Coach Faust's personal ND stationery that he had saved for special situations, reads:

"Dear Lt. Colonel A.J. Scott #18

Congratulations on your retirement after 23 years in the Air Force as an officer for our great country.

You also should be very proud of what you and Theresa have done raising five excellent sons.

I'll never forget the time when I was the coach at the University of Notre Dame, and we were playing the Air Force in 1985. We were driving for a touchdown with a few minutes left in the fourth quarter leading 15-14. We had a penalty that put us back so we decided to have John Carney kick a field goal to seal the game. One of our lineman blocked the wrong way and Terry Maki got thru and got his hands on the ball, which popped up in the air and was picked off by #18 A.J. Scott and ran by our sidelines, 77 yards for an Air Force touchdown which sealed the game for the Academy. The question I have, why didn't you retire in 1984 rather than 2008. I would have been much happier on Oct 5, 1985 rather than having to ride back on the plane to South Bend without a win.

May the rest of your life be filled with happiness, loving God, your family and our great country.

A.J., I'm very proud of your accomplishments, when Colonel Berry called me to ask if I would write you on your retirement, I didn't hesitate and this letter is on my stationery that I have saved over the years for very special occasions like your retirement party.

God bless you, my good friend, and good luck.

Gerry Faust"

(See a copy of Coach Faust's original letter below)

Final Statistics: AFA vs Notre Dame

Score	1	2	3	4	Final
Air Force	0	10	3	8	21
Irish	3	6	6	0	15

Scoring Plays:

ND – Carney	28-yrd FG, 1/12:46	
ND – Carney	33-yrd FG, 2/14:12	
AFA – Pittman	24-yard pass from Weiss (Ruby kick), 2/4:47	
ND – Carney	40-yrd FG, 2/1:59	
ND – Pinkett	2 run (pass failed), 3/7:33	
AFA – Ruby	35-yrd FG, 3/2:53	
AFA – Scott	77-yard blocked FG return (Weiss run), 4/5:16	

Team Statistics:

Category	AFA	Notre Dame
First Downs	21	24
Rush-Pass-Pen	49-21-6	43-36-13
Rushing Yards	292	197
Passing (C-A-I)	11-21-1	20-36-1
Passing Yards	142	223
Punt Avg.	47.3	37.5
Fumbles-Lost	1-1	4-3

Penalties-Yards   6-43   13-97

Individual Statistics (Leaders only):

Rushing (Att-Yds):   Weiss (AFA) 17-122
                            Smith (AFA) 9-72
                            Pinkett (ND) 31-15
Passing (C-A-I-Yds):   Weiss (AFA) 11-20-1-142
                            Beuerlin (ND) 20-36-1-223
Receiving (#-Yds):   Carpenter (AFA) 5-62
                            Pittman (AFA) 2-24
                            Ward (ND) 4-57
                            Miller (ND) 4-51
Tackles: Maki (AFA) - 30 !!!

52,153 fans watch Air Force beat Notre Dame . . . **_again!_**

Scott Thomas sets up his blockers for a punt return against Notre Dame.

Halfback Kelly Pittman picks up big yardage against Notre Dame!

Air Force' John Ziegler and Steve Spewock apply an awesome pass rush that stymies Notre Dame QB Steve Beuerlin!

Maki and Hennings shut down Notre Dame's Allen Pinkett!

QB Bart Weiss reads the Irish Defense.

QB Bart Weiss looking to go deep against Notre Dame.

Illegally grabbing the Facemask? . . . maybe.

The scramble after the block . . . A.J. Scott has the ball and is off to the races!!!

** A.J. Scott (with a little help from Terry Maki) makes it 4-in-a-row for the AFA over the Irish!

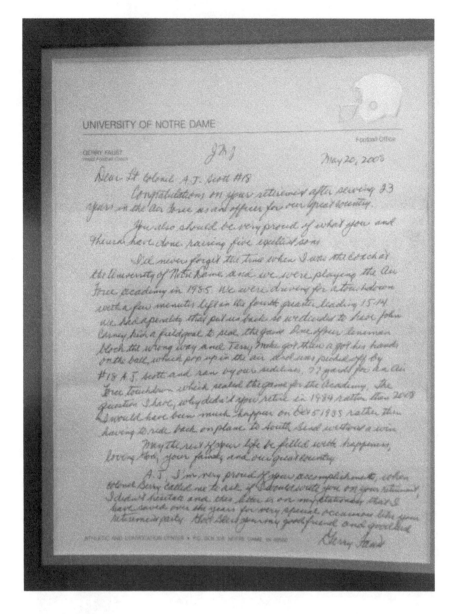

Personal, hand-written letter from Notre Dame Head Coach Gerry Faust to Lt. Colonel A.J. Scott, #18 on the occasion of his retirement from the U.S. Air Force after 23 years of service. Gerry Faust, another "Leader of Character"!

NAVY - AIR FORCE

OCTOBER 12, 1985
NAVY - MARINE CORPS MEMORIAL STADIUM

Chapter Six

The Goats

"The will to win is important, but the will to prepare is vital."

-Joe Paterno

Oct 12, 1985   AFA @ Navy   W 24-7

The Commander-in-Chief's Trophy was not in the possession of the Falcons. To win it back, they must first beat Navy.

The first quarter was scoreless. In the second quarter, things looked better as the AFA scored twice.

Highly touted Navy running back Napoleon McCallum was help to only 67 yards by outstanding defensive plays by Terry Maki, Pat Malackowski and Mike Chandler.

Quarterback Bart Weiss rushed for over 100 yards for the second straight week and completed two passes for 113 yards in the 24-7 victory.

Ralph Routon/The Colorado Springs Gazette:

Air Force completed only two passes here Saturday against Navy, which isn't surprising when the wishbone's triple option is stuck in the gear called "M" for "monotonous."

But those two passes had much to do with the Falcon's 24-7 victory over the Midshipmen.

One, a 60-yarder to wide receiver Ken Carpenter, set up Air Force's important, first touchdown of the day. The other, a 53-yarder to tight end Hugh Brennan in the fourth quarter, led to the Falcon's final insurance score.

Bart Weiss, the AFA senior quarterback, has thrown more times and for more yards on other days this fall. But this time, 2 for 113 yards was plenty.

"We kept running the same play (a version of the triple option) and it was working," said Weiss, who kept the ball 24 times for 102 yards and a lot of punishment. "When we can keep making first downs like that, we don't really need to pass.

"But when they started coming up to support too much, we had to make them pay."

The first time came early in the second quarter, when Air Force was finally able to breathe normally for the first time all day. After making 10 yards and no first downs amid horrible field position through the first 15 minutes, the Falcons needed to take the pressure off their defense.

They punched out a pair of first downs, moving from their 7 to the 35. Then Weiss found Carpenter, who was double-covered but still made the catch and ran to the Navy 5-yard line. Two plays later, Air Force had a 7-0 lead and a lot more confidence.

Even though that would be Carpenter's only catch of the day, it was a sufficient thrill since his father, General William Carpenter (the former All-America for Army) was watching.

"I wish it could have been a touchdown," said Ken . . ., "because I took some heat from Dad. He said, 'They never would have caught me.' I just said, 'Yes, they would have, Dad, because you're 47 years old.'

"But that pass was really set up perfectly. Their corners were coming up so strong that we couldn't even block them, and that's when you can burn 'em. I knew it would work the second time, too."

That came in the fourth period, with Air Force nursing a 17-7 lead but Navy still thinking an upset was possible. That all changed, though, when Brennan slipped behind the Middies' free safety and turned a mid-range pass into a 53-yard gain.

"I had been crack-backing their free safety, "said Brennan, "and it got to the point where they were expecting it when I was split out. So that time I just faked the block and kept going. I don't know where the backside cornerback (who tackled him) came from, but that's OK."

On the sidelines, offensive coordinator Bob Noblitt felt the same satisfaction.

"That call came down from the coaches' box, and it was perfect," Noblitt said. "Navy did some things that slowed us down, but in our type offense, when the defense starts to get a little anxious, the pass is open."

Noblitt seemed most pleased about the fact Air Force suffered no turnovers. In fact, he agreed that was the day's most important statistic.

"We needed a game like that," Noblitt said. "I just wish we could have taken some of the pressure off the defense a little quicker. But as soon as we were able to punch out a few first downs, we went for it."

And what if opposing defenses continue to key on the triple option?

"We'll throw," said Weiss.

"We've got the guys who can catch it."

Two for 113 yards. 56.5 yards per completion.

Not a bad average.

Mike Burrows/The Colorado Springs Gazette:

Napoleon McCallum went dancing Saturday at Memorial Stadium.

The problem for Navy in its 24-7 setback to the Air Force Academy was that McCallum said he danced too much.

It all added up to a waltz for the 13th-ranked Falcons.

"I made some terrible cuts, and it really cost me," said McCallum, the Midshipmen's fifth-year senior tailback from

Milford, Ohio. "When I got the ball on pitch plays and just straight isolation plays, I danced around a little too much."

"I run my best when I just take the ball and go, make a cut and go again. I didn't do that against Air Force. There were a lot of times when I was uncertain where I should go."

McCallum's long run of the day was an 18-yarder early in the third quarter. It was the second play of a 10-play, 80-yard scoring drive that Navy used to cut the Falcons' lead to 14-7.

In that march, which quarterback Bill Byrne capped with a 15-yard touchdown pass to tight end John Sniffen, McCallum carried four times for 36 yards.

Those were the only heroics for a 6-foot-2, 214-pounder who earned consensus All-America honors two years ago.

McCallum entered the game with a per-game average of 122.5 rushing yards.

He got 67 yards on 15 carries against the Falcons and added 20 on two pass receptions, 27 on three punt returns and 20 on one kickoff return.

He stayed bust, all right. But everything was not all right for Navy, which dropped its fourth consecutive game to Air Force.

After playing inspiringly well early – Air Force had 10 total yards and no first downs in the first quarter – Navy was sapped of its defensive strength down the stretch.

The culprit was Air Force's wishbone offense, which had 367 total yards and several time-consuming drives at the finish.

"You can't point fingers," said Navy free safety Marc Firlie, a 6-1, 204=-pound junior from Cumberland, Md. "The offense didn't generate many points, but we gave up some yards, too.

"It can get real frustrating trying to defense a wishbone attack like Air Force has. You really have to play your assignments, and we had a few lapses.

"That first quarter, we really played intense. We just weren't able to keep that intensity. Air Force wore us down."

Firlie finished with a game-high 22 tackles. Navy linebacker Vince McBeth, a 6-1, 218-pound junior from Camden, Ark., had 21.

It was the tackles Air Force laid on McCallum, though, that McCallum remembered most.

"There were a few times I got the ball and there were already Air Force guys in the backfield," he said. "But don't blame our offensive line. They did their job.

"It was me. I could've done a much better job of running."

If that's true, Air Force is thankful McCallum danced to the wrong music."

Mike Burrows/The Colorado Springs Gazette:

The say Scott Thomas is a football player with big-play capability.

Saturday at the Naval Academy's Memorial Stadium, he ranked as a big hitter, too.

Air Force's senior free safety set the defensive tone for the Falcons late in the first quarter when he unloaded on Navy wide receiver John Lobb at the AFA goal line.

It was a third-and-goal play from the 4-yard line. Navy quarterback Bill Byrne dropped back and found Lobb across the middle.

Byrne threw a bullet, thinking Navy was about to take a 7-0 lead over the 13th ranked Falcons.

Lobb caught the ball and was immediately greeted by Thomas, whose savage blow knocked the ball loose and Lobb to the ground.

Lobb stayed there, too – at least a few seconds.

"I thought it was one of the better hits I've made," Thomas said, smiling, after Air Force's 24-7 victory. "The receiver just laid himself out for that kind of hit. I was fortunate to get there at the same time the ball did."

"I popped right back up, but he just laid there. He was making weird noises."

One play later, Navy kicker Todd Solomon was wide left on a chip-shot, 21-yard field goal try.

"The play that Scott gave us was a big-time hit from a big-time player," AFA head coach Fisher DeBerry said. "You'd better believe it was a crucial play."

From then on, the Middies stayed submerged – thanks to the AFA defense.

Navy, 1-4, converted only five of 16 third-down plays.

Byrne, a 6-foot-3, 201-pound junior from Pacifica, Calif., completed only nine of 24 passes for 94 yards – when he wasn't running for his life.

The most impressive job, however, may have been done on Napoleon McCallum, Navy's All-America tailback who ranked No. 7 nationally in rushing entering the day.

That average was 122.5 yards.

The AFA defense gave him 67 yards on 15 carries, and Navy's I-formation offense finished with just 224 total yards, almost 200 below its per-game average.

Three Air Force linebackers finished with double-digit tackles – junior Terry Maki (16) and seniors Mike Chandler (13) and Pat Malackowski (12).

Senior tackle John Ziegler had six stops and two of the Falcons' three sacks of Byrne.

"I thought the major key for us defensively was getting in Byrne's face all day. It seemed like every time he threw a pass, he threw under pressure," Ziegler said. "We chased him pretty good.

"Scott got that great hit that saved a touchdown early, and then Navy came right back with a missed field goal that probably should have been a sure thing. Both of those real gave us a big, big lift. I knew we'd be all right defensively after that."

The Middies averaged just 3.3 yards per rush and 3.5 yards per snap.

"I thought we did a good job on McCallum," said Chad Hennings, an AFA sophomore tackle who got his first – and last – look at the Navy star. "We took him out of the game by keeping him from getting the really long gainer on us.

"By taking Nappy out of the game, we took Navy's offense out of it, too. We've really got a hold of momentum now. It's up to us to keep it going."

The 6-5, 245-pound Hennings led Air Force's down linemen with seven stops.

Thomas also had seven, but took a back seat to junior cornerback Tom Rotello with nine.

Rotello also had the game's only interception.

Ralph Routon/The Colorado Springs Gazette:

Steam, sweat, dirty uniforms and wall-to-wall bodies filled the world's tiniest football dressing room underneath Memorial Stadium.

Players cut off the tape, wiped off the grime and took turns in the small shower. Coaches and media squirmed through the mass, talking to each other and anyone else about what they had just seen.

As always for this game, the usual constellation of stars glistened on general's shoulders. The accompanying smiles gave away the fact that one corner of the Pentagon will be a happy place on Monday.

On this Saturday, in this place that has overflowed with tradition for centuries, Air Force had won another football game. This one, making the Falcons a perfect 6-0 for the 1985 season, had been a methodical 24-7 victory over inspired but not-as-good Navy.

Just a day at the office, said some. A successful business trip, said a few others. Exactly like the convincing 23-7 win over Virginia Tech in last year's Independence Bowl, felt head coach Fisher DeBerry.

Air Force had done something impressive on this day, whipping a psyched-up opponent with a solid, mistake-free, consistent effort. Not a 42-point rout, but a strong victory nonetheless.

Everybody in that cramped room enjoyed the moment. Bowl scouts, swarming like hornets now, shook hands with anyone in a blue uniform and salivated over the prospect of picking this ripening plum.

And then, as the excitement finally began to subside, came the biggest victory of all – the one that brought real tears to the eyes of DeBerry and others, the one that made a simple football game pale by comparison.

The blond-haired young man stood silently, his right hand grasping his neck as if to maintain his equilibrium. He smiled, and his mouth quivered with emotion.

DeBerry saw the visitor, grabbed his hand and shook it hard. The look on the head coach's face made it clear he was overwhelmed, almost speechless.

Danny Malm was back. All the way back.

Only the hardiest of Air Force fans will remember Danny Malm. But his story is unbelievable.

He was a promising reserve wide receiver for the Falcons in 1978-79, before deciding to take a break for a year on the Academy's stopout program. All along, though, Malm intended to come back from his Virginia home and be a cadet-athlete again.

Until one fateful day in 1980, when a terrible auto crash stopped his life.

Malm lay in a coma for three months, with nobody giving him a chance at first to live, much less recover. Even if he survived, doctors thought, the brain and physical damage surely would be massive.

Eventually, though, Malm came out of the coma. He began slow, extensive, painful rehabilitation. Obviously, his AFA plans were gone, though Air Force coaches, starting with then-head coach Ken Hatfield and continuing with DeBerry, kept in touch with encouraging letters. But everyone knew Danny was lucky just to be alive

Last year, Malm came to Colorado Springs and visited the Academy for a football game. He had come a long way then, but he still was shaky. People were happy to see him, but their reaction was to feel sympathy instead of gladness. Malm's battle was far from over.

Saturday, Malm was back for another inspection. This time, he was a champion.

Jim Conboy, the longtime AFA trainer, grabbed Malm's hand and shook it hard, clearly testing the young man's strength. Malm matched the squeeze, straining and grinning, then did the same with DeBerry.

His words came slowly, and his right hand stayed close to the neck. He talked about the years of rehab being "tough, real tough," and his watery eyes gave away how much time and effort must have been spent reaching each milestone.

But now, Malm is truly living again. He is an assistant football and soccer coach at a high school in Virginia. He still has impairments, but they are losing the war now. Making the two-hour trip here for Air Force – Navy was Danny's chance to show the world that he no longer wants or needs pity. Only support.

DeBerry was beside himself.

"You are a miracle." He told Malm, almost shouting the words. "A living miracle. Praise the Lord! You look so much better. Last year you were coming, but you weren't there. I just can't believe it."

To a lot of people, that might not have meant very much.

But here Saturday, even after as satisfying a victory as 24-7 over Navy, Danny Malm's story stole the show.

Just ask Fisher DeBerry.

He may be at the nucleus of a wonderful football autumn, in which Air Force has reached the halfway point with no losses and scratching on the verge of the Top Ten.

But is anyone wonders what was the best thing about Saturday, the head coach will not hesitate. Danny Malm made DeBerry's day, his month, his year.

And that says as much about Air Force's extraordinary football program as any 60-minute game ever could.

Final Statistics: AFA @ Navy

Score	1	2	3	4	Final
Air Force	0	14	0	10	24
Navy	0	0	7	0	7

Scoring Plays:

AFA – Smith	3 run (Ruby kick), 2/11:32
AFA – Pittman	3 run (Ruby kick), 2/:55
Navy – Sniffen	15-yard pass from Byrne (Solomon kick), 3/9:01
AFA – Ruby	23-yrd FG, 4/13:39
AFA – Jones	2 run (Ruby kick), 4/6:40

Team Statistics:

Category	AFA	Navy
First Downs	16	13
Rush-Pass-Pen	67-7-3	33-31-5
Rushing Yards	254	110
Passing (C-A-I)	2-7-0	12-31-1
Passing Yards	113	114
Punt Avg.	43.8	35.4
Fumbles-Lost	2-0	0-0
Penalties-Yards	3-15	5-36

Individual Statistics (Leaders only):

Rushing (Att-Yds): Weiss (AFA) 24-102
Pat Evans (AFA) 20-62
McCallum (Navy) 15-67
Passing (C-A-I-Yds): Weiss (AFA) 2-7-0-113
Byrne (Navy) 9-24-1-94
Receiving (#-Yds): Carpenter (AFA) 1-60
Brennan (AFA) 1-53
Sniffen (Navy) 5-47
Tackles: Terry Maki (AFA) – 15
Mike Chandler (AFA) – 13

QB Bart Weiss sprints through a HUGE hole in the Navy Defense!

Form-tackling practice against Navy!

COLORADO STATE vs. AIR FORCE

Oct. 19   1:30 P.M. $1

Hughes Stadium   Homecoming

Chapter Seven

The Rams

"Character cannot be developed in ease and quiet. Only through experience of trial and suffering can the soul be strengthened, ambition inspired, and success achieved." --- Helen Keller

Oct 19, 1985   AFA @ Colorado State   W 35-19

Six wins and no losses. The dream was beginning. Colorado State and fullback Steve Bartalo nearly shattered the dream. Bartalo rushed for 207 yards and forced Air Force to find some new answers. A one point halftime lead by the Falcons brought little comfort. With only 8:58 left in the game, CSU scored. They were now only a field goal away from taking a one point lead.

The Falcons offense came on the field after the CSU touchdown and took charge. Less than a minute later, they crossed the goal line. The game was sealed when Scott Thomas returned an interception 36 yards for the final touchdown of the game.

Mike Burrows/The Colorado Springs Gazette:

Nobody is supposed to survive a fight with Superman.

Yet the 10-th ranked Air Force Academy football team did just that Saturday in front of a near-record, overflow crowd of 31,127 at Hughes Stadium.

Superman was Steve Bartalo, the Colorado State fullback from Colorado Springs.

Bartalo pounded the Air Force defense 47 times, rushing for a career-high 207 yards.

Who won?

The Falcons, 35-19.

"The most important numbers to us, said AFA center Rusty Wilson, "are the numbers you see up on the scoreboard."

This is supposed to be peacetime, but Air Force found itself in a real battle Saturday. And CSU, now 2-5 overall and 2-3 in the Western Athletic Conference, arrived ram-tough.

Before the Falcons' yardage-gobbling wishbone offense could even get its hands on the ball, CSU had a 10-0 lead.

"We respected (Air Force), but we didn't put them on a pedestal, said Bartalo, a 5-foot-9, 197-pound junior who played the part of two-ton wrecking ball. "There was no doubt in mind we would beat them."

The Rams obviously had no doubts, either, especially after firing their early salvo that left Air Force in an embarrassing hole.

This was Air Force, remember. Bowl-bound Air Force. Air Force. Unbeaten Air Force.

Yes, on-the-ropes Air Force.

"I felt like I played the whole game, and I wasn't out there one snap," said AFA head coach Fisher DeBerry, whose Falcons improved to 7-0 overall and 4-0 in the WAC.

"Lord have mercy, we're getting out of here alive.

"CSU took the fight right to us. They fought, scrapped, battled, you name it. My hat's off to them and Bartalo, a truly great runner.

"But this showed we will not be pushed around without something to say about it. I'm proud of our comeback. It took a lot of guts, and a lot of courage."

And a lot of bruises.

Seven personal fouls were called, including six in the first half.

Emotion ran like Carl Lewis.

Bob Arum and Don King, boxing's biggest promoters, should have bought tickets. Spinks-Holmes had nothing on this bout.

When AFA and CSU players were finished tattooing one another, the Falcons had latched onto their 10th consecutive victory, tying a school record.

"It's disappointing when our players go out and play as well as they played today, and still come up short," said CSU head coach Leon Fuller, who dropped to 1-3 against Air Force.

"I'm proud, real proud of the effort we gave. We lost to a good football team. Toward the end, we had some mental errors and mental breakdowns. But I do believe we're becoming a better football team."

The Falcons believe. Oh, how they believe.

CSU took the opening kickoff and plowed 60 yards in 13 plays, with Steve DeLine's 37-yard field goal capping the march. In just over 6 ½ minutes, Bartalo had nine carries for 30 yards.

Air Force's Scott Thomas fumbled the ensuing kickoff, and CSU linebacker Gary Thompson made the recovery at the AFA 23-yard line.

In two plays, CSU had its surprising 10-0 lead. Bartalo scampered 18-yards on first down, and AFA strong safety A.J. Scott was flagged for a late hit. On first-and-goal from the 2, Bartalo followed the right-side block of 296-pound guard Edgar Mitchell for his 26th career touchdown.

That's when Air Force began looking the part of a nationally-ranked team.

Air Force zoomed 66 yards on just four plays with its first possession to make it 10-7 with 5:49 left in the first quarter. AFA quarterback Bart Weiss opened the drive with a 35-yard, down-the-middle strike to lunging wide receiver Ken Carpenter, and closed the drive with a perfect option-play pitch to senior halfback Kelly Pittman.

Pittman's scoring dash covered 26 yards, and got its launch when wideout Tyrone Jeffcoat threw a downfield block that wiped out CSU cornerback Jim King.

Ironically, it was a second-quarter Bartalo mistake that cost the Rams their lead for good.

He had finished the opening 15 minutes with 74 yards on 17 carries. On his 23rd carry, he was smacked for a 2-yard loss by AFA linebacker Pat Malackowski, and fumbled into the welcoming hands of Falcon tackle Chad Hennings at the CSU 47.

Two plays and 12 seconds later, Air Force had command.

Weiss immediately scooted for 12 yards, with CSU victimized even further by a personal foul on linebacker Gary Walker.

On first down from the Rams' 20, Weiss lofted a touchdown pass to the all-alone Carpenter with 6:31 left before halftime.

The Rams fought gallantly to stay close, but their lead was gone for good.

AFA cornerback Dwan Wilson saved a touchdown when he pirated, at the goal line, a pass thrown by CSU quarterback Kelly Stouffer with 1:33 left in the half.

The Falcons ran three plays before Mark Simon mishit a 31-yard punt to the AFA 43.

On the half's final play, DeLine, a junior from Englewood, successfully boomed a 60-yard field goal that could have been good from 70.

It was the second-longest field goal in CSU history, and the longest ever against Air Force.

"Nobody read us the riot act at halftime, said Weiss, who finished with 110 rushing yards, his fourth 100-yard game of a sparkling season. "We just knew we had a job to do.

"I was calm, really. We all were. We said, 'Hey, they controlled the ball in the first half, so let's return the favor in the second half.' I think our experience is really paying dividends."

In the first half, CSU dominated time of possession, with 21:07 to Air Force's 8:53.

The tables turned somewhat in the second half, after DeLine was wide right on a 46-yard attempt late in the third quarter.

Air Force followed with an eight-play, 71-yard drive. Randy Jones topped the drive with a 10-tard scoring run on the second snap of the fourth quarter to give the Falcons a 21-13 lead.

But back came the Rams. Stouffer took then on a 12-play, 70-yard march that he finalized himself on an 8-yard scramble for a touchdown with 8:58 left in the game.

Stouffer attempted a two-point conversion pass to tight end David Harris, but Malackowski made a diving deflection in the end zone, preserving Air Force's 21-19 lead.

CSU then began to fall apart.

Weiss whipped the Falcons 80 yards in just three plays after the kickoff, with fullback Johnny Smith scoring easily on a 30-yard dive play.

Air Force iced the verdict on the Ram's next offensive play, when Thomas, a battle-tough free safety, intercepted a Stouffer pass and returned it 36 yards for a touchdown with 7:41 remaining.

The irony was that Bartalo, Air Force's nightmare, was the intended receiver.

Bartalo walked to the CSU bench like he carried the weight of the world. Meanwhile, with a 35-19 advantage, Air Force finally felt secure.

"They are one of the top teams," Bartalo said afterward.

Again, a major weapon for the Falcons was the punting of Simon in spite of his 31-yarder that preceded DeLine's cross-country field goal.

Simon finished with a 51-yard average on four punts, including a 71-yarder late in the first quarter.

Air Force had three sacks of Stiuffer, but he still was able to complete 19 of 29 passes for 158 yards. However, his two interceptions were costly for the Rams.

"Nobody this year has played us any more physical, any tougher that Colorado State." DeBerry said. "They gave us everything we wanted, and then some. They really came ready to play."

"Give them credit, but then give some credit to our defense, too. When their backs were to the wall, they came through."

Unquestionably, so did Bartalo.

"I would give anything to have him as a fullback in our wishbone," DeBerry said. "He plays with heart, and I believe he could play with anybody in America."

"We threw everything at him, and he just kept coming. He was super. Superman? Heck, yes."

But Air Force found a way to survive without calling for kryptonite.

Ralph Routon/The Colorado Springs Gazette:

This time the statistics won't look so good.

The yards and points allowed, the time of possession and almost any other number involving Air Force's defense ran into the "alarming" category Saturday at Colorado State.

It added up to 19 points, 360 yards, a 207-yard day for CSU fullback Steve Bartalo, a whopping 82-47 edge in offensive plays for the Rams, and a stunning difference of almost 39-21 minutes in possession time.

But the Hughes Stadium scoreboard, which stayed lit into the night as if to remind the disbelieving CSU side, gave Air Force a 35-19 victory.

For the Falcon defense, which had grown accustomed to feeling largely responsible for this year's happy outcomes, this was different.

"Now we know how Notre Dame feels, where every team you play gets so high," said senior linebacker Mike Chandler. "That's what we're seeing now, too, by being ranked and undefeated. Everybody is all fired up to play us."

However, nobody on the defensive side was using that as an excuse for the Falcon's inability to stop CSU.

"We missed a lot of tackles, and we just lost our concentration," said Pat Malackowski, another senior linebacker and the defense's spiritual leader. "It wasn't really a letdown. We just didn't play as well as we can."

But, to a man, the AFA defense felt the experience of a near-defeat would be helpful as the Falcons face a three-game home stand against Utah, San Diego State and Army.

"This game shocked us," tackle John Ziegler said. "It told us we have to get going and work harder if we want to continue winning."

Said Chandler, "We have to go back and do some re-evaluating. It's not as bad as if we had lost, but today we saw that we're not as good as we think we are. The coaches have told us we can't just show up and expect to play great defense. Today we found out that was right."

Despite the defense's troubles, though, there was a good supply of big plays. Senior cornerback Dwan Wilson made a key goal-line interception in the second quarter, and Scott Thomas ran back an interception for the touchdown that finally subdued the Rams.

Another high moment came just after CSU had scored in the final period to cut Air Force's lead to 21-19. On the Ram's try for a two-point conversion that would have tied the game, Malackowski swatted away the pass from intended receiver David Harris.

"We knew we had to stop them there," Malackowski said. "I was just floating on the play, and the tight end (Harris) was my read. I floated with him and waited for him to make his move. But the credit goes to the defensive line for putting such good pressure on the passer."

From there, the Falcons were in control.

"It was good in a way," Wilson said, because this was our worst game but we still won.

"Now we know we've got to play better, and we will."

Mike Burrows/The Colorado Springs Gazette:

Missed tackles, broken pass coverage, a fumbled kickoff and a personal foul.

For the longest Saturday at Hughes Stadium, Air Force Academy free safety Scott Thomas deserved none of the all-America votes that are likely to come his way after the Falcons finish their season.

Even Thomas admitted it.

But his wounds healed quickly in Air Force's 35-19 victory over gallant Colorado State.

"For most of the game," Thomas said, "I played like crap. I was frustrated. There wasn't a whole lot I could smile about."

It was CSU, though, that did the crying midway through the fourth quarter when Thomas came up with a true all-America play.

AFA fullback Johnny Smith had just scored on a 30-yard run to give the Falcons a 28-19 lead with 7:52 left in the game.

CSU was down, but not totally out.

Up stepped Thomas, the acknowledged star of the AFA defense.

On the Ram's first offensive snap following the kickoff, Stouffer fired a pass intended for Steve Bartalo at the CSU 36.

Thomas dashed in front of Bartalo, made the interception and never missed a stride in racing to Air Force's clinching touchdown.

Suddenly, smiles.

The irony was not lost on Thomas. It was Bartalo, a junior fullback, who had gouged the Falcons for a career-high 207 rushing yards.

"I read that pass all the way through," said Thomas, a senior from San Antonio, Texas, who finished with five tackles and a deflected pass, in addition to the interception. "I saw it coming.

"After scoring, I looked back and saw who the pass was intended for. It was Bartalo. The damage he did on us was unbelievable. He ran us over. I should know, because he ran me over more than a few times.

"Before this game, we had faced two great backs in (Notre Dame's) Allen Pinkett and (Navy's) Nappy McCallum. I thought Bartalo was as good, or better, than both. He's really something. He ripped us good."

The first time Air Force touched the ball, Thomas fumbled a CSU kickoff. That turnover led to the Ram's first touchdown, a 2-yard plunge by Bartalo, and their surprising 10-0 lead.

Late in the first quarter, Thomas fielded a CSU punt and tried to return it after first calling for a fair catch.

In this game, that's a no-no. Five yard penalty.

Miffed, Thomas bounced the ball off a CSU player's helmet. Another no-no. Personal foul.

"Not real smart on my part," Thomas said. "It was the frustration. We were already down by 10 points, and my fumble was the big reason. I just lost my cool."

Thomas' personal foul was one of seven called in the game. CSU was flagged for four of them. Other Falcons charged were senior linebacker Pat Malackowski and senior strong safety A.J. Scott.

"It seemed like early in the game," Thomas said, "everybody was too worked up. There was a lot of pushing and shoving, and a lot of elbows flying.

"This game means a lot to both teams. It always does. But it got out of hand. It was starting to look like all-star wrestling out there."

And it was starting to look like the gloomiest day of Thomas' career.

"What can I say? I'm human," Thomas said. I felt bad about the mistakes. Overall, it was not a good day. I guess everybody is bound to have a day like this sometime."

His touchdown return of Stouffer's ill-fated pass was his bail money.

"I was the reason we fell behind in the first place," Thomas said. "When I scored, I thought, 'There goes a big load off me.' Before that score, I guess I proved that nobody's perfect."

Not even all-America candidates.

Ralph Routon/The Colorado Springs Gazette:

Everybody else had changed and gone to the bus, but Fisher DeBerry still was standing there in the Air Force dressing room, shaking like a leaf.

Not because he was cold, either.

These were the shivers of relief. Huge relief. And exhaustion.

On the shelf of his locker was a cold chicken dinner, which very soon would become his first meal of the day.

"I couldn't eat anything this morning," said the AFA head coach. "I'm so weak now I can hardly stand up."

Earlier, after his unbeaten Falcons somehow had pulled out a 35-19 victory over Colorado State, DeBerry had been as humble as ever. He stood outside that dressing-room door and touched or hugged every AFA player as the team came off the field.

This was one of those occasions when winning was the only satisfaction.

Surely, Saturday could have been the big disaster for Air Force. Across the nation, America's other three unbeaten, wishbone teams – Army, Arkansas and Oklahoma – bit the dust. For certain, the Falcons were close to making it a perfect sweep.

But they won the fourth quarter, and that won the game.

Afterward, many of the Air Force players were acting as if they had lost. They knew they had looked like anything but the nation's 10th-ranked team. They were 7-0, and 4-0 in the Western Athletic Conference. But they weren't celebrating.

Still, DeBerry tried to see the bright side.

"Every team is going to have games like this," he said. "No matter what your record."

But if the Falcons needed a fresh dose of reality, this definitely was more than sufficient.

Colorado State was not intimidated in the least, and the Rams came in with a great game plan. Control the ball, be as aggressive as Air Force, and attack the line of scrimmage. If Notre Dame had played that kind of physical game, the Irish almost certainly would have beaten the Falcons two weeks ago.

Again, however, Air Force refused to lose. Finally, the CSU defense began to crack. Once more, the Falcon defense produced a touchdown.

This was not a 35-19 game. It was more like a 21-19 game. The last two touchdowns will prevent the Falcons from slipping in the AP rankings, and they actually might rise a few places after the losses by Arkansas, Oklahoma and Michigan above them.

On the CSU side, the post-game emotions were full of grief. One man inside the Ram program said he never saw head coach Leon Fuller so distraught after a loss – and there have been many. This could have been a turnaround game for Colorado State, but instead it became just another in a series of familiar endings.

Without a doubt, Air Force will learn from the experience. DeBerry and his staff will have no trouble getting the Falcon's attention this week, with an explosive and talented Utah team coming to town.

But for those trying to find chinks in Air Force's armor, don't use this game.

For three weeks now, the Falcons have been adapting to life as the nationally ranked favorite. It's a different psychology, and they haven't grasped it fully yet. Their tendency is to start slowly, but that merely pumps up an excited opponent such as CSU.

Air Force can't afford such a sloppy beginning anymore, if the Falcons want 1985 to be unforgettable. They may be 7-0 now, but they must learn to be ready at 1:30pm if they want to continue rolling.

So far, though, survived every ambush. And that is a good sign, according to the best expert on Air Force football over the years.

"No matter how good you are, there will be days like this," said Ben Martin, the head coach from 1958 to 1977 who has enjoyed watching this Falcon team develop. "If you're going to win 'em all, you have to win the ones you shouldn't, too."

Air Force did exactly that here Saturday. On their worst afternoon of the season, the Falcons still came out on top.

And now, maybe Fisher DeBerry can digest a few meals.

AFA Notepad:

At 7-0, the Falcons are within one game of matching their best start ever, in 1970. Their 10-game winning streak, including the last three games of 1984, ties the Air Force school record. It also was the Falcons' third straight victory over Colorado State.

DeBerry is now 15-4 as the AFA head coach.

****

Colorado State played a special defense Saturday against Air Force's wishbone, but CSU defensive end Terry Unrein had some difficulty describing it.

"I guess it was like playing man-to-man in basketball," said Unrein, who was all over the field making plays for the Ram defense. "It worked for a long time, but the problem with that kind of defense is that when just one man breaks down, you're relying so much on each individual, it's not a 20-yard gain. It's a touchdown.

Unrein came up with a new description as well.

"They're not just a good physical team, they're a good mental team," Unrein said. "They just keep pounding at you until you make the big mistake. Against them, one minute you're dominating and the next minute, boom, they're gone."

****

One of the day's most unusual situations came during the second quarter, just before Air Force scored to take the lead for good. After recovering a fumble at the CSU 47, the Falcons got a quick big play when Quarterback Bart Weiss kept for 12 yards to the 35. Weiss was tackled out of bounds by CSU linebacker Gary Walk, and a scuffle ensued near the AFA bench. When tempers settled, the Rams were assessed a personal foul because officials saw Walk take a swing at Dick Abel, a retired Air Force general and now a U.S. Olympic Committee executive.

But CSU's story was different.

"Somebody punched me, and I heard a voice say, 'Don't do that again.' I reacted, but I didn't even know it wasn't a player," Walk said. "It was a strange thing."

CSU head coach Leon Fuller also felt the penalty was unjustified, saying," Why should we be penalized when some guy in a sport coat is punching one of our guys around?"

Abel was unavailable for comment after the game.

Final Statistics: AFA @ Colorado State University

Score	1	2	3	4	Final
Air Force	7	7	0	21	**35**
CSU	10	3	0	6	**19**

Scoring Plays:

CSU – DeLine	37-yrd FG, 1/8:10
CSU – Bartalo	2 run (DeLine kick), 1/7:33
AFA –Pittman	27 run (Ruby kick), 1/5:49
AFA –Carpenter	20-yard pass from Weiss (Ruby kick), 2/6:31
CSU – DeLine	60-yrd FG, 2/:00
AFA – Jones	10 run (Ruby kick), 4/14:21
CSU – Stouffer	8 run (pass failed), 4/8:58
AFA – Smith	30 run (Ruby kick), 4/7:52
AFA – Thomas	36-yard interception return (Ruby kick), 4/7:41

Team Statistics:

Category	AFA	CSU
First Downs	17	17
Rush-Pass-Pen	39-8-8	53-21-10
Rushing Yards	275	202
Passing (C-A-I)	4-8-1	12-21-0
Passing Yards	93	154
Punt Avg.	51.0	43.4
Fumbles-Lost	2-1	2-1
Penalties-Yards	8-68	10-86

Individual Statistics (Leaders only):

Rushing (Att-Yds): Weiss (AFA) 9-110
Pat Evans (AFA) 8-34
Bartalo (CSU) 47-207
Passing (C-A-I-Yds): Weiss (AFA) 3-6-0-80
Stouffer (CSU) 12-21-1-158
Receiving (#-Yds): Carpenter (AFA) 2-55
Beach (CSU) 5-47
Tackles: Chandler (AFA) – 14
Maki (AFA)

Spewock, Ziegler and Chandler greet CSU's QB!

RB Greg Pshsniak stretches for extra yards against the Rams!

Chapter Eight

The Utes

"I am thankful for all of those who said NO to me. It's because of them I'm doing it myself." --- Albert Einstein

Oct 26, 1985   AFA vs. Utah   W 38-15

The Falcons dominated play for the entire game even though Utah had come into the game with a 6-1 record. The cadets scored first as running back Kelly Pittman capped a drive that featured his own 28-yard run.

Quarterback Bart Weiss provided his fourth-straight 100-yard rushing performance and Johnny Smith contributed 175 total yards. Scott Thomas electrified Falcons fans by returning the opening kickoff of the second half 102 yards for a touchdown. By so doing, Scott became only the fourth man in NCAA history to return a punt, a kickoff, and an interception for touchdowns in the same season.

Ralph Routon/The Colorado Springs Gazette:

Air Force's defense knew exactly what to expect Saturday from the University of Utah.

Lots of speed, lots of long passes and the constant threat of a sudden touchdown.

After last week, when the Falcon defense was abused by Colorado State's offensive line and star runner Steve Bartalo, this clearly was the chance for redemption.

There were many Utah pass completions for many yards – the Utes ended up with 415 in all.

But the most important statistic was the one on the visitor side of the scoreboard. Utah scored only 15 points, and that meant the AFA defense could share in a satisfying 37-15 victory.

"Anytime you hold an offense like that to only two touchdowns, you know the guys are doing their job," said Bruce Johnson, the AFA defensive coordinator. "We also knew that no lead would be comfortable, because Utah had scored 94 points in the fourth quarter alone this year."

Utah scored eight points in the final period Saturday, cutting the deficit to 30-15 with 9:53 to play. But AFA cornerback Tom Rotello made two interceptions after that, wrapping up a day full of big moments for the defense.

There also was a goal-line interception by strong safety A.J. Scott, and a safety when linebacker Ty Hankamer sacked Utah passer Larry Egger. Too, free safety Scott Thomas broke the game open for the Falcons by returning the second-half kickoff 100 yards for a touchdown.

But nobody was happier afterward than Rotello, the junior from Denver. He had watched in shock early when Utah receiver James Hardy, wide open for a touchdown, had juggled the ball from the goal line to the end line before dropping it. But in the end, Rotello's interceptions stopped the Utes from making another of their late comebacks.

"It was a busy day for us out there," Rotello said. "Those Utah guys were like lightening – they're on you before you know it. You can't panic back there or you're dead.

"We knew they would be trying to throw deep on us when they were behind toward the end. Our coaches knew exactly what kind of patterns they would be running, so it was just a matter of guessing and waiting for the right spot to make the interceptions."

Rotello, who had played in recent weeks with painful shoulder problems, said he didn't mind playing a finesse offense for a change.

"It was a challenge for us," he said, "and holding them to just 15 points is something we can be proud of."

Most of the other defenders felt the Colorado State game last week had made this one more important.

"We felt we had a lot to prove, to others but especially to ourselves," said Chuck Kinamon, a senior outside linebacker. "And I think we did that today."

"We just wanted to play our kind of game, which we didn't do at CSU," said cornerback Dwan Wilson. "We knew our offense would be able to move the ball against Utah. The big question was whether we could hold them down."

And now, facing San Diego State next Saturday will be no problem – even with Army and Brigham Young looming immediately thereafter.

"When you're 8-0," said Johnson, "they're all big."

Plus, there is another motivation.

"San Diego State is another WAC game, and that's enough by itself to fire us up," Wilson said. "That's a big goal for us, to win the league. And the closer we get to it – 5-0 now – the more we want it."

That even goes for the underclassmen.

"Winning the WAC definitely does mean a lot to us," said Chad Hennings, the sophomore defensive tackle. "But we really are just playing them one at a time."

And, they're trying not to notice the growing hordes of bowl scouts.

"We don't want to look ahead," Hankamer said, "but in the back of our minds, we know they're here."

"We thought of this game as just like last year at Army," Kinamon said. "The bowls were saying they wanted us, but when we lost, they were gone."

This time, they'll be back.

Mike Burrows/The Colorado Springs Gazette:

Scott Thomas outraced Erroll Tucker and the Air Force Academy wishbone out- dueled Utah quarterback Larry Egger.

So there was nothing really outlandish in Air Force's 37-15 thumping of the Utes Saturday at Falcon Stadium.

Or was there?

The crowd was disappointingly outlandish. Only 32,269 – including officials of the Orange, Sugar, Fiesta, Bluebonnet and Citrus bowls – showed up on a comfortable day to watch the eighth-ranked Falcons:

> Move to 8-0 overall
>> Surge all alone to the top of the Western Athletic Conference ladder at 5-0
>>> Claim their school-record 11th consecutive victory

Thomas, the Falcon's senior free safety, was brilliant. The AFA Wishbone was too, when it didn't make mistakes.

And, not to be forgotten, it was Air Force's defense that checked Utah's high-scoring offense to only two touchdowns. The Utes, now 6-2 and 4-1, entered the WAC showdown ranked sixth nationally in scoring at 35.9 points per game.

You had to feel for Egger, the Ute's big-league lefty.

The Redondo Beach, Calif. native completed 29 of 50 passes for 347 yards and one touchdown – and still took a damaging defeat back to Salt Lake City.

Air Force swiped three of Egger's passes, including two in the final 7:49 by junior cornerback Tom Rotello of Denver that erased Utah scoring threats.

Thomas, though, loomed larger than any other player. He returned five punts for 61 yards, including a 32-yarder early in the second quarter, and took the opening kickoff of the second half 2 yards deep in his own end zone en route to scoring his third touchdown of the year.

His clutch home run lifted Air Force to a 28-7 lead in a matter of seconds – seven on the scoreboard clock – and the hole proved costly to the Utes.

Thomas' heroics even overshadowed a career-best day by Johnny Smith, the Falcons' backup fullback. Smith broke loose for 175 yards on only 14 carries and scored one touchdown, and led Air Force's rush to an overwhelming total of 451 yards on the ground.

Right behind were halfback Kelly Pittman, with 115 yards, and quarterback Bart Weiss, with 105. Pittman scored three touchdowns.

It marked the first time in AFA history that three backs cracked the 100-yard barrier in the same game.

Incredibly, the Falcons won by 22 points despite committing four turnovers. They also gave up 415 total yards to the Egger-led Utes.

"That's the fastest team we've played all year, and probably the fastest team we'll ever see," said AFA head coach Fisher

DeBerry. "We gave up some yards and we made some mistakes.

"But dadgummit, we kept them out of the end zone except for two times. And I believe that's what a defense is for, to keep you opponent out of the end zone. Egger is as good as everybody said he was. He hurt us. But we always seemed like we were able to recover. Rotello's two interceptions helped us a great deal."

Jim Fassel, Utah's rookie head coach, was saddled with disappointment.

On the Ute's ninth offensive snap of the game, Egger thought he had a 47-yard touchdown strike to all-alone wide receiver James Hardy. But Hardy juggled the ball in the end zone and finally dropped it.

In the second quarter, it was Tucker, easily the nation's most feared special-teams performer, who had a non-scoring 92-yard kickoff return wiped out by a holding penalty on the Utes.

"Air Force is an excellent team," Fassel said. "You have to play well to beat a team like that, and we just didn't make things happen when we needed to. We were not very good on special teams and we had a hard time stopping them early.

"We just didn't do a good job I all areas, which is what you have to do to beat a team like Air Force. You have to capitalize, and we didn't. It came down to the fact that they made the big plays. We didn't make them. Yes, this hurts." Utah's mistakes:

>> Egger was sacked four times. AFA linebacker Try Hankamer had two of them, one of which resulted in a third-quarter safety, the first of the Falcon's season.
>> The Utes were penalized 10 times for losses totaling 79 yards.
>> Smith thundered early and often, and too many times the Utes were bruised outside by Weiss' option pitches.
>> Eight – that's right, eight – of Egger's passes were dropped by his receivers.

"I'm not the kind that points fingers," said Egger, all class in defeat. "I surely didn't help us by throwing those interceptions. That much I know."

And Air Force didn't help the Utes by keeping the ball out of Tucker's hands, sans his cross-country kickoff return that didn't count.

Tucker was able to return only one of junior Mark Simon's punts, that being a harmless, 9-yarder. He returned one of freshman Tad McKinney's kickoffs for a 26-yard gain that counted.

In a word, Turner was shackled.

"That was a decision that we made early in the week, and it was a big, important decision," DeBerry said. "We didn't want to give Erroll Tucker a chance to hurt us. So we said, 'Why give him a chance to return the ball?' I thought Mark and Tad did a tremendous job of keeping the ball away from him, as much as they could. He showed on that 92-yarder what he's capable of doing with a football. Thank God for us that it was called back.

"That Tucker, I'm telling you, scares the death out of people."

But so does Thomas.

Saturday, the San Antonio, Texas native became just the fourth player in NCAA history – last week, Tucker was the third – to return a punt, interception and kickoff for touchdowns in the same season.

"All I can say is, 'That's pretty wild,' " Thomas said, beaming. "I thought the touchdown was a pretty big play for us.

"I don't know about a duel or not. Tucker's a great player. On that 92-yarder of his, he put a move on me that sent me sliding."

A year ago, when Utah handed Air Force a 28-17 defeat, Thomas fumbled the opening kickoff of the second half. The Utes took the turnover and scored.

"That's what started our slide against them, "Thomas said. "It was nice to get one back on them."

Especially with so much riding on it.

Mike Burrows/The Colorado Springs Gazette:

In rural northeast Iowa, Chad Hennings' family farms 800 acres and develops hogs and feeder cattle The good life, despite a bad farm economy.

On that farm, Hennings developed a work ethic that has helped build him into one of the Western Athletic Conference's most promising linemen.

"Once you're born a farm kid, you're always a farm kid," said Hennings, a 6-foot-5, 245-pound sophomore defensive tackle on the Air Force Academy's 17th ranked football team. "There isn't a day that goes by when I don't think about my family or about the farm. The same farm has been in the family for more than 100 years.

"I try to play hard, and I try to work hard. That goes back to when I was little. I'd have chores to do before school, so we'd get up every morning about 5:30 or 6 o'clock and do them. Then after school, there was always more work to do. Farm life isn't easy, but it's enjoyable. It's taught me the value of hard work, for sure."

New Mexico quarterback Billy Rucker discovered as much last week, when the Falcons waltzed out of Albuquerque with a 49-12 win. By the time Air Force led, 28-6, at halftime, Rucker had been sacked six times by the AFA defense. Hennings, the hard-working farm kid from Elberon, Iowa, had four.

That's right, four.

If you see the AFA coaching staff doing cartwheels over Hennings' potential, don't be surprised.

"Chad's gradually improved each week," said Tom Miller, the AFA defensive line coach. "He's certainly going in the right direction. He's got the ingredients you see in great players.

"He's got exceptional talent, agility and strength for a young lineman. And then you add his intensity and pride and you've got a very promising football player."

Air Force is no longer waiting for the results of a pivotal off-season experiment. Thanks to Hennings, those results are now safely tucked away in the too-good-to-be-true file.

The Falcons recruited Hennings as a tight end, the position he played as a reserve in 1984. But with the graduation loss of Chris Funk, the WAC's defensive Player of the Year, Air Force found itself with a gaping hole at one of the tackle positions.

So Hennings was moved in the spring.

"Losing Chris created the hole," Miller said. "In Chad, we took who we thought was probably our best freshman player and moved him to fill the hole. He had the size and strength we were looking for, and we thought he had big-play capability as a defensive lineman."

"When I'm not getting razzed about being a farm kid from Iowa, they call me the baby of the group," Hennings said with a smile. "That's true, though. I've still got a lot to learn. The sacks against New Mexico just happened. I took advantage of a one-on-one situation.

"But we all had a good game, not just me. The key is to do your best. If I keep doing that, I think I'll be all right."

Hennings certainly did OK as a two-sport schoolboy star at Benton Community, a consolidated high school 10 miles from Elberon, population 150.

In football, he was an all-state punter and all-conference tight end. In wrestling, he won an Iowa state heavyweight wrestling championship with a 32-0 record.

"Iowa State wanted me to combine football and wrestling," Hennings said, "and Iowa showed some interest, too. I just didn't know if I would have time for both in college, plus schoolwork. And I had a great interest in flying.

"Air Force's football program was coming on strong, so I thought this would be the best place for me. I have no regrets I'm here. The farm will always be my real home. But I think I've found another home here."

Personable and soft-spoken, he might be the pick of the litter among the academy's sophomore class.

"I know he's top-notch militarily up on the hill, and he's top-notch academically," Miller said. "He's something. Football-wise, I'd say he's got a B-plus so far and he's close to earning all A's."

His family and friends back in Elberon will get a chance Saturday to see for themselves. Air Force, 4-0, plays Notre Dame at Falcon Stadium in a nationally televised game.

"I imagine a few people will be watching back home," Hennings said. "The game will be like a dream come true for me. Just two years ago I was still in high school. And now, this."

The Hennings may even shut down the family farm for a few hours.

Ralph Routon/The Colorado Springs Gazette:

Sometimes, the best way to read a story is between the lines.

On the surface, Air Force captured a vitally important 37-15 football victory Saturday over the University of Utah, a team that turned out to be as porous as it was dangerous. It made the eighth-ranked Falcons 8-0, matching their best start ever, and improving their winning streak to a school-record 11 straight.

Air Force had viewed this as a major obstacle in the way of many team goals – the Western Athletic Conference title, an unbeaten season and a berth in a New Year's Day bowl game. Utah certainly had the raw talent on offense to give the Utes a chance, and it was fully prepared to wage an all-out scoreboard war against Air Force and the wishbone at Falcon Stadium.

It didn't come off, for two main reasons. One, whenever the Utes made the kind of big play that might have turned the game their way, something bad happened. A touchdown pass was dropped, a 92-yard kickoff return was wiped out by penalty, and another touchdown pass was nullified. Two, Air Force's defense played a superlative game, refusing to panic or buckle under pressure. When Utah didn't stop itself, the Falcons either stymied the Utes without a first down (that happened seven times, which is excellent) or came up with a drive-stopping play.

Except for the AFA offense's four turnovers, it might have been that peak game that everyone inside the Falcon program has been eagerly anticipating. Those mistakes, three lost fumbles and an interception, kept Air Force from scoring 50 points or more. They also made the fourth quarter far more suspenseful than it should have been.

That transition takes us into reading between the lines. Not of Air Force's victory itself, because that was above reproach. However, no matter what you read or hear, the Falcons definitely did not succeed in overcoming their main problem with the biggest bowls – lack of respect.

In the tunnel outside the Falcon Stadium dressing rooms, some of the bowl scouts in their colored blazers were whispering negative impressions of Air Force's showing Saturday. Nobody wanted to be quoted, of course, but it was obvious the Orange Bowl and Sugar Bowl contingents already had categorized the Falcons as "not good enough – unless their record is 12-0." If the Fiesta Bowl group felt that way too, nobody said so. The Citrus and Bluebonnet folks, obviously, would take Air Force right now.

But the big guys weren't so kind. One, asking for anonymity, criticized the Falcon's lack of a "killer punch" after building a 30-7 lead in the third quarter. Another said he thought Air Force's "run mostly – pass occasionally" offense would be a tough sell in either Miami or New Orleans.

But it was easy to see what they really meant. Even though Utah was 6-1 and explosive, the bigger bowls felt Air Force should have massacred the Utes. They wanted to see 51-15, not 37-15. They wanted 700 yards, not 524. They look at the Falcons as a fluke, and they figure Air Force should wallop anybody in the WAC except for Brigham Young.

Those Jan. 1 representatives had said they were anxious to see the Air Force phenomenon for themselves and make their own judgments on the validity of the Falcons' national ranking. But, in retrospect, at least some of them didn't come here with open minds.

So the bowl visitors interspersed some crafty semantics with their standard comments in media interviews.

They also noticed something else, over which Air Force had no control. They saw thousands of empty seats Saturday in Falcon Stadium, with the announced crowd of 32,000-plus an obvious surprise.

One bowl man, his brow furrowed when kickoff time arrived with no late rush of fans, quietly asked a biting question:

"Is something wrong between Air Force and the city of Colorado Springs?" he wondered.

No, he was told.

This was just Colorado Springs showing its embarrassing true colors once again.

He shook his head in bewilderment and said softly, "You won't find another unbeaten team in the Top Twenty with a single empty seat for any home game, especially against a league opponent with just one loss. Doesn't anybody here appreciate great college football? What's the matter with this place?"

The answer was simple: I don't know. But it would be a horrible thing if the Springs' apathy cost Air Force a major bowl bid.

Those empty seats Saturday told a sad story: Air Force has a decent base of loyal, rabid fans. But still, Colorado Springs for some reason refuses to embrace fully its hottest sports possession.

And that is a sad, sad commentary. Not for Air Force, a winning program bulging with great people and heading for a tremendous season, but for a cynical city that continually refuses to unite behind anything – even a winner.

Someday, you will regret it.

AFA notepad:

Air Force now has won 11 games in a row, and seven in succession inside the Western Athletic Conference. It's the longest winning streak in AFA history, and the 8-0 start ties the Falcon's best ever in 1970.

The crowd of only 32,269 was Air Force's lowest of the season, hurting the chances for the academy setting an all-time home attendance record for a single season.

****

No play Saturday was bigger than Scott Thomas' 100-yard kickoff return to start the second half, giving Air Force a 28-7 lead.

In fact, if the scoreboard clock was right, Thomas would have broken the world record. Starting at 15:00, the clock ran off only seven seconds to 14:53 on the run. But the fastest 100 meters in history, ironically set by Calvin Smith at the AFA track during the National Sports Festival V in 1983, probably is still safe at 9.93 seconds.

As for the return, it wasn't a specific plan. Thomas wasn't even thinking about the fact he fumbled the second-half kickoff last year at Utah, and the Utes scored moments later en route to a 28-17 win.

"We try not to think about breaking one," Thomas said later. "If we do, then we usually try too hard and make mistakes. I just was lucky enough to pop through there, and then it was just the kicker. No way I was going to let him get me, or everyone would have given me a hard time."

Thomas became the fourth player in NCAA history to score touchdowns by kickoff return, punt return and interception in the same season. Utah's Erroll Tucker had just wrapped up the same feat last week. The other two were Dick Harris of South Carolina in 1970 and Mike Haynes of Arizona State in 1974.

****

Air Force officials had promised to give out far fewer sideline passes for the Utah game, and that certainly was the case. It may have been the least cluttered AFA bench in years.

On the field, the Falcons (especially on defense) obviously tried much harder to contain their emotions after big plays. The results were obvious: no personal foul penalties.

****

Is Air Force a viable contender for a Jan. 1 bowl?

"Yes," said Bill Ward of the Orange Bowl. "But we didn't establish that. They established that. They do have some tough games ahead, though. I think they can prove that they deserve to be up there in the rankings. They're quality merchandise."

****

Air Force punter Mark Simon kicked five times Saturday, which should give him enough to qualify for the NCAA statistical leaders (the minimum requirement is 3.6 punts per game). Since his kicks were for a 46.0-yard average through seven games, Simon should become the national leader.

Final Statistics: AFA vs Utah

Score	1	2	3	4	Final
Air Force	7	14	9	7	**38**
Utah	0	7	0	8	**15**

Scoring Plays:

AFA –Pittman	1 run (Ruby kick), 1/11:54
Utah – Richey	28-yrd pass from Egger (? Kick), 2/12:58
AFA –Smith	13 run (Ruby kick), 2/11:49
AFA – Pittman	2 run (Ruby kick), 2/4:09
AFA – Thomas	100 yard kickoff return (Ruby kick), 3/14.53

AFA – Safety   Egger tackled in end zone
               by Hankamer, 3/5:49
Utah – Bennett 3 run (Richey pass from Egger), 4/9:53
AFA –Pittman   36-yard pass from Weiss
               (Ruby kick), 4/3:50

Team Statistics:

Category	AFA	Utah
First Downs	21	20
Rush-Pass-Pen	63-9-4	27-51-10
Rushing Yards	451	68
Passing (C-A-I)	4-9-1	29-51-3
Passing Yards	73	347
Punt Avg.	39.3	42.8
Fumbles-Lost	4-3	1-0
Penalties-Yards	4-55	10-79

Individual Statistics (Leaders only):

Rushing (Att-Yds):   Smith (AFA) 14-175
                       Pittman (AFA) 17-115
                       Weiss (AFA) 9-110
                       Lewis (Utah) 12-69
Passing (C-A-I-Yds):   Weiss (AFA) 4-9-1-73
                       Egger (Utah) 29-50-3-347
Receiving (#-Yds):   Carpenter (AFA) 3-61
                       Richey (Utah) 10-104
                       McEwen (Utah) 8-63

Tackles: Terry Maki (AFA) – 6
Mike Chandler (AFA) – 5
Tom Rotello (AFA) – 5

A.J. Scott and John Ziegler make it tough on Utah's Utes!

Fullback Johnny Smith breaks into the open against Utah.

Chapter Nine
The Aztecs

"There are only two options regarding commitment. You're either IN or you're OUT. There is no such thing as life in-between." --- Pat Riley

Nov 2, 1985   AFA vs. San Diego State   W 31-10

This victory brought national attention to the Falcons. Nine wins in a row gave them their best start ever and brought them top five national ranking in both **AP** and **UPI** polls.

Fortunately, most of the pollsters didn't watch the San Diego State game.

The vaunted Falcons offense was help to just 373 total yards as the Aztecs gave the cadets a real run for their money.

Tom Rotello picked off two Todd Santos passes and returned one for a touchdown. Scott Thomas and the Falcons' all-time interception leader, Dwan Wilson, each added one interception. Fullback Pat Evans led the Falcons offensive attack with 108 yards.

Ralph Routon/The Colorado Springs Gazette:

College football season has reached its fourth quarter, and the two most precious honors of any year possess no shoo-in favorites.

Nobody can hang onto the No. 1 ranking, and nobody can make an advance claim for the Heisman Trophy. Florida, which may be the best team in America, can't play in a bowl game and doesn't deserve the honors because of its many NCAA rules violations. Keith Byars of Ohio State and Bo Jackson of Auburn, who could have staged a tremendous race for the Heisman, instead have defaulted because of injuries and poor games.

Despite its imperfections, the "system" will produce a national champion on Jan. 2, after the bowls are done. But the Heisman remains in a state of disarray, begging for someone to step forward and take command.

With that in mind, herewith is a late but totally deserving nomination.

Bart Weiss, quarterback, Air Force.

No, the senior from Naples, Fla. will not run for 2,000 yards. He won't pass for 2,000 yards, either. He comes from a program that emphasizes the team concept far more than individual honors.

But no player in America means more to his college team, especially in the group of those still eligible for the national championship.

Last week, a Denver writer pulled out Weiss' statistics and put them beside the totals of one Roger Staubach in 1963, when that famous Navy quarterback won the Heisman. Believe it or not, Weiss is having a better year - both running and passing - than Staubach's honorable season.

Of course, the college game has changed markedly in the last two decades. But the basics remain the same, and Weiss clearly has emerged this fall as the nation's most versatile run-pass quarterback.

Consider these powerful conclusions:

- Weiss ranks 27th among the nation's rushing leaders, but among quarterbacks, his 93.3-yard average per game is No. 1 in America.
- In passing, Weiss doesn't have enough attempts to make the national leader board. But if he did, his pass-efficiency rating of 168.1 would rank No. 1 in America.
- NCAA officials confirmed Monday that Weiss, with 160 more rushing yards in his last three regular-season games, could become only the third quarterback in history to run and pass for 1,000 yards in the same season (the other two were Reggie Collier of Southern Mississippi in 1981 and Johnny Bright of Drake in 1950).

No. 1 in rushing. No. 1 in passing.

If more Heisman voters around the nation knew that, they might not be so flustered about their choice.

Last Saturday, Weiss time after time took the best vicious shots San Diego State's defenders could unleash. They speared him, clotheslined him, flung him down by the facemask, aimed for his knees and ankles, held him up while others joined the pile and even taunted him as he staggered to his feet and back to the huddle after each brutal hit.

Their intent was simple. Punish Weiss long and harshly enough, and maybe he'll have to leave the game.

Nice thought. Wrong plan.

If the Aztecs knew Weiss the way his Falcon teammates do, they would not have wasted their time and effort.

"Most guys his size would never be able to take all that and keep going, but Bart does." said fullback Pat Evans.

"He's incredible - just 170 pounds (actually 175 on a 6-foot frame), and he gets killed almost every play by tacklers who weigh 240 or 250," said receiver Ken Carpenter. "Several times (Saturday) he really got ripped. But he wouldn't come out. That just makes him tougher."

Not surprisingly, Weiss has the total respect of his offense.

"Our feeling now is, 'You lead the way, and we'll follow.' "Carpenter said. "He's a good leader. He got mad one time in the huddle, and he went nuts. He just screamed. 'I'm the quarterback. Everybody shut up' " He's never had to do that again."

Weiss himself would rather not talk about the Heisman. He says it embarrasses him, and he's not lying. He honestly doesn't feel worthy, but the list of those who disagree starts with his backup, Brian Knorr, who would be starting for any other option team in America.

This week at Air Force, of course, everybody's first thought is beating Army.

Next week, the singular goal will be to knock off Brigham Young. Still, maybe the AFA sports information office should send a rapid mass-mail flyer to the national media. It certainly seems in order.

Bart Weiss for the Heisman. Why not?

Mike Burrows/The Colorado Springs Gazette:

Everything carried a distinct flavor of generosity Saturday at Falcon Stadium.

San Diego State quarterback Todd Santos was generous with interceptions, and Air Force found no embarrassment with sticking out its hands.

The crowd was generously announced as being 36,503 although it appeared somewhat smaller.

And the AFA wishbone was generous enough to give the Aztecs a chance in the third quarter.

Considering all the give and take, the Salvation Army missed a great show.

What mattered most to Air Force, however, was the final score. The seventh-ranked Falcons nudged their way closer to a Western Athletic Conference championship with a 31-10 beating of the bumbling Aztecs.

Santos' four interceptions helped make Air Force's 12th consecutive victory appear easier than it actually was.

Excluding a 57-yard punt by Mark Simon, Air Force had just three offensive snaps in the third quarter to SDSU's 29.

Even at that, the Aztecs could not shoot down an unbeaten flock of Falcons, who face the real Army next Saturday.

SDSU lost two fumbles in addition to the flagrant piracy of Santos, and lost for the fourth straight week.

Air Force improved to 9-0 overall, its best start ever, and 6-0 in the WAC.

"The turnovers were certainly our undoing today," said Doug Scovil, the SDSU's head coach who dropped to 0-5 against Air Force. "Except for the turnovers, I didn't think our execution on offense was that bad.

"Air Force doesn't have any weak points. Defensively, I think they are better that some of their recent teams. They're an excellent defensive team."

And to be sure, an opportunistic one.

On the third play of the second half with the Falcons holding a 17-3 lead, AFA junior cornerback Tom Rotello stepped in front of SDSU flanker Vince Warren at the Aztec's 30-yard line, picked Santos clean and raced untouched down the SDSU sideline to a back breaking touchdown.

Santos, who completed 18 of 32 pass attempts for 224 yards, then took the Aztecs on a 18 play, 80-yard scoring drive that ace wideout Webster Slaughter capped with a three yard touchdown reception.

Feeling threatened at 24-10, the Air Force secondary stepped forward one more time and once and for all, turned off the Santos-generated heat.

On the first play of the fourth quarter, with SDSU facing a second-and-8 situation at the AFA 38, Santos lobbed an ill-fated pass into the hands of free safety Scott Thomas.

Rotello and Dwan Wilson also made first-half interceptions that did much to derail Santos, who is rated sixth in the nation in passing efficiency.

Fittingly, AFA halfback Kelly Pittman closed out the scoring with a 3-yard touchdown run just1:52from the finish togive the afternoon the deceiving look of a rout.

It was Pittman, the WAC's leading scorer, who gave Air Force a 7-0 lead with a 2-yard scoot on the game's fifth play.

Remarkably, Air Force showed it can win by three touchdowns despite a stale wishbone.

Air Force had 299 first-half yards. The Falcons finished with 373. Eleven of their 15 first downs came in the opening 30 minutes.

But it was a turnover-free wishbone, too.

"We can play much, much better," said AFA head coach Fisher DeBerry. "I don't want to give the wrong impression to you. I think San Diego State should be given a lot of credit, and I think we made some big, big plays and had great effort.

"But I also believe we weren't real sharp. We had a lot of chances to score and came up empty. We did not play particularly well on offense in the second half. As a team, we did not execute as well as we've been known to execute.

"But, hey, the dadgum defense came through when we needed it. We picked Santos four times, and you just don't do that without talent and a belief in each other. We held down a great, great San Diego State offense."

Air Force's victory somewhat cushioned a terribly difficult week for the academy in general and DeBerry in particular.

On Thursday, an Air Force officer and cadet were killed in the crash of a training glider just north of the academy.

On Friday, DeBerry learned that his father-in-law, with whom he felt extremely close, had died unexpectedly from an illness in Cheraw, S.C., DeBerry's hometown.

With an important victory in the bag, DeBerry flew to South Carolina to be with his family. He plans to return either Monday night or Tuesday morning.

These were late-week losses unrelated to any scoreboard.

Even DeBerry's usually loud post-game speech was noticeably subdued.

"It's hard to keep your mind on something like this (the game) when you've already got a lot on your mind." DeBerry said softly. My family is a long way from home. The news of my father-in-law was stunning, to say the very least.

"This is not an easy time for the DeBerrys right now, nor is it an easy time for the academy. The Cadet Wing was really hit hard by what happened Thursday. You feel these losses. You really do.

"But at the same time, you don't feel like you can dwell on it, either. I saw a lot of champions dressed in blue out there on the football field today. Nobody is more proud of this team than me."

"The plane crash, and then the death in coach DeBerry's family... sure we feel it.: Thomas said. "I can't imagine what it was like for coach Deberry today. Before the game, he told us what had happened with his family. He stayed composed. He wasn't choked up. I believe that's because he feels a true obligation to his players. He saw this day through, just like we all did."

Most certainly, include Pat Evans.

Air Force's junior fullback topped 100 rushing yards for the first time this season. He was the game's leading rusher, finishing with 108 yards.

Catapulted by Randy Jones' cornerback-leveling downfield block, Evans opened the game with a 52-yard dash to the SDSU 28. Four snaps later, Pittman scored.

But even Evans paralleled the trek of his wishbone.

In the first half, he had 101 yards on seven carries.

In the second half, he had 7 yards on six carries.

"I thought our defense gave a great effort," Scovil said. "Fisher told me after the game that it was as tough as they've been played defensively all year. Every time out we seem to get a little better at defensing the wishbone.

"We just gave up a couple of big plays early that were costly."

Aided by a strong wind, SDSU senior Chris O'Brien kicked a 54-yard field goal early in the first quarter. He missed a 43-yard attempt seven minutes later however, snapping his WAC-record streak of 18 consecutive field goals.

Air Force senior Tom Ruby kicked a 49-yarder and later missed from 41 yards.

Santos was sacked five times.

"Our pressure was there when we had to have it." DeBerry said. "Santos is a great passer and we held him to 10 points, just one touchdown.

"I notice the points we give up a lot more than the yards. It'd be nice if we can keep this up."

He said it in a generous sort of way.

Mike Burrows/The Colorado Springs Gazette:

Tomislav Zlatich of Belgrade, Yugoslavioa, is Tom Ruby's biggest fan. And nobody appreciates Tomislav Zlatich more than Tom Ruby of Woodland Hills, Calif.

What, you ask, does this have to do with Air Force Academy football? A lot.

Tomislav Zlatich is Tom Ruby. And Tom – Tomislav? - is the fifth-ranked Falcons' top placekicker and author of a stunning career turnaround.

More on that later. First, meet Tomislav Zlatich Ruby.

"That's really the full name I go by," he said Wednesday. "That's part of who I used to be and part of who I am now. I'm Tom Ruby now. I was born Tomislav Zlatich."

He was born Jan 20, 1964, in Belgrade, the Yugoslavs' capital city, which sits by the picturesque Danube River in the northeast corner of the communist country.

Eighteen months later, Ruby said, his family fled Yugoslavia and established residency in Paris. Ten months later, they were on their way to a California home and eventual U.S. citizenship.

The Zlatich family left its homeland for a reason, Ruby said.

During World War II and after the war, Ruby said his grandfather had been a Yugoslav freedom fighter. First, against the Nazis, and then against the incoming purge of Tito's communism.

"My family, I'm told, didn't live in fear or anything like that." Ruby said. "But I'm told they were very cautious about the possibility of something happening to them."

Soon there was no real freedom for which to fight. His grandfather fled to the United States, hoping the rest of his family would follow.

"I'm not real sure of actual dates on this." Ruby said. "but I do know my mother had a passport that would allow us to leave the country, without pressure, if we chose to do so. I was very young, so I have no real memory of living in Yugoslavia.

"I believe my family made up its mind to leave when they heard, through several sources, that the government was considering taking away the passport because of my grandfather's actions. When we were living in California and I was old enough to understand, my mother told me that she'd heard the government came knocking on our door the day after we left for Paris. Just one day after.

Tomislav Zlatich didn't become Tom Ruby until his parents divorced when he was 5 and his mother married John Ruby, a Los Angeles fireman, when he was 9.

It was then that Tomislav became Tom.

"I consider my stepfather to be my real father now." Ruby said. "It's wonderful the way everything has worked out. My mother remarried in 1973, and I was adopted into the Ruby name."

Though he's now a true-blue American, an AFA senior eyeing a post-season bowl game, graduation and pilot training, Ruby said he never will forget his homeland.

Tomislav would never allow it.

"I care too much about Yugoslavia to forget about it." Ruby said. "There are times even now that my mother and I speak Serbian, the Yugoslav tongue, to each other, just for the fun of it.

"All of us went back in 1978, and I can't wait to go back again. There is a lot of the Zlatich family still living there, and we're all very, very close. They are farmers, so they introduced me, the LA kid, to the ways of the farm when we visited. It's a fascinating visit for all of us.

"My impression of the country was not at all what I found. It's a beautiful, wonderful country that has maintained its identity despite communism. Yugoslavia does not answer to the Soviet Union and is not part of the Iron Curtain. The Yugoslavs are a proud people, and they're a resourceful people.

"I have an uncle and an aunt now living in Yugoslavia who have made plans to be at my academy graduation. That will really be something."

They'll miss Ruby's finest hour, though, in football.

A schoolboy all-America kicker at El Camino Real High School in the Los Angeles suburb of Woodland Hills, Ruby actually signed a national letter of intent with Cal State-Fullerton before deciding to heed the call of Air Force's Falcons.

At Air Force, nobody expected him to pull a disappearing act. But that's what happened, until this season.

Ruby sat and watched for three years while Sean Pavlich and Carlos Mateos hogged the limelight.

Now, Ruby is the one getting his kicks. Finally.

In the Falcon's 9-0 start, he's been perfect on 40 extra-point attempts and has hit 7 of 12 field goal tries, his longest being a 49-yarder. He's averaging 6.8 points per game, and his 61 total points trail only halfback Kelly Pittman's 84 among the high-scoring Falcons.

Along with Utah's Andre Guardi, Ruby leads the Western Athletic Conference in kick scoring.

His grandfather was known for resistance, so it's fitting that Ruby has become known for his own kind of resistance.

He resisted giving up.

"I'm very happy for Tom," said Lt Col Dick Ellis, the AFA special-teams coach. "I think he realized this year was a now-or-never situation for him.

"He's come through. There have been people that have said, 'Well, it's now or never for me,' and it's been never. For Tom, it's been, 'Now.' There's a huge difference."

Ruby is quick to credit Ellis, holder Mark Simon and deep snapper Derek Brown for his turnaround.

But only one person could make it happen.

Tom Ruby.

"If I've learned anything here," he said, "I've learned patience and persistence. I've learned success follows hard work.

"I knew I had to make something happen for myself this year, because this year is it. I didn't want to leave here without leaving some kind of mark, some kind of contribution. Besides, I couldn't give up. My family never did. So how could I?"

Tomislav Zlatich applauded the thought.

Ralph Routon/The Colorado Springs Gazette:

Fisher DeBerry sprawled back into his locker in the coaches' dressing room underneath Falcon Stadium. He ran a hand through his hair, which stood out in 14 different directions. His eyes were bloodshot. His face was pale. His legs were limp.

Only two words could properly describe the man in charge of Air Force's football program.

Utterly exhausted.

And not because of football.

He was outwardly pleased after his Falcons' 31-10 victory Saturday over San Diego State. He felt pride in Air Force's 9-0 record, the best start in AFA history. He knew he would have no motivational problems now, with Army and Brigham Young coming up.

But he couldn't truly enjoy any of it.

DeBerry. A man whose life is consumed by the family concept at home and work, had gone through an excruciating week. His son, Joe, suffered a broken hand on Wednesday. The next day, DeBerry and the rest of the academy reeled in grief upon learning of the glider crash near Monument that killed a cadet and an instructor.

Then on Friday, DeBerry took his wife LuAnn to the airport. She was flying home to South Carolina to be with her father, Joe Coppedge, who had undergone surgery. At the airport, the DeBerrys received an urgent phone call. LuAnn's father had died. Despite the surgery, the loss was unexpected.

"I felt so bad," Fisher was saying now. "Having to put her on that plane by herself."

"It was hard to do. LuAnn is a strong girl. She's a wonderful wife. But I wanted to be there to help her through this time. She realized, though, that I had to stay here."

What most people don't understand is DeBerry's relationship with his father-in-law. DeBerry never really had a father, since his parents separated when he was just a year old. But he was close to the Coppedges because everybody knew everybody in Cheraw, S.C.

Without more detail, suffice it to say Joe Coppedge was the father Fisher DeBerry never had.

How stricken was the AFA coach? Enough that he didn't stay with the Falcon players Friday night at a local motel, as he usually does before home games. Enough that he didn't sleep at all, even in his own bed. Enough that he refused to use it as an excuse Saturday, though he certainly could have.

And once the game was over, enough that Deberry was bracing himself for another all-nighter. He left Denver at 10pm on a flight for Newark, N.J., where he arrived at 3am today. After a four-hour layover, he had a flight for Charlotte, N.C., followed by a 2 1/2 hour drive to Cheraw.

If the funeral is this afternoon, DeBerry plans to return Monday. If the service is delayed, he will be back Tuesday.

"But I need to be there," he said solemnly, "I have to go."

Sure Air Force plays Army next Saturday. Sure it's a supremely important game to the Falcon program.

But they'll have to start working on that game plan without the head coach.

When DeBerry returns, it will be all football again. He will be able to concentrate totally on the task at hand, as he always has done so well.

He couldn't really do that, though, Saturday against San Diego State. And, as vibrant and magnetic as DeBerry always is, when he told the team before the game about his family loss, they knew mere sympathy wasn't sufficient.

That was just the topper, really, to a week full of distractions for the Air Force players. Most of them had spent many extra hours studying for GR's (graded reviews) which are tough exams that aren't made easier for athletes. Too, the glider tragedy silenced the whole academy on Friday, usually the day when cadet spirit begins to boil before a game.

Despite all that, and another inspired opponent, Air Force won again Saturday. For all purposes, the Falcons have gone through a minor slump the last three weeks against Colorado

State, Utah and San Diego State. Any could have spoiled the perfect record and the bold dreams. But nobody has.

That slump must end now, and DeBerry surely will come back with fresh perspective – not to mention some much-needed rest – to provide fresh mental energy for a late-season surge.

And while he is gone, with some time to reflect, DeBerry might realize something else.

If the Falcons didn't lose Saturday, who knows if they ever will.

Mike Burrows/The Colorado Springs Gazette:

His position coach, Jim Grobe, calls him "the most underrated football player in the Western Athletic Conference."

His head coach. Fisher DeBerry, calls him "pound for pound, our toughest player. I'd go to war with him."

Well, then, is Air Force Academy outside linebacker Pat Malackowski a wild man?

To those who have seen him play with the eighth-ranked, unbeaten Falcons, the answer is an unsolicited yes.

Malackowski says no.

"I don't play outside the rules, and I don't think I play wild," he said. "But I do play hard. That's the way I've always tried to play.

"I don't have the natural ability that you see in (AFA defensive backs) Scott Thomas and A.J. Scott, guys like that. So I try to hustle my butt off, and I always try to be in the proper frame of mind."

In other words, wildly enthusiastic.

"I start the mental preparation on the Monday of each game week," said Malackowski, a 6-foot, 209-pound senior from Valparaiso, Ind. Then I fall into a mode on Thursday night. I start running the game through my mind. I see myself on the field, and I see myself making the play."

It works, too.

A year ago, his first as a starter, Malackowski had 58 tackles. This year, Air Force is 7-0

Malackowski already has 38.

"Pat's got the perfect temperament," Grobe said, grinning.

"He's extremely aggressive. I know I've never coached a tougher player than Pat. The great thing about him is that he plays with pain, and he plays with so much intensity. Plus, after a game you can count his mistakes on one hand. That's not typical of an intense player.

"Usually, when a guy plays with Pat's intensity, he'll make a lot of mistakes simply because he's so charged up. Pat's different. He's so steady.

He's so in love with the game, too.

"You got it," Grobe said "Pat knows his future is not in pro football. The clock is ticking on him, so to speak. For him, this is it. He lives each game to the fullest. You never have to be concerned with him being ready to play."

Or making a big hit.

It seems Malackowski isn't satisfied unless he sees blood, grass stains and dirt on his AFA uniform.

Just last week, in the Falcons' 35-19 victory at Colorado State, his helmet crashed down on the bridge of his nose, creating a gash that needed to be sewn shut.

"I think it's broken," Malackowksi said, obviously relishing the thought "But it's no big deal. Just a couple of stitches, a little blood, whatever. My nose gets in the way. For some reason,you don't mind seeing your own blood. But you won't find me in med school."

As a Valparaiso schoolboy, he found himself in the role of a block-happy fullback. The AFA staff took one look at his intensity, and switched him permanently to defense.

"I had a great time in high school," Malackowski said. "I loved the blocking part of it, the contact. It gave me a chance, if I was up to the challenge, to really level some people.

"But there's no comparison. I like defense so much better. I'd rather hit all the time than get hit some of the time. I think defense fits my personality. On defense, I believe you never should take a step backward. I try to be a big hitter. I want the offensive player to get up knowing he's been hit."

All Malackowski is doing is releasing some emotion. If it happens to cause some pain, then so be it.

"At the academy," he said, "you have to be polite and orderly in practically everything you do. That changes on the football field. All activities are a release. Well, football is my release. If I feel any frustration during the day, there's always football to look forward to."

Since Malackowski is a throwback to the old line, when linebackers were known more as crazed, carnivorous attackers, you'd think life-sized posters of Dick Butkus and Ray Nitschke decorate walls in his dormitory room.

"Just the opposite," Malackowski said. "My only idols are my teammates. Guys like (linebackers) Terry Maki and Mike Chandler and (nose guard) Dick Clark. The guys on our defense.

They mean more to me than anybody. Just like me, they know what it takes to play this game."

They found their teacher nearby.

Final Statistics: AFA vs San Diego State

Score	1	2	3	4	Final
Air Force	7	10	7	7	**31**
SDSU	3	0	7	0	**10**

Scoring Plays:

AFA – Pittman	3 run (Ruby kick), 1/13:20
SDSU – O'Brien	28-yrd FG, 2/12:58
AFA – Ruby	49-yrd FG, 2/12:36
AFA – Weiss	4 run (Ruby kick), 2/12:39
AFA – Rotello	30-yrd interception return (Ruby kick), 3/13:30
SDSU – Slaughter	3-yrd pass from Santos (O'Brien kick), 3/6:06
AFA – Pittman	3 run (Ruby kick), 4/:16

Team Statistics:

Category	AFA	SDSU
First Downs	15	18
Rush-Pass-Pen	51-14-5	30-32-8
Rushing Yards	316	112
Passing (C-A-I)	9-14-0	18-32-4
Passing Yards	81	224
Punt Avg.	51.2	55.5
Fumbles-Lost	3-0	2-2
Penalties-Yards	5-39	8-52

Individual Statistics (Leaders only):

Rushing (Att-Yds): Evans (AFA) 13-108
Weiss (AFA) 13-91
Pittman (AFA) 11-40

Passing (C-A-I-Yds): Weiss (AFA) 9-14-0-81
Santos (SDSU) 18-32-4-224
Receiving (#-Yds): Carpenter (AFA) 6-64
Warren (SDSU) 4-91
Awalt (SDSU) 4-49
Tackles: Scott Thomas (AFA) – 8
Terry Maki (AFA) – 6
Mike Chandler (AFA) – 8
Tom Rotello (AFA) – 5

LB'er Pat Malackowski brings down another Aztec.

Head Coach Fisher DeBerry introduces an official to "DeBerryisms."

AIR FORCE

NOVEMBER 9, 1985

STADIUM

$2.00

CHAPTER TEN

THE BLACK KNIGHTS

"Beside pride, loyalty, discipline, heart and mind, confidence is the key that opens all the locks."
--- Joe Paterno

Nov 9, 1985   AFA vs. Army (Snow)   W 45-7

It was cold on the field but the Falcons were hot.

A packed Falcons Stadium watched Air Force recapture possession of the Commander-in-Chief's Trophy in a snowstorm.

Falcon's halfback Greg Pshsniak scored the first touchdown of the game and the Army began to wonder what hit them.

Every aspect of the Falcons' game looked good. The defense limited one of the nation's most prolific offenses to only 186 total yards. On the other hand, the Falcon's offense totaled 501 yards.

The first Air Force goal was achieved: win back the Commander-in-Chief's Trophy.

Ralph Routon/The Colorado Springs Gazette:

This story begins on a December day in 1983, with Air Force's football team preparing for its trip to Shreveport and the Independence Bowl.

Already, the Falcons had wrapped up a 9-2 regular season and had appeared on the low end of the wire-service rankings. Everyone was anxious to play Mississippi in the bowl game, with Air Force going for its first 10-win season in academy history.

Life was swirling around AFA football then, just as it is now. Head coach Ken Hatfield talked with a visitor about the pre-game plans, and the mood was totally nostalgic. He dwelled a long time on the memorable senior class that made the 1982-83 successes possible. It was a tingling moment, emotional and nearly tearful, filled with pride and humility.

Then, when it was time to leave, Hatfield walked out of his office and saw something that changed his feelings entirely.

Walking toward his office was a sophomore Falcon player who wouldn't be playing in the bowl game. The cadet athlete had been injured badly in the season opener and had spent that autumn rehabilitating from knee surgery.

Almost any other head coach, in that situation, wouldn't have said more than "hi" to a non-playing sophomore.

Hatfield grabbed the player, mussed his hair and bragged about his progress.

"This guy is gonna be tremendous. He's got the winning edge." said Hatfield, his arm around the embarrassed young man's shoulders. He had knee surgery in September, and three months later he's running the mile in 5:30. He could play in the bowl game, but we'll hold him out so he can get an extra hardship year if he needs it later.

"Just wait. He will be an all–American. And before his group is through, they could make everyone forget about this year."

The player's name: Scott Thomas.

Now, it is two years later. Hatfield is long gone, and Fisher DeBerry has superbly guided the Air Force program farther onward and upward.

With the 1985 Falcons nearing the end of this remarkable season, ranked as high as No. 4 in the nation with their 9-0 record, Hatfield's bold predictions suddenly reappeared from the memory bank's cobwebs.

Today, Scott Thomas is on the verge of national honors as one of the best free safeties in America. He would be leading the country in kickoff returns, except that he has too few returns because the AFA defense has enjoyed such a superlative year.

And what about Air Force's senior class of 1985? Again, Hatfield was right. This group is in position to take a long step beyond the team of 1983, starting with a legitimate shot now at the national championship.

Saturday, Thomas and the Class of '85 will play their final game at Falcon Stadium. Fittingly, the opposition is Army with the Commander-in-Chief's Trophy on the line.

It's the start of a final four-step sequence that could bring Air Force every football goal imaginable: Army, the war for military superiority; Brigham Young, the showdown for the Western Athletic Conference throne; Hawaii, the last obstacle to a perfect regular season and a New Year's Day bowl; and finally, the Jan. 1 game that could produce a national title.

Sure, those are wild dreams. Yet, thanks to these Falcon seniors, all are possible.

Most of the group played apprentice roles during the 10-2 year in 1983. Three of them – John Ziegler, A.J. Scott and Dwan Wilson – were able to crack into the defensive lineup. Only one, halfback Randy Jones, was an offensive starter. And even then, Derek Brown was revered as the best5 deep-snapper anywhere.

Almost everyone else watched, waited and hungered for their chance. Players like Bart Weiss, Ken Carpenter, Kraig Evenson, Pat Malackowski, Dick Clark, Mike Chandler, Dave Sutton, Kelly Pittman, Hugh Brennan, Tom Ruby, Greg Pshsniak, Brian Knorr, Joe Jose . . . the list seems endless.

Others toiled diligently, even knowing that they might be able to play only as backups or as senior starters, including Randy Wilson, Roger Teague, Chuck Kinamon, Chris Vellanti, Rod Vernon, Eric Pharris, J.P. Scott, Steve Allen and Ron Bryant.

All of them benefited from what happened to Air Force football in their first two years here. But now, they could set a standard against which every Falcon team would be judged – forevermore.

Even if they don't go all the way, Air Force's Class of '85 already has moved mountains.

But, having come this close to the ultimate, these Falcons see no reason to stop now.

Ralph Routon/The Colorado Springs Gazette:

Tradition reigns supreme whenever two service academies meet on the football field.

Army and Navy, of course, long have had one of the nation's best rivalries – even when one or both teams have been on a down cycle. Air Force, at age 30, remains the baby kid on the block. Its games with Army and Navy mean more to the Falcons than to the Black Knights or Middies, whose followers still have trouble recognizing Air Force's legitimacy as a proven winner.

That feeling remains strong on the East Coast. Last month, when the Falcons invaded Annapolis to face Navy, everybody back there was convinced that Air Force had not proven itself. Even the major-metro newspapers picked Navy to win. And shock prevailed when the Falcons left with a 24-7 victory.

Army and Air Force appear closer to developing a full-scale rivalry. Their series is tied at 9-9-1, and the two sides admit to feeling dislike for each other.

Yet today, despite its 9-0 record and high wire-service ranking, Air Force remains the ignored stepchild. Otherwise, its home finale this afternoon against 7-1 Army would be televised across America regardless of records. Army-Navy always will be a national TV fixture. But this Air Force-Army showdown won't be seen live anywhere outside Falcon Stadium.

ABC-TV ignored today's game, mainly because of poor ratings five weeks ago when the network showed Air Force-Notre Dame to the entire nation.

If this game doesn't warrant TV coverage, one has to wonder what it would take.

How strong are the credentials? Well, try this: With a combined record of 16-1, this matchup is the best of any service-academy game since 1945, when Army (8-0) met Navy (7-0-1). Navy had tied Notre Dame, which Army had whipped by 48-0.

Army beat Navy 32-13, to wrap up a perfect season.

That was just a few months after the end of World War II. Nothing else in the 40 years of intra-service games since then has been as good as today.

No service academy team has been ranked as high as Air Force now (at No. 4 in UPI and No. 5 in AP) since Army wound up at No. 3 after its 8-0-1 season in 1958.

And when, do you suppose, was the last time an academy won the national championship? Yes, 1945, when Army's 9-0 finish was good for No. 1 with Alabama and Navy trailing in the final AP poll.

Forty years since a national title for an academy, and the same four decades since an intra-service game with as many advanced superlatives as today.

History may be telling us something.

Mike Burrows/The Colorado Springs Gazette:

Bruce Johnson remembers the night of November 3, 1984, like it was yesterday. Not surprisingly, so does the rest of the Air Force Academy team.

Air Force strutted into Michie Stadium on the Army campus at West Point, NY with the idea of bringing home its third consecutive Commander-in-Chief's Trophy which signals football supremacy among the nation's three largest service academies.

In attendance was a near sellout crowd of 39,000 and ESPN television cameras.

In their own words, the Falcons stunk it up. They lost three of four fumbles and suffered two interceptions in a disheartening 24-12 setback to the Black Knights.

The Falcons drowned on the banks of the Hudson. They remember the deathly quiet flight that took them back home to Colorado Springs.

"I can't recall hearing a whole lot of noise, if that's what you mean," Johnson, the AFA defensive coordinator, said Sunday. "Yes, it was a quiet, long trip home.

"They ate us up with all the turnovers. We got our butts beat, plain and simple. When you do that, the trip home is never fun, even if it's just a 30-minute drive.

Now, guess who's coming to dinner.

You got it. Army.

The seventh-ranked Falcons jumped to 9-0 Saturday with a 31-10 victory over visiting San Diego State. Army, 7-1, got its tune-up with a 34-12 whipping of Holy Cross at West Point.

In five days at Falcon Stadium, may the best wishbone win.

Already, an overflow crowd of more than 52.000 is almost assured.

"In a lot of ways," Johnson said, "it'll be like looking at mirrors. We're both wishbone teams, and the stats say we're two of the better running teams you'll see.

"But Army could easily have some new wrinkles for us, just like we could have some new wrinkles for them."

Unchanged, however, will be the weight shouldered by both teams' quarterbacks and fullbacks.

Army fullback Doug Black, a 6-foot, 210-pound senior from Salado, Texas, ranks 23rd nationally in rushing with a per-game average of 94.6 yards. He's carried 154 times this season for 757 yards, five touchdowns and a 4.9 per-carry average.

He carried 21 times for 77 yards last year against Air Force, and finished his junior season with II touchdowns and Army-record totals of 264 carries for 1,148 yards.

This season, AFA junior fullbacks Johnny Smith and Pat Evans have combined for 931 yards, six touchdowns and a

5.8 per-carry average. Evans is coming off a 108-yard game against SDSU.

Air Force senior Bart Weiss may be the nation's No. 1 option quarterback. He ran for 91 yards on 13 carries against SDSU, and is ranked 27th nationally with a per-game average of 93.3 yards. He's averaging 6.4 yards per carry and has an AFA-leading total of 840.

Army will counter with speedy sophomore Troy Crawford, with oft-injured senior Rob Healy ready in the bullpen.

Crawford, a 5-10, 175-pounder from Houston, gained a game-high 134 yards on 26 carries against Holy Cross and scored two touchdowns. The week before, in Army's 45-43 squeeze past Colgate, Crawford needed only 12 carries to get 136.

He's averaging 81.9 yards per game and 5.7 per carry.

Army trails only fifth-ranked Nebraska on the national rushing ladder. NU is No. 1 with a per-game rushing average of 365 yards. Army is No.2 at 358. Air Force is No. 5 at 313.7.

"With the two offenses," Johnson said, "you're looking at bookends. We will have to be as sharp as ever, no question about it."

"I haven't seen much of Crawford on film yet, but the book on him is that he's an excellent athlete. Black is a tough runner, a tough player. He plays like he has no fear of anybody."

"Defensive coaches never have a chance to rest, and this week will be no different. The tough thing for us this week will be changing gears. The past few weeks, we've been going against great passing offenses. Now we face a great running team. It's a transition our defense will have to make, and make smoothly."

Both teams are firmly in the post-season bowl picture. Army was 5-0 and ranked No. 19 before it crashed at Notre Dame, 24-10.

Air Force has beaten the Irish, 21-15.

"There isn't a person on this team that isn't aware of what happened to us last year up at Army." said Pat Malackowski, an AFA senior outside linebacker. "Very embarrassing night. Sure, give credit to Army for whipping us. But I also think we helped. We stunk, and Saturday will be an opportunity to do something about it."

"Nobody, absolutely nobody, has to get us psyched up to play Army. What's great is that I'm sure they feel the same way about us."

Johnson filled in Sunday for Fisher DeBerry during the taping of the AFA head coach's television show. DeBerry is in Cheraw, S C., attending the funeral of his father-in-law. He is expected to return tonight or early Tuesday.

"We've got a coaching staff that's got a lot of years in this business." Johnson said. "We can carry on in Fisher's absence. Our preparation this Week is so important."

Air Force – Army Notepad:

Air Force closes out its home season today against Army, and the fifth-ranked Falcons are bidding to become the first AFA football team since 1963 to race unbeaten through its home schedule.

In 1963, Air Force beat Washington State (10-7), Colorado State (69-0), Boston College (34-7), UCLA (48-21) and Colorado (17-14) at Falcon Stadium enroute to a Gator Bowl bid and 7-4 record.

This year, Air Force has toppled Texas-El Paso, Rice, Notre Dame, Utah and San Diego State.

"I'm not sure how much of a home-field advantage we have," AFA head coach Fisher DeBerry said, "but I do know I'd rather play Army here than up at their place."

DeBerry did not realize until Thursday night that the Falcons have a chance to finish unbeaten at home for the first time in 22 years.

"You can bet I'll tell our players." he said.

"This bunch takes a lot of pride in playing well at home, and this should be an added incentive for us.

"This is our turf, not Army's, and we're going to do everything possible to successfully defend it."

****

Army, 7-1, has scored 40 or more points in five of its eight games.

Air Force, 9-0, scored 48, 49, 59 and 49 in its first four wins, but hasn't topped the 40-point mark since.

****

The DeBerry-coached Falcons are 9-1 at Falcon Stadium. Their only home-field loss was to Brigham Young, 30-25, last season on Oct. 20.

It won't help Army here, but the Black Knights currently boast a 10-game win streak at Michie Stadium in West Point, N.Y.

****

Air Force will move to .500 in all-time Commander-in-Chief's Trophy games if Army loses today.

To date, the Falcons are 13-14 in the Trophy series, which started in 1972. Army is 10-15-1.

Navy slipped to 16-10-1 last month after it lost to Air Force, 24-7.

****

Army is in its 96th year of varsity football, with an all-time record of 539-283-50.

Air Force, the new kid on the academy block, is in its 30th varsity season and has an all-time record of 152-154-12.

****

Among non-seniors, AFA cornerback To Rotello has the most interceptions of any major-college player in the country.

Rotello, a junior from Denver, has seven in nine games.

****

Rotello is the only AFA-Army starter who hails from Colorado, and none hail from New York.

Not surprisingly, Texas has produced 10 starters for the game, easily the most of any state.

****

Other states that have spawned at least three AFA-Army starters are Florida (4), Ohio (3), Arkansas (3), and Virginia (3).

Air Force will have six Texans in its starting lineup.

Ralph Routon/The Colorado Springs Gazette:

If it's possible for the nation's highest scoring offense to feel queasy, Air Force did.

Every Saturday the Falcons had been winning, but something always detracted from the offense's satisfaction. At times the culprit was turnovers, on other days the opposing defense simply covered the wishbone's options aggressively and well.

Just a week ago, Air Force's attack had sputtered far too much in a 31-10 victory over San Diego State. So, going into the final home game of 1985 against Army, the Falcon offense felt it had something to prove.

Not anymore.

Air Force rolled up 501 total yards Saturday, including 396 on the ground and 105 in the air. Also, the Falcons controlled the ball for six minutes longer than Army, a substantial edge in a matchup of two running teams.

Best of all, Air Force went the full 60 minutes in blowing snow and bitter wind without a single turnover.

And so, after romping to a 45-7 victory over Army, the Falcon offense finally could share in the celebration.

"We're not saying we didn't make any mistakes, said quarterback Bart Weiss, remembering several threats that failed to put points on the board, "But to win by that score is the greatest feeling in the world. This definitely feels better for us than the last few weeks."

Weiss had the biggest individual numbers, with 114 rushing yards and two touchdowns. He also got credit from the AFA coaches for calling audibles before almost every snap to adjust to Army's defense.

But the senior from Naples, Fla., like all the other backs and receivers, felt the prime reason for Air Force's control was the line winning its battles up front, play after play.

"There was no way we were going to lose this one." said Joe Jose, the senior right guard. "We just knew it, and everyone was fired up. On the audibles, Bart did a great job of putting us in the right play that would go to the defense's weakest spot. Then, it's just a matter of executing."

Air Force broke several big-gainers, including touchdown runs of 57 and 56 yards against the Black Knights. But the day's longest play was a 64-yard pass from Weiss to Ken

Carpenter, giving the Falcons a 14-0 lead early in the second quarter.

For Carpenter, it was a special accomplishment since his father, Gen. William Carpenter, was an all-America receiver for Army.

The elder Carpenter was unable to make it here for the game, but that did not diminish Ken's thrill in the least.

"That was really a big one for me," Carpenter Said. "I know I'll never forget it, and I don't think Dad will, either.

Everyone on the offensive side of the dressing room agreed the 501 yards and 45 points were a good way to tune up for the next challenge, next Saturday at Brigham Young, with the Western Athletic Conference title on the line.

"Whenever you lose a game, you spend every day for the next year thinking of how you can make up for it the next chance," said fullback Pat Evans. "That's how we feel about Brigham Young. Nobody has to say anything. We know BYU has a great team.

"But if we can play another game like this, with no turnovers, and if the defense can have another great day, we'll have a chance."

Mike Burrows/The Colorado Springs Gazette:

John Ziegler played Saturday like he wanted to leave his mark at Falcon Stadium.

Consider it mission accomplished.

The Air Force defensive tackle was Army's worst nightmare in the first half of the Falcons' 45-7 victory.

The game was only five plays old when Army, not known for trickery in its well-oiled wishbone, tried junior wide receiver Benny White on a reverse with a third-and-seven call from the Black Knights' 35-yard line.

Up stepped Ziegler, and White forgot to zig-zag.

Air Force's 6-foot-3, 247-pound senior promptly threw White for a 9-yard loss.

"I thought that play by John set the defensive tone for the whole game," said AFA free safety Scott Thomas. "It was a big, big play by a great player."

And Ziegler, playing his final game at Falcon Stadium, hardly was through for the day. Two Army possessions later, Ziegler's unrelenting pressure on Tory Crawford forced the sophomore quarterback to throw an interception. Thomas made the swipe, his fifth of the season, at the AFA 46.

Ten plays later, Air Force had a 7-0 lead, and the rout was on.

On the third play of the second quarter, Ziegler sacked Rob Healy, Army's senior quarterback, for an 8-yard loss.

"John Ziegler, practically all by his lonesome, controlled the football game for us in the first half," said Bruce Johnson, the AFA defensive coordinator. "I thought he was spectacular.

"The guy is just so consistent, he never gives you a bad game. I'll have to see the film to really grade his performance. But from the sideline, I thought this was one of his best days ever."

There was not much left of the Army wishbone at the finish.

The stat sheet read like a list of casualties.

Consider:

Army, now 7-2, was ranked No. 3 nationally in scoring with a per-game average of 37.7 points. The Black Knights scored their only points against Air Force with 9:28 left in the game.

Army was ranked No. 2 nationally in rushing with a per-game average of 358 yards.

Army had been ranked No. 14 nationally in total offense with a per-game average of 421.2 yards. Ziegler and the Falcons gave the Black Knights only 186 on 57 snaps, an average of just 3.3 yards per play.

"We do what we can do, nothing less." Ziegler said. "We played our assignments, and did the job. If it sounds simple, there's a reason. It's a simple philosophy. We're successful on defense because everybody does their job.

"We kept our enthusiasm and we kept our intensity. We never got tired because our offense was so good that we had a lot of time for rest."

Ziegler's point was a key one.

Air Force's possession time was 33:04 to Army's 26:56, and the AFA wishbone cranked out 501 total yards and 24 first downs.

"We've got a lot of seniors on this team . . . Ziegler said. "We all knew this was our farewell performance in this stadium. We wanted to go out with a splash."

Ziegler felt at home in more ways than one Saturday. The windblown snow that swept through Falcon Stadium reminded him of his high school days in Excelsior, Minn.

"I played a lot of snow games back home as a kid." Ziegler said. "I thought this was fun." But the score helped, obviously. "I'd rather play in cold weather than hot. We came out for pregame warmups, and the snow was blowing hard already. I thought. 'Shoot, this is Minnesota.' It was my kind of climate."

One of Army's two turnovers was a second-quarter fumble recovered by Ty Hankamer, an AFA junior outside linebacker from Temple, Texas.

Hankamer said Texans don't mesh well with snow storms.

"Yeah, I don't see too many of these down in Temple." he said, laughing. "I'm not like John at all, I like it hot."

"There were times today when I thought my feet had frozen."

Mike Burrows/The Colorado Springs Gazette:

Add one more item to the tailgating menu at Falcon Stadium.

Cold turkey.

The stuffed kind.

In the midst of a pre-winter snowstorm that turned on and off like a light switch Saturday, Army became swept up in the worst type of conditions imaginable.

Air Force authored the atmosphere with a suffocating defense, ball-control offense and a kicking game that's become textbook efficient.

OK, so it wasn't a full-scale blizzard. But try telling that to Army.

We're talking cold turkey, remember.

And fifth-ranked Air Force, obviously playing with a mission, stuffed the Black Knights like they've never been stuffed before in this series.

We're talking dominance as pure as the driven snow. Air Force danced out of Falcon Stadium with a 45-7 rout, and it could easily have been worse.

The obvious: Air Force performed like a football team that knows it's within reach of a national championship.

Floggings like this aren't supposed to happen when the teams waging battle are a combined 16- 1.

Yet that's what happened in front of 52,103 frozen patrons.

"Physically, we just lined up and took it to them." said Fisher DeBerry, the AFA head coach. "Stuffed them? Yeah, you might say that."

Air Force led at halftime, 14-0, and blew the game open with a 14-point third quarter en route to the Black Knights' worst thrashing since they started playing the Falcons in 1959.

The 38-point margin of victory is the Falcons' widest in 20 games of the AFA-Army series, and their 45 points are the most ever surrendered to them by Army.

At the Division1-A level, Air Force now is the only 10-0 team in the country.

"They sure are better. I didn't figure that we would get beat, 45-7," said Jim Young, the Army head coach. "They just beat us, outcoached us, outplayed us, and they made the big plays.

"I thought we had a shot to come back, but they took it to us good in the third quarter." Real good.

Scott Thomas opened the second half for the Falcons with a 39-yard kickoff return. Two plays later, AFA quarterback Bart Weiss raced 56yards down the Army sideline for a quick-strike touchdown and 21-0 lead.

On the Falcons' third possession of the third quarter, Weiss took them on a 10-play, 37-yard scoring drive that Army punter Harold Rambusch set up when he kicked only 23 yards into a strong northerly wind.

Weiss scored on a 1-yard keeper for a 28-0 lead, and Army found itself rapidly losing a grip on the Commander-in-Chief's Trophy it took from Air Force a year ago.

Army had strutted into this clash with per-game averages of 37.7 points and 421.3 total yards.

Hey, so much for the law of averages.

Air Force gave Army just 186 yards, and the Black Knights committed two turnovers. For the second straight week, Air Force was turnover-free.

Through the first eight games, Air Force had committed 21 turnovers.

"They had turned the ball over a lot before, but they didn't today," Young said.

Completely turned over was Army's wishbone.

Meanwhile, the AFA Wishbone thundered throughout

The Falcons finished with 501 yards and averaged a whopping 6.7 yards per snap.

Air Force scored quick, and a lot. The average time of the Falcons' seven scoring drives was just 2:52.

They got a 51.3-yard average on three punts from Mark Simon, two touchdowns and a game-high 114 rushing yards from Weiss and a 64-yard touchdown reception from wideout Ken Carpenter that Weiss made happen with a perfect throw after a brilliant option fake.

They also got spectacular defense.

Army converted only three of 14 third-down conversions and averaged just 3.7 yards per rush.

Thomas, the standout free safety, intercepted a pass that set up a touchdown. AFA outside linebacker Ty Hankamer recovered a fumble. And Terry Maki, Air Force's Paul Bunyan-like inside linebacker, finished with a game-high 13 tackles.

"We completely shut down a great, great offensive machine." DeBerry said. "I'm so proud of our defense that I don't know what to do.

"We continue to play extremely consistent defense. I guess I'm most happy for our seniors. They went out big winners in their final home game."

The victory, achieved with scouts from 13 bowls in attendance, was Air Force's 13th straight in a streak that dates back to last season.

Because Bowling Green was idle Saturday, Air Force no longer shares the nation's longest major college win streak.

Bowling Green's streak remains at 12 games.

"We don't have the time to think about a national championship or this bowl or that bowl," said DeBerry, visibly exhausted but also visibly thrilled with Air Force's latest step toward squeezing reality out of a dream season "If we don't do our homework this next two weeks, all this goes down the drain.

"There isn't a man on this football team that believes he can afford to think foolish thoughts. We've still got a job to do."

Air Force can clinch a share of its first ever Western Athletic Conference title by beating 18th ranked Brigham Young next Saturday at Provo, Utah. On Nov. 23, the first day bowl bids can be issued, Air Force plays at Hawaii.

"We'll enjoy this victory over Army for one night, and one night only."

Tw Air Force running backs, senior Greg Pshsniak and junior Marc Munafo, scored their first touchdowns of the season.

No score, however, was more indicative of a black day for the Black Knights than Chris Vellanti's 57-yard burst for Air Force with 8:09 left.

Vellanti, a senior halfback from Homestead, Fla., shed several Army defenders on a crisscrossing sprint that got a jump-start when second-team quarterback Brian Knorr, another senior, leveled an Army cornerback with a booming downfield block.

Air Force had a 31-0 lead when Army avoided a shutout with 9:28 left.

Clarence Jones, a junior halfback, raced untouched on a 7-yard touchdown run. His score capped a seven play, 67-yard drive that was helped by an AFA personal-foul penalty and Army fumble that the Falcons failed to recover at their 7-yard line.

But Army never had enough to threaten their vastly superior hosts.

"Sure we wanted a shut out." DeBerry said. "But I'll still take what we did as a great accomplishment.

"I don't believe there were any real losers out there. This was college football at its finest, at its most pure. Army's no loser, no sir.

"They kept playing hard, even when it got out of hand."

Air Force made it a waste of energy.

Ralph Routon/The Colorado Springs Gazette:

None of them had spent much, if any, time in the spotlight during this unforgettable Air Force football season.

They had been the backups, the insurance policies, the ones whose main job was to stand and wait until their time would come. That is, if in fact it ever would.

For at least three members of Air Force's senior football class, though, their final game at Falcon Stadium provided a satisfying answer to some hungry dreams.

Sure, everyone enjoyed the 45-7 rout of Army on a snowy Saturday afternoon. But for that trio- Greg Pshsniak, Chris Vellanti and Brian Knorr - it meant even more on a personal level.

There was Pshsniak, the senior halfback who had been a first-teamer during spring practice before dropping back to the second unit with a nagging knee injury this fall.

Pshsniak, pressed into time-sharing duty when close friend and starting halfback Kelly Pittman came down with tonsillitis, scored Air Force's first touchdown Saturday on a 1-yard run.

But it also was Pshsniak's first touchdown as a Falcon.

"It felt like my first touchdown ever," said Pshsniak, who ran for 126 yards last season and has been more recognized for his blocking on the triple option. "But I kinda had a feeling. I bet my girlfriend 10 dollars that I would score today, and I would have had to pay if I hadn't. Now, I can collect."

For Vellanti, the situation was similar. At least, he had scored two touchdowns last year and one earlier this fall. But the halfback from Florida had not gotten many chances this season, carrying the ball only 15 times for 72 yards.

With the score 31-7 early in the fourth quarter, though, Vellanti made the most of his first ball-carrying opportunity. He took an option pitch from Knorr, picked up some fine downfield blocks - the best also coming from Knorr – and outmaneuvered everyone to the end zone for a 57-yard touchdown that broke the game open, once and for all.

"It was nice, mainly because it was the seniors' last game here." Vellanti said. "My family and my fiancee (last year's Orange Bowl queen) came from Miami to see this one, and I wanted to do something to make that long trip worth it.

"I honestly thought something might happen today. Before the play, I was thinking, 'Nobody's gonna bring me down if I get the ball.' When you come in late and you know you're only gonna get to run two or three times, you make the most of it."

Another senior who savored the moment Saturday was senior place kicker Tom Ruby. After spending the last three years as a barely used backup, Ruby emerged this year as a solidly consistent extra-point machine.

With his six conversions Saturday, Ruby raised his 1985 total to 46 of 46, eclipsing the school record of 41 set in 1983 by Sean Pavlich, who ironically was in the crowd to see his mark fall.

"Don't say I have the record, please. Ruby said. "We have the record. Derek (Brown, the long snapper), Mark (Simon, the holder) and I have the record. It takes all three, and those guys have been perfect. Also, the credit goes to the offensive line for our scoring so many touchdowns."

"It does feel good. Some of us seniors waited around a long time to enjoy all this."

Nobody enjoyed Saturday more, however than Knorr. The quarterback from Lenexa, Kan., who began the 1984 season as the wishbone operator, has accepted the backup role since a shoulder injury sidelined him and thrust Bart Weiss into the starting job last October.

Knorr had felt the frustration of not being able to contribute more as the Falcons built their unbeaten record. But, with the score 31-7 and 9:28 left in the game, came the call Knorr wanted to hear.

"They called me to go in with the No. 1 offense." Knorr said. "I couldn't wait to get out there."

In fact, Knorr was too good. He kept on the option for 4 yards, made a perfect option read and gave to fullback Pat Evans for a 19-yard pickup, then doubled up with the pitch and superlative block on Vellanti's touchdown. Three plays. 80 yards.

Then, when the Falcons got another possession with 6:35 left, the No. 2 offense received its chance - and Knorr got to stay. This time he guided an 11-play, 80-yard drive to the final touchdown, which he set up himself with a 39-yard keeper to the Army 6.

Two series, two touchdown drives and 62 yards rushing.

"Every senior wants to have an ending like that in his last home game." Knorr said. "Sure, I have to admit it's been tough not playing more this season. But today I had fun.

"All week, I just knew we would blow Army out. I don't know why. We wanted to make the last home game a good one, and we remembered the Army game last year.

Then, it hit home to us when the seniors realized it would be the last time to eat breakfast before a home game, the last time to stay at the Sheraton, the last time for everything.

"But today, the beautiful thing was that all the seniors got into the game and contributed. We're not finished yet, but this will be a nice memory."

For Knorr, and for the other seniors who shared in a fulfilling final moment at Falcon Stadium.

AFA NOTEPAD:

Air Force established single-season home attendance records, both for total and average crowds, thanks to Saturday's throng of 52,103, the Falcon's second largest ever for one game.

That gives Air Force a total of 245,396 for this season's six home games, topping the former mark of 224,204 set in 1972. The per-game average of 40,899 bettered the previous standard of 40,701, which also came in 1972.

****

AFA head coach Fisher DeBerry, already recognized as having his own unique vocabulary, came up with a new addition Saturday during his post-game press conference.

DeBerry was talking about the difficulty of facing two straight passing offenses, Utah and San Diego State, and then adjusting to Army's triple-option wishbone.

"We had to switch gears in midstream," DeBerry said. Right.

****

Air Force has one of only two defenses in the nation that have not allowed as many as 20 points in any single game. Michigan is the other team. On offense, the Falcons are one of only three teams in the nation that have scored at least 21 points in every game. The others are Miami, Fla., and Bowling Green.

****

For those who support AFA quarterback Bart Weiss's unofficial candidacy for the Heisman Trophy, his totals Saturday certainly were helpful. Weiss ran for 114 yards, giving him 954 yards rushing for the season. He scored two touchdowns, raising his season total to 68 points. And he passed for 105 yards and another score, giving him 1,208 yards passing and seven TD passes.

****

Among the former Air Force players in attendance Saturday was Marty Louthan, the original Wishbone Magician who quarterbacked the Falcons to records of 8-5 and 10-2 in 1982-83. Now stationed at Altus, Okla., but heading soon for McCord AFB near Seattle, Louthan clearly was impressed with this year's Falcons – starting with his wishbone successor, Weiss.

"I don't think there's ever been a wishbone quarterback that had Bart's instincts," Louthan said. "He's a really good athlete to begin with, but he's also got an incredible sense of where he is on the field and where his teammates are. I don't think you can coach that."

****

Perhaps the day's loudest roar came with three minutes to play, when it was announced that the Cadet Wing Commander, with permission of LtGen Winfield Scott, the AFA Superintendent, had called Monday a "down day", meaning no classes or commitments for any cadets.

But the football players won't enjoy the free time as much as the rest. "I'll catch up on homework," said Weiss. "I have to type a paper for a management class."

Final Statistics: AFA vs Army

Score	1	2	3	4	Final
Air Force	7	7	14	17	**45**
Army	0	0	0	7	**7**

Scoring Plays:

AFA – Pshsniak	1 run (Ruby kick), 1/:15
AFA – Carpenter	64-yrd pass from Weiss (Ruby kick) 2/11:34
AFA – Weiss	56 run (Ruby kick), 3/14:07
AFA – Weiss	1 run (Ruby kick), 3/4:29
AFA – Ruby	22-yrd FG, 4/12:28
Army – Jones	7 run (Stops kick), 4/9:28
AFA – Vellanti	57 run (Ruby kick), 4/8:05
AFA – Munafo	3 run (Ruby kick), 4/1:41

Team Statistics:

Category	AFA	Army
First Downs	24	10
Rush-Pass-Pen	65-10-2	46-11-3
Rushing Yards	396	168
Passing (C-A-I)	4-10-0	4-11-1

Passing Yards	105	18
Punt Avg.	51.3	35.5
Fumbles-Lost	2-0	2-1
Penalties-Yards	2-20	3-25

Individual Statistics (Leaders only):

Rushing (Att-Yds):	Weiss (AFA) 19-114
	Evans (AFA) 17-79
	Knorr (AFA) 3-62
	Jones (USMA) 7-39
	Crawford (USMA) 11-37
Passing (C-A-I-Yds):	Weiss (AFA) 4-9-0-105
	Healy (USMA) 4-7-0-18
Receiving (#-Yds):	Carpenter (AFA) 3-93
	Black (USMA) 1-10
Tackles:	Terry Maki (AFA) – 7
	Mike Chandler (AFA) – 8
	Dwan Wilson (AFA) – 5
	Chad Hennings (AFA) – 4

The 1985 Falcon football team with the Commander-in-Chief's Trophy.

1985 Falcon Seniors w/President Ronald Reagan and the Commander-in-Chief's Trophy.

AFA's John Ziegler congratulates the enemy after a great battle.

C1C Tomislav Zlatich, aka Tom Ruby, shakes hands with the 11th USAF Chief-of-Staff, General Charles A. Gabriel, after the Army game.

Derek Brown and Tom Ruby in the White House, Jan 1986

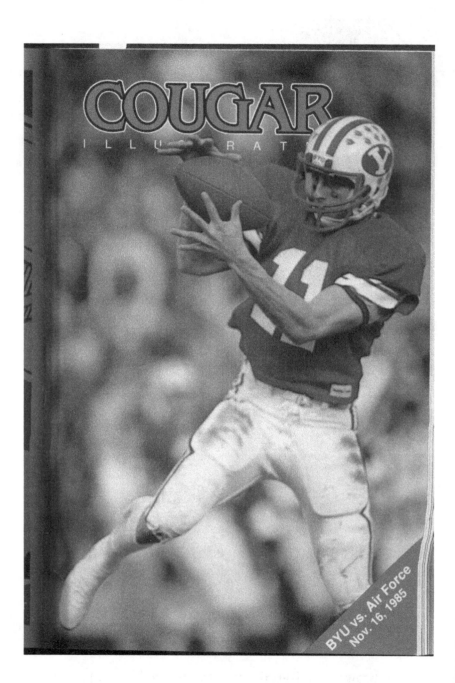

BYU vs. Air Force
Nov. 16, 1985

CHAPTER ELEVEN
THE COUGARS

"Press on – nothing can take the place of persistence. Talent will not; nothing is more common than unsuccessful men with talent. Genius will not; unrewarded genius is almost a proverb. Education will not; the world is full of educated derelicts. Perseverance and determination alone are omnipotent."

President Calvin Coolidge

Nov 16, 1985   AFA @ BYU   L 21-28

The second goal of the Air Force Academy Falcons in 1985 was to win the WAC championship. BYU had the same goal. The Falcons came out in the first half and looked like they were going to put the Cougars away. They led 21-7 at halftime.

Whatever Cougar Coach Edwards told his troops at halftime worked. They tied the score by the end of the third quarter and then took the lead in the fourth quarter with a 69-yard touchdown pass from Robbie Bosco to Vai Sikehema. Less than six minutes remained in the game.

Bart Weiss guided the Falcons 79 yards to the BYU four-yard line on a drive that left only four seconds on the clock. All hope for a perfect season, an undisputed WAC championship, and a shot at a national championship fell as Weiss' pass, intended for Ken Carpenter, was intercepted in the end zone. The Cougars held.

Five words that describe AFA's missed opportunity to compete for a national championship: "Robbie Bosco to Vai Sikehema"

Ralph Routon/The Colorado Springs Gazette:

They knew it wouldn't be easy. They knew Brigham Young's defense could slow down the wishbone. They even realized a late comeback might be necessary.

But, after BYU's 28-21 victory over Air Force Saturday afternoon, the Falcon offense had every reason to feel the brunt of pain.

Air Force made only 13 first downs, ran for only 136 yards, averaged just 2.8 yards per rush, gained just 237 total yards and scored only one offensive touchdown.

Obviously, all of those were season-worsts for the Falcon wishbone. Afterward, the AFA offense blamed both itself and Brigham Young's swarming, superb defense.

"They were good, but it was really just us," said Dave Sutton, the senior tackle. "We started too late. It was frustrating. We just made too many mistakes all day."

Kraig Evenson, the other tackle, agreed. "We showed at the end of the game that we could move the ball on 'em," Evenson said. "If everyone had been playing as a team all along, and we hadn't been having so many breakdowns, we could have done that more. That's all I've got to say."

While the linemen were having problems dealing with the Cougars' front wall, the backs had more trouble outside. Time after time, halfbacks were unable to make blocks on the crashing BYU secondary.

"They just have a tremendous defense," halfback Greg Pshsniak said. "Man, the athletes in their secondary - they hit us harder and quicker than anyone ever has before."

However, quarterback Bart Weiss said the Falcons' problems boiled down to one factor.

"Execution," said Weiss.

"Don't blame the play-calling.

The plays were called well all day. We just put ourselves in bad situations by not executing the plays."

Nobody felt the frustration more than the Air Force fullbacks. Pat Evans ran 18 times for 65 yards, and Johnny Smith 4 times for 7 yards. That wasn't good enough, especially on the first-down plays that mean so much to the AFA game plan's success.

In all, the Falcons ran on first down 21 times for only 44 yards.

On 10 occasions, Air Force faced second down with eight or more yards to go. In one stretch, the Falcons went more than 22 minutes without a first down.

"It was a tough game," Smith said. "They had every avenue covered. We still thought we could win it at the end. But we just ran out of time."

Everybody on the Falcon offense was determined, however, to prove this game was a fluke.

"They were just a good team," Evans said softly, his hands trembling as he tore tape off his legs. "We're gonna keep fighting. We're not through yet. We'll be back, I promise you."

Rebounding starts with the AFA seniors, who realize there is another chance to win the Western Athletic Conference and finish 11-1 for the regular season.

"We're disappointed," said senior center Randy Wilson. "But the world won't stop turning. We just have to pick up the pieces. Today. I guess BYU wanted it a little more than we did. They played a little harder, and we made the mistakes. I know I had a lot of breakdowns, and it hurts.

"But life goes on, and we'll be back."

They also made it clear the AFA trip this week to Hawaii would be no picnic for anyone inside the team.

"We took a vacation there last time." said Pshsniak, who was a freshman defensive back in 1982 when the Falcons wrapped up a bowl bid, then went to Honolulu and lost 45-21.

"This time, the only thing on our minds will be the game. That will be No. 1, and nothing else will matter. Even if we just went over there the day before the game, that would be OK.

"That game means a Jot to us, and we will be ready."

Mike Burrows/The Colorado Springs Gazette:

Chad Hennings ripped the protective padding from his arms and hands much like the Air Force defensive line tried to tear apart Brigham Young quarterback Robbie Bosco.

Saturday, the AFA locker room door inside Cougar Stadium was cluttered with the tools of battle. Fittingly, there were seven occasions during the AFA-BYU collision that the stadium floor was cluttered with Bosco.

Seven sacks.

And that's no typo.

Air Force mixed blitzes into its defensive game plan, and outside linebacker Ty Hankamer responded with two sacks.

But mainly, it was nose guards Steve Spewock and Dick Clark, and John Ziegler and Chad Hennings, the tackles, who were handed the unenviable task of crashing through one of the nation's most protective offensive lines.

There was no mistaking their target, either.

Getting to Bosco, that's what we knew we had to do," said Hennings, a 6-foot-5, 245-pound sophomore from Elberon,

Iowa. "We knew if our secondary was to have a chance, we had to get to Bosco."

Because of the sacks, BYU finished with a net of minus-35 yards on 21 carries. The seven sacks of Bosco cost the 16th ranked Cougars a total of 80 yards.

The score?

BYU 28, fourth-ranked Air Force 21.

"This is tough, real tough to accept," Hennings said. "There's no way you can say how bad we wanted to win this game. Bad, real bad. We went down together as a team.

"I don't think I've ever felt this bad. We could have won, and yet we've got to live with the loss.

"Bosco's good, real good. He's got a lot of poise. But when we got the pressure on him, I don't think he was that impressive."

Bosco rebounded from a horrifying start to throw for 343 yards and three touchdowns. He also threw four interceptions, giving him 22 this season in 11 games.

"I guess the pass rush was not enough," said Ziegler, a 6-3, 246-pound senior from Excelsior, Minn. "We kept after Bosco pretty well, but we had time to throw a few times, and he made the most of that time.

"It's never enough when you lose, and that's what is bad about this. I'd like to think we played pretty well defensively, but the score won't ever let us think that way.

"We wanted to keep BYU from the big play on us, and we gave up three touchdown passes. That shouldn't have happened.

"We worked hard on defense," he said, "and I do feel tired. But I feel guilty. I should feel more tired. The loss tells me our effort wasn't enough."

Bosco's bruises, though, told a different story.

Ralph Routon/The Colorado Springs Gazette:

Even before the drive began, everyone on the west sideline of this den called Cougar Stadium knew how it would end.

Brigham Young had just taken a 28-21 lead over Air Force, on Robbie Bosco's 69-yard touchdown pass to Val Sikahema, with 5:41 remaining. For the first time all day, BYU had taken the lead, and the Falcons' unbeaten record was in dire jeopardy.

But still there was the memory of 1982, when Air Force drove 99 yards with no timeouts in the final 90 seconds to knock off Brigham Young here, 39-38.

"I saw three years ago, all over again." said senior cornerback Dwan Wilson, the only AFA player left who started that day in '82. "It was the first game I ever started. You don't forget games like that.

I just knew we were gonna do it again: score, go for two points and win, 29-28."

Another miracle, the biggest yet in an unforgettable season.

That was the sideline atmosphere, but the offense on the field was even more intense when it began its last-chance series at the AFA 17.

"There was a lot of yelling," said fullback Pat Evans. "Everyone was saying, 'You gotta believe. You gotta believe.' And when we started moving, we knew we could do it."

Two passes from Bart Weiss to Hugh Brennan, and runs by Evans of 9 and 7 yards, moved the ball out to the Falcon 49 with 3:54 remaining. Later, on third and 6, junior halfback Marc Munafo caught a clutch pass for 9 yards and a first down at the 38.

"I wasn't really nervous as soon as the ball was snapped, said Munafo, who knew he might play more with halfback Kelly Pittman sick and unable to make the trip. "Coach Rucker (Ken, the halfbacks' assistant) always keeps us ready."

Now the Falcons were feeling more confident in the huddle – even though Weiss was playing with a painful hamstring pull.

"We knew he was hurting, said tackle Dave Sutton, "but we got past midfield on that drive before I saw that his (right) leg was wrapped. He was still battling, though, like the rest of us."

But much more suspense remained. From third and-13 at the BYU 41, Bart Weiss threw an interception – but a roughing-the-passer penalty against Cougar defensive tackle Jason Buck gave Air Force another chance.

That was the play that really ignited the Falcons, because history really was repeating itself now. Back in 1982, an identical roughing-the-passer call gave Air Force new life just before its winning touchdown with 6 seconds to play.

This time, a dead ball foul on the Falcons cost 15 yards after the play, but Air Force still had a new first down at the BYU 41. The Weiss fired a 23-yard pass to Tyrone Jeffcoat at the 18, and the crowd of 65,000-plus was sweating.

"Tyrone made a great fake on the defender to get open," Weiss said later. "After that, everyone really believed we would win."

Two plays later, with only 45 seconds to go, Weiss hit Jeffcoat with another pass to the BYU 2. But an official ruled it incomplete.

"I knew I caught the ball," Jeffcoat said, admitting that if films showed his feet were out of bounds, he would feel better. "The official said it was no catch, and that's part of football."

On fourth and 3 on the 19, Munafo took an option pitch from Weiss and sped to the 11. But when another option call only took Weiss to the 7, only 0:11 was remaining and the Falcons had no more timeouts.

Next, Weiss threw in the left flat to Munafo, who made a fine falling catch – then smartly dropped the ball. If he hadn't, the clock would have run out then.

"Dropping it was intentional," Munafo said. "I realized it wouldn't do any good to hang on to it. Actually, it was pretty close to a fumble, because I caught it – and then let it go."

Still, there were four seconds remaining. Time for one more play. Head coach Fisher DeBerry called a pass, which Weiss lofted toward the corner of the end zone. But it was off, and BYU's Rob Ledenko intercepted in the end zone at 0:00 – the Falcons only turnover of the day.

"We were really moving the ball," Weiss said, "and I thought we would get in and get the two-point conversion. We all thought that. We came here to win this game."

Instead, it became the miracle drive that wasn't.

Ralph Routon/The Colorado Springs Gazette:

Nobody threw chairs or kicked over benches or screamed profanity.

Nobody refused to talk. Nobody made a single excuse or pointed a single finger of blame, and nobody considered shutting off the media from the dressing room.

There were some wet eyes, and the pain of defeat swept through everyone.

But no bitterness. Just class.

Air Force had lost to Brigham Young, 28-21, and most of the wondrous dreams that had built through 10 victories lay in tatters.

Now there would be no national championship, no playing Nebraska in the Orange or Penn State in the Fiesta for No. 1 in America. Most likely, there would be no clear-cut Western Athletic Conference title.

Outside, as the crowd of 65,393 left Cougar Stadium, the cheers of ecstasy filtered through to add another syringe of frustration to the sadness.

Often, when even the best football teams encounter that most dreaded of nightmares, they retreat in anger. They grope for alibis and they are quick to blame others, starting with officials.

Occasionally, though, there comes a team that shows its truest colors at the height of despair.

Anybody with the slightest sympathy for Air Force could see exactly that here in the losing locker room.

No, that does not mean the Falcons were blasé. It doesn't mean they tried to play down the significance of the moment. It doesn't mean they are without emotion.

You want disappointment, talk to Ken Carpenter, the outstanding wide receiver. Carpenter could have been the hero Saturday. That last-second pass was meant for him in the end zone. It didn't make it.

"Four years, down the tubes. That's how it feels," Carpenter said, biting his lip. "I know It's not really, but that's how It feels right now."

Carpenter was among those who took the defeat hardest, but not a one lost control.

If anybody came close, it actually might have been head coach Fisher DeBerry upon hearing the world's worst-timed question of all time.

"Coach," asked a Salt Lake City TV announcer, "what does this loss do to your season?"

DeBerry's face turned fiery red.

"Whattaya mean, what does this do to our season," he answered in a high voice.

"We're 10-1 right now. That's all I know. And we're not through yet."

Later, the coach marveled at how well the Falcons accepted their fate.

"We don't throw helmets." he said. "You don't see us crying. These players are above that. They're solid people and they can accept a loss."

In fact, some of them were more eloquent in the darkest hour than during the high times. Not just the senior leaders, either.

"We've got a lot of character," said Tom Rotello, the junior cornerback. "I've said all year long that this is one classy football team. And you're seeing it in this locker room today. You won't hear anybody make any excuses.

"We gave 100 percent, and maybe even a little more. Really, that's all you can ask. I'm sure our coaches are proud of our effort. And I know the players are proud of our character.

Just a few lockers down, senior cornerback Dwan Wilson was just as candid and sincere.

"We've been blessed this year, we know that," Wilson said. "We've had a lot of good things happen to us. There comes a day when everything doesn't go your way. When that happens, you have to be a man about it and offer the other team your congratulations.

"I thought we played hard and competed hard, and I also think we showed a lot of class. We never gave up, and that's one thing I'll always remember about this football team. We just don't give up."

They won't give up now, either.

For certain, the offense will have to mend its pride before facing Hawaii next Saturday. Brigham Young's defense did as good a job at swallowing the wishbone as anybody has in a long time. On defense, the Falcons gave absolutely nothing to be ashamed of, including the fact that nobody on that side of the room uttered one word about the offense's inconsistency.

They will drop now in the rankings, probably to about 13th. Brigham Young might crack the Top Ten, as it should.

With a few more breaks, Air Force still could be dreaming today. But obviously, No.1 just wasn't meant to be.

But 1985 isn't over, and the Falcons still can claim some prizes that rate much higher than consolations.

They can win all or part of the WAC championship. They can finish 11-1 for Air Force's best regular season ever. They can try for their fourth straight bowl win, maybe wind up 12-1 and perhaps climb back into the Top Ten.

They lost with pride here Saturday, to Brigham Young, in a game that was a terrific showcase for a league with no respect.

But they aren't losers.

And they will be back.

AFA-BYU Notepad:

Air Force dropped out of the New Year's Day bowl picture with the possible exception of the Fiesta, and nobody was more disappointed than the scouts from the Orange and Sugar who had been planning to follow the Falcons to Hawaii this week.

"I had my bags all packed," said Jim Higgins of the Sugar, "and my wife had even bought some suntan lotion."

"We were looking forward to it," said Bill Ward of the Orange. "But regardless, I can tell you we really enjoyed coming this close with Air Force. They're a class act."

One of the happier people outside the AFA dressing room was Manny Garcia of the Florida Citrus Bowl in Orlando, which tops the list of postseason games that Air Force might take now.

"Nobody knows what will happen," said Garcia, who hinted the Citrus would like Air Force versus either Auburn or Ohio State. "But one thing you learn in the bowl business: If you wait around too long to make your choice, the good teams will be gone."

AFA athletic director Col John Clune and head coach Fisher DeBerry will meet this morning in Clune's office and wait for phone calls, which legally can start coming now. They planned to poll the Falcon seniors on the return flight from here, and Clune said an unofficial agreement could be made no later than Monday.

Air Force most likely will have its choice of the Citrus, Bluebonnet, Liberty, Freedom, Gator, Cherry and Sun bowls.

Brigham Young is hoping for a call from the Cotton but most likely will settle for the Fiesta.

After the game Saturday, though, none of the AFA seniors wanted to give their preference. "It's more important for us to bounce back and beat Hawaii," said safety Scott Thomas, echoing the general sentiment. "I guess that will be the Semi-Aloha Bowl for us. But we still have a chance to have a great season."

****

Air Force was the highest ranked team ever to visit Brigham Young. It also was only the second time when a WAC game matched two rated teams. The other occasion was In 1977, when 7-1 Arizona State at No. 13 scored a 24-13 victory over 7-1 BYU at No. 12.

But this game, despite its hoopla, did not decide the WAC championship for 1985. Air Force is now 6-1, Brigham Young 5-1 and Hawaii 4-1. Utah dropped to 5-2 with its loss at Colorado State, but still could muddle the race further next week at 'Brigham Young. BYU has to face both Utah and Hawaii, while the Rainbow Warriors must face Air Force, San Diego State and BYU - all at home.

Air Force still can clinch a co-championship with a win next Saturday night at Honolulu.

****

Would DeBerry have even hesitated on going for two points at the end, if the Falcons had scored to make it 28-27?

"No. That decision was made before the game," DeBerry said. "We wanted to win."

****

Air Force quarterback Bart Weiss ran for only 32 yards, giving him 986 rushing yards for the season and moving him closer to the unusual 1,000-1,000 double for yards rushing and passing in a single season.

****

How slowly did BYU start?

Well, the Cougars had no first downs and only 2 total yards after the first quarter. At that point, Robbie Bosco was 2 of 12 passing for 10 yards and 2 interceptions.

****

"The most forgettable memory from the BYU game was watching Via Sikahemma return a punt for a touchdown from the sideline and seeing two blatantly obvious blocks in the back out in plain sight for everyone to see. We would have played for and won the national championship, if not for those two blocks in the back, no doubt!!" (Tom Rotello, AFA cornerback.)

****

A peek at what was going on behind the scenes at the AFA:

As mentioned earlier, Lt. Colonel Dick Ellis (AFA Class of 1968) was not only the Falcon's "Special Teams" coach, he also served double-duty as the Associate Director of Athletics, working directly for the Athletic Director, Col. John Clune.

The following information is provided by Ellis as he adds unique perspective to what he calls:

A very real chance to play in the 1985 National Championship Game.

"Granted defeating Notre Dame on a last minute FG block, the overall 12-1 season record, co-champions of the WAC, a big win over Texas in the Bluebonnet Bowl and a final UPI ranking of #5 in the country are more than enough highlights to make that 1985 season very special in the history of Air Force Academy football. However, if we had completed the fourth down pass into the end zone on that last drive against BYU, the Falcons would have played in the national championship game that year against Penn State. So, her is what could have, and should have happened in 1985 that often goes un-reported.

"The week of the BYU game in 1985, Air Force Athletic Director Colonel John Clune was contacted about Air Force possibly being the opponent in the Fiesta Bowl against undefeated and #1 Penn State if we in fact beat BYU in Provo on November 16th. I was one of a very few included in these discussions because of my position in AH administration as well as being on the football staff. However, Colonel Clune, wanted to keep these discussions quiet in order not to put any additional pressure on the coaches or players in what was already a huge BYU game for the conference championship. Unfortunately, we lost to BYU in a game that could have had a different ending if the Falcons' final drive had not ended on an incomplete pass in the Cougars end zone as the clock expired. That loss curtailed the discussions of the Air Force vs Penn State Fiesta Bowl national championship game. Of course, with the loss there then was no reason to make public the possible national championship game negotiations. Any talk of what might have been would be like rubbing salt into the wound. Therefore, this is one of the 'lost' facts of the 1985 season that is rarely mentioned or understood when talking about that special team and the 1985 season.

"Now let me back up and try to put the 'whole story' into a historical format. The end of the year college bowl system was completely different in 1985 from what we have today. There was no BCS or playoffs. The Rose, Cotton, Sugar and Orange Bowls had conference tie-ins, but all bowls (except the Rose Bowl that had the Pac 10 & Big 10 champions) had to recruit/ attract teams to their bowl game. From mid to late November the bowls started lining up the teams, with obviously the Cotton (SWC Champ), Sugar (SEC Champ) and Orange (Big Eight Champ) carrying the most weight in attracting the top ranked teams to play their tie-in conference champions on New Year's Day. The Fiesta Bowl was a big bowl game, but had no conference tie-ins. This allowed the Fiesta Bowl the flexibility to set up a national championship game when the top team was not locked into a conference bowl tie-in. (The Fiesta Bowl later became one of the top four tier games after being selected as a BCS bowl).

"Going into the November 16th game against BYU, Air Force was undefeated, with a high profile win over Notre Dame on national TV, and, highly ranked nationally in all polls. Undefeated Penn State (which was then an independent) was the number 1 ranked team in the country, and could go to any of the bowl games but the Rose Bowl. Joe Paterno held all the cards on where his #1 Penn State would play their bowl game, and the team they would play. Very few people were aware that behind the scenes work started with the Air Force athletic administration in that week leading up to BYU game for a matchup of the Falcons with Penn State in what would have been the national championship game in Arizona.

"That week of the BYU game, the undefeated and highly ranked Falcons were favored over the Cougars team that had already lost two games. Air Force then had the season ending game with Hawaii the following week. The Rainbow Warriors had only won four games, so the long range projection was that the Falcons would have little trouble completing the undefeated season if they could get past BYU. Clearly the stage was set, beat BYU and the pieces would all come together to play for the national championship.

"There was another issue that had to be resolved to set up this national championship game. With a win over BYU, the Falcons would be WAC Champions and required to play in the Holiday Bowl. So, with other behind the scenes work with the WAC conference office, it was resolved that Air Force would be allowed to opt out of the Holiday Bowl in order to play for a national championship in the Fiesta Bowl against Penn State. The Holiday Bowl would then move to fill their bowl with other teams.

"Again, the man with all the cards was still Coach Paterno. He obviously wanted to play an undefeated, conference champion Air Force in the Fiesta Bowl, rather than having to face a 10-1

Oklahoma in the Orange Bowl. The power brokers and the national media would have supported the AFA vs PSU match up because these would have been the only two undefeated teams in the national polls at the end of the regular season.

"Unfortunately, BYU won 28-21 and Air Force's national championship game never happened. Surely as he had feared, Coach Paterno's undefeated team then had to go on to play that one loss Oklahoma team in the Orange Bowl. The Sooners went on to beat Penn State and were crowned the national champions. "With Penn State's loss, they dropped to #3 in the polls and there were no undefeated teams in the 1985 national rankings. Air Force finished at #5 in the UPI rankings with a 12-1 record, behind #1 Oklahoma (11-1), #2 Michigan (10-1-1), #3 Penn State (11-1), and #4 Tennessee (9-1-2).

"Another side light to the season was that with the negotiations to allow Air Force out of playing in their bowl, the Holiday Bowl then invited Arkansas and Arizona State to play in their 1985 game. BYU ended up being the other WAC co-champion and went on to play Ohio State in the Citrus Bowl. It is also extremely interesting that the very next year

in the 1986 season, what would have been an undefeated Air Force playing and undefeated Penn State in that January bowl game actually happened the next year when Penn State played Miami in the Fiesta Bowl for the national championship. Those kinds of negotiations we had in 1985 eventually led to the same kind of Fiesta Bowl matchup after the 1986 season between Miami and Penn State. (Again, that could have been AFA and PSU in 1985). This time, a year later, Penn State won the game and the 1986 national championship.

"With the new national football championship system now in place, it will be extremely difficult for Air Force to ever qualify for the big game. Regardless of what future AFA teams may accomplish, those 1985 Falcons will always be the first team to be oh so close to playing for the national championship."

Final Statistics: AFA @ Brigham Young University

Score	1	2	3	4	Final
Air Force	14	7	0	0	21
BYU	0	7	14	7	28

Scoring Plays:

AFA – Jones	22-yrd pass from Weiss (Ruby kick), 1/12:29
AFA – Rotello	25-yrd interception return (Ruby kick), 1/12:09
BYU – Bellini	22-yrd pass from Bosco (Webster kick), 2/12:49
AFA – Wilson	58-yrd interception return (Ruby kick), 2/8:36
BYU – Sikahema	72-yrd punt return (kick failed), 3/12:47
BYU – Bellini	25-yrd pass from Bosco (Lindley pass from Bosco), 3/4:42
BYU – Sikahema	69-yard pass from Bosco (Webster kick), 4/5:41

Team Statistics:

Category	AFA	BYU
First Downs	13	20
Rush-Pass-Pen	49-18-6	21-49-5
Rushing Yards	135	-35
Passing (C-A-I)	9-18-1	29-49-4
Passing Yards	101	343
Punt Avg.	44.0	49.0
Fumbles-Lost	3-0	1-0
Penalties-Yards	6-49	5-60

Individual Statistics (Leaders only):

Rushing (Att-Yds): Weiss (AFA) 18-32
Evans (AFA) 18-65
Tuipulotu (BYU) 3-15
Passing (C-A-I-Yds): Weiss (AFA) 9-18-1-10
Bosco (BYU) 29-49-4-343
Receiving (#-Yds): Carpenter (AFA) 2-23
Jones (AFA) 2-25
Bellini (BYU) 9-143
Sikahema (BYU) 4-87
Tackles: No Information

DT's John Ziegler and Chad Hennings
pressure BYU-QB Robbie Bosco.

Chapter Twelve

The Rainbows

"There may be people that have more talent than you, but there's no excuse for anyone to work harder than you do." --- Derek Jeter

Nov 23, 1985   AFA @ Hawaii W   27-20

Most teams have trouble staying focused when they play in Hawaii. Air Force was no different, **benching seven starters who didn't respect the curfew** imposed by Head Coach Fisher DeBerry. In fact, the Falcons had *never* won in Aloha stadium, and with the way the game started it looked as if they might have to wait until 1987. On the opening kickoff, Hawaii's Marcel Williams ran 80 yards, but was kept out of the end zone by Scott Thomas. On third-and-one from the Air Force six, Falcons nose guard Dick Clark came up with a huge play to stop the Bows. On fourth down, defensive tackle Chad Hennings applied the hit to squash the Rainbow's first scoring opportunity.

Ralph Routon/The Colorado Springs Gazette:

In the zany world of college football, looking either ahead or backward is unlawful. It's definitely a capital offense, punishable by defeat.

Dwell on the past, whether successful or not, and the result is either complacency or self-pity.

Dream toward the future, no matter how lofty the goal, and dealing with the present loses its necessary priority.

Throughout the major-college scene, teams and coaches try their best to concentrate on this week's game. Forgetting all else, and not considering the good or bad consequences.

Everyone else on the periphery, though, has and uses the freedom or observation and commentary.

Here tonight, as Air Force faces Hawaii in the Falcons' quest to rebound from defeat and wrap up a 11-1 regular season, those who are close to the AFA program have a surprisingly clear advance consensus.

Everyone feels this game will set AFA's course for at least the next year.

If the Falcons win, they will play well in the Bluebonnet Bowl and they will have every reason to project a fifth straight winning season in 1986 - even If nobody knows who the new quarterback will be.

If they lose, watch out.

One man inside the program made a flat prediction. If Air Force loses tonight, he said, this AFA team will finish 10-3 with a three game losing streak (Brigham Young, Hawaii and the bowl) and next year could be no better than 5-6.

"But if they win," the man added, "they will be able to put BYU behind them."

Trouble is, this AFA squad has no previous experience in rebounding from defeat. But if the recent past is any indication, Air Force won't have an easy time. In the two-year stretch of 1983 and 1984, the Falcons' six losses came in three batches of two in a row: Wyoming and BYU in '83, Wyoming and Utah in '84, BYU and Army in '85.

Can this team change that losing pattern? Yes, but only maybe.

For one thing, some of the players are banged up, and Air Force's annual senior syndrome (which wears down some of every year's senior class near the end of their playing days) is affecting a few Falcons.

Senior quarterback Bart Weiss, trying to nurse a pulled right hamstring muscle back to health, is the main worry. His coaches realized afterward Weiss was slowed enough in the second half at BYU to warrant putting in backup Brian Knorr.

This week, Weiss has been careful not to test that hamstring, which means he has avoided making his usual deceptive cuts during practice. "We told him to save it for Saturday night," said head coach Fisher De Berry, "because he will definitely need it then."

Unlike last week, tonight the coaches already are prepared to use Knorr If the need arises. "I think they see now," said one Air Force Insider. "that Knorr at 100 percent is better than Weiss at even 85 percent."

Too, Knorr is the better passer. His throwing has been good In practice here, and pass defense has been Hawaii's main weakness this season. Knorr also has spent at least as much lime as Weiss working with the No. 1 offense, so that would be an easy transition.

Kelly Pittman, still low on endurance after his tonsillitis but able to play for short periods at halfback, should be a boost to the offense. With him, the Falcon offense has enough variety to keep defenses guessing. Without him and with Weiss hobbled, as was the case last week, the wishbone is shaky.

So, if you see Weiss making his usual shifty moves on the option (or Knorr coming in and taking charge), and if Pittman is on the field enough to be a factor, Air Force will have a chance.

What about the AFA defense? If it can hold down Hawaii receiver Walter Murray, probably the best wide-out Air Force has played against all year, then the Rainbows will not score 20 points. They may even have trouble putting more than 10 on the board.

The actual outcome, as was the case last week at BYU, will depend on how well Air Force plays – not the opposition. If the Falcons show any lethargy or if their injuries become a factor again, they could lose.

But if they come back sharp, determined to share or win the WAC title, then they will beat Hawaii somehow. With a strong start, it could be easy. With a slow start, it could be tense, lower-scoring, but still a happy ending.

And then, finally, Air Force will be able to look to the future with optimism.

Mike Burrows/The Colorado Springs Gazette:

Defense wins championships, the football natives always say.

But that doesn't mean the offense can't play a part, too.

Saturday night at Aloha Stadium, the Air Force Academy wishbone decided late In the third quarter that, yes, it wanted a slice of at least a Western Athletic Conference co-championship.

Hawaii trailed, 17-13, but nobody at that point had mistaken momentum for being on the AFA side.

The Rainbow Warriors were surging, and the 13th-ranked Falcons needed a score.

Badly.

They got it on the first play of the fourth quarter, when Greg Pshsniak, a senior halfback, scored on a 5-yard option play to pad the Falcons' cushion to 24-13. Air Force went on to win, 27-20, and will take an 11-1 record into the Bluebonnet Bowl on Dec. 31.

Pshsniak's touchdown, only the second of his AFA career, put the wrappings on a six play, 55-yard drive that debuted with 2:05 left in the third quarter.

"You can't express this feeling, you just can't," Air Force's Joe Jose, a senior offensive guard from Phoenix, Ariz., said afterward. "On the last TD drive of ours, I guess we just sucked it up and said, 'Let's get after it, fellas.' We reached down for something extra.

"We had to do it. We were struggling a little bit at the time, and Hawaii was really coming on strong. We wanted to take some heat off our defense."

Perhaps for the first time all night, Hawaii started feeling the sultry heat of a 77-degree night that baked with 74 percent humidity.

"This is an entirely different feeling from seven days ago when we lost (28-21) at Brigham Young (knocking Air Force out of the Sugar Bowl)," said AFA Tight End Hugh Brennan. "Our defensive line took control when we needed it most, and we put the dang ball into the end zone.

"This is no easy place to play, as we found out. I'm telling you, Brigham Young is in for a test (on Dec. 7), when they come over here to play. Hawaii can beat them if they play like they did against us."

The 'Bows discovered, in a painful way, that Air Force has an aerial option, too, in its ground-gobbling wishbone.

And it was senior Ken Carpenter, the AFA wide receiver, who stepped forward to take a bow. He had six receptions for 115 yards – both game-high figures – in the first half alone and convincingly outplayed Walter Murray, Hawaii's all-WAC wideout and world-class sprinter.

Murray, a possible first-round pick in the next National Football League draft, finished with four catches for 74 yards, including a 33-yard touchdown strike from UH quarterback Gregg Tipton.

In the first quarter, which Air Force closed with a 10-0 lead, Carpenter had four receptions for 79 yards.

Included was a 39-yard strike from AFA quarterback Bart Weiss that helped set up Weiss' 4-yard touchdown run at the 3:22 mark of the first quarter.

"I had a wild first half, didn't I? But I didn't do a whole lot in the second half," a grinning Carpenter said. "Coming in, we wanted to throw the ball more, especially early in the game. That was a big part of the game plan.

When he packs his bags for Houston and the Bluebonnet Bowl, he'll be packing 42 receptions for 869 yards and three touchdowns.

That's figures to an average of 20.7 yards per reception.

Wow.

"Those are nice numbers," Carpenter said. "Still, the big number is 11 -1. We're 11-1, and that's got a nice ring to it. We're assured of a league championship.

This has been one incredible year for us."

That it has.

Mike Burrows/The Colorado Springs Gazette:**

Visiting football teams from the Mainland have come to know Aloha Stadium as a tropical graveyard.

Or something similar, anyway.

Hawaii never breaks from its practice routine during game week, and giggles as its foe usually dines too much, combs too many beaches and sees far too many sights, many of which are shapely curves dressed in grass skirts.

Then, at last, comes the game, and the preparation is all Hawaii's.

"We tend to sneak up on some pretty big names when they come over here," said Dick Tomey, the veteran UH head coach. "First, they think they'll roll over us just because we're Hawaii and because they must think we're not supposed to be very good.

"Then they have a good time while they're here, and I think their preparation slips a little. Many times, that's where we get our edge - In preparation."

Air Force can't afford to find itself digging in a palm tree lined graveyard tonight, starting with the 10:30 p.m. MST kickoff at Aloha Stadium.

Tonight's AFA goal can't become any more basic: If the 13th-ranked Falcons beat surging Hawaii, they assure themselves of at least a Western Athletic Conference co-championship.

"I just hope we play as well as we're capable," said Fisher DeBerry, the AFA head coach. "We're quite capable of being league champions. We've known all season long that we had the ability to win the league. Now is the time to go out and do it."

Just a week ago, Air Force faced the same task, and failed at Provo, Utah, in a 28- 21 setback to Brigham Young.

New week, new game, new foe.

Same horizon.

"There's no question that Air Force will be the best team we've played this season," Tomey said. They are certainly one of the top teams in the country.

"They've got quite a package. When I look at Air Force, I see a great offense, sound defense and solid kicking game. That's a tough combination to beat."

If the Falcons hold any definite pregame edge, it lies among the special-teams performers thrown together by both schools.

Pure and simple, Air Force's kicking game is better than Hawaii's. Actually, in terms of statistics, there's no contest.

Consider:

>> In junior Mark Simon, Air Force boasts the nation's No.1-ranked punter. Simon has a 47.2-yard average on 4.2 punts per game.

Hawaii will counter with junior Ben Maafala, a Honolulu native with a wobbly 36.7-yard average on five punts per game.

>> The Rainbow Warriors have returned 21 punts this year, for a hard-to-believe-it's-really-this-low average of just 4.9-yards per return.
>> Air Force, led by Thomas' sparkling 30.2, is averaging 26.6 yards per kickoff return. Again, Hawaii lags considerably behind with an 18.1-yard average.

What does it all mean?

"Not a dadgum thing if you don't execute the game plan, and block and tackle as hard as you can on every play," DeBerry said. "I'm not sure any team has any edge coming into this game. Hawaii has won their last three games, so you know they're rolling now and playing very well.

"If we want to be considered league champions, we've got to give a championship-caliber effort in this game. We won't be able to afford anything less."

Tomey seemed anxious to see if his 'Bows are up to the challenge of derailing one of the nation's most explosive teams. "I'm not saying Air Force can't be beat," he said. "It's just that we'll have to shut down so many things to realize a victory over them. This Air Force team is legit, in every aspect of the game.

"If we shut down their offense and our defense doesn't play well, we're still in trouble. It works the same way if our defense does the job on their wishbone and our offense struggles.

"I've talked to the players, and I've told them it will take nothing less than our best football of the year' to beat a very talented team. But I think we've got the type of player that lives for a situation like this.

Air Force has laid everything on the table for us. They're not hiding anything. They're coming in here with a lot of firepower."

And fresh from a mini-vacation. Just like so many other victims of Hawaiian hospitality.

TAIL FEATHERS: AFA quarterback Bart Weiss is down to his final opportunity to become only the third player (and second at his position) in major-college history to rush and pass for more than 1,000 yards in the same season.

Since he owns an AFA-high 986 rushing yards Weiss, needs only 14 yards against the 'Bows' to accomplish the feat. He's already passed for 1,309. Yards gained in bowl games are not recognized by the NCAA in official season totals.

Hawaii's offensive line has allowed 26 quarterback sacks in nine games, an alarming total that should excite the AFA defensive line of tackles Chad Hennings and John Ziegler and nose guards Steve Spewock and Dick Clark.

Tomey has said healing UH quarterback Gregg Tipton (bruised shoulder) will play tonight. If so, Air Force should hope Tipton doesn't have a repeat of his UH debut.

Way, way back, on Aug. 31, the transfer junior completed 21 of 38 passes for three touchdowns and a school-record 337 yards in Hawaii's 33-27 loss to Kansas at Aloha Stadium.

"That was the best first-game performance by a college quarterback I'd ever seen," Tomey said. "Greg showed us that night that he had the ability to be a factor at this level."

Because tonight's game will be the first sellout of the season for the 'Bows, plans have been made to televise the action live throughout the Hawaiian Islands.

Mike Burrows/The Colorado Springs Gazette:

Fisher DeBerry won't ever be mistaken for a basketball center, but there the little guy was, standing taller than a 7-footer while beaming from a makeshift pedestal late Saturday night.

The perspiration flowing inside that hot, steamy Air Force Academy football locker room could have filled Pearl Harbor, which flanks Aloha Stadium directly to the southwest.

Air Force had a Bluebonnet Bowl bid tucked safely in its hip pocket, and the 13th-ranked Falcons' record had just zoomed to 11-1 with the 27-20 conquest of Hawaii.

To boot, they had captured at the very least a share of their first-ever Western Athletic Conference championship.

Most certainly, it was time for a speech.

No one stood taller. Yet DeBerry, the Falcon's second-year head coach, chose to keep it short.

His players, who withstood 11 consecutive weeks of constant battering, with one black eye the only real damage, listened intently.

"I told you guys before the start of the season that I wanted us to be known as the best football team in the 30-year history of the academy," DeBerry said, shouting. "You've become just that. I believe you're the best Air Force has ever had. May God bless every last one of you."

Later he would say, in the same high-pitched tone, "Go out, hit the beach and have some fun. But remember who you are, and remember who you're representing.

"Anybody who doesn't show some manners and maturity, I'm telling you, will look pretty dadgum foolish swimming out to that ol' airplane when it's time to leave."

The Falcons roared with laughter. This had become their paradise, and they basked in the warmth of its glow.

Time after time, Air Force either answered the Rainbow' Warrior's escalating tide with points or repelled it with an opportunistic defense that manufactured five UH turnovers, including crucial fourth-quarter interceptions by San Antoinio-spawned AFA safeties A.J. Scott and Scoot Thomas.

Scott, in fact, had two of them in a span of just 57 seconds.

Those two were thrown by Warren Jones, Hawaii's second-year freshman quarterback.

Thomas' interception, at Hawaii's 44-yard line with 1:23 left, was thrown by one stunned Gregg Tipton, the UH junior who needed six stitches at halftime to close a facial wound.

Actually, Thomas' swipe could have been a fourth-down, 14-yard catch for all-WAC wideout Walter Murray and a badly needed first down for the 'Bows.

But AFA linebacker Terry Maki knocked the ball loose from Murray and Thomas was there for the 'Bow-beating pick.

Thomas finished with an AFA-high 10 tackles and returned three punts for 56 yards.

"We had a lot of chances, and in football the team with the least turnovers usually wins," said Dick Tomey, the classy UH head coach whose 'Bows had a three-game win streak snapped while falling to 4-5-1 overall and 4-2 in the WAC. "We had a lot or scoring opportunities that we wasted."

Hawaii self-destructed in spite of its defense, which did an admirable job of slowing the AFA wishbone.

Air Force did finish with 338 total yards, converted eight of 17 third-down plays and never lost a fumble. But the Falcons averaged just 3.6 yards per rush and were allowed only 108 total yards in the second half.

Holes must be fashionable on Oahu. There's a famous crater nearby that's called Diamond Head, and another even closer called Punchbowl.

This one at Aloha Stadium became known as Falcon Crest, and the 'Bows never fully climbed out of it.

After two AFA possessions, the Falcons had a 10-0 lead. It was 17-10 at the half, and the Falcons led, 27-13, with 7:28 remaining after senior Tom Ruby kicked a 24-yard field goal, his second three-pointer of the night.

The 'Bows hardly were finished, but how could they?

Their fans in a frenzied crowd of 44,125 had spent nearly three hours frantically waving 2-foot-long 'ti' leaves, a Hawaiian tradition that is meant to bring good luck to all island natives in sight.

Perhaps enticed by the "ti", Tipton immediately marched the 'Bows to a 27-20 deficit with 4:34 left, completing a seven-play, 70-yard drive with an arching 33-yard touchdown strike to Murray, who had slipped behind Air Force's Mike Toliver, a second-team junior cornerback forced into action by the absence of Tom Rotello.

Rotello, the WAC's leading interceptor with eight, strained a shoulder muscle and bruised a toe in the second quarter and was forced to watch the final 30 minutes from the sideline.

Air Force also played much of the second half without senior Pat Malackowski, an outside linebacker who suffered a bruised elbow.

These Falcons were perilously close to having their wings clipped for the second consecutive week.

That's when Thomas and Scott went to work.

"Every turnover we got was a big one, DeBerry said. "The two A.J. got certainly were biggies, and then the last one by

Thomas kinda wrapped this one up for us. Our defense has been doing that all year."

Ralph Routon/The Colorado Springs Gazette:

Everybody else had left the spacious Aloha Stadium dressing quarters, heading for the buses, the hotel and the beach.

Their voices were jubilant, even though their bodies ached from 11 straight weeks of battle. They talked about moving up in the polls, and they discussed their preference for a bowl opponent.

Behind them all, one person remained in that dressing room. Still wearing his game attire, white shirt and blue slacks, he walked around to the empty lockers, as if he were looking for someone else to hug and congratulate.

Fisher DeBerry didn't want this night to end. He wanted it to last forever. But only with himself recognized as a proud bystander, away from the spotlight. He never would think of himself as the inspirational guiding force, which he was from August through November.

As Head football coach at Air Force, DeBerry had tackled a huge challenge 23 months earlier. On that wintery afternoon of Dec. 27, 1983, DeBerry took over an Air Force program that had just achieved everything many felt it could ever expect: a 10-2 season, a win at Notre Dame, two straight bowl victories and an appearance in the Top Twenty rankings.

Back then, everyone associated with Air Force football would have been satisfied merely to see the winning habit maintained. With all of Air Force's built-in disadvantages, just to be always around 7-4 or 8-3 with a chance for a bowl certainly would be sufficient.

But now, as DeBerry stood alone in that locker room, the Falcons were celebrating a season in which they had attained every realistic dream their coaches placed before them.

They had finished with an 11-1 record, two wins more than Air Force ever had achieved in a regular season. They would go to the Bluebonnet Bowl ranked in the Top Ten, they could claim at least a share of the Western Athletic Conference title, and they came within a hair of challenging for the national title in a New Year's Day bowl game.

They had wrapped up that memorable package here late Saturday night with a dramatic, draining 27-20 victory over inspired Hawaii. It wasn't a peak performance by any means, but it was a classic example of the Falcon's unity and intestinal fortitude.

Afterward, the players talked at great length about the intangibles that had worked in their favor. The younger Falcons began trying to eulogize the departing seniors, who in turn made some initial attempts at describing their final feelings.

But the pleasures of Hawaii beckoned, and with the bowl game another month away, nobody wanted to dwell on that.

DeBerry did, though. Now, his eyes welled up, as he approached the same subjects.

"No way. No way. There is no way we had any business lining up against Hawaii and moving the ball or stopping them like that," the coach said. "I can't put it into words . . . the spirit and character of this team.

"These guys are tired, beat up and worn out. But they haven't complained or looked for excuses. They haven't had open dates through the schedule our other good teams. They've had to play 11 straight weeks. And their attitude . . . they just wouldn't be denied. I'm so proud of them."

If they had been able somehow to win at Brigham Young, the Falcons today would be No. 2 in the country with a 12-0 record. They likely would be heading for the Sugar Bowl, hoping for Penn State to lose in the Orange and then taking a shot at No. 1.

That was just one dream too many.

But, now that the Falcons have rebounder from that loss, it doesn't matter. They still could rise back into the Top Five after the bowls, if they can defeat either Texas or Texas A&M in the Bluebonnet Bowl.

Air Force needs a rest now. Hawaii left the Falcons far more battered than they have been all season. But the postgame mood Saturday was not one looking to the bowl game as a party.

"We have a chance to send off these seniors with four winning seasons, a WAC Championship and four bowl wins." DeBerry said. "After all these guys have achieved, they deserve to go out winning.

"This team . . . it's not any one person. The coaching staff, they did all the work. The players, the seniors, they have been an unbelievable group. I'll never forget this bunch of wonderful people."

And they won't forget Fisher DeBerry, the man who inherited success and inspired it into greatness.

Mike Burrows/The Colorado Springs Gazette:

Air Force quarterback Bart Weiss had just completed first-possession passes of 12 and 14 yards to wide receiver Ken Carpenter Saturday night in Aloha Stadium.

Weiss still needed 14 rushing yards to become only the third player in major-college history to pass for 1,000 yards and run for 1,000 in the same season.

He eclipsed the barrier on his first carry of the night, a pure-wishbone keeper at the 11:56 mark of the first quarter that netted, you guessed it, 14 yards for the 6-foot, 172-pound senior from Naples, Fla.

At that moment, it was easy to imagine seeing Johnny Bright of Drake (1950) and Reggie Collier of Southern Mississippi (1981) out there somewhere, printing a membership card for a new entry.

Tile elite club of Bright and Collier now must make room for Weiss

"This hasn't hit me just yet," said Weiss, who directed the 13th-ranked Falcons to a 27-20 victory over Hawaii in their final pre-Bluebonnet Bowl game. "It's going to take a while for something of this magnitude to sink in."

Against the 'Bows, Weiss completed nine of 15 passes for 140 yards and rushed 12 times for a net gain of 46 yards.

That gave Weiss final-season totals of 1,032 rushing yards and 1,449 passing yards. The NCAA does not recognize bowl-game figures in its official statistics.

Bright's run-pus yardage totals were 1,232-1,168. Collier's figures were 1,005-1.004.

AFA notepad

The week before, Brigham Young held Weiss to 32 rushing yards on 18 carries in a 28-21 loss for the Falcons.

"I was thinking too much about that 1,000-yard stuff against BYU, and I think it showed," Weiss said. "It was hard not to think about something like that, but I should not have let it consume me.

"I thought about it some out there against Hawaii, but I thought I was more in control of myself. It's nice to know I've done it. Now I don't have to worry about it anymore."

"In my opinion," Carpenter said, "there's not a better wishbone quarterback in the country than Bart Weiss."

****

In Air Force, Hawaii was playing its seventh nationally ranked team since 1976, when the 'Bows escalated their football program to the major-college level.

Hawaii's record in those seven games, 0-7.

****

Air Force got a glimpse of William Bell, Hawaii's third-year sophomore tailback from Widefield, Colorado for the first time Saturday night, and the speedy Bell left a first-quarter burn mark on the AFA defense.

In the opening 15 minutes, Bell rushed for 43 yards on seven carries, caught one pass for 14 yards and completed a pass for a 6-yard gain.

He finished with 11 carries for 50 yards and four catches for 41 yards.

"That young man is going to become a great player for Hawaii. There's no doubt about that." AFA head coach Fisher DeBerry said.

"We sure could use some of that speed he's got."

Mike Burrows/The Colorado Springs Gazette:

The Bluebonnet Bowl won't be the end of the football road for Air Force Academy seniors Scott Thomas, Dwan Wilson and John Ziegler.

The three AFA defenders have accepted invitations to participate in two post season all-star games after the 13th-ranked Falcons close their season Dec.31 at Rice Stadium in Houston.

Wilson, a cornerback from Wynne, Ark., will play for the West squad Jan. 12 in the Japan Bowl at Yokohama Stadium in suburban Tokyo.

Thomas. A free-safety from San Antonio, Texas, and Ziegler, a tackle from Excelsior, Minn., will be teammates for the West in the Jan. 11 Hula Bowl, which is played here at Aloha Stadium.

Wilson said he can't wait to get to Tokyo.

"I was very surprised to be selected," he said. "I thought if anybody went to the Japan Bowl, it'd be Thomas. But he's going to the Hula Bowl, so I guessed that opened up something for me.

"This really is a big thrill. I've never been to Japan. I'm sure it will be a great trip, and a fun game. I'll be a long, long way away from my hometown, for sure."

Entering the AFA-Hawaii game Saturday night, Wilson had six interceptions and 46 tackles. His 15 career interceptions ranked No. 1 on the AFA ladder.

Prior to playing Hawaii, Thomas had five interceptions and 79 tackles. He also ranked among the national leaders in punt returns with a 10.1-yard average on 25 returns.

This year, he became only the fourth major-college player in history to return an interception, kickoff and punt for touchdowns in the same season.

Ziegler, a three-year starter, has developed into one of the nation's most feared pass rushers.

Entering the Hawaii game, he had 42 stops and a team-high 10 sacks. Almost half (18) of his tackles caused yardage losses for AFA opponents.

"It's nice to be selected for something like this," Thomas said. "It's a chance for me to play with the guys who are considered the best players in the country. So, it's a chance to see how well you stack up with them.

"I guess what's really nice is that I get to come back to Hawaii, free of charge."

"These selections," Wilson said, "are a credit to our teammates at Air Force. We'll be representing them as much as we'll be representing ourselves."

Thomas and Ziegler will bring to 14 the number of Falcons who have played in the Hula Bowl. In 1964, quarterback Terry Isaacson and Center John Rodwell were the first.

A year ago, defensive tackle Chris Funk and halfback Mike Brown played in the Hula Bowl.

Wilson will be the sixth Falcon to play in the Japan Bowl. Funk played in the game a year ago. Steve Hoog, a flanker, was the first in 1979.

Final Statistics: AFA @ Hawaii

Score	1	2	3	4	Final
Air Force	10	7	0	10	27
Hawaii	0	10	3	7	20

Scoring Plays:

AFA – Ruby	21-yrd FG, 1/7:12
AFA – Weiss	4 run (Ruby kick), 1/3:22
UH – Fasola	1 run (Brady kick), 2/12:48
AFA – Evans	10 run (Ruby kick), 2/9:20
UH – Brady	37-yrd FG, 2/6:19
UH – Brady	48-yrd FG, 3/11:06
AFA – Pshsniak	5 run (Ruby kick), 4/14:55
AFA – Ruby	24-yrd FG, 4/7:28
UH – Murray	33-yrd pass from Tipton (Brady kick), 4/4:34

Team Statistics:

Category	AFA	UH
First Downs	18	16
Rush-Pass-Pen	55-17-6	35-30-5
Rushing Yards	198	123
Passing (C-A-I)	10-17-2	18-30-3
Passing Yards	140	199
Punt Avg.	48.1	48.3
Fumbles-Lost	1-0	2-2
Penalties-Yards	6-47	5-45

Individual Statistics (Leaders only):

Rushing (Att-Yds):	Weiss (AFA) 12-46
	Smith (AFA) 9-45
	Evans (AFA) 12-44
	Fasola (UH) 14-83
Passing (C-A-I-Yds):	Weiss (AFA) 9-18-1-140
	Tipton (UH) 11-17-1-118
Receiving (#-Yds):	Carpenter (AFA) 6-115
	Murray (UH) 4-74
	Dyer (UH) 2-26
Tackles:	No Information

CB Dwan Wilson returns an intercept versus Hawaii!

Chapter Thirteen

The Longhorns

*"You will never do anything in this world without courage. It is the greatest quality in the mind **next to honor**." --- Aristotle*

**Dec 31, 1985   AFA @ Bluebonnet Bowl   W 24-16
(NTV) vs. University of Texas**

<u>*Mike Burrows/The Colorado Springs Gazette:*</u>

Mark Simon repeatedly gave Texas swift kicks in the britches.

Pat Evans rumbled like he wanted to play the party role of ***Bevo***, the Longhorn's bigger-than-life mascot steer.

And on New Year's Eve 1985, football purists everywhere lifted their crystal glasses to toast the heroics of a magnificent defensive display.

Air Force rode off into the Texas sunset that December 31st with a 24-16 beating of the Longhorns in the 27th Bluebonnet

Bowl, and the victory will long be remembered as one of the most cherished in Academy history.

"Aren't you proud," AFA Head Coach Fisher DeBerry asked, "that these young people will soon be defending our nation?"

More Deberry: "Our men give up so much in size. But when it comes to heart, they didn't give up a thing!"

Especially to the over-sized Longhorns.

At the finish, Texas paid with its fourth consecutive bowl-game setback.

In spite of Texas thoroughly derailing the AFA wishbone's outside attack and passing game, *the Falcons won.*

In spite of having to punt a Bluebonnet-record 11 times, *the Falcons won.*

And in spite of Ken Carpenter's absence, *the Falcons won.*

Carpenter, Air Force's standout senior-wide receiver, left the game late in the second quarter and never returned after aggravating a foot injury. With him went the AFA passing game.

Punter Mark Simon averaged a Bluebonnet-record 49.2 yards on the Falcon's 11 punts and single-handedly saved Air Force in a nightmarish second quarter.

Evans, Air Force's junior fullback, scored the Falcon's third touchdown of the game and rushed 18 times for a season-high 129 yards.

They were enough to hold off a Texas team that finished 8-4.

The Longhorns lost despite leading comfortably in first downs (14-9) and total yards (302-194).

Air Force closed a memorable 1985 with a school-record 12th win in 13 games. The Falcons' bowl triumph also was their fourth straight in as many years.

Too, Air Force finished as the only team in the country to win 12 games. And the Falcons later wound up ranked No. 5 nationally in the United Press International poll and No. 8 nationally in the Associated Press poll.

"We did not play well enough to win," said a visibly disappointed Texas Head Coach Fred Akers, whose bowl record with the Longhorns fell to 2-7. "We had the effort, but we did not play as smart as we could have. We gave them too much yardage up the middle with Evans."

"I told our team that we have nothing to be ashamed of. This was the year that a lot of people thought they could get a piece of us, and only a few did. We don't have to apologize for the effort or the season."

These days, no one is asking the Falcons to apologize. For anything.

"I believe our true character came out in this game,: said DeBerry, who pushed his two-year career record to 20-5. "I'll say it again. This was one special group of Air Force players and one special group of Air Force seniors. Mark Simon continually bailed us out of trouble, and we kept plugging and plugging away. We believe in ourselves, perhaps more than any other team in the country believes in itself. This bunch will fight and scrap with you, and they're going to find a *dadgum* way to beat you. Today was no different."

Indeed.

A sun-splashed crowd of 42,000 at Rice Stadium in Houston, Texas watched Air Force fall behind 0-7, after Texas' first offensive possession and regroup enough to take a 21-10 lead into the fourth quarter.

It was UT quarterback Bret Stafford who hit 6-foot-5, 240-pound tight-end William Harris on a 34-yard touchdown strike only 3:46 into the game to give the Longhorns their early lead.

But it was halfback Greg Pshsniak and quarterback Bart Weiss, two AFA seniors, who answered with 1-yard touchdown runs that gave the Falcons their 14-7 halftime lead.

Jeff Ward kicked three short-range second-half field goals for the Longhorns, the last coming with 7:34 remaining in the fourth quarter. But they weren't enough.

However, the three touchdowns Texas missed scoring, leading to Ward's appearances, would have been enough.

As it was, Evans broke loose on a 19-yard touchdown sprint late in the third quarter after AFA cornerback Tom Rotello intercepted Stafford.

Air Force senior Tom Ruby hammered home a 40-yard field goal just 43 seconds from the finish to seal the Longhorn's fate.

"We got behind early," DeBerry said, "but the thing about it was, Texas executed that TD play of theirs really well. So we couldn't feel all that bad about it.

They just executed better than we did at that time. We knew there was a lot of time, and we knew a lot of things could happen. Fortunately for us, they did."

All the first-half points were scored in the first quarter, and Texas completely stuffed the Falcons in the second.

After Air Force's opening three possessions of the second quarter, they had minus-8 yards total offense for the quarter. Texas' defensive might was such that the Falcons finished the 15-minute period with just one first down, 26 total yards and three fumbles, none of which they lost.

Simon was forced to punt four times in the second quarter, and three of them traveled 57, 53, and 56 yards.

"Just an incredible punting exhibition by that young man," DeBerry said. "We would have been in big trouble without him around to bail us out.

I believe we had a lot of MVPs out there, but Mark Simon is as much an MVP as anybody we've got."

Remember, during the season he won the NCAA punting title with a 47.3-yard average!

Against Texas, in order, his punts carried 40, 42, 57, 53, 42, 56, 33, 57, 62, 52, and 47 yards. He wasn't wearing cowboy boots, but the Longhorns still feel the point of his kicks.

"I even got a few good rolls," Simon said afterward. "I guess it was my day. It feels great to beat a team like Texas.

I wasn't tired, really. Whatever the offense needs, I have to deliver. If I have to kick 11 times, then it's my job to do the job 11 times. Sure I felt some pressure. This was a big game for us. You don't always get the chance to play somebody with the great tradition of Texas."

Officially, Evans was voted the Falcon's Most Valuable Player. James McKinney, a 6-4, 242-pound defensive end, was the Texas honoree.

"It was easy for me," Evans said. "My sisters probably could have run through some of the holes our center (Rusty Wilson) and tackles (Kraig Evenson and Dave Sutton) kept opening for me."

Evan's longest run was a 48-yard dash that set up Pshsniak's first-quarter touchdown.

"Pat gave us great effort and determination at a time when we needed it the most." DeBerry said.

Most important, Air Force enjoyed a turnover-free game, though Scott Thomas did fumble two Texas punts. Stafford was intercepted twice and completed just nine of 18 passes for 88 yards.

AFA linebackers Terry Maki and Mike Chandler combined for 27 tackles.

Texas was trailing, 21-16, when the Longhorns had two crucial possessions late in the fourth quarter.

One ended in a John Teltschik punt from the Texas 22-yard line, thee other when AFA cornerback Dwan Wilson intercepted Stafford. Ruby then extended the AFA lead.

"Texas was as physical a team as we've played all year," DeBerry said. "Their defense was outstanding. Texas came after Bart and really did a job on him."

"But we held together, and that's what I'm most proud of. I don't know if it's possible for it to get any better than this."

Only at 13-0.

But when they walked out of Rice Stadium, no one heard the Falcons complaining.

For Texas, however, New Year's Eve became New Year's grieve.

Final Statistics: AFA vs Texas (Bluebonnet Bowl)

Score	1	2	3	4	Final
Air Force	14	0	7	3	**24**
Texas	7	0	3	6	**16**

Scoring Plays:

UT – Harris	34 pass from Stafford (Ward kick), 1/11:14
AFA – Pshsniak	1 run (Ruby kick), 1/3:37
AFA – Weiss	1 run (Ruby kick), 1/1:38
UT – Ward	24 FG, 3/6:19
AFA – Evans	19 run (Ruby kick), 3/3:35
UT – Ward	31 FG, 4/14:14
UT – Ward	28 FG, 4/7:34
AFA – Ruby	40 FG, 4/:43

Team Statistics:

Category	AFA	UT
First Downs	17	14
Rush-Pass-Pen	9-8-0	10-4-0
Rushing Yards	189	214
Passing (C-A-I)	1-5-0	9-18-2
Passing Yards	5	88
Punts (#-Avg.)	11-49.2	6-44.5
Fumbles-Lost	1-0	0-0
Penalties-Yards	6-45	8-67

Individual Statistics (Leaders only):

Rushing (Att-Yds): Stafford (UT) 6-63
Evans (AFA) 18-129
Passing (C-A-I-Yds): Stafford (UT) 9-18-2-88
Weiss (AFA) 1-5-0-5
Receiving (#-Yds): Harris (UT) 3-65
Pittman (AFA) 1-5

Attendance: 42,000

Weather: Partly cloudy, 70 Degrees, Wind N 10-20 mph

All-WAC, All-America Punter,
Mark Simon launches another beauty!

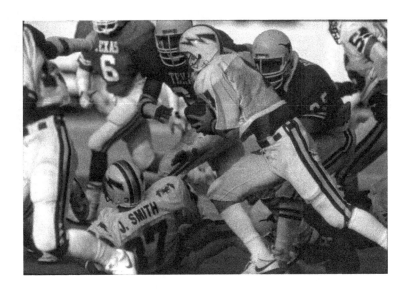

QB Bart Weiss running the option against the powerful Longhorns.

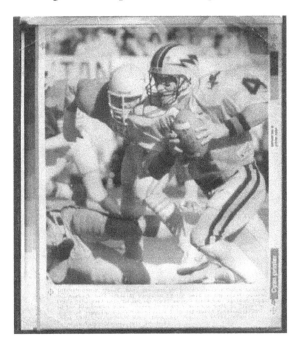

From the archives, QB Bart Weiss moving the chains!

QB Bart Weiss comes to the end of the road!

Air Force Falcons, 1985 Bluebonnet Bowl Champions!

PART THREE

Leaders of Character

BENJI 53

On February 17th, 1991, **Captain Scott "Spike" Thomas**, flying with the 19th FS and 363rd TFW temporarily based at King Khalid Military City, was flying a night interdiction mission in his F-16C with the codename of "Benji 53". As the package was coming off of station (egress), his F-16 experienced engine problems. Early reports suggested he had been hit by a Surface to Air Missile (SAM), but it cannot be confirmed. Thomas's wingman, 1LT Eric "Neck" Dodson, came to his aid and helped him nurse his plane closer to the Iraq-Saudi Arabia-Kuwait border, nearly 40-60 miles south of their position. Dodson assumed control of most radio communications between AWACs (Bulldog), leaving Thomas free to fly his injured plane.

With less than 50 miles to go to the border, and his plane leaking what appeared to be fuel, Thomas and his wingman realize his F-16 is beginning to develop a catastrophic engine fire. With a valiant effort to get as close as he could, Thomas finally decides to eject over enemy territory. His radio contact is spotty once he is on the ground, but Search and Rescue helicopters (a package of 2 UH-60 Blackhawks and 1 MH-53J

Pave Low, along with F-15E's providing Close Air Support), located his position roughly 2 hours later. The F-15E's were called in to engage an approaching Iraqi truck with cluster bombs during the extraction.

During debrief, it was realized that an SA-7 Surface to Air Missile (SAM) had been shot at the rescue helicopter in which Thomas was riding, but the missile was out of range and landed short. It was also learned that Thomas had less than 1 hour of freedom, as there were Iraqi troops within 2 miles of him in 2 different directions.

Crew/Description

Benji 53 (F-16C Block 25C, Serial 84-1218)

- Pilot: Captain Scott "Spike" Thomas (**BEN53**)

Benji 31 (F-16C, ?)- Wingman

- Pilot: 1LT Eric "Neck" Dodson (BEN31)

Bulldog (XX)?

- AWACs E-3 Sentry (BULL)

Actual Transmissions

UKN1-	"Benji 31, Victor."
BEN31-	"Go ahead."
UKN1-	"Roger ah, you headin' for Hafr Albatin?" (Emergency divert airfield, Hafr Albatin (OEPA)
BEN54-	"Ah, negative. Right now we are going straight towards the border, the closest route. You've got the--I've got the nearest divert for you, Hafr Albatin for one-thirty-four, is that what you've got?"
BEN53-	"Yeah I got it, I'm not gonna make it."
BEN31-	"Why not?"
BEN53-	"I won't make it there, I'm ah looking to do a crossing and get out."
BEN31-	"Is there something wrong still?"
BEN53-	"This is all I can get man. Neck, I'm gonna go a little bit--I'm going less than max range. I guess I should go max endurance."
BEN31-	"What's your FTIT and, ah, RMP rate?"

BEN53- "Okay, my FTIT rate is 870, RMPs 94, I'm just not gettin' any thrust. Oil pressure's at 40."
BEN31- "Okay, lemme come back and look at you again, okay?"
BEN53- "Cool."
BEN31- "Dude, I'm gonna punch my tanks out (interrupted "No we're good) so I can stay with you, all right?"
BEN53- "Cool."
BEN31- "Ah, what's your gas rate at?"
BEN53- "46."
BULL- "And Five-three, you have some friendlies north four."

{SOUNDS OF EARLY WARNING RECEIVER, FRIENDLY F-16's LOCKING BENJI 53 ON THEIR RADAR}

BEN31- "You are leakin' tons of fluid and it looks like gas, that's why I am wondering what your gas is."
BEN53- "Okay."
BEN31- "It's all comin' out right where the hook meets the engine."
BEN53- "Copy. Okay, how far do I have to go . . . to the border?"
BULL- "Border is 60 miles."
BEN53- "I might make it Neck."
BEN31- "Yeah, you will Homer, man, don't worry."
BULL- "And Benji, ah, your friendlies are tally with you."
BEN53- "Copy."

BEN31- "Is this all the airspeed you can get?"
BEN53- "That's it man. I can dump the nose, but I really don't want to. I wanna keep this wing goin' for me."
BEN31- "Yeah."
BULL- "Five-three, ah, confirm you're a single-ship?"
BEN53- "Negative. I've got a wingman here."
BULL- "Roge."
BEN31- "Ya know Spikey, if you need some more lift, you might want to throw your flaps down."
BULL- "Five-three, border is, ah, 55 miles."
BEN53- "Copy. Think I'll hang out for a little while, Neck."
BEN53- "Okay."
BULL- "Roge."
BEN31- "Say distance to border, Bu-Bulldog."
BULL- "Border 54."
BEN31- "Understand you've got, ah, choppers in the air?"
BULL- "Benji, you want choppers?"
BEN31- "That's affirm (?). You guys better scramble them now!"
BULL- "Roge."
BEN31- "Vector 'em to where we're gonna be."
UKN1- "(?) Five-one, did you copy that?"
BEN31- How you doin' Homer?"
BEN53- "Hangin' in man."
BEN31- "Cool. I'm with you all the way."
UKN- "Roger, did copy."
BEN53- "I'm gonna try the flaps (interrupted)."

BULL-	"Benji, border 50."
BEN31-	"Copy 50. Bulldog, Benji."
BULL-	"Benji, go ahead."
BEN31-	"Copy, understand that ah, this border area is pretty clear with threats?"
BULL-	"That's affirm, I'll check for ya."
BEN31-	"Check please."
BEN53-	"Flaps up a little bit Homie."
BEN31-	"Cool."
BEN53-	"That and my AOA is down a little bit."
BULL-	"And Five-three, we're checkin' for ya."
BEN53-	"Okay."
UKN1-	"Benji 41." Did he mean Benji 31? UKN1 is the same pilot from the beginning of recording.
BEN31-	"Go."
UKN1-	"Anything we can do to help?"
BEN31-	"Say again?"
UKN1-	"Anything I can do to help?"
BEN31-	"Ah, you might wanna get on a tanker, get some gas and be able to, ah, help with SAR."
UKN1-	"Okay."
BULL-	"Five-three, border 44."
BEN31-	"Eight staff (?), left ten."- "Benji 1, Benji 2 Victor."
BULL-	"Benji Five-three, if you could squawk emergency please."
BEN31-	"Do you got that Spike or do you want me to do it?"
BEN53-	"Yeah, I got it. I dunno if that's such a good idea, is it?"

BEN31-	"I dunno. Bulldog, Benji, is that a good idea right where we're at?"
BULL-	"That's what I was instructed, ah, I'd say no, I've got good contact."
BEN31-	"Okay, good, keep that contact. Do you got choppers in the air?"
BULL-	"Affirm, they are on their way."
BEN31-	"Copy that."
BEN53-	"Bummer dudes."
BEN31-	"Wh-What's goin' on man?"
BEN53-	"Just bummer."
BEN31-	"Okay, now you've got fire comin' out of your engine. Looks like it's failin'."
BEN53-	"What's failin'?"
BEN31-	"Well, it looks like you've got sparks and shit comin' out of your engine now."
BEN53-	"Okay. Bulldog."
BULL-	"Go ahead."
BEN53-	"Okay, I-I'm havin' a more serious problem now, okay?"
BULL-	"Roge."
BEN31-	"Understand, choppers are in the air?"
BULL-	"That's affirm. Border 40."
BEN31-	"Neck, you tell me if you see any fire."
BEN31-	"Okay, it's red sparks poppin' out right now."
BEN53-	"Okay, just tell me if you see a fire."
BEN31-	"Okay. Stay with it dude."

{Fire Begins}

BEN31- Okay, you're-"
BEN53- "I-I'm gettin' out!"
BEN31- "Okay, you're on fire."

{Ejection seat}

BEN31- "Okay, Bulldog, we've got him out, we've got him out!"

{Unknown Horn} Possibly stall horn, or engine-out horn in Benji 53 cockpit (plane is now gliding pilotless, did not explode)

BEN31- "Bulldog, we have a good chute. Bulldog, Benji, do you copy?"
BULL- "I copy, marked."

{Sound of rushing wind, still recording inside Benji 53?}

By Irv Moss
The Denver Post

When Scott Thomas saw the open door on the side of the helicopter and the blur of uniformed people directing him to get through the door, his mind flashed back to the 1985 football season at the Air Force Academy. He envisioned his Air Force teammates leading the way for him to run into the end zone after an interception.

The 1985 season was special for him, and for the Falcons. They finished 12-1, in large part because of Thomas, an All-America safety whose spectacular career at the academy will be capped Tuesday night with his induction into the College Football Hall of Fame in New York City.

"I'm accepting the Hall of Fame recognition on behalf of that team," Thomas said. "I was lucky enough to be singled out, but I'm representing the team, the coaching staff and this institution."

Scott Thomas was a pilot in the Air Force and was forced to bail out of his damaged jet during Operation Desert Storm. A special forces team rescued him from enemy territory. (National Archives)

With the helicopter in sight, Thomas wasn't anywhere close to a football field. He was caught in hostile surroundings in northern Iraq in 1991 during Operation Desert Storm. He had been flying an F-16 fighter plane that developed engine trouble and caught fire, forcing him to eject behind enemy lines.

Thomas doesn't talk much anymore about his harrowing experience, but he has relayed details over the years. Upon ejection, his parachute hit on a rocky hillside where U.S. military personnel would be shot on sight.

"The ejection part was very loud," Thomas said. "I remember looking down and seeing my plane disappearing into the clouds below me."

Once on the ground, Thomas tried to assess his bleak situation while reminding himself to remain calm.

"I had been in pressure situations," Thomas said. "I had felt the pressure being in Notre Dame Stadium and fielding punts with a bunch of big Notre Dame players bearing down on me. Things are so connected."

This, however, went far beyond anything he dealt with on the football field. As Thomas focused on the helicopter, his mind snapped back to reality. The forms he saw weren't football teammates but special forces personnel, who quickly got him on board, and out of danger. It was the ultimate in teamwork, all that he had trained for in his years at the academy.

"It was unbelievable," Thomas said. "They sent 14 guys in there to get one."

The rescue mission arrived just in time. As the helicopter lifted off the ground, it was fired upon by Iraqi forces.

Thomas arrived at the academy in 1982 a bewildered teen unsure of what he was getting himself into. He grew up in San Antonio and developed into a star high school running back who had his heart set on playing at the University of Texas. His dream faded as Texas did not offer a scholarship.

"I wanted to go to Texas since I was 3 feet tall," Thomas said. "The Air Force Academy always had been straight with me, so I decided to go where they wanted me."

Scott Thomas was an All-America safety for the Air Force Academy. (National Archives)

Thomas entered the academy as a running back, but soon found himself buried on coach Fisher DeBerry's depth chart. Soon after, he went to DeBerry requesting a move to safety, where there were fewer players stacked above him. It proved a prudent request.

Thomas, 6-foot-1, 195 pounds, became a three-year starter and earned All-America honors after his senior season in 1985. That fall he became just the seventh player in NCAA history to have touchdown returns of a punt, a kickoff and a pass interception in the same season.

And to top it off, Air Force defeated Texas, the team he longed to play for, 24-16 in the 1985 Bluebonnet Bowl.

"Players like Scott Thomas are the reason I'm in the Hall of Fame," said DeBerry, also a Hall of Famer. "We had some very good players. Scott Thomas could have played at any school in *the country. He played with a little bit of a chip on his shoulder. He played it hard, tough and with class."*

Emblematic of Thomas' approach was a game against Colorado State. The Falcons weren't playing well, and DeBerry chewed him out.

"I told Scott that he'd be watching the game standing next to me if he didn't get it going," DeBerry said.

Thomas didn't come off the field, and Air Force rallied to win.

Thomas is the fourth Air Force football recipient to enter the College Hall of Fame, following Brock Strom, Chad Hennings and DeBerry.

As he looks back, Thomas feels blessed he chose the academy.

"I wasn't very mature when I left high school," he said. "I probably would have made some poor decisions along the way, and I don't think I would have been as successful if I had gone to Texas. I didn't learn how to conduct myself until I got here."

Thomas, having retired from the military, is now a commercial airline pilot. And he'll always have his memories of his Air Force days, and the good fortune of changing his position.

"I'll always remember playing in Notre Dame Stadium and playing Army and Navy," Thomas said. "I also think what if I had sat back and been a second-string running back."

But his belief in the importance of teamwork that he learned at Air Force has never wavered.

He owes his life to it.

Indeed, USAF Captain Scott "Spike" Thomas, was and is the "Benji 53" in this true story from Iraq, just one of thousands of former USAF Academy graduates, including hundreds of former intercollegiate cadet/athletes (many from the 1985 football team) who prepared mentally, physically, and emotionally to do their job, their duty, when called upon, and stepped up to the challenge, wherever it was . . . whatever it was . . . certifiable *leaders of character*.

Playing for Coach Fisher DeBerry, **Scott Thomas** ('86) is one of only five **Consensus All-American Football players from the USAF Academy**. The other four are:

Brock Strom ('59),

Ernie Jennings ('71),

Chad Hennings (also Outland Award winner – '88), and

Carlton McDonald ('93).

Scott Thomas was also recently inducted into the **College Football Hall of Fame** class of 2012, joining Coach Fisher DeBerry (2011), Brock Strom (1985), and Chad Hennings (2006), representing the USAF Academy.

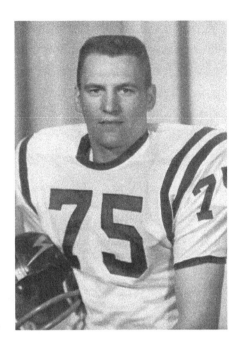

Brock Strom, AFA '59

Brock Strom was co-captain of the Falcon football teams of 1955, 1957, and 1958. The 6-0, 217-pound tackle became the Academy's first All-American football player and the Associated Press described him as "the bulwark of the team that almost literally came from outer space to go through the season undefeated and land in the Cotton Bowl opposite Texas Christian on New Year's Day."

After the Air Force Academy, Storm studied at MIT, earning a masters degree in Astronautical engineering. He served in Southeast Asia, flying 105 missions as a navigator. He was decorated with two Distinguished Flying Crosses, two Bronze Stars, and three Air Medals. Achieving the rank of Colonel, he served as Deputy for Space Defense Systems, responsible to the Secretary of the Air Force for the entire U.S. Space Defense Program.

Before retiring, Brock worked on the anti-satellite program and was the director of engineering during the building of the satellite based NAVSTAR Global Positioning System that is now used in ships, cars, trains and planes.

During his professional, post-Air Force career, he taught mathematics and management at the Academy as a visiting professor.

Brock lives in Colorado Springs, CO with wife Claire.

Ernie Jennings, AFA '70

Scott Thomas, AFA '86

Chad Hennings, AFA '88

Carlton McDonald, AFA '93

"Soon after returning to base, the media asked how scared he was. Scott said, 'I wasn't near as worried about the Iraqis as I was about Notre Dame's toss sweep when I was playing football at the Academy.' Scott went on to talk about all the lessons he learned in football at the Academy, how his Survival, Evasion, Resistance and Escape (SERE) Training after his freshman year helped him survive behind enemy lines, as did his experiences in the football program.

"Ironically, who was among the group rescuing Scott? One of his former classmates at the Academy. The classmate was willing to risk his life to save his 'brother'. That commitment and the commitment Scott Thomas showed in his courageous mission are beyond words. Like we say, 'Brothers are hard to beat.' If you shoot down Scott Thomas' plane, his brothers are coming to save him, and they'll be back the next day to even the score!" (Jim Armstrong/Denver Post)

Epilogue

About the 1985 Falcons

The key members of the 1985 USAFA football team, the Administrative leadership, the Coaches, the Players ... their careers, and what they're doing now ... thirty years later:

Superintendent: USAF Lieutenant General (Ret.) Winfield W. Scott, Jr.

Winfield W. Scott, Jr. was born in 1927, in Honolulu. He graduated from high school in Lewisburg, West Virginia, in 1945 and entered the United States Military Academy at West Point, New York in 1946. Upon graduation from the academy in 1950, he received a bachelor of science degree in military science and a commission as a second lieutenant. General Scott earned a master of arts degree in international law and relations from The Catholic University of America, Washington, D.C., in 1963. He completed the Armed Forces Staff College in Norfolk, Virginia, in 1964 and the Naval War College in Newport, Rhode Island, in 1967.

He received his wings upon completion of pilot training in August 1951 at Craig Air Force Base, Alabama. After advanced fighter pilot training at Luke Air Force Base, Arizona, he was assigned as a tactical reconnaissance pilot at Kimpo Air Base, South Korea, where he completed a combat tour of duty in F-51 Mustangs.

From 1952 to 1959, General Scott served in many operational and maintenance positions flying F-80s, F-86s and F-100s. In 1958 he won individual honors as high man in the Pacific Air Forces Fighter Weapons Meet flying the F-100 Super Sabre.

Scott was assigned as an Air Force Reserve Officer Training Corps instructor from May 1959 to July 1962, and then as professor of aerospace studies at the Catholic University of America until August 1963. He completed the Armed Forces Staff College in February 1964 and then transferred to Royal Air Force Station Lakenheath, England, as commander of the 492d Tactical Fighter Squadron. He entered the Naval War College in August 1966 and after graduation completed transition training with the 476th Tactical Fighter Squadron at George Air Force Base, California, where he was top gun in the F-4D Phantom.

He was assigned to the Republic of Vietnam in January 1968 as assistant director of operations, 366th Tactical Fighter Wing, Da Nang Air Base, where he flew 108 combat missions in F-4s. In August 1968 he became chief of the Current Operations Division, Tactical Air Control Center, Headquarters Seventh Air Force, Tan Son Nhut Air Base.

From 1969 to 1977, Scott held various command and staff positions: action officer on the Air Staff, wing commander, division commander, vice commander of an air logistics center, and commander of a technical training center.

Scott served as assistant deputy chief of staff, plans and operations, Headquarters U.S. Air Force, Washington, D.C., from August 1977 until June 1978. He then took command of the Alaskan Air Command, with additional duty as commander of the Alaskan North American Air Defense Region, Elmendorf Air Force Base, Alaska. In April 1981 he was assigned to Seoul, South Korea, as deputy commander, United States Forces Korea; deputy commander in chief, United Nations Command Korea; chief of staff, Combined Forces Command; and commander of the Air Component Command. He became Air Force Academy Superintendent in June 1983.

The general is a command pilot with more than 5,300 flying hours in more than 25 different aircraft including F-4s, F-15s and F-16s, and is jump qualified.

His military decorations and awards include the Defense Distinguished Service Medal, Legion of Merit, Distinguished Flying Cross with two oak leaf clusters, Bronze Star with "V" device, Meritorious Service Medal, Air Medal with eight oak leaf clusters, Air Force Commendation Medal and the Republic of Korea Order of National Security Merit (Kukson and Cheon Su medals). In May 1980 he was inducted into the Air Force Order of the Sword by the noncommissioned officers of the Alaskan Air Command and in July 1980 the Air Force Sergeants Association awarded General Scott the L. Mendel Rivers Award for Excellence.

In 1985, while serving as the 10th Superintendent of the U.S. Air Force Academy, Scott accomplished the Academy's freefall parachute training. At nearly 60 years old, he was the oldest and highest-ranking person to earn jump wings through that program, said to be the only training program in the world where the student's very first jump is accomplished as solo freefall (as opposed to solo static line or tandem freefall).

During that same period, as the Air Force Academy's Superintendent, General Scott made the extraordinarily difficult decision to suspend the Honor Code for a short period and grant amnesty to any/all cadets who voluntarily reported themselves for an Honor violation, including toleration. This self-imposed "timeout" was made possible by the General's experiences (good and bad) with the Honor Code while he was a cadet at West Point. Most historians believe that his actions, as difficult as they were, both personally and professionally, created an opportunity for the academy to pause, review, and correct issues that were plaguing the institution, virtually saving the honor and ethics "institutions" that are so very important at the USAF Academy.

General Winfield W. Scott, Jr. retired on August 1, 1987 and lives in Colorado Springs, CO with his wife Sally.

Commandant of Cadets: USAF Lieutenant General (Ret.) Marcus A. Anderson:

Lieutenant General Marcus A. Anderson's last duty assignment was as the inspector general, Office of the Secretary of the Air Force, Washington, D.C. He oversaw Air Force inspection policy; criminal investigations; counterintelligence operations; the complaints and fraud, waste and abuse programs; intelligence oversight and two field operating agencies--the Air Force Inspection Agency and the Air Force Office of Special Investigations.

The general graduated from the U.S. Air Force Academy in 1961. He has held a variety of operational and staff assignments including commander of a fighter wing in Europe, commandant of cadets at the academy (during the 1985 football season), commander of a Numbered Air Force in Europe, and commander of the Air Force Operational Test and Evaluation Center. He is a command pilot with more than 4,400 flying hours in the F-100, F-4, F-15 and A-10 aircraft, flew 240 combat missions in Southeast Asia, and is jump qualified.

General Anderson's major awards and decorations include: Distinguished Service Medal, Legion of Merit with oak leaf cluster, Distinguished Flying Cross, Defense Meritorious Service Medal with oak leaf cluster, Meritorious Service Medal with two oak leaf clusters, Air Medal with 13 oak leaf clusters, Air Force Commendation Medal with oak leaf cluster, Vietnam Service Medal with three service stars, and the Republic of Vietnam Gallantry Cross with Palm.

General Anderson retired on April 1, 1996 after 35 years of service to his country and lives in Fair Oaks Ranch, TX with his wife Ginger.

Dean of Faculty: USAF (Ret.) Lieutenant General Ervin J. Rokke:

Lieutenant General Ervin J. Rokke is president, National Defense University, Washington, D.C., whose mission is to ensure excellence in professional military education and research in the essential elements of national security. He is responsible directly to the chairman, Joint Chiefs of Staff, and exercises jurisdiction over all organizations, establishments, facilities and personnel assigned or attached to the National Defense University.

The general was commissioned as a second lieutenant through the U.S. Air Force Academy, Colorado Springs, Colo., in 1962. After receiving a graduate degree in international relations from Harvard University, he completed intelligence training at Lowry Air Force Base, Colo. Several intelligence assignments in Japan and Hawaii were followed by a tour as an instructor at the academy. He returned to Harvard University and received a doctorate in international relations in 1970. General Rokke was the U.S. air attache to the United Kingdom before being selected as the dean of faculty at the academy in 1983. He witnessed the last days of the Soviet Union as the U.S air and defense attache to Moscow between 1987 and 1989, and later served as director of intelligence, U.S. European Command. Prior to assuming his current position, he served as assistant chief of staff, intelligence, Headquarters U.S. Air Force, Washington, D.C.

General Rokke's major awards and decorations include: Defense Distinguished Service Medal with bronze oak leaf cluster, Distinguished Service Medal, Defense Superior Service Medal with bronze oak leaf cluster, Legion of Merit, Meritorious Service Medal with bronze oak leaf cluster, Air Force Commendation Medal with bronze oak leaf cluster, National Intelligence Meritorious Unit Citation, Air Force Outstanding Unit Award with bronze oak leaf cluster, and the Air Force Organizational Excellence Award.

General Rokke retired on July 1, 1997 after 35 years of service to his country, currently serves as the Senior Scholar for the AFA's Center for Leadership and Character Development (CCLD) and lives in Monument, CO with his wife Pamela.

Football Officer Representatives (ORs): The AFA's secret weapons!

The Duties and Responsibilities for the Officer Representatives include:

- Monitor cadet/player academic and military performance throughout academic year.
- Chair Football Eligibility Committee for fall and spring semesters.
- Provide corrective measure academic and military deficient cadet/player academic & military performance to the Academy Board's four Class Committees at mid semester and end of semester for fall and spring semesters.
- Solicit /coordinate cadet/player input on tutors [faculty members] to take on away football trips to provide extra instruction.

Results:

- Strong support from coaching staff and in particular, Coach DeBerry, resulting in improved cadet/player performance in both academic and military performance.
- Implemented numerous improvement programs to assist cadet players maintain proficiency in academic, military and athletic performance. During a 13-year period the team GPA improved from 2.30 [1983] to 2.74 [1997] and the academic performance continued to increase. In 1994, implemented a Get-Well Plans to track cadet player performance more efficiently... and it's still working today!

USAF BGen (Ret.) Marcos E. Kinevan (USAFA/OR: 1967-1987)

A member of the USMA class of 1947, General Kinevan, completed tours at Hamilton AFB; Pusan, Korea; McChord AFB; and the Pentagon before coming to the USAF Academy, where he was Chairman of the Social Sciences Division and lead the Law Department for twenty-one years before retiring as a Permanent Professor in 1988. During those 21 years at the AFA, General Kinevan also served as the Officer Representative (OR) for the Falcon Football Teams (including the '85 team), working tirelessly to develop and coordinate programs that helped literally thousands of academy athletes stay as competitive in the classroom as they were on the field, and never missing any of the 234 games while he was an OR. Mark's wife, Barbara (Bobby), passed away in 2005 after a long battle with Alzheimer's. General Kinevan passed away on July 25, 2008. He and Bobby are interred at the AFA Cemetery.

USAF BGen (Ret.) David Swint (USAFA/OR: 1984-2000)

Thirty-nine years as an Air Force officer with assignments ranging from base and major command civil engineering, commander of heavy construction squadron, to faculty and leadership duties at the Air Force Academy. Served at March AFB, Cannon AFB, Forbes AFB, Phan Rang AB in South Vietnam, Kunsan AB in South Korea, Offutt AFB, and the USAF Academy. General Swint earned his PhD at Michigan State University.

At the AFA, General Swint served as the Permanent Professor for the Department of Civil and Environmental Engineering from May 1982 – July 2000, and was the Co-OR for Football with BGen Mark Kinevan Fall 1984 - Spring 1987, continuing in the Fall of 1987 through July 2000.

General Swint is married to his wife, Sharon, and they live in Colorado Springs, CO where they own/operate Swint Realty Company.

Director of Athletics: Colonel John J. Clune

John J. Clune (October 29, 1932 – April 4, 1992) was the fourth Director of Athletics at the United States Air Force Academy (1975–1991). The Clune Arena at the Academy is named in his memory.

A native of Jersey City, New Jersey, Clune graduated from St. Peter's High School where he earned all-state honors in basketball. He was a 1954 graduate of the United States Naval Academy, where he earned All-American honors in basketball, and held scoring records that lasted for 30 years. He earned a master's degree in electrical engineering from the University of Southern California, completed the Armed Forces Staff College in 1959 and the Industrial College of the Armed Forces in 1972.

His initial assignments were in missile operations, missile maintenance and administration. He served as an Air Officer Commanding at the Air Force Academy from 1965 to 1968. Prior to returning the Academy, he was Chief of the Electronics and Equipment Division, Air Force Logistics Command and Chief of the Logistics Engineering Branch, Headquarters U.S. Air Force.

During his tenure as the Air Force Academy athletic director, he arranged for the Academy to become a member of the

Western Athletic Conference, the first service academy to join a conference. He was responsible for initiating a 10-sport intercollegiate program for women when the first class was admitted in 1976. Once joining the WAC, Col. Clune served on the Compliance Committee, Finance Committee and the Extra Events Committee. Clune served as president of the National Association of Collegiate Directors of Athletics and as a member of the NCAA's Postseason Football Committee. He is the former Chairman of the Board of Directors of the College Football Association and served as chair of the NCAA Voting Committee.

He was also instrumental in working with Colorado Springs civic leaders in bringing the United States Olympic Training Center, Olympic House and two Olympic Sports Festivals to Colorado Springs. He served as the president of the Air Force Academy Athletic Association and was one of the 10 board members designated by Congress to serve on the Academy Board, which is the governing body of the Air Force Academy. While in the military, Clune was rated as a senior missileman. Among his military decorations the Legion of Merit, two Meritorious Service Medals and the Air Force Commendation Medal.

John Clune died of cancer in 1992 after serving 16 years as the director of athletics at Air Force.

Head Coach: Fisher DeBerry

DeBerry was born in Cheraw, South Carolina in 1938. In high school, DeBerry was a four-sport varsity letter winner, lettering five times in baseball, three times each in football and basketball and twice in track. He was also an all-state selection in baseball and football. DeBerry graduated in 1960 from Wofford College in Spartanburg, South Carolina, where he lettered in football and baseball. He was also active in the Kappa Sigma Fraternity while in college.

After six years of coaching and teaching in the South Carolina high school ranks, DeBerry returned to Wofford, where he coached for two years as an assistant when Wofford won 21 consecutive games and was ranked first in the NAIA. For the next nine years, 1971 to 1979, DeBerry was an assistant coach at Appalachian State University. While DeBerry was there, Appalachian State was ranked in the top 10 nationally in either rushing, total offense or scoring offense three times. In 1974, the team ranked sixth nationally in pass defense when he was defensive coordinator.

Ken Hatfield hired DeBerry in 1980 as the Air Force Academy quarterbacks coach. The next year, DeBerry was promoted to offensive coordinator. By 1982, Air Force posted an 8-5 record and beat Vanderbilt in the Hall of Fame Bowl while averaging 30.4 points per game. After the 1983 season, Hatfield left Air Force for Arkansas after the Falcons' 10-2 season and Independence Bowl victory. DeBerry was promoted to head coach.

During DeBerry's tenure as head coach, Air Force won at least eight games 11 different seasons. DeBerry's first team, in 1984, was 8–4 and beat Virginia Tech in the 1984 Independence Bowl. The next year, the Falcons won 12 games, and were ranked as high as #4 nationally until a 28–21 loss at BYU. In the final Associated Press poll, the Falcons ranked sixth. DeBerry has coached the Falcons to three conference championships, winning the Western Athletic Conference championship in 1985, 1995, and 1998. The 1998 team's 12–1 record completed the first back-to-back 10-win seasons in school history, and finished the season ranked 10th nationally.

DeBerry's Falcons have dominated the Commander-in-Chief's Trophy series with arch rivals Army and Navy. Air Force has won the trophy 14 times and shared it once in DeBerry's 21 seasons. He is a combined 34–8 against the Black Knights and Midshipmen and is the winningest coach in service academy history. Since the Commander-in-Chief's series began in 1972, Air Force has gone to 16 bowl games, compared to a combined 13 for Army and Navy. DeBerry has led the Academy to 12 of those bowl games and has a 6–6 record.

Now "retired" in Oklahoma and South Carolina, he continues working for less fortunate folks through his church, and leading the Fisher DeBerry Foundation which was founded by Coach DeBerry and his wife Lu Ann. The Fisher DeBerry Foundation provides support and education of single moms and their children, as well as other charitable causes, including parenting development, mentoring programs, after school activities and funding for academic scholarships. In addition, Fisher has been active in the Fellowship of Christian Athletes and in 2004 was inducted into its Hall of Champions. He and his wife LuAnn have assisted fund-raising efforts for the Ronald McDonald House, American Cancer Society, Easter Seals, March of Dimes, Salvation Army and the American Heart Association. Coach DeBerry continues to practice what he preaches, by giving truly motivational speeches, and writing best-selling books like: <u>For God and Country</u>, Foundations of Faith, and <u>The Power of Influence</u>, Life-changing lessons from the coach.

Jim Bowman: Associate Athletic Director for Candidate Counseling

Graduate and football player at the Univ of Michigan / USAF pilot of B-47 Stratojet, the Strategic Air Command's first nuclear-capable delivery platform/ long-time AFA Head Frosh/JV Coach. "Bo" was responsible for developing and managing the AFA's athletic recruiting machine, for nearly 30 NCAA sports, for over 40 years. Now retired in Corvallis, Oregon with wife Mae.

Bruce Johnson: Defensive Coordinator

Graduate of Wofford College / coached at North Carolina State, Furman, Marshall, Citadel and LSU prior to AFA. Later coached at Univ of North Carolina after leaving the Academy. Died while jogging in North Carolina.

Bob Noblitt: Offensive Coordinator

Graduate of Kansas State University / coached Sothern Illinois, Yankton, Washburn (also head coach at Washburn) and UT Arlington prior to AFA. Now retired in Texas.

Cal McCombs: Defensive Secondary Coach

Graduate of the Citadel / coached at Univ of South Caroline and the Citadel prior to AFA. Later, became Falcons Defensive Coordinator. Went on to be the Head Coach at VMI and Southland Conference Coach-of-the Year after leaving the Academy. Now retired in South Carolina.

Lt. Colonel Dick Ellis: Varsity Special Teams Coordinator and Head JV Coach

1968 graduate of the Air Force Academy, coached football at the Freshman, Junior Varsity, and Varsity levels at the AFA as well as being the Head Coach at the AFA Prep School. Also, served as the AFA Associate Director of Athletics under AD, Colonel John Clune. Coached at Universities of Arkansas, Clemson, and Rice and became the Director of Athletics at Baylor University after leaving the Academy. A scratch golfer, Dick is now enjoying retirement (Colonel/PhD) in East Texas with wife Cecilia.

Ken Rucker: Running Backs Coach

Graduate of Carson-Newman / coached at Appalachian State and Richmond prior to AFA. Went on to coach at Baylor, Texas A&M and Univ of Texas after leaving the Academy. Now Director of Player Relations at University of Texas.

Dick Enga: Tight Ends coach

Graduate of Univ of Minnesota / coached at Lackland AFB, Texas, Spangdahlem AB, Germany, and Edwards FTC, Calif. and at AFA he served as Head Coach of the Prep School before moving to the Varsity coaching staff.

Charlie Weatherbie: Quarterbacks and Fullbacks Coach

Graduate of Oklahoma State / coached at Oklahoma State and Wyoming prior to AFA. Later became the Head Coach at Utah State, Navy and La-Monroe after leaving the Academy.

Captain Carl Russ: JV Defensive Coordinator

Graduate of Univ of Michigan. Went on to a successful Air Force career after leaving the Academy.

Tom Miller: Defensive Line Coach

Graduate of Portland State / coached at Bridgeport, Davidson, Citadel, and Dartmouth prior to AFA. Later coached at Univ of Southern Colorado after leaving the Academy. Now businessman in Colorado.

Darrell Mastin: Head Coach at the AFA Prep School

Graduate of Air Force Academy. Went on to become Head High School Football Coach in Oklahoma.

Jim Grobe: Outside Linebackers Coach

Graduate of Univ of Virginia / coached at UVA, Emory & Henry, and Marshall prior to AFA. Later became Head Coach at Ohio, Wake Forest and 2006 National Coach-of-the-Year at Wake Forest after leaving the Academy. Now retired in North Carolina.

Captain Rick Brown: JV Defensive Coach

Graduate of Air Force Academy. JV offensive line coach, defensive coordinator, and Varsity assistant defensive coach. Went on to a successful Air Force career after leaving the Academy.

Sammy Steinmark: Receivers Coach

Graduate of Univ of Wyoming / coached at Wyoming prior to AFA. Later coached at Navy after leaving the Academy. Now in business in Maryland.

Jack Braley: Defensive Ends and Strength & Conditioning Coach

Graduate of Nebraska / coached Defensive ends for AFA Varsity before moving to key position as AFA's first Strength & Conditioning coach . . . providing crucial knowledge and focus on that key part of the AFA's football (and other NCAA) program(s) that make AFA athletes much more prepared to compete and win.

Jack Cullitin: Head Equipment Manager

Longtime AFA equipment manager. Passed away in Colorado.

Levy "Peewee" Cordova: Assistant Equipment Manager

Good friend to all. Passed away in Colorado.

Jim "Iggy" Conboy: Head Athletic Trainer

Under head athletic trainer Jim Conboy's leadership, the U.S. Air Force Academy's athletic training program expanded to serve the Academy's 41 intercollegiate athletic teams and 17 intramural sports. Conboy, who was with the Academy when it opened its doors in 1955, retired in 1998.

National Athletic Trainers Association Hall of Fame – 1980.

Air Force Academy Athletic Hall of Fame inductee – 2011.

Jim Conboy was more than an ankle-taper to Air Force Academy athletes. He was a friend, a confidant, a father figure, a soul mate.

Conboy dispensed wisdom as effectively as he dispensed medical care.

Conboy spent 43 years with cadets, 43 years nursing their aching bodies and often-ravaged psyches. It's not easy being an academy cadet. For the young men and women he tended to with a never-wavering smile, Jim Conboy made it easier.

From 1955, before a single cadet set foot on the AFA campus, through 1997, when health problems forced him off the sidelines and into an advisory capacity, Conboy was the academy's head trainer. He worked with all cadet athletes, but mostly with football and basketball players.

Conboy's failing health was one of the only negatives of the 1998 Air Force football season, a season when the Falcons won 11 games and their first outright Western Athletic Conference title.

But when Conboy finally succumbed at age 74 in a Colorado Springs hospital in October, 1999, his friends and colleagues chose to remember the good times. They spoke of a man who nourished their lives with good words and good deeds.

"He was one of the most unusual people I've ever known," said Dean Smith, an assistant basketball and baseball coach at Air Force in the late '50s before becoming a legend at North Carolina. "He was one of the most caring people in the world, and he was great company. That's a great match."

He spent several years as chief of physical therapy at a pair of veteran's hospitals before signing on with the newly formed Air Force Academy in 1955.

Conboy and the academy were a perfect fit. He loved his job, worked at it tirelessly, smiling all the way. With his wife, Jeanne, who died in 1972, Conboy had seven children of his own. He had hundreds more who loved to hang out with him in the AFA training room.

"He really taught us that we live in an unranked human system, meaning there is nobody better than anybody else," said Conboy's son, Brian. "With all the brass and the notables around here, he never forgot the equipment managers or the assistant trainers, or the children of the coaches. We're pretty proud of that."

The Conboy clan richly deserves to be proud. Jim Conboy was one of the good guys.

(Randy Holtz, The Rocky Mountain News)

Jim Conboy, USAFA Head Athletic Trainer 1924-1999

1985 FALCON FOOTBALL PLAYERS

Bradford James "BJ" Shwedo #88

Then: 6-foot-2, 211 pound, Tight End from Concord, N.C.

Now: **Major General**, Director, Capability and Resource Integration J8, United States Cyber Command, Fort Meade, MD. General Shwedo leads the development and has oversight for the Cyber Mission Forces' integrated master plan and schedule covering three mission areas: Defend the Nation in Cyberspace, Provide Support to Combatant Commands and Protect the DoD Information Networks.

Prior to his assignment to U.S. Cyber Command, General Shwedo was the Air Combat Command, Director of Intelligence, A2. General Shwedo's other staff assignments include Headquarters U.S. Air Force, Special Programs Division; Joint Chiefs of Staff, J-3, Special Activities Division; intelligence support to SAF/AQ; Executive Assistant to the Deputy Director of the Central Intelligence Agency and the Director for Cyber Planning and Operations within the Office of the Secretary of Defense for Policy. General

Shwedo's commands include Detachment 2, 18th Intelligence Squadron, Osan Air Base, South Korea, and during the initiation of Operation Iraqi Freedom, he commanded the 566th Information Operations Squadron, which provided direct combat support through the National-Tactical Integration Program. General Shwedo's group and wing commands were within the 67th Network Warfare Wing, whose mission was to operate, manage, and defend the U.S. Air Force's global networks. Within the 67th NWW, General Shwedo also commanded the 67th Network Warfare Group, whose mission was to train and ready Airmen to execute computer network exploitation and attack. Throughout his tenure at the 67th NWW, this unit was in direct support of operations Enduring Freedom, Iraqi Freedom, and the greater war on terror. General Shwedo also led an intelligence team to Al Kharj, Saudi Arabia in support of operation Desert Shield/Storm.

"BJ" gives credit to what he learned as a player/coach at many different athletic levels: "you've got to win with what you got!" He and his wife Alison currently live in Hampton, VA.

Dick "Bandstand" Clark #52

Then: 6-foot-0, 224 pound, Nose Guard, from Richmond, VA. Helped Falcon defense allow school-best 2.8 yards/carry.

Now: **Major General**, Vice Commander, Air Force Global Strike Command, Barksdale Air Force Base, Louisiana. The command organizes, trains, equips and maintains all U.S. intercontinental ballistic missile and nuclear-capable bomber forces. The command's mission is to develop and provide combat-ready forces for nuclear deterrence and global strike operations -- safe, secure and effective -- to support the president of the United States and combatant commanders. The command's six wings control the nation's entire inventory of Minuteman III intercontinental ballistic missiles, B-2 and B-52 bomber aircraft.

Dick's previous commands include the 34th Bomb Squadron, Ellsworth Air Force Base, South Dakota, and 12th Flying Training Wing, Randolph AFB, Texas. He has also served as the Vice Commander, 8th Air Force (Air Forces Strategic), Barksdale AFB, Louisiana, and **Commandant of Cadets, U.S. Air Force Academy, Colorado Springs, Colorado**. Prior to his current assignment, he served as Senior Defense Official, Defense Attaché, Cairo, Egypt.

General Clark is a command pilot with 4,200 flight hours, primarily in the B-1 bomber.

Dick smiles when he says, " . . . everything I know about leadership has a foundation in the leadership lessons I learned while playing football at the Air Force Academy."

Dick and wife Amy have two children, son Milo and daughter Zo, and currently live in Houston, TX.

Roger "Horsehead" Teague #84

Then: 6-foot-3, 232 pound, Tight End from Flagstaff H.S. in Flagstaff, AZ.

Now: **Major General**, Director, Space Programs Office of the Assistant Secretary for Acquisition, Office of the Secretary of the Air Force Pentagon, Washington, DC. He directs development and purchasing on space programs to Air Force major commands, product centers and laboratories dealing with acquisition programs. His responsibilities include crafting program strategies and options for representing Air Force positions to Headquarters U.S. Air Force, the office of the Secretary of Defense, Congress and the White House.

His career includes a broad range of assignments primarily acquiring, operating and supporting space control, missile warning, and communications systems. He has commanded at the squadron, group and wing levels and served on the staffs at Air Force headquarters. He commanded the 4th Space Operations Squadron, Schriever AFB, Colorado, where he led his unit during launch, test and operational activation of three Milstar communications satellites. He also commanded the Space-Based Infrared Systems (SBIRS) Space Group and the SBIRS Wing, leading development, launch, test and on-orbit checkout of the final Defense Support Program satellite, the first two SBIRS polar orbiting payloads, and the first SBIRS geosynchronous satellite. He served as Vice Commander, Space and Missile Systems Center, Los Angeles AFB, California, and prior to his current assignment, he was the Director of Strategic Plans, Programs and Analyses, Headquarters Air Force Space Command, Peterson AFB, Colorado.

Roger and wife Kimberley have one son, Brett.

Pat Malackowski #48

Then: 6-foot-0, 200 pound, Linebacker from Valparaiso, IN. Rivaled Maki as team's hardest hitter.

Now: **Brigadier General** Patrick C. Malackowski, Military Deputy for Total Force-Continuum, Deputy Chief of Staff Strategic Plans and Programs, Headquarters U.S. Air Force,

Washington, D.C. He is the active-duty member of the tripartite leadership team leading the Total Force-Continuum efforts for the Secretary and Chief of Staff of the Air Force. His leadership directly contributes to the One Air Force and Balance lines of effort that support a more unified regular Air Force, Air National Guard and Air Force Reserve. These efforts include a high velocity analysis of all Air Force mission areas as well as a review of legislative, policy, operations and education total force initiatives that support an improved Air Force organization.

His commands include a Fighter Squadron, an Air Expeditionary Group, an Operations Group, a Fighter Wing, and an Air Expeditionary Wing. His staff experience includes tours in 13th Air Force and the Pacific Air Forces. Prior to his current assignment, he was Commander, 455 Air Expeditionary Wing, Bagram Airfield, Afghanistan.

General Malackowski is a command pilot with more than 3,800 flying hours in the A-10A/C Thunderbolt II. Pat and wife Carol currently live in Alexandria, VA.

Bart "Scooter" Weiss #4

Then: 6-foot-0, 172 pound, QB from Naples, FL - Directed record-setting offense, WAC Offensive Player of the Year, 1985.

Now: The Director of Athletic Operations at the Community School of Naples (CSN), an independent, Pre-K through Grade 12 college preparatory day school in Naples, Florida. CSN is the largest independent school in Collier County, Florida with a student body of approximately 1000 students.

Bart recently retired from the United States Air Force after nearly 30 years of service (Colonel and Command pilot) and during his career in the Air Force he led and commanded flying squadrons and multiple operational units worldwide. In addition to these leadership experiences, he served in Washington DC, working alongside both military leaders and members of Congress to include piloting AF-1 and AF-2 during the Clinton/Gore administration. Over the last 15 years, he has deployed to the Indian Ocean, Iraq, Afghanistan, Turkey and Saudi Arabia. During the last 5 years, he led 480 cadet-candidates through a balanced curriculum of military training, academic education and athletic competition + 67 faculty. As Deputy Athletic Director of the USAF Academy, he transitioned the Academy's Athletic Department from a government-based organization to a $42 million non-profit corporation, oversaw 27 NCAA Division I athletic teams and supervised physical education and fitness programs to 4,000 USAF Academy cadets. He is married to the former Kathy Terry of Naples and they have three sons and one daughter (Tyler, Cooper, Parker and Olivia).

Scott "Spike" Thomas #29

Then: 6-foot-0, 183 pound Free Safety from John Jay HS in San Antonio, TX. Consensus All-America football in 1985, NCAA Football Hall-of Fame.

Now: Scott flew as a Mission Commander during Desert Storm where he was decorated with the Distinguished Flying Cross for heroism. The story of his war-time ejection from his burning F-16 and the subsequent team rescue effort has inspired his motivational speeches ("Shared Sacrifice" and "Surrounded by Excellence") across the country as the

President of his company, Mach 2 Seminars and Management Consulting.

"Ultimately, it has nothing to do with flying," Thomas said. "We take what we learned in military aviation and show how it applies to the business world. We promote team building and show how the different parts of organizations can function as a team."

Retired USAF Lt. Colonel, served as a member of the Air Force Reserve 97th Flying Training Squadron at Sheppard Air Force Base, Texas, Scott was the Commander responsible for Euro-NATO Joint Jet Pilot Training.

Today, Scott lives in Wichita Falls, TX with wife Kelly (whom he met at UPT), flies 767's for American Airlines on international routes out of Dallas-Ft. Worth (DFW) in Texas.

Terry Maki #67

Then: 6-foot-2, 227 pound, Linebacker, from Libby, MT. His 30 tackles keyed win vs. Notre Dame in 1985. Maki was second-team all-conference his sophomore year and first-team all-conference his junior and senior years. He was also first-team Kodak All-American, second-team Football News and first-team Associated Press.

Now: Retired USAF Lt. Colonel, living in Missoula, MT. Football coach at Florence HS, Florence, MT. Founder/owner of Bitterroot Services and Technology, LLC, providing high-level training services to J-9, Joint Forces Command, and FEMA, plus regional product sales responsibility for several high-tech health-related products. Previously, as an Air Force Special Operations/Combat Controller, Maki took part in the invasion of Panama in 1989, and while stationed at Rhein-Main Air Base in Germany, he participated in Operation Desert Storm in 1991. He was assigned to Fort Bragg, N.C., from 1993 to 2000 and was deployed to Afghanistan in 2001-2002 and then again to the Middle East Region for Operation Iraqi Freedom.

Terry and wife Amber (West Point grad) have five children: Kahlan (West Point 2013), Preslee (USAFA 2015), Melody (currently on a mission in Mexico), Caroline (JrHS), and Luke (5th Grade).

Alton "AJ" Scott #18

Then: 6-foot-3, 192 pound Defensive Back from Winston Churchill H.S. in San Antonio, TX. In the Air Force served as an Acquisition Officer, Program Manager, Head FB coach at the USAFA Prep School, and Director of Honor and Honor Education at USAFA.

Now: Retired Lt. Colonel, Regional Director and Director of Diversity Recruiting in USAFA Admissions. A.J. has five (5) sons and lives in Colorado Springs with wife Theresa ('85 Classmate).

Brady Glick #93

Then: 6-foot-2, 220 pound, Linebacker/Special Teams, from Green Springs, Ohio.

Now: Retired Lt. Colonel is a Command pilot who became the first pilot ever to fly over 5,000 hours in an A-10 Thunderbolt II, now flies for the Indiana National Guard, and works as a senior consultant for Composite Engineering, Inc., responsible for Combat Systems Development and Advanced applications for high performance Unmanned Combat Aerial Systems (UCAS). Has five children: Connor, Sadie, Keegan, Hallie, and Sophia.

John Ziegler #74

Then: 6-foot-3, 246 pound, Defensive Tackle, from Excelsior, Minn. (where he is in the Minnetonka High School Alumni Hall of Fame), a scrappy defender, who gave up 30 pounds to AFA opponents each week.

Now: USAF Colonel continuing to serve as part of the Air Force Office of Special Investigations (AFOSI), including (1) Director of the Strategic Counterintelligence Directorate – Iraq (SCID-I), in which we provided direct actionable intelligence to Special Forces and US Army maneuver elements engaged in kill/capture missions throughout Iraq, (2) Director, Strategic Counterintelligence Directorate, Multi-National Force – Iraq, Baghdad, Iraq; (3) Commander, AFOSI Region 8, Peterson AFB, CO, supporting US Northern Command and NORAD, Air Force Space Command, and the Air Force Global Strike Command; Inspector General, HQ AFOSI; and as the (4) AFOSI Senior Representative to the Defense Intelligence Agency, Bolling AFB, DC. John has one daughter, Katharine and lives in Woodbridge, VA.

Chad Hennings #87

Then: 6-foot-5, 237 pounds, Defensive Tackle, from Elberon, Iowa. Was named to the WAC All-Decade Team, was a consensus All-America selection, inducted into the GTE Academic All-American Hall of Fame, and both the College Football Hall of Fame, and the Outland Award winner in 1987. Chad flew A-10 Thunderbolts on 45 combat and humanitarian missions during the first Gulf War, played defensive tackle (#95) for Dallas Cowboys for nine seasons, earning three Super Bowl rings.

Now: Chad Hennings and wife Tamara (Tammy) live in Flower Mound, TX (a suburb of Dallas) with son Chase and daughter Brenna. Chad's the President of Hennings Management Corp., the founder of Wingmen Ministries, the author of two books (It Takes Commitment, and Rules of Engagement), a philanthropic leader in the Dallas-Ft Worth area as a member of the board of directors of Christian Community Action, and a popular values and motivational speaker to youth and business groups, not to mention a wonderful role model for young men and women everywhere.

Dave Sutton #55

Then: 6-foot-2, 245 pound Offensive Tackle/Center from Jefferson H.S. in Lafayette, IN.

Now: Dave is a retired USAF Colonel, and currently the Director for L-3 Interstate Electronics Corporation (IEC), Navigation Solutions in Anaheim, California. Previous responsibilities at L-3/IEC include Capture Manager, Proposal Manager, Program Manager, Acquisitions and Mergers and Business Development. When he retired from the Air Force as a Colonel, he was the Chief of Staff, Space and Missile Systems Center, Los Angeles Air Force Base, California. He directed an 800-person staff responsible for all activities supporting a Product Center with over 6,500 people and an annual budget exceeding $12B providing joint warfighters with navigation, communication, weather, warning, force application, and space control capabilities. He interfaced with Air Force Space Command, the Air Staff, the National Reconnaissance Office, the Joint Staff, the Office of the Secretary of Defense, and other Department of Defense and Federal agencies, local community leaders, defense industry corporations, and international partners. Dave and wife Wendy live in Foothills Ranch, CA.

Mark Simon #39

Then: 6-foot-0, 202 pounds Punter from Whitewater H.S. in Whitewater, WI. A Homecoming King who played the Trombone in both the Classical and Jazz bands, Mark was selected as an All-American, won the '85 National Punting Championship (47.3) and set a new Bluebonnet Bowl punting record (49.2).

Now: Mark was one of the first Satellite Operations Officers at Schriever AFB near Colorado Springs, "flying" high-priority payloads for the Air Force (GPS) and other DoD "customers". At the same time, he had opportunities to kick for the Raiders, Patriots, Packers and Broncos on the weekends . . . but the USAF wasn't very accommodating in those days. He did, however, plow the ground that would help allow many highly-talented, future AFA athletes to combine participating in professional sports with performing their duty in the USAF. Mark has leveraged his Air Force Satellite Operations (SatOps) experience into increasingly responsible civilian jobs supporting huge technology developments for many highly-classified satellite programs, now with a major role as a Program Manager with the Aerospace Corporation, operating out of Schriever AFB near Colorado Springs, where he and wife Merrellee live today.

Steve "Speeknocker" Spewock #63

Then: 6-foot-3, 233 pound, Nose Guard from Highland. Mich., selected 1st-Team All-Academy (AF, Army, Navy), 2nd-Team All-WAC and Honorable Mention All-American (Defensive Line), AP/UPI. Finished Senior year tied for second-most QB sacks (10) in a season, and member of record-setting most QB sacks (31) in a single season by three interior lineman (shared with Chad Hennings and John Steed).

Now: Steve became a self-taught Builder/Remodeler in the Metro-Boston area. After securing state licensure as both Contracting Supervisor and Remodeling/Renovation Expert, he founded his own small-business, focusing on custom projects ranging from design and installation of kitchens, doors + windows, decks + outbuildings, and small/large home additions.

After becoming an 'official' Writing Professional in 2007, Steve has published over 50 articles in multiple Regional + National magazines, provided technical input for two "how-to" manual books focusing on architectural construction, contributed to marketing brochures, helped initiate/contribute to various business Twitter campaigns, and now has seven concept story ideas under initial screenplay development--with three of those scripts under initial writing contract.

Previously, Steve served as a System's Acquisition Officer while stationed at Hanscom AFB, MA. Over 7 years, he gained many professional accreditations (R+D, Test, Budgets, Cost Scheduling, Logistics, etc.) as a System Procurement Specialist. Holding various positions (Site Director, Asst. Test Director, Asst. Program Manager, etc.) on multiple programs (with budgets ranging from $3M to over $600M) led to his selection as Program Manager for a Weapon Launch Planning System for the B-52 bomber, where he exceeded system spec. performance ahead of schedule and 15% under budget--despite executing a mid-program Top-Secret Source Selection for contract award.

Steve lives in Yarmouth Port, MA.

Russell "Rusty" Wilson #56

Then: 6-foot-0, 218 pound, offensive Center from a strong military family in Jacksonville, Ark. As a senior at Jacksonville HS, Russell's football and track teams won their respective state championships with considerable help from Russell who won all-conference and all-state honors, respectively. At USAFA, Rusty struggled to successfully reach a starting position as the center on the Varsity, after much help from Coach Jack Braley to significantly increase his strength and conditioning.

Now: A retired USAF Colonel, with Communications responsibilities that include: commander of the Karatas Radio Relay location near Incirlik, Turkey, SC Director of the 422nd Air Base Squadron at RAF Croughton in England, Chief of Staff for the Joint Staff Support Center (JSSC) in the Pentagon, Director of Strategic Planning for the Air Force Operational Test and Evaluation Center (AFOTEC) in New Mexico, Chief Information Officer for AFOTEC, Director for Knowledge Operations Initiatives for U.S. Forces – Korea, Commander of 721th Mission Support Group at Cheyenne Mountain Air Force Station, and DISA's Deputy Chief Information Officer located at Fort Meade, MD. Today,

Rusty spends most of his "free" time as a Scout Master in the local (Hartland, Maine) Boy Scout troop.

Rusty and wife Elyse have six children, including sons: Robert, John, Russell, Christopher, and David, plus one very special daughter: Elyse, of course!

Derek Brown #53

Then: 6-foot-1, 195 pound Center/Deep Snapper from Decatur H.S. in Federal Way, WA. Was the critical first link in the most successful punting/kicking teams in AFA history. Won a national football foundation and Hall of Fame scholarship as well as an NCAA post graduate scholarship. Went to the University of Washington and earned a masters degree in civil engineering. Served as an Air Force civil engineer for 10 years and then went to work for Mortenson Construction.

Now: Construction Executive at M. A. Mortenson Company, a highly experienced, partnering-focused leader in construction. Expertise in project and program management including DoD, Air Force / airfield programs, airfield redevelopment programs, engineering in land development - planning, environmental oversight, civil engineering and entitlements, and wind energy projects. Leads large scale wind energy projects across the country, and oversees about $300-million in projects per year. Derek and wife, Krystal, are currently in the process of moving back to Denver where he will be Project Director on the Sterling Ranch development; which is a 3400-acre mixed-use development project located just south west of Denver up against the foothills.

Tyrone Jeffcoat #1

Then: 5-foot-10, 175 pounds, Wide Receiver, from NATO school in Naples, Italy. Three Sport Letter Winner (Track, Football, Basketball) All Conference in each Support, team Captain Football and Basketball; Honors classes. At AFA, was a talented receiver and blocker in the Falcon's high-powered option offense.

Now: Air Force career included returning to USAFA as both a Squadron Air Officer Commanding (AOC) for Fightin' Fourth Squadron and later as a Military Arts and Sciences instructor. Civilian career features being a "turn-around specialist" in the printing and packaging industry, leading the management teams in six different manufacturing facilities, mentoring and coaching them to be better leaders and lead with a servant mindset.

Tom Rotello #45

Then: 5-foot-11, 186 pound, Defensive back from Mapleton H.S. in Denver, Co. Tom had 17 interceptions as a Falcon (the most ever in a 4-year career), 8 interceptions during the '85 season alone, earning him All-WAC and All-America honors.

Now: In his 17th year flying for Delta Air Lines, living on a small horse farm near Lebanon, Ohio with wife Jami (classmate @ USAFA), plans to move back to Colorado when he retires.

Dwan Wilson #24

Then: 6-foot-1, 185 pound Defensive Back from Wynne H.S. in Wynne, AR. A strong Christian, Dwan was the youngest of eight children. Signed with Oklahoma State until he met Ken Hatfield and saw USAFA. Number three on AFA Career interceptions list with 15 picks. Started at cornerback all four years against Notre Dame, and had interceptions in three of those games.

Now: Taught Undergraduate Pilot Training (UPT) as an Air Force T-38 Instructional Pilot (IP) before going to United Airlines where he has worked for over 22 years, now flying 747's on international routes (mostly to the Far East) out of San Francisco International (SFO) airport. Dwan and his wife Maria live in Carmichael, CA.

Chuck "Ironman" Kinamon #38

Then: 6-foot-0, Linebacker from Marcos De Niza H.S. in Tempe, AZ. Flew KC-135's and KC-10's and participated in every conflict from 1988 through 1998. Served in AF Reserves until 2010.

Now: An Admissions Liaison Officer for the AF Academy and a pilot for Delta Air Lines.

Pat Stoll #79

Then: 6-foot-3, 216 pound Defensive Tackle from Los Alamitos H.S. in Los Alamitos, CA.

Now: Living in Capistrano Beach, CA, with wife Maria, finishing 17 years as a wealth management manager for Northwestern Mutual.

Rod "RV-aka-Winnebago" Vernon #23

Then: 6-foot-0, 181 pound Defensive Back from Farragut H.S. in Knoxville, TN. Air Force experience included jobs as a scientific analyst and an Economics professor at USAFA.

Now: Civilian career includes experience with Proctor and Gamble and Dell/Austin where he is a Marketing Manager with aspirations to open his own business someday. Rod lives in Austin, TX with wife Bonnie.

Eric "Rocky" Pharris #7

Then: 5-foot-11, 185 pound Wide Receiver from Hickman County H.S. in Centerville, TN. Flew T-38, B-52, and B-1 aircraft in the Air Force.

Now: Retired USAF Lt. Colonel who flies 737's for Delta Air Lines. Eric and wife Deborah live in Cibolo, TX.

Greg Pshsniak #28

Then: 5-foot-10, 183 pound Running Back from Salem H.S. in Salem, OH. Roomed with Spike Thomas for 3 years. Was a cost analyst in the Air Force.

Now: Lives in Ramona, CA with wife Delores. Greg is a Sr. Program Manager with L-3 Communications in San Diego, CA.

Steve Hendrickson #75

Then: 6-foot-2, 240 pound Offensive Guard from Louisville H.S. in Louisville, OH. Flew F-111 and F-15E Strike Eagles, completing combat missions, as well as "no fly zone" missions over northern Iraq and in Bosnia.

Now: Retired USAF Lt. Colonel who now flies for FedEX, Steve and wife Sharon live in Poquoson, VA.

Kevin Palko #12

Then: 6-foot-0, 180 pound Quarterback from Dearborn, MI. T-38 Instructor Pilot (IP), helped standup the USAF Reserve's first C-17 squadron, ended up logging combat time in Bosnia, Afghanistan, and Iraq. Flown for both FedEX and Delta Air Lines.

Now: GS at USAFE-AFAFRICA in the Theater Strategy Branch. Kevin also serves as the C-VEO aviation expert for Africa, plus helping buy aircraft for and train our African Partners. Kevin lives in Charleston, SC.

Brian Knorr #6

Then: 5-foot-11, 183 pound Quarterback from S.M. Northwest H.S. in Lenexa, KS. Talented #2 QB on the 12-1, '85 AFA Falcon Football team.

Now: Brian is the college football Defensive Coordinator for the Indiana Hoosiers football team. He also was an assistant at the Air Force Academy before going to Ohio University to work with head coach Jim Grobe. He was the head coach of the Ohio Bobcats program from 2001 to 2004. Brian Lives in Lewisville, NC with wife Julie.

Elijah "EJ" Jones #42

Then: 6-foot-3, 195 pound Defensive Back from Cranbrook H.S. in Detroit, MI.

Now: Senior IT Project Manager for Visa, Inc., living in Ypsilanti, MI with wife Wanda.

Mike Chandler #60

Then: 6-foot-0, 204 pounds, from Waterloo, Iowa. Second-leading tackler to Maki.

Now: Lives in Oviedo, FL with wife Joan.

Kelly Pittman #47

Then: 5-foot-9, 180 pound, Running Back from Houston, TX. Bart Weiss' wingman in the Falcon backfield.

Now: A pilot with American Airlines, living in Superior, CO with wife Mary Jo.

Pat Evans #36

Then: 5-foot-11, 196 pound Fullback from St. Aloysius H.S. in Vicksburg, MS. Voted AFA's Most Valuable Player in 24-16 win over Texas in the Bluebonnet Bowl, having rushed 18 times for a season-high 129 yards.

Now: A District Business Manager for Bristol-Myers Squibb, Pat and his wife Aimee live in Wildwood, MO.

Tom Ruby # 5

Then: 6-foot-2, 194 pound Kicker from El Camino Real H.S. in Woodland Hills, CA. Holds AFA "Best Career Kicking Conversion" Percentage for, '84-'85, 57-57, 1.000.

Now: Retired USAF Colonel, PhD from the Univ of Kentucky, CEO – Bluegrass Critical Thinking Solutions, lives in Junction City, KY with wife Laura.

Ken Carpenter #83

Then: 6-foot-1, 180 pound, Wide Receiver form Ft. Lewis, Wash. Led '85 Falcons in receiving.

Now:Retired USAF Lt. Colonel and pilot with Delta Airlines, living in Atlanta, GA.

Joe Jose #70

Then: 6-foot-3, 248 pound Offensive Guard from Thunderbird H.S. in Phoenix, AZ.

Now: Lives in Lumberton, NJ with wife Pam.

Steve Siegler #22

Then: 6-foot-1, 190 pound Defensive Back from Clear Creek H.S. in Houston, TX.

Now: Lives in Austin, TX with wife Erin.

Steve Allen #19

Then: 6-foot-1, 191 pound Wide Receiver from Birm. Rice H.S. in Bloomfield Hills, MI.

Now: Regional Sales Manager for St. Jude Medical Center. Lives in Matthews, NC with wife Shelly.

Tyler Barth #24

Then: 5-foot-9, 165 pound Wide Receiver from Barrington H.S. in Barrington, IL.

Now: Lives in Crystal Lake, IL.

Hugh Brennan #89

Then:6-foot-4, 224pound Tight Endfrom Cary Grove H.S. in Cary, IL.

Now: Lives in Joliet, IL.

Peter Browning #41

Then: 6-foot-0, 183 pound Defensive Back from Kettle Moraine H.S. in Wales, WI.

Now: USAF Lt. Colonel serving in the Air National Guard, lives in Oklahoma City, OK with wife Trudy.

Larry Bruce #21

Then: 5-foot-11, 190 pound Defensive Back from Denton H.S. in Denton, TX.

Now: A retired USAF Lt. Colonel, living in Argyle, TX.

Ron Bryant #21

Then: 6-foot-0, 177 pound Wide Receiver from Crescent H.S. in Iva, SC.

Now: A retired USAF Lt. Colonel, living in Anderson, SC with wife Mia.

Rip Burgwald #54

Then: 6-foot-1, 217 pound Linebacker from St. Paul Academy in St. Paul, MN.

Now: Lives in Denver, CO.

Marlon Camacho #2

Then: 5-foot-7, 160 pound Kicker from Hooks H.S. in Houston, TX.

Now: Retired USAF Colonel, Acquisition Officer, now living with wife Angela in San Pedro, CA.

Bob Collins #86

Then: 6-foot-2, 220 pound Tight End from Delta H.S. in Sacramento, CA.

Now: Retired USAF Major, Principal Engineer, Systems Engineering Group, Lockheed Martin Space Systems Company. Now living in Franktown, CO with wife Stacey.

Roger Creedon #90

Then: 6-foot-2, 237 pound Defensive Tackle from Cupertino H.S. in Santa Clara, CA.

Now: Now lives in Santa Clara, CA.

Scott Curtis #64

Then: 6-foot-2, 215 pound Linebacker from Spring Woods H.S. in Houston, TX.

Now: Lives in Moorpark, CA with wife Christine.

Jerry Duhovic #63

Then: 6-foot-2, 250 pound Offensive Guard from Mary Star of the Sea H.S. in San Pedro, CA.

Now: Owner/EVP of Centaurus Financial, Inc., lives in Rancho Palos Verdes, CA with wife Rosanne.

Kraig Evenson #65

Then: 6-foot-2, 240 pound Offensive Tackle from Burges H.S. in El Paso, TX. Kraig was selected on the '85 All-WAC Offensive Team.

Now: A retired USAF Lt. Colonel, Kraig is a Vice President for HD Power Supply Solutions, in San Antonio, TX.

Chris Findall #66

Then: 6-foot-3, 244 pound Offensive Guard from DeSmet Jesuit H.S. in St. Ann, MO.

Now: Retired USAF Lt. Colonel, Program Manager at Weston Solutions, resides in Bennington, NE with wife Kami.

Steve Flewelling #97

Then: 6-foot-4, 230 pound Defensive Tackle from Interlake H.S. in Bellevue, WA.

Now: Lives in Renton, WA with wife Betsy.

Chris Forseth #72

Then: 6-foot-2, 235 pound Offensive Tackle from Shorecrest H.S. in Seattle, WA.

Now: Retired USAF Lt. Colonel, MIT Fellow, Director for Harris Corporation, lives in Colorado Springs, CO with wife Daylene.

David Gaines #50

Then: 6-foot-3, 223 pound Offensive Center from Wasson H.S. in Colorado Springs, CO.

Now: Retired USAF Lt. Colonel and works for the Cortac Group in Versailles, KY, where he lives with wife Darcy.

Roy Garcia #76

Then: 6-foot-1, 238 pound Offensive Guard from Burgess H.S. in El Paso, TX.

Now: Retired USAF Lt. Colonel, Senior Program Manager at Composite Engineering, Inc. Lives with wife Amy in Roseville, CA.

Blake Gettys #51

Then: 6-foot-2, 238 pound Center from St. Edwards H.S. in Berea, OH.

Now: Colonel in the USANG, commands the 176th Operational Group, and flies for Delta Air Lines. He's been living in Eagle River, AK for the past 20 years with wife Kathleen, and with the exception of getting mauled by a very large brown bear at the end of 2012, he's really enjoying life!

Ashley Glitzke #26

Then: 5-foot-9, 1880 pound Running Back from Manitou Springs H.S. in Manitou Springs, CO.

Now: Lives in Oklahoma City, OK.

David Goldstein #86

Then: 6-foot-5, 224 pound Tight End from Hinkley H.S. in Aurora, CO.

Now: USAF Colonel with a PhD from the University of Colorado, David is the Commander of the Phillips Research Site at the Air Force Research Laboratory (AFRL) in Albuquerque, NM, where he lives with wife Julie-Ann.

Scott Haines #52

Then: 6-foot-3, 205 pound Defensive Back from George Washington H.S. in Denver, CO.

Now: Flies for Delta Air Lines and lives in Lakewood, CO.

Ty Hankamer #94

Then: 6-foot-1, 217 pound Linebacker from Temple H.S. in Temple, TX.

Now: Lives in Salado, TX.

Bruce Hawkins #34

Then: 5-foot-9, 160 pound Defensive Back from Pennsauken H.S. in Pennsauken NJ.

Now: Lives in Simi Valley, CA.

Doug James #73

Then: 6-foot-3, 228 pound Defensive Tackle from Perkins H.S. in Monroeville, OH.

Now: Retired USAF Colonel, now serving as the Division Chief for the VA at Wright-Patterson AFB in OH. Doug and wife Pamela live in Beavercreek, OH.

Forrest James #12

Then: 6-foot-3, 177 pound Defensive Back from Highlands H.S. in San Antonio, TX.

Now: Works for Best Transport Corp. and lives in Spring Branch, TX with wife Erika.

Randy Jones #15

Then: 5-foot-11, 190 pound Running Back from Carroll H.S. in Corpus Christi, TX.

Now: National Account Manager for Freddie Mac. Lives with wife Maria in Arlington, VA.

Derick Larson #54

Then: 6-foot-2, 210 pound Linebacker from El Camino Real H.S. in Canoga Park, CA.

Now: Lives in Denver, Co and flies for United Air Lines.

Mike Loughman #62

Then: 6-foot-2, 243 pound Offensive Tackle from Immaculate Conception H.S. in Elmhurst, IL.

Now: A Civil Engineer for the FAA, living in Schaumburg, IL.

Tom Manion #49

Then: 5-foot-10, 175 pound Defensive Back from Washington H.S. in Massillon, OH.

Now: Retired USAF Lt. Colonel, pilot for American Air Lines, lives in Warner Robins, GA with wife Karen.

Kevin Martin #85

Then: 6-foot-3, 201 pound Linebacker from Mullen H.S. in Denver, CO.

Now: A chemist for the Environmental Protection Agency, Kevin lives in Baltimore, MD.

Frank Martini #92

Then: 6-foot-2, 220 pound Defensive Tackle from Roseville H.S. in Rocklin, CA.

Now: A pilot for UPS, Frank lives with his wife Lacye in Roseville, CA.

Grant Morris #31

Then: 6-foot-0, 192 pound Fullback from Clark H.S. in San Antonio, TX.

Now: A pilot for Southwest Air Lines, Grant lives in San Antonio, TX with wife Cindy.

Marc Munafo # 46

Then: 5-foot-11, 188 pound Running Back from Huron H.S. in Huron, OH.

Now: Lives in Tavernier, FL with wife Jennifer.

Greg Myers # 78

Then: 6-foot-1, 235 pound Offensive Tackle from Clyde H.S. in Green Springs, OH.

Now: Lt. Colonel with the AR USANG, Director of Operations for the 154th Training Squadron, lives in Sherwood, AR with wife JoAnn.

Trent Pickering # 86

Then: 6-foot-4, 210 pound Linebacker from Clinton H.S. in Janesville, WI.

Now: USAF Colonel, Pentagon, Haf-A300B, lives in Alexandria, VA with wife Elise.

Matt Rathsack # 77

Then: 6-foot-1, 245 pound Nose Guard from Midland H.S. in Midland, MI.

Now: Retired USANG Colonel, VP of Federal Programs for Tetra Tech, Inc. Lives in Marysville, MI.

Johnny Smith # 37

Then: 5-foot-9, 192 pound Fullback from Fayette County H.S. in Fayetteville, GA.

Now: Retired USAF Lt. Colonel living in Havre de Grace, MD with wife Jolene.

John Steed # 65

Then: 6-foot-2, 219 pound Nose Guard from Central H.S. in Little Rock, AR.

Now: Retired USANG Lt. Colonel, Program Manager for INRange Systems, lives in Collinsville, IN with wife Martina.

Mike Toliver # 43

Then: 5-foot-10, 1885 pound Defensive Back from Eldorado H.S. in Albuquerque, NM.

Now: Pilot for UPS America, Inc., lives with wife Nicole in San Diego, CA.

James Tomallo # 10

Then: 5-foot-11, 176 pound Quarterback from Centerville H.S. in Centerville, OH.

Now: Pilot for Southwest Air Lines, lives in Spring Branch, TX with wife Tricia.

Chris Vellanti # 32

Then: 6-foot-0, 194 pound Fullback from Columbus H.S. in Homestead, FL.

Now: Lives in Tampa, FL and is a Property Management Specialist.

Mike Walker # 95

Then: 6-foot-4, 226 pound Linebacker from Auburn H.S. in Auburn, AL.

Now: Retired USAF Lt. Colonel, Principal with PCT Cos, and lives in Washington, DC.

Jeff Weathers # 61

Then: 6-foot-1, 211 pound Linebacker from Red Bank H.S. in Chattanooga, TN.

Now: Lives in Franklin, TN.

A Toast to the Host

"A Toast to the Host" is part of the original Air Force song. Many times this is sung as a separate piece, as it is sung to commemorate *those who have fallen* in the name of service to our great country. This is the reason for the difference in melody and the reverent, reflective mood.

After every football game, at home and away, the AFA Drum and Bugle Corps plays "A Toast to the Host" as the entire football team gathers together on the field, joins hands and stands at attention. (Often joined by members of the opposing team's players and coaches, a true sign of respect for not only the way the AFA players played the game that day/night, but *their commitment to go forth and serve their country* . . . most notably Army, Navy . . . and even BYU.)

"*A Toast to the Host*", by Robert Crawford

Here's a toast, to the host

Of those who love the vastness of the sky,

To a friend, we send, a message of his brother men who fly.

We drink to those who gave their all of old,

Then down we roar to score the rainbow's pot of gold.

A toast, to the host, of men we boast, the U.S. Air Force!

Go Falcons!

Gone . . .

But Not Forgotten!

- Brian Bullard* Class of 1986
- Gary Chandliss Class of 1987
- Tim Sweterlitsch Class of 1987
- Marty Tatum Class of 1987

****The Brian Bullard Memorial Award***, established in 1984, is the highest honor given annually to an Air Force Academy football player. This prestigious award is voted on by the team, based on the criteria that typifies Brian Bullard – unselfishness, 110 percent effort, total team commitment and pride in his role on the team whether he's a starter or not.

Bullard was a 1982 graduate of Air Academy High School in Colorado Springs. He attended the Academy the following year and played on the football team for two years. During Thanksgiving vacation in 1983, Bullard and his girlfriend, fellow cadet Dianne Williams, died from carbon monoxide poisoning while returning from a trip to Kansas in a snowstorm.

LEADERS OF CHARACTER...

"Air Force, Army: If they can defend the nation like they play ball, the United States is in safe hands!"

Cover headline from the Oct. 29, 1985 issue of Football News.

"Aren't you proud, that these young people will soon be defending our nation?"

AFA Head Football Coach **Fisher DeBerry**.

"Everything I know about leadership has a foundation in the leadership lessons I learned while playing football at the Air Force Academy."

MGen Dick Clark, a former AFA cadet, football player, and Commandant of Cadets at the Air Force Academy.

"The Air Force Academy came first for Coach DeBerry. As a country, we've allowed college football to take on its own persona. It can be pretty easy to let it get away from centering on the student athletes. A lot of suitors came and offered Fisher big dollars to leave Air Force. But he was committed to this program and our players. Coach DeBerry did more for the institution of college football than most people realize."

AFA Superintendent, **Lt. Gen. Mike Gould**, a former AFA cadet and football player at the Air Force Academy.

"The game should be all about the players who are involved and the institutions they represent.... We need to re-examine what college football is all about. It seems to be going in a crazy direction right now. It starts with commitment."

Fisher DeBerry, former Air Force coach (Associated Press file).

"Coach DeBerry was an amazing molder of men. You always knew where Coach DeBerry stood with his faith and ethics. Every year, I look back and realize that he did it the right way."

Jemal Singleton, former AFA cadet and football player, now assistant football coach at Oklahoma State University.

"Coach DeBerry told us to count on adversity and more importantly count on overcoming it. It's not how many times you get knocked down it's how many times you get up."

Tyrone Jeffcoat, former AFA cadet and football player, now an industry "turnaround specialist."

"The Gulf War was the highlight of my AF career. Probably the closest experience to being on that 85' team. Being deployed and flying combat missions was in a lot of ways like being with teammates . . . we practiced during the week and went to battle Saturday afternoon. We depended on each other and trusted each other. A lot of those Saturday afternoon pregame thoughts came back to me while preparing for missions during the war. There is no question in my mind that the closest you can get to combat is competing on athletic fields, especially a football field."

Chuck Kinamon, former AFA cadet and football player, now flies for Delta Air Lines.

My fondest memory of Fisher DeBerry? His Deberryisms. "Don't 'dampen' the eye of the team", "that was the greatest kicking game expedition (versus exhibition)", "remember who you are when you are out in town representing the team", *and* "this is the day the Lord hath made, let us rejoice and be GLAAAAD in it!" *to start every pre-game meal talk at the hotel. His energy, love and devotion to the team, and the way his words got ahead of his thinking at times to create some classic phrases.* "By gosh men . . . . . ." *was how he started many of his post-practice talks as he checked off his talking points on his 3 by 5 note cards."*

Patrick Stoll, former AFA cadet and football player, Air Force career working on Titan 4 space launch vehicles, now a wealth management advisor.

"Football. Ate drank and slept football. Loved my coaches (especially coach McCombs and his wife Lynn and his children Lainne and Will), my teammates, Jack, PeeWee, Moose, Kathy, Col Clune . . . etc. It was my life blood, and the only reason I survived the Place (USAFA). I learned more about leadership and teamwork from my experiences in the football program than any leadership course I ever took in my air force career."

Tom Rotello, former AFA cadet and All-America football player, tactical airdrop and Special Operations (SOLL-II qualified: Special Operations Low Level), now a Captain at Delta Airlines.

"Fisher DeBerry, what an amazing man, coach, and mentor. The most impressive thing about him is his true love for his players both current and past (all past now that he is out of coaching), his family, and God. I remember his emphasis that life was much more important than football. To live our lives with character, selflessness and to always "call your Mom and Dad".

Kevin Palko, former AFA cadet and football player, T-38 Instructor Pilot, flew combat missions as C-17 Pilot, FedEX Pilot, Delta Air Lines Pilot, helped start up United States Air Forces Africa (AFAFRICA).

"Bottom line, for me, I'm the airman I am today, the man that I am today and the leader I try to be today while thinking of that Team, that brotherhood, that drive, that foundation of being a Falcon on that Team for 4-years."

BGen Pat Malakowski, former AFA cadet and football player, Military Deputy for Total Force-Continuum, Deputy Chief of Staff Strategic Plans and Programs, Headquarters U.S. Air Force, Washington, D.C

... in a culture of commitment,

and a climate of respect!

Go Falcons!
Go Air Force!

Count The Helmets

The story of the 1985 Falcon Football Team

*Leaders of Character
in a
Culture of Commitment
and a
Climate of Respect*

Neal Starkey

"*May the lessons learned from these very true stories of character, leadership and commitment help current and future generations at the Air Force Academy succeed as they serve America.*"

Count The Helmets, **by Neal Starkey**

Printed in the USA
CPSIA information can be obtained
at www.ICGtesting.com
LVHW091336200724
785991LV00001B/59